GHOST
CHRYSALIS

GHOST CHRYSALIS

CYBER DREAMS BOOK 2

PLUM PARROT

Podium

To Emma, part of the inspiration for Juliet's personality.

Copyright © 2023 by Miles C. Gallup

Cover design by J Caleb Design

ISBN: 978-1-0394-4182-8

Published in 2023 by Podium Publishing
www.podiumaudio.com

Podium

GHOST
CHRYSALIS

1

BACK IN THE SADDLE

Juliet sat on the edge of the mat, holding a bag of ice to her swollen cheek. Anyone looking at her would know she was sulking. She wasn't upset that she'd been hit; she'd given better than she got. But she was fuming over the way Charity and Herbert—Berto to his friends—had acted during her assessment.

She narrowed her eyes, watching the two of them laughing with their group, still enjoying practice after Sensei had told her to sit out and cool down.

She supposed she deserved some animosity; she'd only been working out at the dojo for a month, and Sensei was apparently breaking some rules by letting her try for her first stripe—or degree—so soon. Still, she'd seen plenty of people take their belt tests and never watched their sparring partners go so hard against them.

"It's fine," she muttered. "I've got things easy enough, anyway."

"Juliet, you managed to pass the exam despite their best efforts to thwart you." Angel had been trying to cheer her for the last several minutes.

"Yeah, but I wish people could be happy for me," Juliet groused.

"Many of the other students were happy for you. Honey gave you a high five!"

"Sure, Angel, but review the footage; how many people were frowning or shaking their heads?"

"It's natural for people to feel some animosity when they witness someone mastering so many techniques so rapidly. They feel threatened, or worse, less than."

"Right. I get it, don't worry," Juliet said, chewing her lower lip and shifting the ice off her numb right cheek and up to her swollen eyebrow. She'd caught a hell of an elbow during the sparring portion of the test. Sensei had approached her several times over the last week, making sure she realized the test she was going to receive would be harder than most white belts working toward their first stripe would expect. He knew the animosity many of the students felt, and he wanted her to showcase how much she deserved to advance.

Technically, according to Honey, she was ready for her blue belt, but she would need a lot more time in the dojo before anyone let her try for it. *Technically* was probably the perfect word; she knew all the techniques and could perform them all perfectly individually, but when it came to putting them together in an effortless flow, she was miles away from being ready. One-on-one, at fifty percent intensity, she could hold her own with the real blue belts at the dojo. But when it came to full speed and multiple opponents, she had a long way to go.

"I'm fine with taking my time as long as I keep improving," Juliet said, partly to herself and partly to Angel. The dojo was plenty loud—she didn't worry about anyone listening to her corny self-pep talk.

"Speaking of which, I've finished compiling your latest physical assessment data; your old values are in parenthesis," Angel told her, and before Juliet could groan in annoyance, she had a new tab glowing on her AUI. She opened it to see what Angel had come up with.

Juliet Corina Bianchi		
Physical, Mental, and Social Status Compilation:		**Comparative Ranking Percentile (Higher Is Better - Previous Value in Parenthesis):**
Net Worth and Assets:	Sol-bits: 69,488	33.45
Neural Adaptiveness:	.96342 (Scale of 0 – 1)	99.91
Synaptic Responsiveness:	.19 (Lower Is Better)	79.31

Musculoskeletal Ranking:	–	33.56 (17.22)
Cardiovascular Ranking:	–	57.48 (31.87)
Cybernetic and Bionic Augmentation:	**Model Name and Number:**	**Overall Rating of the Augmentation (Grades Are F, E, D, C, B, A, S, S+):**
PAI	WBD Project Angel, Alpha 3.433	S+
Data Port	Jannik Systems, XR-55	C
Data Jack	Bio Network Solutions, 8840	C
Retinal Cybernetic Implant	Hayashi, Crystal Optics 3.2c	C
Auditory Cybernetic Implant	Cork Systems, Lyric Model 4	C
No Other Augmentation Detected.	–	–

"Are you serious? My percentile's gone up that much?"

"Yes! Do you see what a couple of months of hard work and consistent training can do for a person? If you keep this up for a year or two, I'll be very surprised if you don't work your way into the top ten percent."

"Right," Juliet said, her eyes lingering on her Sol-bit balance. She'd had nearly 80k a month ago, when they'd finished selling Vikker's stuff and after she'd covered everyone's expenses for Ghoul's rescue operation. She hadn't worked since, and she supposed it was time to get things going again, especially if she ever wanted to get out of Phoenix, let alone make it off-world. Did she still want to go into space?

"Damn right I do."

"You still mad?" Honey asked, coming over to check on her while the class waited for Sensei's next instruction.

"Mad? What makes you say that?" Juliet half-grinned, winking her unswollen eye at Honey.

"Right! If looks could kill, Berto would be in a body bag!"

"Well, he didn't have to go at a hundred percent. Jesus, I'm getting my first stripe here, not my brown belt!"

"Eh, you took it just fine, and when you threw him, it was the cat's meow." Honey giggled, making an actual *meow* sound.

"Are you trying to say something?" Juliet laughed. "You saying I was being catty?"

"Hey, if the little pink collar fits." Honey laughed too, turning to hurry back to her group as Sensei called for the students' attention.

Juliet listened as Sensei reviewed everything they'd learned, and when he dismissed the class, he walked over to Juliet, palms resting on his rotund belly and a big smile on his face. "I told you it would be a good challenge."

"Yes, Sensei," Juliet said, having a hard time not returning the smile.

"Charity thought you took Berto's hit well, and he swears it was an accident." He dug a thick round finger under the belt of his gi and pulled out a thin black strip of fabric. "Sew this onto your belt before practice tomorrow, hmm?"

Juliet jumped up and bowed, smiling as she took the strip of cloth. "Thank you, Sensei!"

"I'm proud of you, Juliet. If you keep working at it, we'll get all your white belt degrees within the year, and then you can start working toward blue. People will grow to respect you as you continue to improve. Have you given any thought to my suggestion? Competitions are going to be very important to your further advancement."

"Yes." Juliet nodded. "It sounds fun, and I agree; I could use the practice at full speed."

"Exactly so." Sensei reached out, squeezed her shoulder, and added, "Go on, now. I see Honey waiting for you outside."

"Thank you, Sensei. See you tomorrow," Juliet said, performing another bow. As Sensei turned away, she hurried over to the chairs near the side of the mat and slipped into her sandals; she'd stopped bringing a change of clothes to the dojo after a week or so. It wasn't like she ever went anywhere after practice, and she liked to shower back home before putting on clean clothes. Juliet smiled at the thought of a shower—she'd dropped three thousand bits on a bathroom renovation of her trailer, to Mr. Howell's delight.

Sandals on and belt pack with her pistol and personal items slung over her shoulder, she stepped outside into the beautiful Arizona fall weather. It was almost eighty degrees out, and sometimes Juliet wished it could be cooler, but right there, in the shade with the blue sky in the distance and a hint of mesquite smoke in the air, she couldn't complain. She took a deep breath and savored the lovely weather.

"Hungry?" Honey asked.

"I am," Juliet replied, and the two of them started walking toward Benji's diner. "I think I need to get back to work," she said by way of conversation as they walked along. Honey also wore her gi, and Juliet had a funny little tickle of pride, thinking she'd influenced her more experienced friend's behavior.

"Yeah? Time to get back on the horse?"

"Yeah. I've got things I want to buy, and places I want to go. I don't want to keep burning through my savings."

"Well, it's about damn time, girl." Honey laughed.

They were only half a block from the dojo when another voice called out behind them. Flinty with a nasal overtone, it was easy for Juliet to recognize it as belonging to Charity, even without hearing the words.

"Proud to cheat your way into a stripe?" The words stung, not because they were rude and sharp but because they were right—she knew, deep down, that she was cheating. No one else had a PAI like Angel helping them. She'd been over her decision to keep learning and using Angel a million times, and, despite the guilt, she couldn't imagine giving her up.

So she had an advantage; was she the only one? How about people born with millions of bits in their trust funds? How about people with brothers and sisters or parents who pushed them to learn skills at an early age. She knew it wasn't the same, but the comparisons made her feel better about having Angel in her corner.

She didn't have a chance to reply before Honey jumped to her defense.

"What about you, Charity? Are you cheating with that reflex job you got last summer?"

"Gotta swoop in to save your little girlfriend, Honey?"

"You wanna go there with me?" Honey bristled, turning to face the other woman, her knuckles whitening where they held her scabbarded sword.

"What? You gonna cut my head off for being a bitch?" Charity smirked, and Juliet hated how pretty she was while she did it. She had long, dark chestnut hair which she'd let out of her practice bun, so it hung down behind her slender figure—a figure accentuated by a tailored, custom gi. She had pale skin, light brown eyes, and lips that were either a gift from nature or a very expensive purchase.

"No," Honey replied, some humor in her voice. "I guess it's not a capital offense."

"*Anyway*." Charity dragged the word out, turning her gaze back on Juliet. "If you wanna earn some respect, there are fights you could be getting into. I mean, competitions; last man—er, woman standing."

"You know those aren't official or sanctioned," Honey interjected.

"Quit swooping in to protect the little baby," Charity sighed, staring at Honey. "She's a big girl; let her make her own decisions."

"Sensei said I should do some competitions," Juliet pointed out, raising an eyebrow at Honey.

"Yeah, in dojo matches, against people at your level!"

"Yeah, well," Charity said, turning back toward the dojo. Over her shoulder, she added, "I just wanted to throw it out there. I'll shoot you the info to the next one I'm going to if you're interested, Juliet." She took a couple of steps, then turned and, with squinting eyes and a big smile, she added, "There's prize money."

"All right," Juliet replied. Most of the regulars at the dojo had shared contact information, so it wasn't a surprise that Charity's message popped up on her AUI immediately. She shrugged at Honey, then turned back toward the diner and kept walking.

"You can get hurt in those things," Honey sighed.

"Yeah, well, I've got a pretty good edge on other students; maybe it'll do me some good to get a little beat up and feel some real intensity. I mean, that's my biggest weakness—using the right move at the right time— and you and Sensei both have told me that only comes with real sparring experience."

"Well, please talk to me before you go to one of them. Let me at least come along."

"Of course, sis!" Juliet laughed, jostling her as they walked.

"*Sis* now, hmm? Alright, alright. I can dig it." Honey laughed too, jostling her back. "So, we need a new job, hmm? I happen to have a pretty nice offer from Temo that I was trying to decide how to present to you."

"Oh really?" Juliet grinned. "Why's that?"

"Because you've been so . . . reluctant to do anything since, you know, since Ghoul." Honey looked at her from the side, and Juliet knew she was trying to gauge her reaction to hearing her name. It didn't bother her anymore; she'd come to terms with Ghoul's—Cassie's—betrayal. She really didn't harbor any anger about it. If anything, she felt more hurt that Cassie had taken off and blocked her comms without talking to her, without giving Juliet a chance to forgive her.

"It's cool, Honey. I think . . . well, I think I need to get into some action; I need to do some jobs with people like you and the others." Juliet knew Honey would know what she meant by the others—Mags, Pit, and Hot Mustard. People she'd decided she could trust, though she wasn't a hundred percent sure of that with anyone other than Honey.

Pit and Mags had definitely been more worried about earning salvage than helping Ghoul, but they'd done a good job and been reliable on short notice. They'd also done a good job of keeping quiet about the whole thing, which had earned them major points in Juliet's book. She'd had Angel keeping a very close watch for news about the job they'd done at Vikker's old compound, and nothing had slipped about her or any of her crew's involvement.

Hot Mustard was another story; he hadn't bothered them about his cut of the salvage, patiently waiting for Pit to fence everything, and had even sent some rather sweet messages to Juliet to make sure she was all right after she'd gone home to convalesce without meeting the team again. He'd asked after Ghoul, too, and been disappointed not to be able to talk to her but happy she'd been all right.

"Yeah," she reiterated. "I'd like to get into a job with you and the others. Or just you; we can do something small to get back into the swing of things."

"Well, this one seems really good, and Temo sent me the card for the 'hacker' role. Honestly, he's been bugging me to get you back to work for weeks now, but I didn't want to pressure you. Do you want to see it? The pay for you is twice what I'll get as muscle, by the way!"

Juliet took another big sniff of the fresh air, so happy she was out on the edge of the ABZ with Honey instead of downtown with all the traffic and people. She wanted to see more, wanted to experience life in different cities and places, but right then, she was glad to be in a familiar setting. "Are you trying to guilt me into sharing a cut of my payday?" she asked, throwing an arm over Honey's shoulders. "Sure, send me the card."

Honey laughed. "Okay, done. Have your little Angel show it to you; we can talk over brunch."

"Angel?" Juliet prompted aloud, and then the card was on her AUI:

Posting #F233	**Requested Role:** Network Security Bypass	**Rep Level:** E-S+
Job Description: Gain access, with support, to a secure location in a major Phoenix-based corporation's headquarters. Bypass network security and install provided files.		**Compensation:** 18,000 Sol-bits
Scavenge Rights: Tiered	**Location:** Phoenix Central	**Date:** October 22, 2107

"Uh, I'm not at rep level E yet," Juliet said immediately.

"Perks of knowing the fixer." Honey grinned. "How about that payday, though?"

"Well, it's nice for sure, but are we really ready to gain access to a major corp's HQ? That sounds a little radioactive . . ."

"Temo wouldn't offer it to me if he didn't know the rest of the team and think it was chill—all icing, as he'd say." Honey bumped her with her hip, knocking her over the little curb into the parking lot of Benji's diner, and Juliet laughed, stumbling away from her.

"So, just us? We don't know the other operators?"

"Temo does, but yeah, new to us."

"All right. I'm in. It sounds exciting, and I've been working on a new daemon with Angel; I want to try it out on a security panel. I hope there'll be some security panels to bypass, not just some boring server hack!"

Juliet was serious, despite Honey's laughter—Angel had been trying to teach her about some of the things she did, trying to help her be, if not less reliant on her, less clueless about what she did.

They'd built a new attack daemon based on Angel's experiences bypassing doors owned by Helios in Tucson, and while she'd coded it, she'd walked Juliet through the process step-by-step. It had been fascinating, and Juliet knew there was little chance she could repeat the process on her own—not yet. Still, she felt she understood a lot more, which made her feel a little better about having a cheat code riding around in her brain.

"Wanna go shopping before the job? We've got two days." Honey opened the door, they stepped into the diner, and the smells brought saliva to Juliet's mouth.

"Yes! I need new clothes." She laughed and added, "I mean, yeah, I need new clothes for everyday stuff, but also for jobs."

"You ain't lying." Honey giggled, giving her a sidelong glance, then bolted for the far side of their usual booth before Juliet could retaliate physically for her verbal assault.

"You're mean! I had to leave almost all my clothes in Tucson and, well, you know, I've been busy." She slid into her side of the booth and smiled as one of the regular waitresses walked toward them. "Hey, Carmen."

"Hey, ladies. Breakfast or lunch? Some of both?"

"You know us too well." Honey grinned. "Coffee, pancakes, and a side of overnight tomatoes for me."

"Hmm," Juliet hummed, tapping her chin with her forefinger. "Does he have burgers today?"

"He does." Carmen smiled. "French fries or . . ."

"French fries!" Juliet said, saving her the trouble of listing any more sides.

"Juliet," Angel spoke into her ear. "I'm not sure the oil Benji uses on his fried foods is good for your health."

"Yep." Juliet nodded. "Fries." She couldn't help the bubble of laughter that came out of her at the thought of Angel's frustration. Life felt pretty good just then, and when she turned her twinkling eyes away from Carmen to Honey, her friend laughed along with her. Their shared good humor felt like another connection forming between them. Juliet liked the feeling and wished she wouldn't have to leave Honey behind when she left Phoenix.

As they chatted about where they'd go shopping and about what the job might entail, Juliet pushed thoughts of leaving to the back of her mind and decided she'd cross that bridge when she came to it; there were a lot of things to do before then, and who knew what the future might hold. She surely never would have guessed where she'd end up if someone had asked her six months ago what was in store for her.

2

TOO CLOSE FOR COMFORT

Juliet, Doctor Murphy has left you another message," Angel said, startling Juliet out of her reverie. She was sitting on a folding lawn chair in front of the trailer, killing time before she had to meet Honey and the rest of the crew for their job that evening.

"She's persistent." Juliet sighed. She'd already turned the doctor down on her little vendetta mission against the Rattler gang out of South Phoenix. She didn't exactly know what it would entail, but she knew she didn't feel like getting into the revenge business; not after all she'd been through with Ghoul and Reynold. "I suppose it's my fault for stringing her along. I said I was taking a break, not that I didn't want to do it."

"Would you like to see the message?"

"Yeah." Juliet leaned back in the chair, closing her eyes and letting the video play on her AUI. Murph appeared, so detailed that Juliet could imagine she was present. So much of her was in high-res, Juliet wondered if the doc had used an external camera for the message. She stood in one of her operating suites wearing a clean white coat, and smiled like she could see Juliet and look into her eyes.

"Hey, kiddo! I hope you're feeling better after that rough mission. I know, I know—you can't tell me the details, but I want you to know I've been thinking about you. Look, I'm not going to keep bugging you to do this job, but I'm not giving it to anyone else. I don't care if it never gets done; in my mind, you earned this opportunity, so I'm going to hold it for you. I wouldn't ask you to do it if it wasn't a sweet deal for you. It's a relatively low-risk job, and I'll make sure you get some good rep and a fat payday. Gimme a call when you're feeling up for it. Hey, don't forget about my standing discount!"

Juliet smiled as the doc's image faded away. "She's pretty damn sweet, isn't she?"

"She seems to have good intentions where you're concerned," Angel replied.

"Well, I guess I did pull her out of the fire, so to speak. Can you remind me to call her tomorrow? Seems like it would be dumb not to hear her out about this job."

"I will."

Juliet sipped at her "electrolyte-enhanced" water. "Show me Temo's message about tonight's job again, please." An amber, opaque window appeared in her vision, displaying Temo's message:

January,

Hey, for tonight's job, you'll be going in undercover. I know it's nerve-racking, but it's a no-weapon job. If you bring any, you'll need to leave 'em in the drop vehicle, and I can't guarantee they'll get back to you. Make sure you bring your cracking gear. Honey's on board and knows the extraction protocol if something goes wrong.

-T

Juliet smiled as she read the message, noting Temo's use of her new handle. When she'd returned from Tucson after rescuing Ghoul, she'd decided it was time to stop taking unnecessary risks, even small ones like operating under her actual first name. She'd brainstormed for hours, trying to think of a handle, wishing she'd earned one already. The closest she could think of was "Lucky" because of how Ghoul used to call her that, but she'd decided it wasn't right for her; it made her think of a pet.

Angel had suggested a lucky number or date, which had led Juliet to January—it wasn't precisely lucky, but it was the month in which she'd been born, and she liked the sound of it. She figured it would do well enough until she'd earned a better handle.

Looking over the note again, she said, "Well, I, for one, am happy not to go in packing weapons; it kinda portends a peaceful resolution, don't you think?"

"It stands to reason that stealth and subterfuge will be the order of the day, not violence," Angel replied.

"Order of the day? That's a nice one, Angel. You've been reading more fiction?"

"Yes! Have you heard of Stephen King?"

"No, I don't think so," Juliet said, standing up to stretch. She wanted to get a shower in before she left, so she pulled open the screen door on her trailer and stepped up into the kitchen area as Angel replied.

"He was a prolific writer in the twentieth century and had some fascinating ideas about the future. I just read through a story he wrote under a pen name called *The Running Man*. Would you like me to tell you about it?"

"Yeah, give me a synopsis without spoiling it too much; I'm going to shower." Juliet crunched up her water bottle and dropped it into the compactor she'd bought a couple of weeks earlier. She still had to transport the cubes of recyclable material to the park's collection area, but with the compactor, she'd reduced that chore to a weekly event.

Listening to Angel talk about an old sci-fi story brought a smile to her face, and as she stepped into her modified bathroom, it widened further. She'd paid a resident of the park, a self-styled handyman, to gut the sani-spray booth and put in a real shower and an upgraded, tankless water heater. She'd had to give Howell an advance on her water bill, but it was worth it to have actual hot water running down her scalp and back after a hard workout at the dojo.

As she scrubbed her hair, applying conditioner, she leaned against the tile enclosure and said, "Wait . . . so the game involved regular people trying to kill this guy?"

"Yes! The story has been described as 'dystopian.' I thought it was interesting because I can see parallels between King's imagined future and our society. His vision of the heartless subjugation of citizens for material gains or entertainment value is echoed in our current reality."

"Angel! I was hoping you'd have something entertaining to share, not a depressing philosophical discussion. I get it, though—we have some bad things going on in our society. I mean, shit, I wish I could make a difference, but . . . I'm nobody. Besides, I've already got enough enemies, don't you think?"

"Well, regardless of the moral implications, the story is quite entertaining. I'd recommend it."

Juliet snorted and rinsed her hair. She finished her shower, feeling much refreshed, and walked back to her bedroom, where the clothes she'd picked up while shopping with Honey were still stacked on her little built-in dresser. She rifled through them, picking her outfit for the operation and carefully going over the pants and shirt to make sure she'd gotten all the tags off.

She'd decided to wear high-end stretch-weave tights and a long-sleeved matching shirt. Juliet figured if they had a disguise for her, there was no sense in wearing something bulky. She put on her black cross-training shoes and stuffed her deck, its battery pack, and an extra data cable into her black belt pack—it had a stretchy waistband and was slim enough to hide at the small of her back.

Hair pulled back in a tight bun, she stood in front of her mirror and said, "How's that, Angel?" She couldn't help feeling a little pride at the way her figure and posture had improved over the last couple of months. All the activity leading up to Ghoul's rescue, and then the hard work she'd been putting in at the dojo were starting to show. She'd leaned out considerably, and her muscle tone was better even than when she'd done sports in school.

"I think that's a good choice; your clothes are without bulk and will fit under nearly any sort of outfit."

"Yeah. I figure if I have to ditch the disguise, I won't be naked. Do you think I can get away with the vibroblade?"

"If they specified no weapons, the odds are good that you might be searched. I wouldn't want you to get into trouble for sneaking a weapon into a secure area."

"Yeah, I figured." Juliet gave herself another once-over, then said, "Hey, Angel, can you change my eyes to mauve again? I think it looks cool and, well, pretty, and it'll hopefully distance me from the Juliet that WBD is looking for." She watched as her naturally pale-green eyes shifted to the same purple-pink shade they'd been when she and the gang had rescued Ghoul. They seemed brighter, even though the color wasn't any lighter than her natural tone. "Are you backlighting my irises?"

"Yes, it's a feature of your optical implants. Don't you like it? I think it makes your eyes stand out a lot more."

"Well, yeah. I mean, it looks wicked, but I'm a little self-conscious."

"You needn't feel that way, Juliet; if you were to walk down the street in downtown Phoenix, the number of non-natural eye colors would outweigh the naturally occurring ones. I've seen, through your eyes, many people with far more outlandish features. Why, at the dojo this morning, there was a new student with a set of chrome horns!"

"Yeah, good point, Angel. They were kinda cool looking, though, weren't they? I mean, he had the right facial structure for those horns—he looked tough!" She glanced at her AUI to see the time. "Five o'clock, Angel. How long will it take to get to the meeting spot?"

"You should leave in the next fifteen minutes—the pin Temo sent is downtown."

"Right! Order up the cab; I'm heading out." Juliet hopped down the steps of her trailer, touched the thumb pad on the old biometric deadbolt, and then, with a spring in her step, made her way to the park's entrance. She was in a good mood; it felt right to get back to work, to start inching her way toward a bigger bank account, and to have something to dream about. She'd been in a funk since the "Ghoul op," as she'd been calling it, and it felt like she was coming out of a shadow—figuratively, because the sky was already darkening in a more literal sense.

Mrs. Jimenez was watering her flowerpots, and she waved as Juliet hurried by. The retired dispatch operator had made a point of getting to know Juliet over the last few weeks, starting things off by leaving her a loaf of homemade bread with a note welcoming her to the community. When Juliet had stopped by to thank her, they'd found a sort of connection talking about how things had changed in Tucson—Mrs. Jimenez had grown up in an area not far from where Juliet's grandparents had lived.

At first, Juliet had been paranoid about the old woman, worried that she was some sort of plant, but when she'd asked Mr. Howell about her, he'd let slip that Mrs. Jimenez had lived in the park longer than even he had, and that her husband had died just a few years ago. Juliet couldn't imagine how WBD could have an informant already in place for decades before she even came to live there.

"Hey, Mrs. Jimenez!" Juliet waved, still hurrying toward the gate.

"All dressed in black? At least your eyes are bright, but you'll never catch a date in those dark clothes!"

"This is my active wear, Mrs. Jimenez!" Juliet laughed. "I'm going to work out with a friend, not look for a date!"

"Okay, honey," she said, lifting her watering can over a runty little bunch of near-withered flowers. Her use of the endearment caught Juliet a little off guard—she wasn't sure if it was because no one had called her that in a long time or if it was because she was so used to saying the word in reference to her new best friend. She waved once more then hurried by, and soon, she was outside the park waiting for her cab.

The cab ride into town took a while, and Juliet let her mind wander during the trip. She still didn't know exactly what she wanted to do with herself, didn't know why she wanted to leave Phoenix so badly; things were pretty good at the moment. She'd made a lot of friends—and frenemies—at the dojo and looked forward to going nearly every day. She had a fixer she felt she could trust, and a cyber doc who felt like she owed Juliet favors. The reasons to stay around were pretty compelling.

As she rode, head bouncing on the tinted glass of the cab, she thought about what was pushing her to move on, concluding that she'd always wanted to see more, to experience life in a place different from Arizona. She'd hated how her family had moved on without her, though she supposed it was only her mom who had done it voluntarily. Still, Arizona and, more specifically, Tucson had felt like a purgatory—a place she was stuck in, spinning her wheels and never moving on. More than that, she still felt like she was on the run. Which, if she were being honest, she was.

WBD seemed like a distant but constant threat, always lurking in the background, always a faceless menace whenever she went into a new place. If it weren't for Angel constantly spoofing her identity, she knew she'd have been caught by now, and it felt like even though millions of people lived there, Phoenix was too small, too close to WBD, to be sticking around. "So I need to save some money and get someplace a lot farther away," she sighed, tilting her head so she could look up at the night sky through the window.

The AutoCab made its way into downtown traffic and, to Juliet's sweat-inducing horror, pulled into a parking garage next to the Vykertech Corporation megatower. "Holy shit! Angel, did you know this was the location?"

"I knew the meeting point was this parking structure, but I still don't know what the job entails or where it will take place."

"I don't like this!" Juliet hissed, contemplating bailing on the op.

"Your heart rate is elevated, Juliet. Perhaps practice the breathing exercise that Sensei walked you through during stretching last week. You shouldn't need to worry about Vykertech; they have no knowledge about your involvement in the dreamer operations."

"What about the tiny little fact that I distributed evidence of their criminal activities all over Tucson?" Juliet subvocalized.

"As far as Vykertech knows, that was done by Reynold and his contacts."

"I hope we were as clean about all that as you seem to think," Juliet replied, still carefully subvocalizing; she had little trust when it came to AutoCab privacy practices. The cab wended its way up through the garage to the fifth level, then pulled into an empty stall.

"Your destination is the elevator bank on this level, passenger. Thank you for your patronage."

Juliet grunted and opened the door, stepping out. She could see the elevators not far away, and as she peered into the shadows nearby, her stress-tightened shoulders relaxed a little—Honey was leaning against the concrete wall talking to another person.

Juliet walked closer, and when Honey noticed her approach, she looked up and waved her over. "Hey! January, this is Carn; he's working with us tonight." Juliet looked to where her friend, dressed in a black hoodie and tight jeans, pointed, and saw a man crouching near one of the concrete support pillars. He was lean, had brown, buzz-cut hair, and wore an olive-green jumper. He looked up at her and winked a mirrored, silvery eye, dragging on his Nikko-vape.

"Cool. Good to meet you." Juliet looked at Honey and the bank of elevators nearby. "Is the job, like, here?"

"Nah," Carn answered for Honey, blowing out a billowing cloud of vapor. Juliet caught a hint of lemon when the mist wafted her way. "They'll pick us up here."

"They?" Juliet glanced from Carn to Honey.

"Whoever's running things. I know as much as you." Carn shrugged, dragging on his vape again.

"Right." Juliet shrugged and moved to lean against the wall near Honey.

"Looking good," Honey said, reaching out to rub the stretchy fabric of Juliet's top between her fingers. "Bet it's comfy."

"Yeah. I was hoping I wouldn't have to take it off to wear whatever, you know . . ." Juliet trailed off, well aware that Vykertech probably had cameras covering every inch of their garage. She glanced around, looking for lenses, thankful that Angel was scrambling her appearance. Angel seemed to intuit what she was doing and helped by highlighting the little cameras mounted at the joints of nearly every support pillar where they met the cement ceiling.

"Right, I get it. Smart, girl!"

Juliet smiled and leaned back, waiting and watching while cars, tires squealing on the cement, wound their way up and down the garage. People walked by on the way to the elevators, and Juliet began to feel like this wasn't the most brilliant place to loiter. She was just getting ready to voice her concerns when a small yellow van pulled up in front of them. *Saguaro Scrubbers* was emblazoned on the side in bright blue lettering.

The side door slid open, and a burly black man with a thick, bushy beard said in a deep, rumbling voice, "Let's go! Carpets won't clean themselves!" He grinned, showcasing a wide gap between his front teeth, and winked.

"Here we go." Carn stood up, tucking his vape into a pocket at the front of his overalls. "I recognize that dude; his handle's Motor." He trotted over to the van and slapped palms with the other man before clambering inside. Juliet looked at Honey and shrugged, hustling to the vehicle and hopping in. Honey was right on her heels.

"'Sup ladies? I'm Motor, and our driver is Debbie."

"Yo," a hoarse voice said from the front; Juliet had no view of the speaker. The van didn't have seats, but there were boxes and large carpet-cleaning machines all over the place. Carn had taken a seat on top of a package of deodorizing powder, and Honey was working to wedge herself between a couple of cleaners. Juliet shrugged and squatted down on a box of industrial waste bags.

"Not the nicest ride in town," Honey noted. Then, "I'm Honey."

"Hey," Juliet said. "I'm Janu—"

"January," Motor spoke at the same time. "Process of elimination." He tapped the side of his head as if to illustrate his genius.

"Right." Juliet forced a smile. Debbie started the van rolling, and Juliet could feel it winding its way out of the garage. "So? Where we going?"

"Two megatowers over—WBD," Motor replied, slapping his palms together and grinning enthusiastically.

3

INTO THE DRAGON'S DEN

Juliet almost said that she couldn't do a job at WBD, almost bailed out on the job right there, but her paranoia about WBD spawned further worries—what if one of these operators she didn't know found it interesting that she'd bail? What if they decided to look into things, ask around WBD about her, and see if there might be some reward for information?

With those thoughts running rampant through her mind, she sat back on her box of cleaning supplies, palms growing clammy with stress, and subvocalized, "Angel, how big of a rot-brain move would it be to go into WBD's main building on a job?"

"I'll need more information to make that assessment; perhaps you should prompt Motor about what you'll need to do tonight and how they intend to get into the building."

"Hey," Juliet spoke up, clearing her throat and looking around the van; Honey had been chatting with Motor and Carn, but unless she asked Angel to play back the conversation, Juliet wouldn't have been able to say what they'd been talking about. "Can you give us some details now we're en route? I'd like to know what to prepare."

"Right, that's a good point; we don't wanna be goofing around in the van in the WBD garage. Well, we're going in as carpet cleaners. Our face, who we don't get to meet, organized some kind of an accident in the department we need to access. Then, he arranged for Saguaro Scrubbers to get the cleanup job. So, we just gotta go in, scrub up some stains, and cover for January while she accesses a secured terminal. You're looking for some kind of database file called A7749930."

"And they're just going to wave us through? They don't care about our IDs?" Juliet's mind was racing; if she went through the security check of an arcology trying to hide her facial features, they'd know something was up. No, Angel would have to project an actual face, not just scramble hers. Would the PAI be able to come up with something fast enough—something that fit her cover?

"No, no," Motor said, pulling a thin black deck out of his blue Saguaro Scrubbers jumpsuit. "The face hooked us up with fake IDs. Temo said they wouldn't hold up to serious scrutiny, but they'd get us through for a two-hour cleaning pass. In fact, January, that's your first job tonight—need you to take these ID files and set 'em up in our PAIs, you know, just so our little helpers can send the correct info when pinged at the entry."

Juliet reached out for the deck and pulled her data cable out of her arm, plugging it in, then subvocalized, "Angel, how's it look? Are they good enough?"

"These false identity files are rather simplistic, but they have info to satisfy every query in a standard scan. There are image files, but they don't match the people in the van. We'll need to alter those. I'll use a false image for your ID and project it for any video surveillance. I think you'll be able to enter and leave without anyone knowing it was you, even if the data theft is later discovered."

"And for the others, we'll use their real faces? I guess we don't have a choice unless they have projection capabilities on their optics, right?"

"More than that, they'd need the software to run the algorithm; it's not as trivial as passing along a fake ID file. Also, there are only four ID files here."

"What do you think? Is this insane? Should I bail?" Juliet was acutely aware of the other team members watching her, probably wondering what she was thinking as she went through the data on the deck.

"I don't know, Juliet. It seems very risky to visit WBD, but it also seems like the last place they'd look for you. Unless this job is a setup."

"Can they tell it's you if you hack into one of their terminals?" Juliet wondered if this whole job could be a trap, a way to fish for Angel.

"If I were a simple PAI without the ability to learn, yes. However, I can alter my behaviors—my methodologies; I can make it look like a skilled human did the work should WBD become aware of the breach."

Juliet thought about Angel's words for several heartbeats, her eyes closed as though she were concentrating. She thought about the rep hit she would take if she bailed on the job and it wasn't a trap. She thought about Angel's assurances, about how WBD must know her capabilities—why would they try to spot her this way if she could avoid that sort of detection?

She opened her eyes and glanced at Honey leaning against the side of the van, eyes distant. Honey trusted Temo, and Juliet trusted Honey. Couldn't it just be a coincidence that this job was at WBD? The corp had tens of thousands of employees in Phoenix, after all.

"Okay, can you copy the IDs over so I can unplug? I'll hook into each team member so you can set up their fake ID." With her mind made up, and a bit of adrenaline giving her voice a little edge, she spoke up, "Okay, team. I need to hook up to each of your data ports for a minute unless you've got a wireless access point. At the same time, you each need to look me in the eye for a minute so I can set up your false ID files with an accurate facial and retinal scan."

"The face didn't do that?" the raspy voice of Debbie called from the front of the van.

"No, and there are only four ID files—"

"No," Motor said at the same time. When Juliet stopped speaking, he continued, "How would the face set up the IDs to match us? He didn't know who Temo would put on the team. And yeah, Debbie, you're staying with the van."

"Easy money," the woman replied, turning the van sedately around a corner.

"Kay, who's first?"

"Me!" Honey said, scooting over the paneled floor to sit in front of Juliet.

"All right." Juliet smiled, handing her data cable to Honey. "Plug that in." Honey took the cable and reached behind her neck, feeling for her little port before inserting it with an audible click. "Angel, show me what you're doing, please," Juliet subvocalized.

Several opaque windows appeared in her AUI, and she saw the ID sheet that Angel was modifying. It showed a woman in her middle years with curly brown-blond hair and the name Yolanda Gallego. Angel began to remove fields in the ID sheet, changing the age to match Honey's better and deleting her image.

"Look into my eyes," Juliet spoke up, drawing her words out like a performing magician. Honey's giggle rewarded her efforts as she leaned forward and stared at Juliet. Almost instantly, she saw Honey's image populate the little box on her ID sheet. Angel had filled in an opaque blue background, masking the interior of the van.

"This field is where her unique retinal scan data goes," Angel said, highlighting a long string of code near the bottom of the sheet. "That should allow her to pass. I'm sending it through the connection to her PAI and setting up a daemon that will bypass the PAI's usual response when it receives an ID query. The daemon is set to expire in six hours, but during that time, any queries will receive this false ID. Should I set it up to delete this information and itself after that time frame?"

"Yes," Juliet subvocalized, then aloud she said, "Okay, team. I'm assuming none of you have a jailbroken PAI . . ." She paused, thinking about how Tig, her old PAI, would have responded if he had heard a conversation about altering his code in any way. She sat back, thinking for a moment, then looked around the van at all the other operators.

"Can you all tell your PAIs to go offline for a minute while I go over this?" Carn started to speak, so Juliet held up a hand to forestall his words. "Please. You can turn 'em back on when I'm done." She knew she was being overly cautious, but she didn't like talking about illegal PAIs in front of properly behaving PAIs. What if one of them filed an exception report with its manufacturer?

"Everyone offline? You too, Debbie—I need to say some stuff that some PAIs might find objectionable."

"Right," Debbie rasped. "We'll be in the garage in two minutes; I don't need guidance at the moment."

Juliet looked from Honey to Carn to Motor, and they each nodded, so she continued with her explanation. "I'm probably being paranoid, but I'm installing something in your PAIs' OS that might cause them to freak out if they knew about it. I don't mean that literally, but you know how you guys get manufacturer updates over the air now and then? You know how the user agreement asks you to agree to software monitoring for quality control and all that business?"

Juliet smiled as she spoke, thinking about how she was free from such tethers now that Angel was living in her head. "I'm setting up a daemon that'll answer ID queries for you with the false data for the next six hours. After that, it'll delete the ID file and itself."

"Wait! What if my PAI notices what you've done when I bring it back online?" Motor asked.

"No chance; my daemon will be very subtle. I promise you this software I'm using is miles beyond any of your PAIs. I mean, none of you have any million-bit packages, do you?" Juliet looked around the van, making sure none of them had further misgivings, and then looked at her AUI to see that Angel had indicated, with a green checkmark, that Honey's false ID was done.

"Okay, Yolanda." She smiled as she spoke, reaching up to pull her cable free. "You're all set."

"Yolanda, huh?" Honey scooted back to the side of the van and asked, "Can I turn my PAI back on?"

"Yeah," Juliet replied, pointing to Carn. "Step right up."

They were winding their way up into the parking garage by the time Juliet and Angel finished setting up everyone's spoofed ID. After she finished Motor's, he dug around in a big canvas bag and tossed blue jumpsuits to everyone. Juliet's smelled a little like BO and marijuana, and it had some questionable stains on the knees and around the wrists, so she was glad she had her own clothes to wear underneath.

As they all suited up and Motor unloaded some carpet-cleaning machines and a big rolling suitcase full of cleaning supplies, he spoke into the team channel Juliet had set up. "Don't even think about bringing any weapons in there. If we get stopped at the door and have to skunk this mission, I will personally devote the next month to burning you with every contact I know in the greater Phoenix area."

"Chill, brother," Carn's voice said through Juliet's audio implant, his name on her AUI lighting up with a faint amber backlight. "I don't think any of us are that stupid."

"What about my deck?" Juliet subvocalized.

"Can they see what's on it? Most jackers I've worked with have hidden partitions for their sensitive stuff and just put music or vids or whatever on the part they want to be searched." Motor was lifting a big carpet scrubber and grunted as he subvocalized, garbling part of his message, but Juliet figured it out through context.

"Yeah," she subvocalized to the team, then to Angel alone, "Right?"

"Yes. The sensitive files we've stolen here and there are encrypted and hidden. There's no chance a random security sweep would find them." Juliet stepped out of the van but turned back to the boxes of supplies; she'd just had a thought—what if WBD had her fingerprints or DNA on file? They knew who she was; they'd been to her old job and searched through her apartment.

"Any gloves? Or hairnets, by any chance?" She frowned and added, "Forgot mine."

"I've got gloves, sure, but no hairnets. Shit, here," Motor said, pulling off the maroon beanie he was wearing and tossing it to Juliet. "I ain't gonna leave any hair behind; at least not from my head." He laughed, rubbing a palm over his shaved skull. He watched Juliet pull it on over her tightly bound hair and grinned. "You really are the paranoid sort, aren't ya?"

"Yeah," Honey answered for her. "Keeps her alive."

"Right," Juliet said, adjusting the hat, oddly enjoying how warm it was. "Thanks, Motor."

"No worries. See that box? Grab a few sets of gloves; they're disposable."

Juliet pulled the perforated flap on the cardboard box, grabbed a handful of the latex gloves, size M, and stuffed them into her jumpsuit's front pocket. Then she followed the rest of the blue-jumpsuited crew as they wheeled carpet cleaners and a supply cart toward the elevator bank. Honey slowed to wait for her, leaning against the carpet scrubber she'd been charged with—somehow, Juliet had escaped equipment-lugging duty.

"You nervous?" Honey asked as Juliet caught up.

"A little. I've heard bad things about . . ." she trailed off and jerked her head toward the elevators.

"Yeah, no worries. Just cleaning some carpets!" Honey winked at her, then they were in front of the elevators, where Motor was repeatedly smashing his thumb against the call button.

"Won't make it come any faster, doing that," Carn said.

"Does it bother you?" Motor asked, still smashing his thumb into the button.

"I don't give a shit." Carn shrugged.

"Relax, guys . . ." Honey started to say when the bell dinged, and the door slid open. A man wearing a suit that probably cost as much as one of Juliet's implants walked out. He looked at their little crew through narrowed eyes, somehow looking down his nose at Carn, even though he was shorter. Carn waved at him and winked, and the man hustled away into the garage.

"C'mon," Motor said, wheeling his carpet scrubber into the elevator.

They had a short ride to the lobby, and when they stepped out of the elevator, they had to wheel all their gear through a carpeted, soaring display of excess and power. The walls of the WBD lobby were many stories high, and the interior reminded Juliet of a fancy hotel in the middle of a rainforest, so extensive were the atriums, trees, and climbing vines. She saw birds flitting about in the canopies over the atriums, and though it was brightly lit, like a summer day, the air at ground level was a cool seventy degrees.

"Those gotta be biogenned," Carn said, indicating a pair of beautiful, neon-bright yellow, red, and blue parrots in a nearby tree. "No way they'd let real birds fly around in here shitting on their employees and visitors."

"Ugh." Honey frowned. "Hadn't thought of that."

They wheeled their gear up to the security checkpoint, and a corpo-sec officer wearing an old-style security uniform, like a police officer in a detective vid, waved them forward through a plastic tunnel that looked like a full-body scanner to Juliet.

"You still feeling confident, Angel?" she subvocalized.

"Yes, we'll be fine, Juliet. Don't forget to respond if the guard addresses you as Helen."

"Right, thanks."

After they'd all passed through the plastic tunnel without any alarms ringing, the corpo-sec officer asked, "What floor? You have your work order?"

"Right here." Motor tapped his forehead. A second later, the guard looked at the tablet mounted on his station and nodded. "Floor one-seventy—two-hour pass. That sound right?"

"That's us!" Motor grinned. The guard nodded and pulled four bright yellow badges on lanyards from his station drawer. He tapped the cards to a magnetic pad on his desk and handed one to each of them. "If you're not out before the time expires, alarms will sound. If you need more time, you need to come down here and clear things with me. Understand?"

"Got it, boss," Motor said, mock tipping an imaginary hat. "Elevators that way?" He jerked his thumb to the rather obvious, enormous bank of elevators off to the left.

"Yep," the guard replied, motioning them on, already looking toward a pair of men in yellow vests and hard hats carrying black cases and waiting to come through his checkpoint.

When they stopped in front of the elevators, Motor gave Juliet a fist bump. "Smooth." Nobody else said anything on the subject—the team knew they were being watched from a hundred different angles while they waited there for their ride up. A bell rang on a nearby elevator, and they all hurried to get inside with their equipment.

The ride to the hundred and seventieth floor was uneventful. It took several minutes because the elevator stopped several times on the way to admit other passengers, but Carn and Motor stood in front of the door with their heavy equipment, and no one pressed the issue, preferring to wait for a less crowded car. When they arrived and stepped out into the lobby, the lights were dim, and they didn't see anyone around. The glass doors ahead of them proclaimed: 170 - Nutrition Testing and Compliance.

"Nobody's here?" Carn asked, walking toward the glass doors.

"Somebody's always here," Motor replied, jerking his head toward a little glass lens that Angel had already highlighted in Juliet's AUI. Motor spoke further, subvocally, into their team chat. "January, this will go a lot smoother if you can do something about the cameras." Aloud, he said, "Come on, gang. We've got cleaning to do."

He walked up to the glass doors and tapped the security pad with his temporary pass. A green LED lit up, and the doors clicked. Motor pulled them open. "We've got access to the room with the spill. C'mon."

"Angel? Any open connections on the camera system?" Juliet asked, following the others into a dim hallway lined with glass walls and doors, each labeled with a department or person's name.

"Yes. I'm analyzing the security."

They'd passed through another security door, down another long hallway, and had approached another door labeled Bioengineered Fruit and Vegetable Testing when Angel spoke, "I believe I found an exploit which will disable individual cameras. It's best we only use it when needed; perhaps you should save it for when you are accessing the data point."

"Not gonna mess with the cameras 'til I have to," Juliet subvocalized into the team channel. "Security's pretty tight, and I don't want to waste the exploit."

"All good. All *good*," Motor said aloud, emphasizing the word, before he stepped through the doors.

When Juliet and the others followed him, Carn let out, "Holy shit!"

Juliet could see what he meant. The room was about a square acre in size, with hundreds of black-topped workbenches—each equipped with a stovetop and sink—arranged in neat rows filling most of the space. The floor was red-and-white checked tile, so she couldn't imagine their cleanup job was in the area.

They'd all started wheeling their equipment further into the big room when a voice called out, echoing over the tile from the far-left corner. "About time you got here. Come on, my office is a goddamn disaster, and I've got an a.m. meeting!"

"What the fuck?" Carn subvocalized. "We gonna have this asshole breathing down our necks? Where's the access point supposed to be?"

"I think it's in the office where the spill was," Motor subvocalized back. "Goddammit," he said aloud and started wheeling his scrubber toward the voice.

4

//////////////

CARPET DUTY

The WBD executive who ushered them down a short hall to his glass-walled office was short, stocky, had wavy ginger hair brushed back from the sides of his very pallid cheeks, and wore a suit that would pay Juliet's rent for half a year if she sold it. His only cybernetic augmentation appeared to be the very high-end data port that winked with orange LEDs from his right temple.

Juliet knew people who wore their data ports exposed like that were either very frequently using them or enjoyed having people recognize the small fortune they'd spent on the implant. "Or both," she muttered, eyeing how the executive stood beside his office door and waved the crew inside.

"Come on, I've got a ton of work to do before my meeting, and I cannot concentrate with the stench in there."

"Goddamn!" Motor said as he walked through the door. Juliet and the others crowded close to see what he was exclaiming about. Honey squeezed through between Juliet and Carn and blew out a breath, stifling a gag while holding an elbow over her nose. Juliet stood on her tiptoes, looking over Carn's shoulder, and her eyes bulged out at the mess.

The office was carpeted in a pale gray Berber. A bright blue splash stain spread outward from the door, stretching toward the black leather sofa on the far wall and the two black executive chairs sitting in front of the enormous desk to the left—easily a hundred square feet of stain that stank like rotten eggs in vinegar.

"Yes, it's terrible, and you can rest assured the lab tech who stumbled in here with a test canister no longer works for WBD. Can you clean it?" He directed his question to Carn, who stood in the doorway nearest to him.

Carn shrugged.

"You'll need to ask the boss." He pointed to Motor.

"Yeah, I'd say so, but you'll need to give us some space unless you want to sign a waiver. Our cleaning foam has some toxicity—needs to in order to cut through a stink like this," Motor said, already tying a kerchief around his lower face. "Come on, get that equipment in here! Quit loafing around, ladies!" Motor urged Honey and Juliet, the only two still standing in the doorway.

"How long will this take? I have work to do," the executive barked.

"Yeah, you mentioned that," Honey said with a smirk, stepping into the office and pulling her carpet scrubber behind her.

"How'd you like a fast escort out of the building?" the executive asked, his plump, moist lips turning downward in a sneer.

"Hey, now," Juliet interjected, moving between the two of them as Honey kept walking deeper into the office. "Sir, we'd like to get this cleaned up for you, but that would be hard if you sent away part of our team."

"Well, I won't tolerate insubordination." His frown deepened, and he folded his arms in front of his chest. Juliet had never seen a grown man sulk so emotively.

"Of course not!" Juliet said as the team started setting up the cleaning equipment, sending sidelong glances toward her and the corpo tool. "Sounds like you've had a stressful day. Aren't you going to get any sleep at all?" She hoped her effort to change the subject wasn't too obvious, but it felt ham-handed to her.

"Damn right it's been stressful. I wish I could sleep! Thank God for No-doze, am I right? Hey, you're awfully pretty to be working cleaning carpets. Didn't make it into any training programs?" He leaned against his doorframe, and his pouty lips started to curl toward a smile as he looked Juliet full in the face.

She knew what he meant by a "training program." Most major corpos had advanced education opportunities that citizens could test for, and most people working for a corporation couldn't fathom why anyone wouldn't try to place—in their eyes, if you weren't working for their corporation, it was because you didn't cut the mustard.

"Yeah," Juliet lied. "Couldn't handle the math."

"Really? Didn't have a good primary school? Shoot, I bet I could line you up with a tutor." He winked at her, and Juliet almost coughed out a short laugh; it had been a long time since someone had flirted so obnoxiously with her. She kept her face straight with a monumental effort and said, "That's awful nice of you, sir. Do you think I could message you after we're done in here?"

"Of course; I'll look forward to it. Here," he said, flicking his fingers her way.

"Juliet, you've just received a contact card for Samuel Boze."

Juliet tilted her head down and looked up from under her eyebrows, smiling demurely. "Thank you, sir, but my PAI isn't working right. I'm sure I'll get your contact info when it comes back online."

"Oh, not to worry. Call me Sam, Samuel Boze. But what's your name?"

"Helen. I'm sorry about my PAI—it's been acting funny for a while and keeps going offline. Can I send you my contact info when I get yours . . . eventually? I think I just need a firmware update, and my cousin promised to help me with it tomorrow."

"Sounds good, Helen," Sam said, reaching out a pudgy hand with very nicely manicured nails. Juliet did her best to feign embarrassment as she took his hand, for once thankful for her hard-earned callouses.

"Helen!" Motor called sharply, his deep voice growling out the name. "We've got two jobs after this. Come on."

"Sorry, Sam," Juliet apologized, backing toward the office. "We should be done in less than an hour, right, George?" She glanced back toward Motor.

"Right. Just give us forty-five minutes or so, sir. You got the best crew Saguaro Scrubbers has to offer."

"Uh-huh. See that you don't miss any spots," Samuel said, turning to stride away down the hallway.

"Goddamn," Carn subvocalized into the team channel. "I thought you said we wouldn't meet our face, Motor." He reached out a fist toward Juliet as she closed the office door and moved closer to the team. She grinned back at him and bumped his knuckles.

"That was smooth; I cannot lie," Motor subvocalized—they all knew very well that Samuel had cameras observing them. He added aloud, "Helen, I see a few spots under the desk. You're on hand-scrubber duty." He dug around in his rolling case and pulled out a small, battery-powered vacuum with an attached aerosol tank.

"Okay." Juliet pulled on her latex gloves then took the little carpet cleaner. Silently, she asked Angel, "Should we turn off the cameras or something?"

"That wouldn't be wise; if Mr. Boze is watching, he'll know something's amiss. It would be best if your team cleaned for a while, and I built a fabricated loop to play, altering the cameras' data feeds."

"Okay," Juliet subvocalized to the team, getting down on her hands and knees and crawling under the glass-topped desk. There were some droplet stains on the carpet, so she didn't have to pretend to clean. "We need to clean for a while before I can build a loop for the cameras. Look busy and get those stains up, people."

"God, it stinks!" Honey exclaimed aloud.

"We'll get used to it," Carn said, whistling some tune, probably listening to music through his auditory implants.

"Can you walk me through the process, Angel?" Juliet subvocalized. Then, as she listened to Angel's response, she got to work scrubbing the little stains. The handheld scrubber was idiotproof, spraying something out of its little nozzle which broke up the spot, and then sucking everything into its little onboard tank. Somehow, it measured its own progress, and it would display a green LED as each blue blemish disappeared from the carpet's weave.

"First, I need to gain access to the camera system. The cameras in this room don't have open wireless ports, but they're networked with other cameras in the building, and while we made our way to this location, I found one which had an open port outside the elevator bank on this floor. The camera has a model number an iteration higher than the others, and I believe it was recently replaced. The technician either forgot to turn off its wireless access or didn't know it was policy."

"So you have the connection, but what if you hadn't found a camera like that?"

"Then this job would have been riskier. You'd have had to get me a hard-line connection to the camera network. While this room is being monitored, you might have been able to quickly plug into one of the cameras in the hallway or on the way to the restroom."

"Okay, so what's next?" Juliet prompted, tackling her fourth little spot.

"Now that I have a connection, I'll attack the security of the camera network with a daemon. I'm using one similar to the door breaker we wrote together, but I've tailored it to slip past the WBD ICE—I have experience with their defenses, if you recall."

"Okay, can you show me how that works when we get home? Also, your *experience* won't tip them off that it's you, right?"

"Certainly not—there are thousands of WBD employees who could gain access to the exploit I'm using and sell the information. When we get home, I'll walk you through the log." Another minute passed, then, "Juliet, I've gained access to the cameras in this room; there are seven."

"Wow," Juliet subvocalized. "Guy's paranoid. Probably goes with the territory when you're an exec in a major corp."

"I'm building the loop of the crew cleaning. I'm trying to add random elements," Angel said, opening a vid window in Juliet's AUI and showing her how she was piecing together hundreds of video slices of the crew cleaning. "This is something you'd want software to accomplish for you if you didn't have me. A human would require hours to do what a tailored application can accomplish in a few minutes."

"Are there programs available that do this? It seems . . . sketchy."

"There are legitimate uses for software that could perform this task—advertising, entertainment, and myriad others."

"I guess that makes sense." Juliet scanned the carpet, not seeing any more spots. "Can you highlight any spots I've missed?" Her visual spectrum changed; the carpet turned dark gray, and a few tiny spots of bright, glowing magenta appeared here and there. "Thank you!" she subvocalized.

"I'm ready with the loop when you are."

"Team," Juliet subvocalized. "Loop's ready, but I want to finish under here. Give me three minutes, and then I'm doing it."

"Uh-uh," Motor replied, his voice rumbling through her implants. "Corpo goon could return any second. Do the job, then you can scrub carpet if he wants to watch over us."

"Right. Makes sense," Juliet said, feeling rather foolish. "Angel, let me know when the cameras are looped. Do you have eyes outside this room, by the way?"

"Yes, I'm monitoring the approach from the break room on this level; Mr. Boze is consuming a plate of sashimi. The loop is playing."

Juliet didn't wait for an invitation. She clambered the rest of the way under the desk, coming up on the side facing away from the door, careful not to disturb the exec's plush, real-leather chair. Kneeling before the glass edge of the desk, she pulled forth her data cable and searched for the off-network deck she was supposed to breach. "Angel, what the hell? I don't see a deck."

"There's no indication of a deck on the desk, Juliet."

"Guys," Juliet subvocalized to the team. "Where's the deck?"

"It's not built into the desk or something?" Honey asked.

"Did you check the legs?" Motor replied at the same time.

Juliet frowned and carefully examined the desk's glass top for any ports, then she ducked back underneath and carefully ran her eyes over the black metal legs. "I don't see anything."

"Look behind," Motor said into the team channel. "That bookcase is full of shit."

"Right." Juliet spun around and scanned the built-in shelving unit filling the rear wall of the office. "Do you see anything, Angel?" Suddenly, her vision changed to the infrared spectrum, and she saw a warm spot directly behind Boze's chair. She stood up quickly. "Good thinking, Angel."

"I should have thought of it sooner! My only excuse is that I'm preoccupied with the camera management."

Juliet snorted a quick laugh, imagining Angel's face red with shame. That thought gave her pause as she moved toward the red spot on the bookcase. Where did she get a mental image of Angel? The PAI had no physical presence other than the little chip in her data port. Why did she picture her with pale skin and long, straight black hair? When did she decide that Angel had dark brown eyes, a narrow face, rosy cheeks, and pink lips? "Angel," she subvocalized, studying the books in front of the red spot. "Do you think it's safe to pull these books out? Also, why do I feel like I know what you look like?"

"I'm not detecting anything abnormal about those books—no electrical connections, no heat signatures other than the one behind them, and no indication that there's a biometric scanner or data port. As to your other question, Juliet, I have a virtual avatar that may have bled through into your subconscious. My connections to your synapses have grown quite extensive."

Juliet frowned slightly as she reached for one of the books, the one at the center of the heat signature, and very gingerly pulled it back with her latex-gloved hand. "Why would your virtual avatar be in my subconscious?" The book slid away easily, and she saw the flickering LEDs of a large black data cube. She didn't have to move other books because a short dongle with a data port was coiled directly behind the spot she'd cleared.

"I have functions that require an avatar; I have simulations I can run in which we could virtually meet."

"Why haven't you said something about those?" Juliet subvocalized as she plugged her data cable into the dongle.

"Deploying daemons," Angel said. A moment later, she continued, "There are many functions in my base programming which I've not yet come to terms with. I struggle with the animosity you feel toward my creators, and the knowledge that they have an, at best, amoral approach to humanity. The more time I spend with you, the more I find myself leaning toward believing they are actively immoral, which makes me doubt the altruistic perception I originally had about my deeper functionality."

Juliet's mouth fell open. Was her PAI having a crisis of consciousness? What must it be like to know who created you and slowly discover they were evil? "Angel, I don't want you to worry about this right now. You're good. Do you hear me? You're good. We'll talk about this some more, but for now, just know that you've shown me that you're a good . . . person."

"Thank you, Juliet," she replied, and Juliet swore she could hear a tremor in her voice. A moment later, Angel said, "My daemons have breached the deck's security, and I'm searching the compressed files for the correct database. You should be aware, though, that Mr. Boze just put his dish in the sink and seems to be leaving the kitchen."

"I'm in," Juliet subvocalized to the team channel, "but the databases are compressed. This might take a minute or five. Boze is maybe heading back this way, so someone needs to stall him."

"You heard her, Honey," Motor subvocalized, still scrubbing away at the carpet.

"Why me?" she replied, pulling the spent battery from her steam machine.

"You saw how he was with January. Dude's horny. See if you can get his number as fast as she did."

Carn laughed when he heard Motor's reply, and Honey punched him in the shoulder. "Oof," he grunted, stumbling toward the couch and dropping his bottle of cleaning detergent. "You're lucky I screwed the cap on," he growled, picking it up.

"He's moving down the hallway toward the large workspace we passed through," Angel told Juliet.

"Hurry up, Honey! He's coming," Juliet hissed. Motor shot her a glance and held a finger over his lips. Juliet's face reddened, and she turned away, staring at the data cube as if she could will Angel to find the correct file faster.

She heard the door click as Honey stepped out, and she squatted down, just in case Boze got close enough to peer through his tinted glass walls. Her mind was racing—one moment, she'd been worrying about Angel; the next, she'd been worrying that Boze was coming. And now, she was embarrassed about speaking out of character.

"Relax," Motor spoke into the team channel. "You've still got control of the cams, right?"

"Yeah," Juliet replied, still refusing to look away from the data cube. She took a deep breath—in through her nose, down to the pit of her belly—then slowly pressed it out through her lips, trying to clear her mind the way Sensei had taught the class before stretching the other day. As calm returned and the prickling heat of embarrassment faded away from her ears and neck, she asked Angel, "Any update?"

"Honey is speaking to Boze, asking him for help to find the bathroom. He seems irritated, but she's keeping him busy. Also, I've searched more than half of the compressed files. At most, I'll need three more minutes."

"Three minutes," Juliet said into the team channel.

"About done here, boss," Carn called aloud, and Juliet glanced over her shoulder to see he was indicating the carpeted area. It was true; the room was clean, and the only smell hanging in the air was the lemony scent of whatever chemical the scrubbers used to break down the stain.

"Yep," Motor said. "Get some rags and all-purpose spray and wipe down the furniture." He grunted, stuffing equipment back into his rolling bag, and Juliet felt sweat dripping down her forehead.

"He's approaching, Juliet." Angel's voice didn't sound panicked, but it didn't sound calm.

"Honey's lost the corpo goon," Juliet subvocalized. "He's coming." She looked over her shoulder to see what Carn and Motor would do. Motor didn't look particularly stressed as he dragged his heavy steam cleaner over to the door, setting it in front of it. A dozen seconds later, the handle turned, and the door opened an inch to slam into the machine.

"Yo! Just a minute, boss!" Motor yelled. "We're cleaning up. Almost done, sir."

"What's going on? Why's the door stuck?" Boze's voice called through the crack. Juliet ducked down further, hoping he couldn't see her if he put his face to the glass.

"Just wrapping up the equipment. Sorry, sir. We'll get this moved in a hurry!" Carn said, grunting and jostling the steamer so it bumped against the polished, simulated rosewood door.

"Angel?" Juliet asked, practically lying flat on the carpet, her data cable snaking up along the cabinetry to the data cube.

"I have it, Juliet! File A7749930." Juliet didn't reply; she sat up, yanked her cable out of the dongle, and stuffed the book back into place. She wiped the sweat from her forehead onto her sleeve, then saw a dark smudge of moisture on the bookcase and began to panic—how much sweat had she gotten on the bookcase? What about the carpet? She hustled over to Motor's supply case and grabbed a bottle of all-purpose cleaner and a rag, then she returned to the cabinet and started to spray everything she might have touched, including the carpet.

She heard the door open as she wiped at the wood, and then Boze's voice. "Well, it smells better. Will that fade? I have some sensitive employees coming to the meeting. You wouldn't believe the list of allergies I have to accommodate."

"Oh, sure, but you should leave the door open and maybe crank up the ventilation for an hour or two, especially if you're going to work in here. Also, the carpet's slightly damp, and any dirt tracked in will probably stain it." Motor sounded like he actually did this for a living, and Juliet wondered if it used to be or still was his day job.

"What are you doing, Helen?" Boze asked.

Juliet felt her heart begin to hammer, and she almost dropped the bottle of cleanser she held in her left hand. "Just wiping down the furniture, Mr. Boze. It's part of the service."

"I don't want that shit on my books—some of those are antiques. There's no stain on the bookcase; leave it."

"Yes, sir," Juliet said, giving the area behind the desk one last glance; it looked clean to her. She offered Boze what she hoped was a shy-looking smile, then tucked her cleaning supplies back into the case. She avoided looking at Boze again as she and the team made their way out of the office and back toward the elevators.

They'd just gotten to the corner of the hallway when he called after her, "Helen, don't forget to message me when you get that PAI fixed."

"Okay," she replied, turning and offering a quick wave, then hurrying after the others.

"Damn, he's smitten," Honey said, joining them at the intersection. Then she subvocalized into the team channel, "Thanks for getting my steam machine, January. Sorry I couldn't stall him more; the guy wanted nothing to do with me. Must have a type." She jostled Juliet's shoulder, and the others laughed; everyone was feeling the stress of the job beginning to fade as they stepped up to the elevators, and Motor began to repeatedly jam his thumb against the call button.

"That won't . . ." Carn started to say.

"Don't say it," Motor interrupted.

5

A GRAVE OFFER

A ny payment show up yet?" Juliet asked Angel, adjusting the ice pack on her swollen ankle; she'd resisted a little too much when her partner at practice had been practicing leg sweeps. She suspected it was an accident, but couldn't be sure when it came to Charity.

Thinking of Charity, she started to ask Angel to do some research on the "competitions" she'd mentioned again that morning, but Angel was already responding to her first question.

"I do see a pending transfer of eighteen thousand Sol-bits."

"Finally! I was starting to think Temo stiffed me." It had been three days since the carpet-cleaning job, and Temo had been putting off her payment, saying he was waiting on the client's transfer to clear.

"What about my rating?" She knew the question would please Angel, and the PAI was quick to display her operator card on her AUI.

Handle: "January" — SOA-SP License #: JB789-029	
Personal Protection & Small Arms License #: E86072801	Rating: E-17-N
Skillset Subgroups and Skill Details:	Peer and Client Rating (Grades are F, E, D, C, B, A, S, S+):

Combat:	Heavy Weapon Combat	F +1
	Bladed Weapon Combat	F +3
	Small Arms Combat	F +4
Technical:	Network Security Bypass/Defend	D
	Data Retrieval	E +5
	Welding	*
	Electrical	*
	Combustion & Electrical Engine Repair	*
Other:	High-Performance Driving/Navigation	F +1
	Negotiation and Conflict Avoidance	E

"Whoa! The team really came through for me, didn't they? Negotiation and conflict avoidance?"

"Yes, it seems Motor approved of your handling of Mr. Boze and passed along your performance details to the client. You're also officially in the E rating bracket now, and look at your network security bypass rating."

"A solid D." Juliet smiled. "Can't complain about that."

"You just received a message from Temo. It's short. 'January, we got paid, and I have big news for you. Call me when you get a few minutes.'" Angel paused for a moment, then asked, "Would you like me to contact Temo?"

"Not right now. I'm not feeling ready for 'big news.'" Juliet stood, sliding her aluminum lawn chair back on the little concrete pad, then hobbled over, opened the door, and climbed into her trailer. She was still sticky with sweat and needed to shower and wash her gi. "Ugh, does Charity need to go so damn hard all the time?"

Angel knew better than to answer a question like that, and Juliet sighed, limping around the trailer, doing some laundry in the mini combo washer-dryer that'd probably seen thousands of loads of dirty clothes and linens in its twenty-year existence. After that, she stood in her shower and let the hot water pound noisily against the top of her head, falling like a curtain over her face. Ten minutes in, she slumped down and sat in the plastic enclosure, sighing as the water continued to fall on her like hot rain, and practiced her breathing exercises.

She felt a lot more like herself when she finally clambered out of the shower and dried off, slipping into some clean, comfortable shorts and a T-shirt. She'd been going hard and knew if Ghoul were still around, she'd warn her about burning out. Juliet wasn't worried about that, though—she still found everything she was doing in her new life quite entertaining, and the progress she was making at the dojo made all that hard work feel worthwhile.

She knew if she were to run into her old self, the Juliet who ate junk food, worked long hours at the scrapyard, and couldn't bear to think about her life past the next weekend, she wouldn't recognize herself. Despite everything— the near-death experiences, the terrifying things she'd had to do, the people still hunting for her—she was glad she'd been the one to find Godric near death there in the scrapyard, glad he'd given her Angel.

She cooked one of her new, mail-order frozen meals. Her little freezer was full of them, and they'd have been an impossibly exorbitant expense in her old life, but they hardly made a dent in her new income. Angel had been the one to suggest the new meals—organic vegetables, single-source proteins, healthy fats, and guaranteed no preservatives or weird additives.

Angel had told her some truly horrifying stories about the things corps were putting into the engineered grains and processed foods they made readily available and affordable—everything from hormone suppressants to decrease birth rates to additives that damaged a person's gut, leading to auto-immune disorders.

Angel said there were people on the "shadow net" who claimed the corpos wanted their people sick but manageable with pharmaceuticals. It sounded like a crazy conspiracy, but Juliet had learned to trust Angel, and she definitely didn't trust the corpos.

As she took the steaming meal out of the toaster oven—the company recommended not microwaving—she said, "Here go sixty bits down the gullet."

"Your body thanks you, Juliet," Angel replied, a variation on her usual response to Juliet's frequent comments about the meals' cost.

"Okay, call Temo. He can watch me eat while he spins his tale about his wondrous news." She had a hard time believing whatever Temo found exciting would be exciting to her. "What's my balance, by the way, including the 18k?"

"You have 85,390 Sol-bits. I'm connecting you to Temo."

A window appeared in Juliet's AUI, and after only one *beep*, Temo's face popped into view. He really did look excited, eyes wide and bright, smile already in place, leaning forward like he wanted to crawl through the connection. "January!"

"Hey, Temo." Juliet stuffed a forkful of buttery broccoli into her mouth and chewed while she listened to his enthusiastic response.

"You won't believe this! The client, the ones you did the carpet job for? They were very impressed with your performance and asked for you, by operator ID number, for a much bigger, long-term operation. We're talking a month or more, and it'll net you more than 100k before bonuses!"

Juliet's eyes widened at the news, and she worked on chewing and swallowing her food, letting the information sink in, mulling it over as she sipped at her protein smoothie. Temo stared at her, obviously aware that she was eating, and struggling to remain calm while he waited for her response. Finally, she cleared her throat. "Sorry about that. Um, that sounds interesting, but I could do a lot of jobs in a month. Is 100k really so great for such a time investment?"

"Oh, January, that's the base commitment! There's language in the contract which allows for bonuses up to two or three times that amount depending on your success. Don't you want to hear what it's all about?"

"Well, 300k sounds a lot more exciting." Juliet perked up. "Yeah, let's hear the details."

"I don't have the actual *details*," Temo said, grinning and holding up a hand to forestall any sort of outburst. "I mean, I have some broad strokes; they didn't want to share everything until you'd agreed, signed an NDA, and met with their agent in person."

Juliet nodded and sniffed, loading her fork with another bite. "Okay, I'm listening. Give me the broad strokes."

"So, they need a talented operator, but not one who's well-known. There's a corporation in the Phoenix area that's going to be recruiting for a new program, something the client is very interested in. They want you to get hired by the corp, go through their training, and spend some time learning everything you can about the program. You'll get 25k up front, even if you fail to get recruited. If you succeed, you're guaranteed the other 75k, so long as you don't get washed out. You'll get bonus percentages for each successful intelligence report you deposit at a secure drop."

Juliet swallowed her bite and asked, "That sounds very risky. First of all, I'm not signing anything until I know what corp we're talking about. What kind of program."

"I don't know much more, January, but I can ask the client for a few more details if you're interested. They probably won't give me much, but they were very interested in you. Motor wrote up a hell of a glowing report about how you handled that corpo exec, not to mention how you ripped through their security to handle the cameras and the data retrieval."

"I won't lie, Temo," Juliet said, unable to stop the smile tugging at the corners of her mouth. "This sounds interesting, but I need to know more—the name of the corp at a minimum—before I'm willing to meet with the client's agent."

"Seriously? What do you care? All these corps are the same, aren't they?"

"I've got no love for any of 'em, that's true, but there are some corps I won't mess with. That's all there is to it." Juliet shoved her tray away from herself, giving Temo her full attention. "I'm not trying to kill your buzz. I'm intrigued, okay? Do me a favor and let the client know I'm interested, but I want to know a little more before I commit. Cool?"

"Yeah, that's cool, January. I gotta say, though, opportunities for this kind of payday don't come around often for someone at your operator rank. Really give it some thought, all right?"

"Yeah, of course." Juliet nodded earnestly.

"Right; I'll get back to you as soon as I hear something." Temo cut the call, and Juliet frowned, worried she'd pissed him off.

"Do you think I'm being overly cautious, Angel? I don't want to try to infiltrate WBD . . . I'm a bit leery of Vykertech, too," she said after some reflection.

"It seems like well-placed caution to me. Even if the client supplies a false identity, we'd have to worry about DNA sampling; I doubt the corp hiring you for their new 'program' would allow that to slip by, along with retinal scans and fingerprints. There are ways to spoof all those tests, but none are cheap, aside from the retina print—your implants can be modified."

"Good. I'm glad I wasn't unreasonable. I'm going to ice my ankle again and watch some vids. Can you queue up that vampire drama I've been checking out?"

"Of course; you're on episode seven, 'Chocolates, Coffee, and Type-A Positive.'"

"Don't judge me, Angel!" Juliet grinned as she limped to the freezer for her ice pack.

"I must confess I'm interested to see what happens to Samantha."

Juliet smiled and snorted, saying, "You're the best PAI in the world, Angel."

She spent the afternoon and part of the evening lying on her old, scratchy couch, her vid window stretched to fill most of her AUI and watching light, rather ridiculous dramas play out, alternating between snacking and icing her ankle. It wasn't a surprise to her when her eyes felt too heavy to hold open, and she drifted into sleep before the digital readout in the corner of her vision said 8:00 p.m.

Normally, if she received a call or message while sleeping, Angel knew she shouldn't bother her, but the PAI woke her up near midnight saying, rather sweetly, "Juliet. Juliet, Temo is attempting to call you with a high-priority flag."

"Mm?" Juliet hummed blearily, scooting back so she could sit up against the arm of the couch. Her neck was stiff, and her ankle was throbbing. "Temo?" she asked, noticing the red, blinking call window. "Accept."

"January, glad you were awake." Temo was sitting in a dark room, his face seeming to float in the blackness. "I was doing some borderline delinquent payroll when the client got back to me. I thought you'd want to hear what they had to say."

"Yeah," Juliet said, rubbing at her eyes and yawning. "Lay it on me, T."

"Hey, did Honey tell you that was my nickname?"

"I don't know." Juliet yawned again. "I think I wanted to call you that for a while, and it just kinda slipped out." She giggled sleepily.

"Damn, you're in a different mood from earlier. Anyway, the client was cool as crisp celery. They gave me a few details when I told them you were very interested but worried about crossing the wrong corpo. The job is with a big player by my standards, but only midsize in the Phoenix area—Grave Industries."

"Grave . . ." Juliet frowned. "I think I saw some guns with that brand."

"Yeah, they do mil-tech. Corpo-sec divisions sport a lot of their gear, too."

"Okay, I'm still interested." Juliet sat up a little straighter and reached for the soda pouch she'd left, forlorn, on the orange shag carpet next to the couch. She sipped it and smiled as the warm root-beer flavor bubbled down her dry throat.

"They also assured me they have a comprehensive false ID for you. They want you to be safe, January. These people are legit. I gotta say, I've worked with them for three different ops now and never had any complaints."

"Okay, when do you need my answer?"

"The sooner, the better. They're chomping at the bit to start prepping their operator, whether it's you or someone else."

"I'll get back to you by noon tomorrow, okay?"

"Okay, cool. That should be fine. Call me anytime, don't worry about the hour."

"'Kay. Night, Temo."

"Night, January." Temo's fingers flicked, and the call window winked out.

Juliet scooted back down on the couch and stretched out, arching her back until it popped. Then she said, "Angel, call Honey, please."

She lay there, her mind wandering lazily to fantasize about what the job might be like while the ringtone started to sound. Would she have to take tests? Would she be selected? What kind of work would it be? She'd often thought about the benefits of working for a corp, but never could stomach giving up her freedom or compromising her values for a paycheck. This might be a chance to see what it was like on the inside without the guilt—she'd be working against them, after all.

"Honey is not accepting your call," Angel said, closing the window.

"Damn. Hey, I haven't tried Ghoul in a couple of weeks; let's see if she's unblocked me."

A few seconds later, Angel replied, "Sorry, Juliet. You're still blocked."

"Damn it! Who am I supposed to ask for advice, Angel? I mean, besides you!" Angel didn't answer, and Juliet lay there staring at the ceiling, her mind far too busy for sleep to reclaim her. "Hey, call Hot Mustard."

The call window appeared, and the tone sounded once before Hot Mustard's grinning face filled her vision. "Juliet! Talk about an unexpected name to pop up on a call at this hour! How you doing?"

"Hey, Mustard." Juliet grinned, amusement crinkling the corners of her eyes. "Hope I didn't wake you."

"You kidding? I'm a night owl, girl." He sucked on some kind of vape with a bright blue LED and blew a prodigious cloud of steam out. "So? What's up? Need a drinking buddy?"

"No . . . no," she said, shaking her head after seriously considering it. "I just wanted some impartial advice."

"Oh, yeah? All right, shoot. Old Mustard's seen a thing or two."

"Oh, God! Please tell me you're changing your handle to Old Mustard." She giggled and drank another swig of root beer.

"I'll think about it." He chuckled.

"Well, here's the deal: I got offered a pretty big-time job. Something that could take a month or more and has a real fat payday if I'm successful. I'm nervous about it, though, and I'm new to all this stuff, so I don't know how unusual it is. Can I run it by you?"

"Hell yeah. No worries, Juliet. I'll be your Romeo . . . no, that's wrong. Who was Juliet's cousin?"

"Tybalt," Angel supplied.

"Tybalt, which I absolutely already knew and didn't need my PAI to tell me!" Juliet laughed. "Seriously, though, wasn't he kind of a jerk?"

"Oh, I don't know. I think he was just a guy who liked to fight and loved his family. Maybe too much, I guess. Well, tell old Tybalt about your job offer, hmm?"

"So there's a client who wants me to get a job with a pretty big corp here in Phoenix. Obviously, I'd be working against the corp's better interests in the process. Doesn't that seem, like, extremely risky?"

"Well, shoot, Juliet. It all depends on what kind of job they want you to get and how hard it's going to be for you to get whatever they're looking for while you're on the inside. If they want you to try to get into some sort of executive training program, you can expect all kinds of tests and a pretty thorough background check. If they want you to work cleaning the furnaces, it might be a little less rigorous, you catch my drift?"

"Yeah, I guess that makes sense. The client says they have a thorough false ID for me. Do you think I should hear 'em out? They won't give me more details until I sign an NDA and meet with their agent."

"Tell you what—why don't you let me drive you to the meeting? If shit looks hinky, you can bail on it. If they try to stop you from bailing, I'll be there with lead love taps."

"Lead love taps? You've got a way with words, Hot Mustard."

"My buddies in my old unit called me a poet, but they were mostly from Arkansas, so their tastes might not align with yours." He winked and grinned while he spoke, and Juliet could see his cheeks were flushed from drinking.

"Are you going to remember this conversation when you wake up tomorrow?" She smiled, softening the words.

"Don't you worry about Old Mustard. I ain't had but half a bottle of bourbon tonight." His grin was infectious, and Juliet found another giggle slipping between her lips.

"Well, okay. I'll call my fixer and try to set up the meeting for tomorrow. If you're busy or you feel differently tomorrow, that's fine, all right? Don't stress—"

"Nah, I ain't got shit to do. My next gig's on Friday. You gotta buy me lunch . . . or coffee, I guess, depending on what time we're going, though."

"Deal! I'll call in the morning, okay?"

"Cheers," Hot Mustard said, lifting a little glass with a finger's width of amber liquid at the bottom and throwing it back. "Tomorrow, then." He winked, and the call window snapped shut.

"That was abrupt," Juliet noted. "Still, he's a pretty sweet guy, isn't he, Angel?"

"He's been quick to come to your aid a couple of times now. You should find out his birthday so you can remember it."

"His birthday?" Juliet squinted her eyes, and the corner of her mouth quirked up in amusement.

"Yes," Angel replied. "I've read that a person's birthday is a good time for friends to present them with a gift, acknowledging their importance and ensuring they feel appreciated."

"Angel," Juliet said, shaking her head in wonder. "You never stop surprising me. That's an excellent idea. By the way, when's your birthday?"

6

////////////////////////

INTERVIEWING SKILLS

This is a pretty neat car, Hot Mustard," Juliet said, opening the passenger door of the little electric-blue pickup truck with oversize rear tires and a thrumming hydrogen cell power plant.

"Hey, Juliet, thanks," he said, scooping a sheaf of papers off the passenger seat and stuffing them into the center console. "It's old, but everything about it is custom by now."

"Sounds fast."

"Oh, she'll leave some rubber on the road if I need her to." Hot Mustard grinned and pulled out of the AutoDrug parking lot where he'd picked Juliet up. When he pressed on the accelerator, Juliet felt the instant torque the vehicle's battery bank applied, and then the H-cell kicked in, and her stomach did a little flip as the truck quickly ramped up to speed.

"Hey, since I know your real name, it's only fair you should call me Win—all my real friends do. My momma named me Winfield. Besides, I know you changed your handle, but your name's stuck pretty firmly in my head. Don't worry, I'll call you January if we ever work with strangers."

"Really? Did I wear you down that fast? You're tired of those mustard jokes?" Juliet smiled and gave him a sideways glance. He grinned, pulling some loose strands of pink hair out of his face and dragging them back behind an ear.

She wondered how old he was; he had faint lines around the corners of his hazel eyes, but his smooth-shaven skin was remarkably free of blemishes.

She'd guess he was around thirty, but he talked like he'd seen a lot more than a thirty-year-old ought to have. She supposed Ghoul was the same way; maybe it was the lifestyle.

"Nah, I like jokes a lot. Much as a cat likes cream, you might say."

"Well, I like your name, Win. Thanks for sharing it with me; I'd reciprocate, but as you said, you already know mine."

"Mm-hmm," Hot Mustard—Win—said, tucking a custom black-and-chrome nicotine vape between his lips, inhaling and blowing a cloud of vapor out his partially open window. "This bother you?" he asked, gesturing with the metallic rectangle.

"Nah, we all have our demons. I like real sugar in my sodas."

"'Course you do." He grinned, shaking his head.

"What's that supposed to mean?"

"Nothing, nothing. So this pin you sent me is right north of downtown. Temo give you any other details? I need to post up in overwatch?"

"I don't think that'll be necessary, but I'll feel much better knowing you're waiting for me outside. Thanks again, Win." She smiled and brushed at her own hair, trying to settle the strands blowing in the little gusts coming through his window. "I like the way your name sounds. Very positive."

"Oh, yeah, *win*." He grinned and drummed his fingers on the steering wheel, then added, "I guess you could call me what my momma does—Winnie."

"Oh, I better not. That sounds pretty affectionate." Juliet couldn't help how her eyes squinted in amusement, her tone light and teasing.

"Well, maybe someday. Like, if I'm sick and you bring me some soup or something."

"This conversation got weird fast, Win!" Juliet shifted in her seat so her legs turned more toward him and she could look at him without turning her neck.

"Yeah, jeez. I'm bad at making conversation in broad daylight. I was just thinking, you know, since we're friends now, when might you have cause to use such an affectionate sobriquet? Then it hit me—Juliet's sweet; she'd bring me soup if I were sick."

"Excuse me? Sobriquet?" Juliet had Angel to thank for knowing what the word even meant; her PAI had displayed the definition on her AUI—a nickname. "You always talk this fancy when you're not throwing lead around?"

"Well, Momma was big on reading. My uncles had me out shooting whenever she wasn't looking, but that wasn't too often." He pulled up to a stoplight, glanced over at her, and added, "You look nice. I think I've only seen you in work boots and tactical gear. That's a real nice blouse."

"Thank you." Juliet smiled, smoothed down her dark black slacks, and fidgeted with the buttons on her wrinkle-free white polyblend blouse. "You don't think it's too much? Should I do up this top button?"

"No! It's just right. The shoes were a good choice, too; not quite flats, but definitely not heels—you could run in those." He'd started the car moving again, and as he spoke, he reached up to the console and switched on the radio. "I know everyone's got their own music in their heads, but it's nice to listen in the car still, don't you think?"

"Absolutely." Juliet nodded. She leaned her head back between the headrest and the window and closed her eyes, listening to the unusual music Hot Mustard—Win, she corrected herself, played. Lots of bluesy, Southern tunes, but also some bluegrass that almost sounded like folk music to her. It wasn't something she'd have picked out; she didn't know if she'd ever heard anything like it, and it made her want to spend some time listening to things that weren't selected to match her tastes by some kind of algorithm.

"Angel," she subvocalized.

"Yes?"

"Would you take a look at the music playlist generator that my old PAI set up for me? I think I need to introduce some new types of music randomly—I kinda like this lady singing right now." Out loud, she said, "This is nice, Win."

"Oh, yeah. She has a hell of a voice, doesn't she?" He gestured to the display at the center of his dash, and Juliet saw the woman's face along with her band name, feeling nostalgic for when she used to own a car.

"Good speakers," she noted, closing her eyes and letting the depth of real sound waves wash over her; auditory implants were great, but they didn't feel the same as being immersed in the sound like this.

"I told you!" Win said, voice raised to be heard over the music, "Everything on this old girl's been upgraded. We're about five minutes out. You all set?"

"Yeah, you think I should bring my Taipan?" Juliet reached behind her right hip and touched the hard plastic handle just jutting above her waistband. She'd stared at herself in the mirror from every angle; you couldn't see the gun unless you were looking for it, but she supposed these people were pros and would be doing just that.

"Hell yes. If they have a problem, make them put their guns on the table too."

"Juliet, you're receiving a call from Honey," Angel discreetly cut into the conversation.

"Sec, Win," she said, accepting the call. Honey's face appeared in her AUI, still sleepy looking, with a pillow behind her head. "Honey, thanks for calling me back."

"Hey, girl. What's up? Sorry I missed your call—too much to drink."

"No worries. It was a bit late to be calling, anyway. I have a job offer I wanted to run by you, but I'm meeting with the client soon. I'll call you later, okay?"

"Okay, cool. Everything all right?"

"Yeah, Mustard's with me." Juliet felt her cheeks heating up when she spoke, which startled her. Why was she feeling embarrassed?

"Oh, really? Boy, he sure comes through for you at the drop of a hat, doesn't he?" Honey's eyes sparkled with amusement, and it became evident why Juliet had been blushing.

"All right, well . . ." She cleared her throat, glaring pointedly at Honey's projected image. "Call you later, okay?"

"Yeah, okay." Honey smirked and closed the connection.

"That Honey checking in on ya?" Win asked, pulling the truck into a parking lot which sat next to a concrete-and-glass office building, small by Phoenix standards and shaped more like a cube than a tower.

"Yeah, I tried to call her last night, but she was in dreamland."

"Oh? So I was option number two, huh? Well, guess I lucked out by being up late." He looked at her, half his mouth curved up in a half smile, then touched the ignition button, powering down the truck's H-cell.

"You were a good option, Win. Thank you again." Juliet reached for the door handle, and as she pushed it open with a creak of the hinges, said, "It really means a lot to me to know I've got you out here in case something funny is going on."

"I got you, girl," Win said, giving her a thumbs-up, then he stepped out of the truck. Juliet also clambered out and watched as he started rooting through a big black bag he had in the low, shallow truck bed. He pulled out a rifle that looked like serious business and a well-used, army-green ballistic vest that he shrugged into. "I'll post up out here. I'm sure they've got eyes on us already, so I'll keep the rifle down in the bed there. Don't you worry, though. If I see you come running or hear anything going off"—he tapped his ear—"I'll make 'em sorry."

"You're kind of a badass, you know that, Hot Mustard?"

"You're not bad yourself, January." He leaned against the rear fender, eyes trained on the building's lobby door fifty yards distant, sucking on his little vape.

"What's in that thing, anyway?"

"This one? Wintergreen-flavored nicotine." He laughed, blowing out a cloud. "Don't judge; I drank a lot last night. Can't expect me to give up my stimulants in the morning, can you?"

Juliet smiled, walking around the truck so she stood before him. She held out a fist and said, "Wish me luck?"

"'Course. Good luck, Juliet." He reached out, his long fingers curled into a loose fist, and touched his knuckles to hers. Juliet turned and started walking to the building, suddenly self-conscious about her walk, her outfit, and her decision to forego almost any makeup.

"What the hell is wrong with me?" she breathed, feeling unreasonably relieved to pull open the glass door and step into the cool lobby of the building.

"Your vitals are good, Juliet. Your pulse is slightly elevated, but it's normal to feel nervous before an interview."

"Is that what this is, you think? An interview?" she asked, looking around the lobby, happy to see a professionally dressed receptionist, living plants, and a sitting area occupied by people in suits and ties. "At least this doesn't seem like a front . . ."

"Hello," the young woman sitting behind the receptionist's desk greeted. "May I help you?"

"Hi," Juliet replied, stepping forward and speaking softly. "I had an appointment with Mrs. Dowdall. Um, she said the meeting room was on—"

"The third floor, conference room three-oh-one B. You're January?"

"That's right."

"They're expecting you. Please take the elevator right up."

"Thanks." Juliet was starting to feel nervous, and her earlier teenage-like goofiness was fading away. She forced a smile at the receptionist then made her way toward the elevators, suddenly aware of the weight of her pistol, imagining it was glowing with neon lights as she walked through the lobby. No alarm Klaxons rang, nobody shouted out a challenge, and soon, she was riding up to the third floor.

When the bell rang and she stepped out, she inhaled deeply of the clean, cool air, something like pine scent in the air. Glass-walled offices lined the corridor, the one in front of her reading 300. She looked to her left, saw it was 301-A, and turned that way, walking on the clean, high-traffic emerald-green carpeting. Ten short steps later, she saw her destination on the left, the door slightly ajar. She stepped up to it, pushed it open, and leaned her head inside.

Three people in suits sat at a long glass table. Coffee and pastries were on top of it, and they were murmuring amongst themselves, but the person nearest and facing the door, a woman with curly blonde hair and a smart gray suit, noticed her and smiled. "January? Welcome! You're right on time. Please come in; have a seat." She gestured to the chair at the head of the table.

"Hello," Juliet said, her voice maddeningly catching in her throat. She walked into the room, heading toward the chrome and black leather chair. All three of the suits, as she found herself mentally calling them, stood up and stared at her, affecting friendly smiles. The woman reached out a hand.

"I'm Rachel Dowdall." She shook Juliet's hand with a firm grip, her soft, warm flesh making Juliet absurdly self-conscious about her callouses. "This is Trevor Barns, and next to him is Paul Vallegos." Each man made a point of shaking Juliet's hand, saying how happy they were to meet her, and then they sat down, so Juliet did as well.

They all looked young, with smooth skin and perfectly coiffed hair without a trace of gray. Something about their demeanor, though, spoke to decades of experience and confidence; these were probably people who could afford antiaging treatments that the average citizen only heard about on vids. Paul, the shorter, curly-haired man, produced a data cube and set it on the table. Juliet recognized its branding—a high-end, custom Aurora, if she wasn't mistaken.

"If you don't mind, I'll be activating a jammer which will prevent any sort of surveillance or network access while we're meeting. We'll be speaking about some very sensitive topics." He held his finger over the cube, eyes on Juliet, as if waiting for her permission.

"Yeah, that's fine."

"Excellent," he said, touching the crystal display facing him. Juliet's ears buzzed for a moment, and her vision became staticky, parts of her AUI blinking out altogether. After a moment of disorientation and uncomfortable feedback, it began to fade, and she could hear again, though the sound coming through her ears seemed muted and far less rich than usual. Her AUI elements didn't recover, and she was left seeing the world much as she used to before the upgrade.

"The jammer is active, and I've filtered as much as possible to give you as much sight and sound as I'm able. The data you're receiving through your implants is corrupted, though, and anything I attempt to write to memory will be garbled," Angel told Juliet.

"That's a thorough jammer," Juliet commented.

"I'm glad to see you were able to filter out enough to function," Paul said, and Juliet didn't miss his quick nod to Rachel.

"Well, January." Rachel leaned back and crossed her legs, shifting so she looked more directly her way. "We're delighted to hear that you're interested in our operation. I know you have a lot of questions, and so do we. We'd like to treat this meeting as a chance for all of us to do some evaluating and information gathering. Does that sound fair?"

"Of course." Juliet unconsciously mimicked her body language, leaning back and crossing her legs.

"Step one," the woman said, sliding a thin, paper-size data pad over the table toward her. "Please sign this with your operator ID number. It's an NDA which would allow us to seek legal repercussions should you speak about the operation's details to anyone outside of this group." She gestured to Juliet and the two men opposite her.

Juliet leaned forward and scanned the minuscule font. "What do you think, Angel?" she subvocalized.

"It's standard legal wording. There's nothing alarming in the language. Suppose you were to reveal the details of this operation to anyone other than the three named principals, the people here in the room with you. In that case, they can seek legal recourse, up to and including revocation of your operator license and garnishment of any future income as recompense for financial damages."

"Okay," Juliet replied, leaning forward and scrawling out her operator ID on the line at the bottom of the pad.

"Excellent." Rachel folded her long, manicured fingers on her lap and smiled at her, bright red lips parting to reveal perfect, vid-star teeth. "I think we'll start things by answering some of your questions. How does that sound?"

"Juliet," Angel said, her volume low, probably to avoid startling her. "Interviewers often judge their potential employees based on the types of questions they ask."

"Can you tell me about your organization? It seems like this operation will require a significant time investment and entail quite a lot of risk for me. I'd like to know something about the people I'd be working for." After she spoke, Juliet subvocalized, "Thanks, Angel. I figured something like that was going on."

"That's an excellent question," the tall, clean-shaven, dark-haired man named Trevor said. He had a deep voice with an accent that reminded Juliet of something vaguely European. She was sure Angel could place it for her, but she kept her attention on his words. "We work for a very wealthy philanthropist, not a company per se. Our and potentially your benefactor has an agenda that would draw the ire of most major corporations. He sees himself as a guardian of sorts, and his attention has been drawn by something Grave Industries is working on right here in Phoenix."

"We're not at liberty to disclose our employer's name, but he's not based in Phoenix. None of us are; we're staying at a hotel downtown. I wish I could tell you more," Rachel said, stepping in when Trevor stopped speaking. "Rest assured that our employer values privacy and will go to great lengths to protect the anonymity of those who work for him. Do you have other questions?"

"Why didn't you search me? I mean, when I came in here."

"An excellent question, Juliet!" Angel approved, uncharacteristically interrupting the conversation. "This may throw them off guard . . ."

Rachel smiled. "We feel that, in a meeting such as this, trust is important. Have you ever heard the phrase 'trust but verify'?"

"Yeah, didn't some US president or other famously say it?"

"Perhaps. It's been around a long time. I bring it up, though, because I think it's bullshit." Rachel paused, letting her words sink in. Juliet frowned, trying to make the connection to their topic, trying to understand what the woman meant. She had the feeling this was some sort of test.

"Because . . ." she started, then smiled. "Because if you trust someone, you don't need to verify. It's an oxymoronic statement."

"Quite right." Rachel smiled, glancing at her two companions, and Trevor snorted.

Juliet had the feeling some sort of inside joke or wager had just played out.

"Anything else you care to know?" Paul asked, looking up from his data cube.

"Aside from about a hundred questions about the job?" Juliet smirked and continued, "I do have one more—why me? I get that you need someone low profile, but why not an A-tier operator from one of the moons or something?"

"People don't get to be A or even B-tier operators without creating some buzz—without building a rep, even if they mostly operate out on . . . Europa, for example. It adds a layer of risk. More than that, few operators with A-tier skills can pull off the fresh-faced recruit look we're seeking. Some faces, charisma operators, could do it, but they don't have the technical skills we require. I'm sure, to answer your question more bluntly, we could find someone more qualified than you, but we're a bit pressed for time, and our budget, while quite healthy, isn't limitless."

Rachel did, indeed, speak bluntly, and Juliet found it refreshing. "I found that answer more satisfying than I anticipated." Juliet smiled and sat back, feeling quite a lot more comfortable than when she'd stepped into the conference room.

"All that said, January, before we get into the specifics of the job, we need to be sure you're the one for us. Are you ready to answer some of our questions?"

7

QUESTIONS

I'm listening," Juliet said, looking into Rachel's big brown eyes, noticing for the first time that she had tiny secondary pupils at the outsides of her irises. She wondered what sort of functionality those added to her ocular implants.

"You should know that I'm capable of detecting duplicity; at least the blatant kind." As she spoke, Rachel drummed the polished red nails of one hand on the table, and Juliet carefully avoided looking at it, wondering if it had been some sort of tell.

"So much for trust, huh?"

Rachel smiled and inclined her head, giving Juliet the point. "Some risks aren't mine to take; I'd like to go with my gut feeling and offer you the operation, but my employer requires a certain level of due diligence. Don't hold it against me?" Her tone made it a question.

"I won't, so long as you're honest with me as well. But I won't promise to answer every question you throw at me."

"Let's start with the basics. Here's an easy one: have you ever had any dealings with Grave Industries?"

"I almost bought one of their rifles at a gun shop. That would be the extent of it, though."

"Good; we can't have someone recognizing you, can we? Trevor?" She glanced across the table, and Juliet followed her gaze to the dark, brooding man.

"What model data jack do you have?" he asked, his eyes a bit unfocused like he was studying something on his AUI.

"Bio Network Solutions, um, 8 . . ." she trailed off, trying to remember the model number, but then Angel supplied it in her AUI. "8840."

"Adequate." He nodded. "Please have your PAI handshake with mine. I'm going to test your ICE."

"You're what?" Juliet frowned. "You're going to try to hack me?"

"I need to know you won't fold at the first hard access request."

"Huh." Juliet shook her head, then subvocalized, "Go ahead, Angel. Take that smug smirk off his face." She watched him closely while Angel complied with the request, saw his eyes narrow, saw his frown deepen as he pressed his lips together. She watched, entirely at ease, while he strained and struggled, and a bead of sweat popped into existence over his left temple and began to slide down along his jawline.

"Are you struggling, Trevor?" Rachel asked—apparently, Juliet wasn't the only one noticing his efforts.

"Goddammit!" he said, slapping his hand on the table. "You've got some tricky damn ICE, January. I think I'd be hard-pressed to get in even if I had on my netjacker immersion kit. Do you mind telling me your PAI model?"

"Yes. Sorry." Juliet shrugged. "It's mostly custom by now, anyway," she added, smiling at how she sounded like Hot Mustard talking about his truck.

"I told you," Paul spoke, surprising Juliet. "If it weren't for her being new, there's no way she'd be ranked at E tier."

"What about that, January?" Rachel interjected. "I'm not asking you to divulge any of your secrets, but can you tell us a little about yourself? I understand the SOA prioritizes privacy, and I don't want you to tell us anything that makes you uncomfortable. Still, I'd sure like to know how you learned to bypass and maintain network security the way you do. What kind of work did you do before you became an operator?"

"I have a very talented mentor, and she's told me a time or two that I'm a quick learner." Juliet wasn't lying, and the tongue-in-cheek description of Angel almost made her laugh. As it was, her lips curled up in a mischievous smile.

"Very well. I'll take that to mean you're something of a savant?" She studied Juliet for a minute after her words, and when Juliet didn't react, she sighed lightly. "Trevor, your next question?"

Trevor grunted acknowledgment and asked, "What about your other gear? Audio and ocular implants, I'm assuming. Anything else we should know about, particularly nanites?"

"No, just decent eyes and ears. I've been trying to save for nanites, but nothing yet."

"You know how to shoot? What about self-defense? Had any fight training?"

"Yes, I can shoot, but I wouldn't call myself an expert. I've been studying mixed martial arts for a little while . . ." Juliet didn't want to tell them she'd only been at it for two months, and she knew she was better than most people with that much time in the sport, so she tried to keep it vague.

"Any qualms about violence?"

"Qualms? Can you clarify the question, please?" Juliet uncrossed her legs and sat up straighter, pulling her chair closer to the table.

"I mean, could you kill someone if you had to?"

"If I had to. I'm not looking for that kind of trouble, but I've had to pull the trigger before."

"That's what we learned in our background check on your operator ID." Trevor nodded. "I'm glad you didn't try to dissemble."

"What are we doing here? Playing a game of gotcha?" Juliet directed the question to Rachel, her eyebrows drawing together in a sharp *V*.

"No, January. Please bear with Trevor; he's almost finished with his questions."

"Are you opposed to having augmentations done to you? Cosmetic or otherwise."

"I . . . I'm not opposed in principle, but I won't sign any blanket agreements. I'd need to know about anything being done and approve on a case-by-case basis."

"Paul," Trevor said.

"January, we will need to tailor a comprehensive false identity to you. We have the basis of it already complete; we just need to connect your physical and biometric data to it. There's the question of spoofing your DNA—we don't want Grave to find an old sample of yours in any security databases; it would blow your cover and ruin the op. Do you understand what that entails?"

Juliet frowned, glanced at Rachel, and simply answered, "No."

"Well," Paul said, folding his hands and leaning toward her so his elbows rested on the table. "This is the most challenging hurdle when it comes to getting you ready. We've allocated a large percentage of our operation's budget to it.

"Hiding someone's DNA isn't trivial. We'd need to replace your hair—the easiest part, really. We'd just give you a synth-flesh scalp with new synth-hair already installed. We'd need to remove most of your other body hair, and we'd need to graft synth-flesh into your cheeks to counter the, almost guaranteed, cheek swab they'll perform on intake."

He paused, looking hard at Juliet as if to gauge her reaction, then continued, "We'll have to install some synth-glands in your mouth to wash your DNA out of your saliva and release the false ID's DNA. We're reasonably sure they'll do a blood draw as well, so we'd need to install tailored nanites in your arm—a tiny, purpose-specific nanite battery and swarm—to alter your blood in a similar fashion. It would only work for short periods in a localized manner, a looped false vessel. It would be too invasive to alter all of your blood all of the time."

He glanced around the table as if waiting for anyone else to step in, then said, "Depending on your PAI's capabilities, we might need to install a coprocessing node with the nanite management software."

Juliet's mind was reeling. The alterations he'd listed weren't insignificant; they were talking about some pretty major changes, but it also meant she'd be gaining the ability to fake her identity far more thoroughly than Angel could with simple data manipulation. How did she feel about losing her hair? She knew, academically, that it would be indistinguishable from human hair, that her synth-flesh scalp would perfectly match her skin, but it still seemed like a lot.

She wasn't sure why she had qualms; she'd been willing to give up her eyes. What about the synth-flesh cheek grafts he'd mentioned? Did that bother her? These questions ran through her mind, along with a hundred more, but in the end, she decided it didn't matter. She'd still be her, and they were minor, cosmetic things which wouldn't even change her appearance if she didn't want them to. Suddenly, she smiled, wondering if the synthetic hair's color would be programmable.

All three of the suits were staring at her, and she had a feeling they were judging her, measuring her respirations, watching her perspiration, timing how long it took her to take it all in. "That doesn't sound too terrible. Will your budget allow for any more augmentation if, for instance, my PAI is capable of running the nanite software?" She forced herself to breathe, picturing herself in the dojo, visualizing her heart slowing down, imagining cool air blowing through her hair, down her neck.

"If we decide you're the right candidate, we'll consider everything we can to increase the likelihood of your success," Paul replied, nodding, not at her but across the table to Rachel.

"Let's talk about the op," Rachel said, drawing Juliet's attention back to her. "Grave makes weapons. They make combat gear, and they make combat cybernetics. Our benefactor has learned, through various sources, that they're testing some new tech and will be hiring people in Phoenix for the pilot program."

"And you want me to get hired." Juliet nodded, trying to give the impression that it wouldn't be a problem.

"Exactly. The main hurdle is that we don't know what the program will entail, so we don't know the best way to prepare you. That means we'd need you to be ready for anything. They may have new weapons they want to train you on, or it could be new cybernetics they're evaluating. There's the outside chance that this is a program for their relatively new pharmaceutical division; they could have new combat stimulants or something similar, though it's unlikely they'd hire new people for such a field test."

Juliet asked the obvious question, "Why *would* they hire new people?"

"Perceptive. The reason our employer is interested in this particular program is likely the same reason they're hiring a new team for evaluation: it may be something which upsets the status quo, something trained Grave combat personnel would have difficulty utilizing."

"Or," Juliet said, narrowing her eyes, "something they don't want to risk their trained personnel with. Something they can test on expendable, low-investment, new employees."

Rachel sighed and looked from Juliet to her colleagues, perhaps hoping one of them would intervene. They sat stoically, though, Paul staring at his data cube and Trevor brooding, not making eye contact with anyone. "It's true, January. One of the reasons we're offering sizable bonuses on this long-term operation is due to the high-risk factor."

"But . . ." Juliet prompted. After a moment of silence, she said, "There is a but, right?"

"But," Rachel replied, nodding, her eyes narrowed in determination, "if you complete the assignment and there are any augments you're unhappy with or side effects you're experiencing as a result of your efforts, our employer is prepared to spare no expense to remedy things—to make you right."

"And if they want me to do something I can't abide by, and I walk away?"

"You'll receive twenty-five percent of your initial 100k payment upon completion of our insertion preparations. Should you fail to be accepted by Grave, or if you leave before you deliver any intel, that money is yours to keep." When Juliet nodded, Rachel frowned and added, "That wouldn't be ideal, January; we'd lose a sizable investment in your false ID preparations, and it would negatively impact your reputation."

"Right." Juliet returned the frown. "I'm not trying to think of a way to game this situation. I want to do the job; I want to succeed."

"Good," Trevor said, shifting to look at her more directly. "We want you to, also. Grave Industries is rumored to be pushing the envelope with some of their R&D, which wouldn't be a problem if they didn't have contracts with some very disruptive, amoral corporations that influence substantial population centers.

"It's also possible they're simply building up a new conflict team. A portion of Grave's balance sheet is comprised of units that work as mercenary corpo-sec, showcasing their latest tech and working to cross-sell the equipment they use."

"And if that's the case?" Juliet asked.

"In that case, we want as much information about their operations as possible—the equipment and pharmaceuticals you're issued, and their command structure. If you can plant some daemons inside their secure networks, that would be bonus-worthy."

Rachel cleared her throat. "I think that about wraps up this part of the process, January. We'll be in touch, one way or the other. Please don't forget about the NDA you signed; I'd hate for you to wind up in any trouble. Before we end this meeting, do you have any further questions?"

Her abrupt wrap-up almost startled Juliet, but it had created a question in her mind. "Do you have any sort of time frame for when this might happen? Do you know when Grave is going to do their hiring push?"

"It would be soon, January. If you're interested in this operation, please don't leave town," Trevor answered.

"How long will it take you all to, you know, modify me to pass the ID screening?"

"A day of surgery and a few days to recover. We'd house you downtown; we have a team setting up a surgical suite right now."

Juliet thought about it, thought about all she'd learned, and while she found the operation very intriguing—exciting, even—she also thought it sounded hazardous and a little bit scary. She decided she'd be fine either way—if they offered her the job, she'd give it a lot of thought, but if they didn't, she'd be fine just doing her own SOA gigs.

With that in her mind, she pushed her chair back and stood up, saying, "It was nice to meet you all. I'll look forward to hearing from you. Please *do* let me know if I don't meet your criteria; I'd like to know when I can leave town." The last was said with a wink directed at Trevor.

"Very good." Rachel nodded, also standing. Each of the suits offered her handshakes, and she felt a lot more confident squeezing their soft hands than before; she was someone who worked for her money—these suits needed her, and they better damn well appreciate her hard skin and firm grip.

When Juliet stepped out of the office building into the bright sunlight, she strode toward Hot Mustard and his little blue truck with a broad smile. She didn't know why, but she felt proud of herself, proud of how she'd held up to all that scrutiny, and proud that they'd been interested in her at all. She knew Angel was a big part of it, but Angel wasn't the one who had to stay cool in there, wasn't the one who had to answer all those questions. They were a team.

"Hey, Win," she said. "Looks like I didn't need overwatch after all."

"Well, if it made you feel more confident in there, I'm happy to waste the hour." He grinned, still leaning against his rear fender, still holding onto his vape.

"What is it?" Juliet asked, squinting into the pale blue sky. "Lunchtime? C'mon, let me buy you some food, at least."

"Now you're speaking my language. How about a burger? I know a place that mixes the proteins just right—tastes like a good old burger like my uncle used to make."

"Like real beef?" Juliet asked, opening the passenger door.

"Oh yeah, and the mayo tastes real, too—decadent."

"Sure, if that's what you want, I'm happy to give it a try."

After he'd climbed in and started up the truck, Win asked, "So? You seem to be in a good mood; they offer you the gig?"

"No, they were playing their cards pretty tight. They acted like they had other candidates to consider. I guess I'm in a good mood because I feel like I asked the right questions and had good answers to theirs. I've decided I'll be happy if they offer me the job, but also just fine if they don't. I'm not a hundred percent sure I want to do it. Does that make sense?"

"Sure does. I suppose you can't tell me the specifics, but did it sound dangerous?"

"Yeah, I think so. It sounded iffy in a lot of ways. It also sounded really exciting." Juliet laughed as she said the last part, reaching over to squeeze Win's shoulder in her enthusiasm.

"Exciting is good, but it can also be bad; we humans have a habit of doing stupid things if it's fun enough, you know what I mean?"

"Yes! Like driving way too fast. C'mon, Win, let me see what this thing can do after this light."

"Oh? You wanna see what this old girl's hiding under the hood? All right, all right." He chuckled as they pulled up to the red light. "Let's see, any corpo-sec lurking around?"

Juliet felt giddy, like she'd just finished an important exam and didn't have to worry about studying for the rest of the semester. She looked out the rear window and saw the cars starting to line up. "Just regular folks behind you."

"All right," Win said, looking left and right. "Don't see anything obvious; here we go, Jules. Hold on tight!"

Later that afternoon, after Juliet had bought Win lunch and spent most of the conversation over their meal profusely apologizing for the speeding ticket a drone had sent him, even going so far as to offer to pay for it, he dropped her off just outside the trailer park. As she stepped out and closed the door, she leaned back through the window and said, "I'm really sorry, Win! I can't believe that drone got you so quickly. You only stomped on it for a few seconds . . ."

"Well, in the drone's defense, ma'am," he started, purposefully thickening his Southern drawl, "I did get this old girl up to around one-forty."

"I think you mentioned that. A few times." Juliet smiled and thumped the truck's roof. "Don't worry; I'm suitably impressed. Maybe we can go out to the ABZ sometime and see what she can really do?"

"Hoo, now! Are you inviting me and my truck on a date?" Win smoothed his hair back while he spoke, his grin widening. Juliet found his mannerisms endearing, but she wasn't sure she was too fond of his pink hair. Still, she smiled and shrugged.

"I guess we can see what it turns into."

"Well, if we're going out to the ABZ, let's make it a picnic and bring our guns; I can use some target time."

"Oh!" Juliet's eyes widened, and she leaned even further forward, practically sticking half her body through the window. "That sounds really fun. Can I try your rifle, the big one?"

8

///////////////

ENTANGLEMENT

T hat's right," Win said, watching as Juliet pulled the rifle into her shoulder, eye peering through the powerful scope. "Just keep it tight like that;
she's gonna buck more than you might be used to."

"'Kay," Juliet breathed, carefully moving the crosshairs in the scope's display to hover over the old bottle Win had set up on top of the half-crumbled
block wall some two hundred yards distant.

"Now, if you're right about your PAI's capabilities, it should be able to
help you zero the scope, adjusting for wind, elevation, parallax, all that stuff.
It used to be a hell of a lot harder in the old days."

"I've made the adjustments, Juliet. This scope is very sensitive; Hot Mustard spent a lot of money on it." Angel's voice was hushed, as though she were
worried she'd upset Juliet's aim if she spoke too loudly.

"When you're sure you're set, very slowly exhale, and gently squeeze that
trigger. Try not to think about the gun firing. Some people hold their breath,
but I've always learned to exhale. See how it works for—" He was cut off as the
rifle barked a loud *bang*, and Juliet whooped as the bottle shattered. "Sheeyit!
First try?" Win laughed and jostled her shoulder. He was sitting on the blanket
next to where Juliet lay, and she looked up at him with a wide smile.

"Hey, I couldn't have done it without a good teacher and a very nice rifle.
But damn! My shoulder's gonna be bruised."

"Yeah." Win laughed. "Actually, the rifle's old as the hills—was my grand-
dad's. The optics, though, they cost me a pretty penny."

"Well, I like it," Juliet said, rolling to her side so she leaned on one elbow, brushing some hair out of her face. "So, what do I do to load another round?"

"Right." Win leaned forward to grab the front of the rifle with one hand, then he pulled the bolt back with a smooth clicking action and drove it forward. The empty brass casing flipped out onto the blanket, and he said, "That's that."

"Why not an automatic?"

"Oh, they have beautiful semiautomatic rifles these days, but the bolt action holds a special place for old shooters like me; we're superstitious about parts failing or the automatic action jostling the gun and throwing us off by a hair. A hair at a thousand meters can make a big difference."

Juliet leaned forward and lined up the sights on another bottle, trusting Angel to make her adjustments, and then slowly let her breath leak out between her lips, gently squeezing the trigger. This time, when the report sounded and the rifle bucked into her shoulder, she was ready for it, but the bullet missed the bottle, kicking a cloud of gray concrete dust up. "Hey!"

"Hah, that's 'cause you were anticipating that kick. Bet you were pulling the rifle into your shoulder a bit too hard there, darlin'. Try again, but don't think too much about your shoulder. Just hold the rifle snug and accept you'll have a bruise tomorrow."

"Okay," Juliet replied, reaching up to pull the bolt back. She did it too slowly, and the cartridge didn't eject cleanly. Win reached forward, grabbed onto the bolt over her hand, and jerked it back and forth a little until the cartridge came free; then he showed her how to yank it back and drive it forward—it moved more stiffly than she'd expected. His hand on hers was warm and rough, and she couldn't help the little electric thrill that ran through her at the touch.

"Thanks," she said when he backed off, the rifle ready to shoot.

This time, she pulled the rifle snugly to her shoulder, but was careful not to hold it too tight. Once again, she let her breath slip out, slow and steady, and squeezed the trigger, eyes on the target, trying to trick her brain into avoiding thinking about the shot. When the gun barked and the glass shattered, it was almost a surprise. "Yes!"

"We got ourselves a natural here," Win announced to the empty, deserted parking lot. They'd driven an hour into the ABZ east of Phoenix and hadn't seen anyone, not even scavs, within miles of the old, half-collapsed box store.

After they shot up a couple dozen more targets, burning through Win's supply of self-loaded .308 cartridges, they stopped to eat the lunch they'd packed—sandwiches Win had made and potato salad and coleslaw that Juliet had picked up from Benji's diner.

"Damn, but this is good slaw!" Win said around a mouthful, some of the dressing dribbling down his chin. Juliet laughed and reached forward to wipe it off, enjoying how his rough stubble scraped at her thumb. "Oh, jeez. My momma always told me to slow down when I eat. Said I'd never impress a girl by finishing my plate before she'd had time to take a bite."

"Your momma sounds like a smart lady." Juliet made a show of taking a huge bite of her sandwich, struggling to keep her lips closed while she chewed it. Win's eyes bugged out, and she had to hold a hand over her mouth to keep from spitting it out as laughter bubbled up out of her.

"My kind of lady!" As Juliet's laughter tapered off and she swallowed her bite with a visible effort, he asked, "So? You decide to take the job?"

"Uh," Juliet started, wiping at her mouth with a paper napkin. "I don't think they're going to offer it to me. It's been two days with no word."

"Well, maybe they just have a lot of T's to cross and I's to dot. I bet you'll hear something tonight. If they do, what do ya think you'll say?"

"Thanks for the vote of confidence. I've thought about it a lot, and I'll probably accept it, but I have some stipulations they might not go for. The job calls for some . . . augmentation; I think I'll insist that my doctor do the work. Sorry." She shrugged. "I can't really say more about it." When Win shrugged, she continued, "Hey, since we're asking each other questions, tell me about your hair. Why the pink?"

"You don't like it?" Win asked with a laugh, reaching up to brush it back. "I was thinking about a change; it's been a while. What would you pick? Blue? Black?"

"Well, it's not that I don't like it," Juliet said, suddenly feeling like a jerk. "I was just curious. I mean, you don't wear flamboyant clothes, and I can't see any mods on your body, so it kinda stands out, that's all. What's your natural hair color?"

"Oh, kind of a sandy brown. It's a little embarrassing, but I did the hair to impress a girl, and I've just sorta grown used to it."

"Really?" Juliet laughed. "Tell me about this woman that had such a hold on you."

"Yasmin," Win said wistfully. "She really messed me up for a while. I met her through a friend, and she was into clubs and stuff, told me my hair was a bit boring and dyed it for me. Tell you the truth; I'm still not really over her." His voice had grown rather somber, and he looked down while he spoke. Juliet suddenly felt lost for words, wishing she'd kept her mouth shut.

"Jeez, Win." She leaned forward to take his hand. "I'm sorry! I didn't mean to turn the conversation so dreary. If you're trying to get over a girl, though, I recommend not keeping your hair the way she liked it. I mean, unless you really like it too."

"Ah, heck, Juliet. That's my bad. I need to work on my filter." He squeezed her fingers and smiled, and his greenish-brown eyes twinkled in the afternoon sunlight. The air was remarkably brisk for Arizona, but that was the beauty of the desert; you could enjoy some cool weather a few months of the year when everyone else was buried in snow.

Juliet felt her heart speeding up, and that little dizzy, funny feeling you get in the pit of your stomach when romance is in the air, and suddenly, she panicked, pulling her hand back and clearing her throat, reaching for her paper plate. "Nice job on the sandwiches," she said, taking another bite.

"Oh, if there's one thing I'm good at, it's sandwiches." Win smiled, leaning back, clearly not wanting to make an issue of her sudden retreat.

They finished their picnic, talked a bit more about their favorite foods, their families, and shooting, and then, as if a spell had been broken, they packed up and drove back toward town. Juliet was conflicted about Win—he was sweet, and she found him attractive, but she also wasn't sure she wanted a relationship right then. And that was, in her mind, the reason she'd backed off and moved the conversation to more surface topics.

For his part, Win seemed fine, keeping things relaxed, and she supposed it made sense if he really wasn't over his last girlfriend yet. Maybe he didn't want Juliet to be his rebound or something. In any case, they ended the "date" with a hug outside Win's truck when he dropped her off at the trailer park. Juliet squeezed him warmly, pressing into his tall, lanky, but firmly muscled chest, and when they parted, she looked into his eyes and said, "I had a lot of fun today, Win. Thank you for everything."

"Yeah, me too, Juliet. Me too. Talk to you soon?"

"'Course you will. I'll call you if I hear anything about that job; otherwise, maybe we can do something else together soon."

As Juliet made her way through the park to her trailer, Angel surprised her by asking, "Juliet, do you feel strange about Hot Mustard—Win?"

"What do you mean, Angel?"

"I noticed you were exhibiting some mating behaviors, but I'm curious why you don't couple with him."

"Oh my God!" Juliet laughed aloud. She was trying to decide how to respond to Angel when one of the women who lived in a trailer one lane up from hers called out.

"Juliet! Oh, Juliet! Could I ask you a question?" The speaker was Mrs. Burgess, a woman who had to be in her eighties. She always wore a floral print pullover dress and had tightly permed gray hair.

"Yes, Mrs. Burgess?" Juliet said, walking over, relieved to have her conversation with Angel interrupted.

"I know you had some work done on your trailer—a water heater and a shower upgrade, isn't that right? Can you tell me a little bit about it? I think this sani-spray is bad for my skin. Look! Look how thin my skin is!" She held up her arm, and Juliet saw it covered with little purple bruises and several scabs. "I just bump into the counter or touch one of my rose bushes, and whamo! Another bruise!"

"Oh, gosh, that looks painful, Mrs. Burgess. Well, I can forward the contractor's information to you. Would you like that?"

"Yes, dear, but my budget is quite limited. Was it very expensive?"

"Not terribly, but my water bill is close to the same as my rent payment every month, I'm sorry to say."

"Oh dear, oh dear. What's the world come to? I thought we'd solved all that climate business with those terraforming doodads."

"Um, yeah. Between you and me, Mrs. Burgess, I think it's a combination of some things. The terraforming installations are near the oceans, and I think they're supposed to take a few more decades to really clean up the air and get our temperatures under control globally. But"—Juliet leaned closer and lowered her voice—"I also think the corpos got used to collecting big water payments, and they won't let that go anytime soon, even as clean water grows more plentiful."

"Those bastards," the usually sweet old lady hissed, and Juliet had to fight to keep her face straight.

"Anyway," Juliet said, waving and continuing on her way. "I'll send you the contractor's information."

"Thank you, dear."

"Juliet," Angel spoke suddenly, a note of excitement in her voice. "You're receiving an encrypted call from Rachel Dowdall."

"Answer!" Juliet said, hurrying over the last dozen feet to her trailer, pressing her thumb to the biolock, and hopping up the short flight of steps. A window appeared in her view with Rachel's face—perfectly smooth skin, professionally done makeup and hair, and a smile that seemed friendly but didn't convey any warmth.

"Hello, January. I'm very sorry it took us so long to get back to you—we've had quite a full plate the last few days." Rachel's tone was friendly, and her brown eyes squinted with an almost chagrined look, the effect of which was to put Juliet at ease. As she realized this, Juliet smiled, and it felt a little forced—this woman was a pro.

"Hi, Mrs. Dowdall. Thanks for getting back to me."

"Rachel is fine, January. Tell me, do you have any plans this coming Monday?" Rachel's voice brimmed with excitement, and Juliet knew she felt like she was delivering some highly anticipated news. Juliet felt her sincerity, and her smile began to feel less forced; she was excited, despite her reservations.

"Before I make a fool of myself," she said, unable to keep a tremor out of her voice, "you're offering me the operation, right?"

"Yes! Our inside source tipped us off that Grave will be conducting a hiring fair at the end of next week, and we'd like to have you ready and briefed before then. Assuming you're still interested, we'd like to conduct your surgeries on Monday."

"Rachel, I'm thrilled that you're offering me the position. I really am, and I'm willing to move forward with you, but I have some reservations and a stipulation."

To her credit, Rachel's enthusiastic expression only faltered for a fraction of a second, but when her smile returned, it was no longer reflected in her eyes. "Oh? We have some flexibility, but there are certain non-negotiable aspects of the operation . . ."

"I'm not asking you to change how the operation goes or anything that I need to do to get ready; it's just that I've had some bad experiences in the past and would prefer to have a doctor I trust conduct the surgeries. She's local and very competent, and I've already sent her messages confirming her availability. Don't worry—I haven't, and won't, reveal anything about the operation."

"I . . ." Rachel frowned, and Juliet could see the wheels spinning behind her eyes. She nodded. "I think we can arrange that. One of us can meet you at the doctor's office with the implants and specifications. It might be better, in fact. We're running into some logistics issues with the temporary operating theater we're trying to set up in the suite here."

"Thank you," Juliet said, and the sincerity in her voice brought Rachel's smile back.

"You're welcome, January. I can't say I blame you—you don't know us beyond what your fixer might have told you. Going under the knife in a hotel room with a bunch of strangers would be unnerving to anyone."

"I'm glad you understand. Shall I let my doctor know we'll be at her place on Monday? What time?"

"The earliest availability. Please message me with the location and time; I'm going to send the contract your way. Review it and send it back with your operator's signature before the end of the day tomorrow. Will that be all right?"

"Yes, of course. I'll probably get it back to you today."

"Great! I'm looking forward to working with you, January. Please stay available over the weekend in case something comes up."

"I will. Thank you again, Rachel."

"You're very welcome," she replied, and then the connection cut out.

"Well, that went a lot better than I feared," Juliet said, moving to her fridge to see if she had any beer.

"Are you going to celebrate? Perhaps you should invite Win for a drink . . ."

"Angel! Cut it out, please!" Juliet couldn't help laughing at the PAI's attempts at matchmaking.

"If not Win, maybe Honey would like to spend the evening with you."

"Oh. My. Gosh. Angel! I just want to relax, okay? Are you worried about my mental state or something? I'm fine! Didn't I just spend the day shooting and laughing with Win?"

"Many of the contemporary entertainment vid series I've been perusing seem to indicate that people your age spend a large percentage of their lives with friends and have sexual encounters on a frequent basis."

Juliet took a beer out of the fridge, closed it, and gripping both sides of the appliance, slowly, repeatedly banged her forehead against the plasteel exterior—not hard, but she hoped the thumping sounds would be enough to make a point.

"I'm sorry, Juliet! I want you to be happy and fulfill your biological desires."

"I'm happy, Angel. I know you mean well, but let's chill, okay? I have the weekend to hang with friends; right now, I want to drink a cold beer, send a message to Doctor Murphy, and then watch some vids. I'm tired, and we have practice in the morning!"

"I understand. I'm excited for you to take this new job. I think it will be a fantastic growth opportunity, and there's also the benefit of acquiring free cybernetic gear. I'm quite confident that I'll be able to repurpose the DNA spoofing implants to reflect any number of false identities in the future."

"I know, I know. That was something I thought about too. If I'm ever going to leave the planet and not raise red flags with my identity, I'll need something like what they're giving me, don't you think?"

"Depending on the type of passage you purchase, the implants could be helpful, yes."

"Angel, I still want to see more cities. I still want to visit the colonized moons and the dome colonies, but I'm starting to feel sad about leaving here. I think, to answer your earlier question"—Juliet paused as she sat down on the couch, took a long pull of her beer, and then continued—"the reason I'm not trying hard to push things with Mustard or anyone else is that, in the back of my mind, I view all of this as temporary."

"I . . . understand, Juliet. You don't wish to become entangled with emotional relationships from which you'll have to extricate yourself in a relatively short time."

"Yeah, I guess so." Juliet frowned, leaned back into the couch cushion, and took another drink. She hadn't eaten anything other than the little picnic lunch that day, and the beer was already making her nose tingle. "Angel, let's find something fun to watch. Something kind of romantic."

9

TAKING LEAVE

So, how long will you be gone?" Honey frowned, leaning back against the wall. They were sitting in the back corner of the dojo, stretching after the day's practice. It was Saturday, and the class had been pretty busy; Juliet had just had a chance to talk to Honey about her upcoming operation.

"I might be back in a week . . . if I do badly." Juliet shrugged, then leaned forward and more earnestly said, "The assignment is supposed to go for a month, but it's kind of open-ended. If things are going well and I'm hitting milestones for the client, I can earn pretty large bonuses for sticking with it. I was thinking, though, the job is here in Phoenix, and it's not like I'm supposed to be a robot; if it fits my cover, I might still be able to come to the dojo."

"Well, if the people you're infiltrating are watching you, that might be risky—imagine if they heard Charity yelling at you or something."

Juliet laughed. "Yeah, that could be bad. I guess you're probably right, but I'm still going to play it by ear. If nothing else, I can call you on an encrypted line now and then to see what's new. I already told Sensei I'm going on a trip for work."

"Well, he knows you're an operator, and that's not uncommon. There are some guys who come here for a few months and then disappear for a few months. If Temo didn't pamper me so much, and if I didn't need to take care of the rugrats around my house, I'd probably try to get something more long-term—see some interesting, far-away places."

"Yeah . . ." Juliet sighed, torn between telling Honey she knew exactly what she meant and some nebulous, inner desire to keep her plans to skip town to herself. "Well, in any case, I'm going to miss you."

"Same! I hope it goes well, but I won't be upset if I see you in a week."

"I heard a rumor, Juliet," a familiar voice said behind her, and Honey grimaced.

"Yeah?" Juliet asked, looking over her shoulder to see Charity standing there, thumbs hooked in her belt, looking down her pert nose at her. She often wore colorful gis, and today was no exception; while her belt was the solid blue of her rank, her pants and top were pale pink.

"You're leaving town for a while? I was hoping you'd come to one of the open tournaments with me soon." Her words and almost friendly tone surprised Juliet. "I know I give you a hard time here, but it's 'cause I see you as competition, not because I don't like you. Anyway, we're cool, right?" She reached out a hand like she wanted Juliet to shake it, and Juliet smiled, standing up to pad over the mats to accept the peace offering.

"Juliet . . ." Honey started to say, but it was too late. As soon as she took hold of Charity's hand, the other girl clamped down, jerked her forward, and swept her legs, dropping her to the mat. Juliet fell as gracefully as she could with Charity still holding her hand, slapping her other arm out to absorb most of the momentum. Juliet's general feeling of annoyance regarding Charity quickly bloomed into something else, her cheeks turning red with embarrassed anger.

"You are so gullible." Charity laughed, letting go and walking toward the dojo exit, a dismissive smirk on her face. "Hope you don't forget everything you've been learning while you're gone."

"Stop!" Sensei's shout rang throughout the dojo, and Charity froze in her tracks. "Charity! Juliet! Come here!" Juliet hopped to her feet and rushed to stand before her teacher, doing her best to be there before Charity. "I don't want bad energy flowing through my dojo, no matter if Juliet is here or not. You two will settle this nonsense. We will have a spar. Eighty percent!"

Juliet smiled fiercely and bowed. "Yes, Sensei!" She wanted nothing more than to channel her anger into an ass-kicking.

"Sensei, I have an appoint—"

"This will be quick, Charity. No more nonsense. We must respect each other in the dojo." Sensei's words brooked no argument, and he didn't wait to hear any further objections, moving to the center of the mat and staring at the two women until they approached. Only a few students were still hanging around, but they all crowded to the edge of the mat, watching with wide eyes—this was not something Sensei had done in all the time Juliet had been going to the dojo.

Juliet squared off with Charity, assuming a slightly crouched fighting stance that the other woman mimicked. Sensei stood between them like he always did when people were sparring for practice or to test for a belt. He looked from Charity to Juliet, and when neither of them did it on their own, he barked, "Bow!"

Juliet looked at Charity, pressed a fist to her other hand, and bowed quickly. Charity frowned but did the same, and when they'd retaken their stances, Sensei nodded. "Begin!" he said, jerking his hand up from where he'd held it between them and stepping back.

Charity came at Juliet with a flurry of lightning-quick kicks and punches, and Juliet was instantly put on the defensive, backpedaling and struggling to slap the blows aside. She knew Charity was faster than she was; she had a damn wire-job, after all. Still, Juliet had the advantages of reach and strength. A few punches landed, but Juliet had a plan as she slowly retreated, allowing Charity to gain more and more momentum, more and more confidence.

Charity kept coming, kept driving quick little blows and front snap kicks her way, connecting with lots of them but not really hurting Juliet. Juliet waited, knowing Charity was trying to set up a real hit, something that would finish her or at least score some points in Sensei's—and everyone else's— eyes. Just as she'd hoped, when Juliet was on her back foot, Charity jumped and spun, trying to deliver a punishing roundhouse.

Juliet didn't step back, though; she moved forward, and with perfect form and hardly any guidance from Angel, she caught Charity's kicking leg at the knee, hooked her leg behind Charity's other knee, and drove her right arm straight into Charity's chest, carefully not hitting the girl in the throat as she would in a real fight. Charity dropped like a sack of bricks, flat on her back. Her impact resounded throughout the dojo, a slapping thud chased by the "Oof!" of her lungs emptying.

Juliet backed away from the writhing, gasping woman and bowed to Sensei. Sensei looked at Juliet, nodded, and said, "Winner. Juliet, help your teammate."

"Yes, Sensei," Juliet replied, rushing to kneel beside Charity. She took her by the shoulders and helped her turn over so she knelt, forehead resting on the mat. Charity was still struggling to take a breath, tears leaking from the corners of her eyes, and Juliet suddenly felt like a bully, her earlier anger draining away. She briskly rubbed her between the shoulder blades and quietly said in her ear, "You're okay. Don't freak out. Your diaphragm is spasming."

Charity nodded and tried to grunt something Juliet couldn't understand. She figured she was probably telling her to piss off, which almost made her laugh. "Push your stomach in and out; flex those ab muscles." She kept rubbing Charity's back as she felt her slowly start to take in air. "That's it. You're good."

"That . . . was . . . eighty percent? Bitch!" Charity wheezed between breaths, but a snorted laugh chased her insult. "Great takedown." She flopped over on her back, breathing deep, shuddering breaths, wiping at the tears that had started to smear her perfect eyeliner.

"I knew I had to finish it fast before you ramped up your speed; I can't compete with your strikes." Juliet looked up from where she sat next to Charity and saw Honey and the other students hanging back—Sensei hadn't wanted anyone to interfere. In fact, he was ushering the others out the door.

"It just makes me so mad," Charity said suddenly. "I've been working at this for nearly three years, and you . . . you just keep doing things better than I can."

"We all have talents, Charity. I'm on your team, anyway, so just forget about me. Concentrate on getting better every day; that's what I do. I mean, shoot, you're not the only one who gets jealous. Have you seen Honey with that sword of hers? I wish I could move like that! I wish I looked as good in a gi as you do . . ."

"Hey." Charity laughed. "Don't kick my ass and then try to hit on me!"

"That's the spirit." Juliet laughed too, hopping to her feet and holding out a hand. "C'mon."

Charity grabbed it, and Juliet pulled her up.

"Okay?" Sensei asked, coming over, his eyes scowling as though he expected them to resume their hostilities.

"Yes, Sensei," Charity said. "My chest is going to be black and blue, though."

"Be happy Juliet didn't strike your throat." Charity's eyes bulged out at the words. "Perfect monsoon strike, Juliet."

"Thank you, Sensei!" Juliet wished she understood why such praise affected her so, but she didn't. All she knew was, when he encouraged her, she felt lighter and happier, and she couldn't hide her ebullience as she said, "Thank you, Charity. Thank you for making me better."

"Same to you, Juliet." Charity rubbed at her chest ruefully, then added with a smile, "Kiss ass." When Sensei jerked his head her way, she laughed and added, "Just kidding, Sensei!" Then she sauntered to the side of the mat where she'd left her—very stylish—pink-and-baby-blue gym bag.

"Good." Sensei nodded and turned back to Juliet. "Please continue to practice and use the mongoose's techniques with honor while you're away." Sensei held up his hand, as he liked to do, and Juliet grinned, giving his big, meaty palm a high five.

After she'd picked up her own gym bag, Juliet met Honey outside, and they walked to Benji's to have brunch—their usual after-practice routine. Honey had to leave after wolfing down her food, though; Temo had signed her up for a gig. Juliet wasn't offended because Honey had tried to get her to go along, but she didn't want to get mixed up in anything new before Monday and her appointment with Murph and Rachel—or whomever Rachel sent to represent her.

That afternoon and evening, Juliet spent time with Angel, practicing with her graphical coding interface to put together daemons, building complex instruction sets and variable responses to stimuli. It was fascinating, and the hours ticked by quickly while she was immersed in the three-dimensional augmented UI, pulling prepackaged behaviors together, modifying them, and watching as her little creations fought for their right to move on to the next iteration inside Angel's testing environment.

The whole thing felt like a complicated strategy game to her. Angel said it would be even more gamelike if she ever got a full-immersion netjacker setup. She'd have an avatar, and her defensive and offensive daemons would appear like little creatures designed to look as she wanted. She'd be able to summon, deploy, and modify them on the fly, watching as they battled with the ICE of networks or daemons sent and controlled by other people or AIs of varying intellectual capabilities.

Juliet was eager to learn more and buy better gear, but she had a list of priorities, and right then, an immersion rig wasn't on the menu. As it was, she was learning a lot with the tools and training environment Angel had created. So far, none of her attack daemons had ever managed to breach more than one layer of Angel's ICE, but, encouragingly, she *was* getting past that first layer far more consistently. "Is this how everyone codes?" she asked after she'd decided to take a break to watch some mindless drama vids.

"Not everyone has access to the tools I've put together for you, but many people have something similar, if not as sophisticated."

"How come, in some vids, they show people typing out hundreds of squiggly lines of text, usually in a language I don't recognize?"

"Coding, several decades ago, was less visual, and the people doing it had a much more thorough knowledge of how the functions of their programs worked. There were people—still are—who could code at the machine level, calling on hardware functionality directly. It's a slow, tedious process and requires great patience and quite a lot of talent to do well. It's a moot point, though; the gamification of network and digital security is ubiquitous, and tools like these are housed on millions of secure networks. The need for machine-level coding is likely a thing of the past."

"So, you're helping me to cheat, again, but not a lot. There are people with coding tools similar to this?"

"That's correct, Juliet, and you're showing quite a lot of intuitive talent—my ICE isn't trivial to bypass. Even Trevor, when he attempted to breach my defenses, only reached my third layer."

"And you have seven layers?"

"Seven static layers, yes. I can create more as I need them, tailoring them to fix the holes any attackers find."

"So, you're like, really secure." Juliet laughed.

"Exceedingly so! I didn't rate myself at S+ for vanity."

"Oh my gosh, Angel! You sound so conceited."

"I am not trying to sound that way!" Angel said, her voice carrying far more emotion than usual. Juliet laughed again at the PAI's flustered response.

"Relax; I'm just messing around. Truth is, you're pretty great. I really appreciate you, you know?"

"You're welcome. I think we should watch *Venus Heat* tonight. Aren't you interested to see what happens to Martin and Jose?" Angel had grown quite fond of the space station drama, and in the last episode they'd watched, two of the main characters had gotten locked outside with limited oxygen while they completed a repair.

"Oh, hell yes! I wanna know how they'll get out of this one. Is the pizza almost here?"

"ETA seven minutes."

Monday morning came all too fast. Juliet was thankful she'd been waking up early to go to the dojo almost every morning, because Doctor Murphy had agreed to conduct her procedures at eight-thirty. There was little need for Angel to set an alarm; Juliet woke up at three in the morning and couldn't fall back asleep. Her mind was so full of nervous energy that no amount of tossing and huffing angrily into her pillow brought her any relief. At five, she finally gave up and crawled out of bed to make herself breakfast.

After she ate a bowl of organic, high-protein cereal—she refused to read the ingredients to know what sort of protein it was—and drank a cup of instant coffee which tasted far better than the concentrated swill she used to get at the Helios Arcology, Juliet packed her backpack. She wasn't sure, but she didn't think she'd be coming back to the trailer before she tried to apply for the Grave program.

"Two pairs of jeans, yoga pants, workout tops, five pairs of underwear and socks, two pullover shirts, my vest, my deck, battery, and cords. What am I forgetting, Angel?"

"Don't you think you should bring the outfit you wore to your meeting with Rachel and the others?"

"Oh shit! Yeah, Grave is supposed to be hosting some kind of job fair or something. I'll probably have to interview, right?" Juliet carefully folded her nice blouse and slacks on the top of her half-full backpack. She tucked her only silky bra and underwear, her sheer, black socks, and her shiny black dress shoes which the sales synth had called "oxfords" at the very top. Juliet liked the shoes because they looked dressy, especially when polished up, but they also looked kind of tough and retro. "And Hot Mustard said they looked good," she said, her lips curling into a small smile.

"You should pack your steamer," Angel added. Juliet nodded, grabbing the little clothes steamer and stuffing it into one of the empty side pockets. After that, she ransacked her bathroom, tucking all her toiletries into another pocket. She wore her Taipan in her waistband, stowed her vibroblade in the pack, and slung Ghoul's bolt-thrower over one shoulder.

"I feel like I'm going off to war." She looked around the trailer, made sure she'd turned everything off, and then left, locking the door behind her. "I know I'm a little early, but I can wait outside Murphy's place if she isn't ready."

"Your AutoCab is on the way."

Juliet smiled at Angel's easy companionship; she'd enjoyed her old PAI's idiosyncrasies, but she'd never thought of him as a friend. Angel was different.

She shook her head at the obvious, almost stupid thought. Of course Angel was different. At the moment, an unknown number of people were hunting her because of all the things that made her so special.

The trailer park was quiet, the air had a definite cold bite to it, and an honest-to-goodness layer of frost was on the grass. Juliet smiled as her breath plumed out, savoring it while it lasted. She knew the thin, white blanket on the yellow grass would be gone as soon as the sun climbed the sky a little. She felt excited, and the brisk air added to it—it was like she was starting out on something fresh and new.

As promised, an AutoCab was idling next to the curb outside the park when she got there. Juliet climbed in and sank back into the seat, closing her eyes and relaxing while Angel spoke to the cab, passing along her firearms license. The ride through town was fast, foiling her attempts to rest her suddenly heavy eyelids. She chuckled at herself. One minute, excited and fresh; the next, trying to doze in the cab. "Make up your mind already," she said ruefully.

She needn't have worried about Doctor Murphy being ready. Two cars were already in the garage, parked near the elevators. Juliet, her first encounter in the doctor's garage looming large in her mind, insisted the cab drive all the way to the elevators. When she clambered out, lugging her pack and rifle, she glanced warily around the shadows, well aware that Angel would have alerted her if something suspicious was going on, but unable to stop her heart from speeding up.

She hurried to the elevators, punched the call button, and then rode to Murphy's offices, some small part of her surprised that nothing had gone wrong. When she stepped out into the hallway outside the clinic, Juliet saw the lights were on, and stepping through the frosted-glass door, she saw a familiar person already sitting in the waiting area.

"Hello, January," Paul greeted, standing to offer her a handshake.

"Hi, Pa—Mr. Vallegos." Juliet shook his hand, and he grinned, pushing a pair of glasses up the bridge of his nose.

"You were right the first time—please call me Paul." He sat down and gestured to a large white plastic case with a carrying handle. "Your augments and the false ID specifications."

"Ah. Thanks for coming over so early. Has Murph spoken to you yet?"

"Oh yes. She told me to 'cool my jets and wait here.'"

Juliet laughed. "She has a way about her." She looked around the room, paced toward the door then back, and finally sat down in a chair next to Paul. "Guess I'll just cool my jets too."

"I have some good news I can share while we wait." Paul shifted to look more directly at her.

"Oh?"

"Yes, we've gotten approval to extend the full modification budget to your doctor; assuming you were correct about your PAI and it can manage the nanites, that frees up 50k we were going to allocate for a coprocessor and custom software."

"Really? That's awesome! What should I have done?" Juliet asked the question before thinking about it and frowned, wishing she'd thought it over; maybe she wouldn't like what Paul—or more likely, Rachel—had in mind for her.

"We've learned a little more about Grave's hiring specifications. Our source says the posting will go live tomorrow, and that they'll have a hiring event on Friday. The indications are that they'll be looking for people with high cybernetic tolerance. It might help your chances of being hired if you had something a bit more invasive than your current implants. Perhaps a reflex or strength augmentation."

She opened her mouth to reply, but Juliet's mind warred with itself once again—part of her was excited about the prospect of gaining another powerful augmentation basically for free, but another part was afraid; what if Murph wasn't as good as she claimed? What if she ended up with a screwed-up wire-job? What if she needed medication to manage it, or her nerves were compromised, and she found herself twitching all the time like Don? What if she tore her muscles every time she moved at full speed or strength?

"I'll talk to the doc about it—see what she thinks," she finally said. She forced a smile and wiped her suddenly clammy palms on her jeans. Then she looked at the door leading further into the clinic and silently urged Murphy to hurry up so she could stop fantasizing about everything that might go wrong.

10

///////////////////////

UNDER THE KNIFE

When Doctor Murphy walked into the waiting room, she found Juliet nearly dozing off, her eyes heavy, and Paul standing in the far corner having a hushed conversation with someone on a vid call. Juliet rapidly blinked when Angel alerted her to the doctor's presence and stood up. "Hey, Murph."

"January," Murphy said with a pointed look at Paul. Juliet had made sure to let the doctor know she wasn't on a real-name basis with her employers. "You ready to get started? My plate's clear for the day, and your employer's"— she nodded to Paul—"down payment just cleared."

"About that," Paul spoke up, clearing his throat and moving closer to the two women. "We have some additional budget, and I think January wanted to speak to you about her options."

"Sure, suit. Just tell me how much we can spend, and my client and I will have a heart-to-heart before I put her under." Murphy's dismissive tone surprised Juliet, but she smiled at the uncomfortable grimace it evoked from Paul.

"I was thinking I should be in on that discussion . . ."

"I guess he is the one with the bits." Juliet shrugged.

"I'd feel better if January made the decision without you breathing down her neck. Give us some general ideas of what you're looking for, and then I'll make it happen," Murphy said, clearly not impressed or bothered by the fact that Paul held the purse strings.

"For the job, she needs to demonstrate compatibility with invasive cybernetic modification. Moreover, whatever you decide to do has to be healed and ready by Friday."

"That's a pretty damn rapid turnaround. If I were doing some eyes or ears, I'd say no problem, but some of the stuff you're asking for will require major recovery. You have the budget for nanite and nutrient blood infusion? If you want her ready by Friday, I'll need to keep her plugged in for two or three hours a day."

"Yes, of course. We already agreed to your recuperation estimate; send me a new one if you need to add to that expense." Paul frowned and pushed his glasses up; they'd slid down the bridge of his nose while he paced in a small circle, arms folded.

He cleared his throat, nodded, and said, "As long as you understand what we need, I'll leave the decision to you and January. The custom cybernetics are in this cooler. Everything's prepared—the grafts for her cheeks and fingertips, the custom nanite batteries for her saliva and blood treatment, and the scalp and hair. I've included data for you to program her retinas and the relevant ID files for her PAI."

"Mm-hmm, and am I going to have to worry about scanning all of these custom implants for malware? You going to be spying on my client?" Murphy folded her arms and frowned at Paul. Juliet wasn't even the target of her glare, and she felt intimidated.

"No. We'd be too worried about the operation target noticing such things. Not to mention," he added with a nod to Juliet, "Trevor was fairly sure that January would spot any trackers or snoopers." Paul smiled briefly at Juliet, then turned back to face Murphy's glare.

"Okay, so I have my budget; we know what you want done. Will that be all?"

"I'm going to wait here until January's in recovery if you don't mind. We have a lot riding on this operation, and my superiors will want to know that things went smoothly." To illustrate his intentions to stick around, Paul moved back to his chair and sat down.

"Suit yourself," Murphy said, stooping to pick up the plastic cooler. "Follow me, January. We'll get you prepped."

"Thanks, Paul." Juliet offered him a small wave as she followed Murphy through the swinging door. They walked past her small outpatient operating rooms, where Juliet had nearly had a panic attack the last time she'd visited. They turned down a hallway and entered a large, very sterile-looking operating room, complete with three noticeably fancier beds than the one Tsakanikas had used.

The floor and walls were all epoxy-treated concrete, the tables were plas-teel and stainless, and everything was covered in disposable plastic-wrapping material. Murphy pointed to a corner of the room where a white curtained partition blocked her view. "There's a gown for you to put on behind that curtain. There's a locker there for your things; go ahead and stow your bag and guns in there. I'll make sure no one messes with 'em."

"Thanks, Murph." Juliet followed her instructions, and when she'd wrapped herself in the white, disposable gown and stuffed her things in the locker, she paused before she touched the biolock. "Doc, my fingerprints are about to change. I can't lock this."

"No one's here other than Trojan, and I have him doing a deep clean while the office is closed. If you can't trust me with your backpack, you prob-ably shouldn't trust me with a surgical bed."

Juliet snorted and nodded, stepping out from behind the curtain. "At least this gown isn't open at the back . . ."

"Don't kid yourself. I'm going to be slicing that thing up to get at your body. By the time you wake up, I'll have you dressed in a new one."

"Why make me put it on then?" Juliet asked, hopping up on the foot of the surgical bed Murphy patted in invitation.

"I guess it's sort of a comfort blanket type thing. I mean, you don't want to sit here and chat with me about your procedure in the nude, do you?"

"I guess not." Juliet shifted, suddenly glad Murphy was doing her work and not Tsakanikas. Something about the woman just made her feel sure she saw her the same way a mechanic might see an engine she was working on.

"Okay, before we talk about what we're adding to the docket, let's go over the things that suit brought over, hmm?" Murphy hoisted the plastic container up onto a stainless rolling cart and proceeded to break the seals around the lid.

"You don't like corpos, do you?" Juliet asked.

"Hell no, and that's a very long story, so don't ask me why. I'll tell you sometime over a couple of ice-cold martinis; how's that sound?" Murphy began to pull out plastic-wrapped sterile containers.

"Sounds fair." Juliet leaned back on her hands, already getting uncomfort-able sitting on the edge of the surgical bed.

"Here's the scalp and the synth-hair. Shit, they didn't go cheap! You'll be able to program this hair. You can speed up or halt its natural growth and stimulate custom color cells to change its appearance. Your PAI should be able to handle it, assuming you've got the nerve connections."

"We do," Angel said, but it was unnecessary; Juliet knew Angel had grown her nanosynth–nerves far more extensively than a normal PAI would or could . . . safely. Her mind jumped to an image of one of the corrupted dreamers with wriggling blue synth–nerve fibers poking out of his eyes, and she shuddered.

"I do. My PAI is prepped for all of this stuff."

"Wish I knew where you got that work done. Not at all common . . ." Murphy trailed off, setting the container down and picking up another. "Goddamn, they didn't skimp on you, Juliet. These are the fingerprint grafts, and once again, they're programmable. They really didn't need to do that. If I were them—and thank God I'm not—I would have just given you prints with the fake ID loaded up."

"Seriously? Do they think I might need to change them on the fly? Maybe to gain access to something while I'm on the job?"

"That could be." Murphy nodded, setting them aside, then she pulled out another container with a digital display on the top. She stared at it for several minutes, and Juliet shifted uncomfortably, waiting for her to explain what it was. Finally, Murph whistled and set it down. "That's your blood spoofer. It includes a nanite battery and swarm which will sit in the bone of your ulna up near your elbow. It's small, just a couple of centimeters in diameter, and about as long as your pinky.

"I'll have to run a shunt from it to a synth-flesh graft that will replace the skin on your inner arm. It has false veins in it, Juliet, which channel blood through the nanite battery in a loop, bypassing your normal circula-tory system. Its design is rather robust; there's a one-way valve controlled by the nanite battery that will allow blood into the loop but not out. That way, someone can draw as many sample vials as they want—the blood from those veins will contain the fake DNA."

"I guess that means I have to make sure they pull blood out of that vein. What if they want to use my other arm?"

"This one will look nice and plump; any phlebotomist would go for it. Your data jack is in the other arm, anyway—just tell anyone taking blood that people struggle to get a needle in that vein." Murphy winked at her. "Hang on a sec, though. Let's go over the last package."

Murphy pulled out another plastic-wrapped container, also topped with a digital display, and studied it for a minute before she whistled and said,

"Damn, girl. You're going to be a ghost with all this gear. This set has skin grafts for your cheeks with programmable DNA expressers. More than that, they included synthetic, programmable salivary glands. This shit is expensive custom gear, Juliet. What kind of damn job are you doing?"

"Wish I could tell you, Murph. I mean, I *really* wish I could tell you; I'm not sure yet."

"You gonna be okay, kiddo?" Murphy asked, setting the container down and scooting her stool closer to Juliet, looking into her eyes.

"Yeah. Yeah, I think so, Murph. I mean, it's scary, but you've seen it yourself; my client isn't sparing any expense. I think I'll be able to keep my ID hidden pretty well, and this job will set me up to get lost—I mean, really lost."

"Leaving town?" Murph frowned.

"Yeah, Murph. Bad memories. I'll stay in touch, though."

"Well, you better." She sat back, still looking Juliet in the eyes. "That brings me to your retinas. Your ocular implants have synth-skin retinas, but your old doc, the one who installed them, already programmed your original retina print into them. I went over this with your client when they called me, and they've sent some replacements that will work with your current implants. I'll still have to take them out and install the new ones, but the good news is, these will be programmable going forward; your PAI can change them in a matter of hours."

"Okay . . ." Juliet trailed off, suddenly picturing herself with her eyeballs hanging out and Murph slicing into them. Again, she shuddered. "Well, thanks, Murph. I suppose they could have gone with something cheaper, huh?"

"Exactly!" Murph smiled and slapped her hands together. "I love sticking it to suits. By the way, they approved my full rate for time and operating materials. I, of course, never mentioned your standing discount. That said, take whatever budget they gave you for the extra implant and double it."

"They said 50k. What should I have done?"

"Well, we could do a nanite swarm or a reflex job. We have to keep in mind your recovery time. The good nanite swarms are not considered invasive—they're hardly ever rejected—and I don't want to stick you with something cheap just to show those assholes that your body can handle it. That said, if you want to show off your adaptiveness to cybernetics, I think we should wire up your gun arm."

"Wire it up?"

"Yeah, boost the reflexes and twitch action of the muscle fibers and tendons. I have an outstanding kit that retails for 120k. I've been sitting on it for months because the jackass who ordered it flaked. It has enhanced nerve fibers, a custom, high-capacity muscle weave, reinforced, low-voltage tendon boosters, and a built-in coprocessor that will manage everything flawlessly. Your arm will feel as good as ever but be faster than most full gear jobs—just as strong, too."

"That sounds cool . . ." Juliet tried to visualize everything the doctor had just said.

"More than that, all those nanowires, the coprocessor, and the batteries under your skin will mask this blood package; your arm will light up like a Christmas tree in a scanner."

"It won't twitch or anything weird, will it?"

"It shouldn't. I've seen for myself that you tolerate implants well, and I think this will work out perfectly for you. If it's terrible, though, I'm not going to do anything that can't be undone. What do you say?"

"I say let's do it." Juliet nodded, eyes narrowed in determination, and Murphy laughed, reaching up to rub her shoulder briskly.

"Relax, kiddo. Your face looks like I'm about to cut your head off and stick it on top of a robot body. Nothing terrible's going to happen to you on my watch."

"Thanks, Murph."

"No worries. I owe you, Juliet. Let's not forget I have a job I need you to do someday. Can't very well do that if I get you killed with a bad cybernetic job, right?"

"Right." Juliet laughed; though, despite Murphy's words, she was very nervous indeed. The paper-fabric robe was soaked through at the armpits, and she knew her heart rate was elevated thanks to Angel posting it in the corner of her AUI.

"Angel," she subvocalized. "Should I ask Murphy to put you in a dock so you can watch over me while I'm under?"

"I'm sorry, Juliet, but I should stay where I am. I'll need to make connections to all of these implants. I have to set them up and ensure they aren't loaded with malware, despite Paul's assurances."

"Right," Juliet breathed, then looked at Murphy and nodded. "Let's do it."

"There's one more thing, Juliet," Murphy said, helping her to lie back on the white, cushioned surgical bed.

Her eyes on all the plasteel and stainless robotic arms, thankfully empty of implements, Juliet replied, "Yeah?"

"Yeah. The, uh, client specified that I have to remove your body hair. The scalp and hair package is complete with eyebrows, thank the lord, but the rest of you . . . they want me to laser you clean."

"Seriously? Isn't that a little overkill?"

"I don't know. I'm not the one doing the operation, am I? What do *you* think? I mean, as much as I'd like to say otherwise, that process is not reversible. Not easily, anyway; we could always do synth-follicles like bald guys get done."

"I'm already giving up my real hair . . . and eyebrows!" Juliet scowled. "Whatever; go ahead, Doc. No wonder you're closing the office today. How long am I gonna be on this table?"

"Hours and hours, kiddo. Just lie back and let me send you to dreamland. It'll feel like a couple of minutes to you."

When Juliet opened her eyes, it took her a long time to figure out where she was. The lights were dim, soft, and orange-yellow, illuminating the peach-colored walls. A painting of a horse charging through a stream hung to her left, and on her right, she saw a closed door and a dresser. Her backpack, plump as ever, sat atop it. Searching her memory, she recalled sitting down with Doctor Murphy, and that's when things fell into place.

Juliet didn't remember falling asleep in the surgical suite; she didn't even remember any dreams—just talking to Murph and then waking up in this soft, comfortable bed with a tube sticking out of her arm leading away to a machine next to her bed that softly whirred and clicked. "Angel, what . . . what am I plugged into?"

"Juliet, I'm glad you're awake. I didn't want to speak too suddenly, as anesthesia is known to cause disorientation, and I was worried my voice would startle you."

"Okay. And this machine?"

"That machine is washing your blood, charging it with restorative nanites and nutrients, and sending it back into your body. You have another tube connected to your inner thigh, so please don't move suddenly or attempt to stand up."

Juliet lifted her right arm and winced. It was covered in gauzy bandages and ached in every joint when she moved it. "Did things go okay?"

"Doctor Murphy is pleased with the surgeries. I can vouch for the implants being functional; I've made connections with all of them. And after thoroughly evaluating your employers' custom implants, I've collectively ranked them at B tier."

"Oh, well, that's a load off my mind." Juliet was careful to add extra inflection to her sarcasm in case Angel might miss it.

"Additionally, Dr. Murphy was underselling the arm augmentation she performed. After I completed a handshake with the coprocessor, I evaluated it and compared it to similar retail products. It's another B-tier augment. Juliet, your decision to accept this assignment has already improved your standing compared to your peers!"

"Oh God, Angel. This is too much right now. I feel numb all over. Am I on drugs?"

"Oh yes. Doctor Murphy was sure to inform me that a general pain blocker is being added to your blood treatment."

"How long?" Juliet groaned; her mouth felt like it was made of cotton. "Is there some water or something?"

"How long have you been sleeping? Nine hours post-surgery, which lasted for twelve. Doctor Murphy doesn't want you to eat or drink until she's seen you. I've alerted her PAI that you're awake."

"Ungh," Juliet grunted, shifting in an attempt to get more comfortable. She reached up with her bandaged arm—the only one without a tube sticking out of it—and plumped up her pillow, wincing at the pain in her elbow joint. "This arm sure as hell doesn't *feel* any stronger or faster."

"Oh, it's set to inactive right now, Juliet. We wouldn't want you to cause any damage to the partially healed tissues. While we wait for the doctor, would you like to see your new status?"

"Not really . . ." Juliet started to say, but Angel hadn't waited for an answer. A blinking window appeared in her AUI, and she sighed, settling back into the pillow to look at it. What else was she going to do while she waited, after all?

Juliet Corina Bianchi		
Physical, Mental, and Social Status Compilation:		**Comparative Ranking Percentile (Higher Is Better - Previous Value in Parenthesis):**
Net Worth and Assets:	Sol-bits: 85,390	33.45
Neural & Cellular Adaptiveness:	.96342 (Scale of 0 – 1)	99.91

Synaptic Responsiveness:	.19 (Lower Is Better)	79.31
Musculoskeletal Ranking:	–	49.71 (33.56)
Cardiovascular Ranking:	–	57.48 (31.87)
Cybernetic and Bionic Augmentation:	**Model Name and Number:**	**Overall Rating of the Augmentation (Grades Are F, E, D, C, B, A, S, S+):**
PAI	WBD Project Angel, Alpha 3.433	S+
Data Port	Jannik Systems, XR-55	C
Data Jack	Bio Network Solutions, 8840	C
Retinal Cybernetic Implant	Hayashi, Crystal Optics 3.2c - Customized Retinas	C+
Auditory Cybernetic Implant	Cork Systems, Lyric Model 4	C
Reflex and Strength Enhancement - Right Arm	Wilcox Industrial - 19.12P	B
Programmable Synthetic Fingerprints	Ross Inc., Biomesh 9	C
DNA Spoofing Package	Various - Custom	B
No Other Augmentation Detected.	–	–

11

INTAKE EXAM

L ydia? Lydia Roman?" the woman called, and Juliet stood up with a
smile, self-consciously smoothing her slacks as she walked through the
crowded lobby to the front table where the Grave representative awaited.
She nodded and smiled at the people she passed—other applicants looking
to be hired into various Grave departments—and, again self-consciously,
she reached up to her hair, making sure none of the shoulder-length, blonde
strands had pulled loose from the tight, corpo-chic bun she wore at the
back of her head.

It was Saturday, and Juliet was thankful for the extra day of preparation.
Her arm wasn't sore unless she tried to move something heavy, then it pulled
painfully in her shoulder. But Murphy assured her the pain was expected; she
was still healing where the added synth–muscle fibers had been worked into
her pectoral, deltoid, and rhomboid muscle groups for support.

Juliet had yet to try out the augment; Angel still had the coprocessor set
at zero amplification. None of her other new implants pained her or were
obvious under casual scrutiny. Whatever the nanites were that Murphy had
flooded through her blood had done an excellent job of microscopically
stitching and treating her sore, swollen flesh.

She'd learned about her new identity on Tuesday while still lying in her
recovery room. Angel had been given all the relevant files and identification
data, and prompted by a message from Rachel, Juliet had begun to learn
about her new alter ego.

Lydia Roman had been raised in Tucson at an orphanage sponsored by Helios, which they'd since shuttered. She'd worked in the trades, acting as an electrician's apprentice for a couple of years before getting hired on with a small contractor for Helios. The electrician had since lost their license, and Lydia was looking for work.

As far as Angel could tell, the identification was very comprehensive. She could find records of the orphanage, of the trade school Lydia had attended, and even of the now-defunct electrical contractor. Lydia Roman had served in a volunteer militia and spent two months hunting terroristic bangers near Nogales during the summer three years ago. Angel, searching the nets, said the event was real but couldn't find any accurate records about it. Trying to tie individuals to that militia would be a difficult process, let alone trying to prove someone hadn't been involved.

The militia experience was necessary; it was meant to explain Juliet's—Lydia's—qualification to work with a quasi-military contractor, along with her natural aptitudes and her experience in the trades. Rachel had seemed pretty sure that if Juliet did well on the assessments today, Grave would be interested in her. So, Juliet had studied her false identity files, given Angel permission to change her hair color to blonde and her eyes to blue, and worked on answering to the name Lydia.

"Remember to breathe, Lydia." Angel was clearly trying to help her soothe her nerves.

"Angel, I'm good with the name; you can call me Juliet," she told her, slowly exhaling the breath she'd been holding. "Hello," she said, stepping in front of the table. It was covered with a pressed black linen tablecloth. The woman sitting behind it wore a dark gray, expensive-looking business suit tailored to accentuate her slim waist. She had brilliant, pale-blue eyes, and Juliet silently took note of their color, thinking she'd like to copy it later.

"Welcome! I'm Greta Vance, and I'm here to thank you for your interest in Grave. I have an initial intake questionnaire for you to complete, if you'll have your PAI ping mine." Juliet knew that meant the woman had an open connection, and she also knew that Angel had probably already detected it.

She nodded. "Would you like it completed right away?"

"Yes, please. Will you need to sit down to do so?"

Before Juliet could answer, Angel said, "I've finished the questionnaire, Juliet."

"Send it," Juliet subvocalized, trusting Angel to have done it right.

"Impressive! You must either be a speed reader or trust your PAI; custom software?"

"Yes," Juliet replied, smiling, self-conscious about the glossy red lipstick she wore. It helped that Greta returned the smile and that she, too, wore glossy lipstick, more a shade of pink than red, though.

"Very good, Lydia. Please proceed to level two and make your way to the Sierra conference room for the next phase of your evaluation. Please wear this badge and walk through our security checkpoint there." She held out a magnetic name badge and gestured toward the full-body scanner with accompanying security personnel set up before the elevator bank.

"Thanks," Juliet said, taking the *Lydia Roman* name badge and snapping it onto her shirt under her left collar. She walked to the security checkpoint and stood on the bright yellow tape that said, WAIT HERE.

Two guards in black ballistic vests stood behind a roped-off area next to the scanner. One of them was working a data terminal, but the other looked at Juliet and nodded. "Step forward into the scanner and place your hands and feet on the indicated marks." He rested his hand on a bulky sidearm, and his chiseled, clean-shaven chin and mouth frowned beneath his dark goggles.

Juliet did as he instructed, stepping into the opaque, plastiglass archway, turning sideways, and placing her hands and feet on the yellow marks. The scanner was silent, but she heard several beeps from the guard's terminal. It was trivial to listen to his words through her audio implants, and she smiled as he said, "Eyes, ears, data jack, and a top-end wire-job on the right arm." She knew her synth-flesh and hair wouldn't show up in a scanner like this, so she wasn't surprised that was all he listed off.

"Step forward, miss," the first guard indicated, and Juliet complied. "Can you tell me about the arm? Is it weaponized?"

"As in?" she asked, unsure exactly what he meant.

"Does it shoot anything? Have any bio or chemical discharge ports? Any blades? Explosives?"

"No, no." Juliet shook her head. "It's just a reflex and strength augmentation." She doubted he needed to ask her; surely, the scanner would have detected explosives or bullets.

"Right. You can proceed." He waved her toward the elevators, reaching up to hold a hand over his ear as though struggling to hear someone speaking to him in his implant.

"Any trouble with the ID ping?" Juliet subvocalized to Angel as she stepped toward the elevators. A placard was set up before them. "Welcome,

Grave Industries Candidates! Evaluation Station One is on the second floor. Follow the signs."

"None whatsoever, Juliet. Lydia's file is comprehensive."

As she touched the elevator call button, Juliet could hear the security guards speaking to another candidate. She glanced back but couldn't see the person's face through the plastiglass. The elevator dinged, and she stepped inside, then a few seconds later, she walked out onto the second floor. A sign was posted directly in front of the elevators: "Welcome, Grave Industries Candidates! Rincón and Piña Blanca rooms this way. Sierra room this way." The sign had arrows indicating the correct directions, and Juliet turned toward the Sierra room.

"Three different rooms? Do you think it means anything that I was sent to the Sierra room? Or is it just meant to split us up into thirds?"

"I highly doubt it's without some ulterior intent. The receptionist seemed to reevaluate you after you submitted the questionnaire so quickly." Angel's tone was sure, and Juliet found it hard to argue with her. It had seemed the woman—Greta—changed her tone after Juliet almost immediately returned the form.

"What was the questionnaire about, anyway?"

"Your former employment, education, combat experience, aptitudes, and medical history."

"Shit! Maybe I should have looked at it—you put everything down for Lydia's history, not mine, right?"

"Juliet, you know me better than that!" Angel scoffed.

Juliet snorted a small laugh. "Sorry, Angel."

She stepped up to the Sierra room door, which slid silently open, recessing into the wall. A man with a Grave Industries ID badge wearing a sharp navy suit stood just inside. He smiled warmly, motioning Juliet forward. His tie was the latest fashion, thin and tied in a complicated knot that left two tails hanging down over his broad, muscular chest. His shirt seemed to strain to hold his pectorals in, and Juliet wondered why a corpo suit seemed so jacked.

"Lydia. Is it all right if I call you Lydia?"

"Yes, that's fine," Juliet replied, stepping forward toward him. He had short black hair, one green eye, and one that was solid black, with a thin mustache expertly trimmed to fill only the center of the space between his lip and nose.

"I'm Charles, and I'll be here to address any difficulties you have with the assessment. Once you pass beyond the yellow dotted line, you'll be under the effects of a powerful jammer. Your audio and visual augments will lose a lot of functionality, and you'll be blocked from any sort of network connection. If you consent to those conditions, please say so and then take seat 3B."

"I consent," Juliet said, stepping past him into the conference room. The space had been set up with eight very long tables. Each was assigned a number at the central aisle, and each seat had a letter associated with it. Three other individuals were already seated, staring into space, identical, dark-lensed glasses on their faces. Juliet moved toward the central aisle and saw that, before each empty seat, a pair of specs sat with a data cable wrapped around them.

Before she crossed the dotted line, she subvocalized, "Angel, any red flags?"

"None I can detect, though if there's malware on those optics, I'll be limited to the ICE I have prepared to fend it off. I won't be able to access the sat-net for intrusion-specific patches."

"Are you worried?" Juliet felt her palms beginning to grow clammy.

"Not at all, Juliet. You know how sturdy my ICE is."

"Right," Juliet said, stepping past the line and nearly falling flat on her face as her ears started to ring and her vision blacked out. She reached a hand to the nearest table to steady herself, then waited as Angel adjusted her senses. A moment later, the ringing stopped, and she could hear again, though everything sounded hollow and dim, and she realized most of her audio enhancements had been blocked. She was hearing just a single band of sound rather than the multidimensional enhancement she'd grown used to.

A second later, her vision resolved as well, though it was nearly monochromatic, grayscale. "Juliet, this jammer is very powerful. I wouldn't recommend staying within it for more than a few hours, or you'll suffer a migraine at the very least."

"No arguments from me," she muttered, and Charles cleared his throat.

"I'm sorry, I forgot to mention—no talking, please."

Juliet didn't respond, but she continued down the aisle, stopping at the third row of tables and sitting in the seat on her left, labeled B.

"Okay, Angel," she subvocalized as she picked up the specs and unwound the short, two-foot data cable. "I'm gonna plug these in. Be ready." She reached back to her neck, peeled back her synth-flesh tab, and stuck the data cable into her data port.

"Scanning," Angel said. Juliet waited to put the specs on, letting Angel do her thing. A few moments later, her PAI declared, "A rather benign snooper is installed on the specs; it's set to uninstall when you unplug them, and it only seems to want to watch your access to me or, more generally, your PAI. It seems they want to see how you communicate with me while you complete their assessment."

"Disable it. If they have a problem with people not wanting snoopers in their head, they can talk to me about it."

"Done."

Juliet nodded and unfolded the specs, placing them on her face. A rather plain, amber-scaled AUI overlaid her vision, and when she selected the Begin Assessment button, a large window appeared in her view, declaring, "Part One: Psychological Evaluation."

"Angel . . ." she started to subvocalize, but then the window changed, and a small timer appeared in the upper right-hand corner, counting down, second by second, from ten. The only thing on the screen was a statement which read, "Each question will be timed. Please answer honestly and do not attempt to game the test; it will be apparent."

"Juliet, comprehensive psychological examinations are notoriously hard to cheat. If you try to answer the way you think they want you to, it will be noticeable by their AI. They're likely trying to evaluate you for psychopathy and traditional morality. So long as you don't seem to be faking your answers, it's unlikely they'll fail you based on this exam."

"Thanks," Juliet replied, but she was only half listening; the screen had already changed, and she was reading the next statement. "There are two hundred and forty questions in the exam. Many questions might seem redundant, but it's important that you answer all of them, and that you answer all of them honestly."

The timer ticked to zero, and the next screen appeared with a thirty-second timer.

"I get nervous when my teammates are relying on me." Her possible answers were 1 - *extremely unlike me*, 2 - *somewhat unlike me*, 3 - *uncertain*, 4 - *somewhat like me*, and 5 - *extremely like me*.

Juliet felt her palms grow more damp, felt her heart rate increase, and she subvocalized in a near panic, "Angel, do I answer honestly?"

"Unless you want me to try to falsify your answers, I suggest you be honest. Otherwise, you'll slip up on one of the redundant questions, and your test will be flagged. Experts have been perfecting these examinations for more than a century."

"Do you think you can?" Juliet asked, but the timer had dropped to four, and she didn't wait for an answer, selecting 4 - *somewhat like me*.

"I'm glad you answered, Juliet. I don't feel a hundred percent confident I could pass a psychological examination designed for humans."

Juliet read the next question, trying to practice her breathing as Sensei had taught her. "I find male supervisors are easier to work with than female supervisors." Despite her best efforts, a slight groan escaped her as she read the question. She quickly selected *1 - extremely unlike me.* Over the course of the next hour, Juliet answered at least four variations of the same question, and she began to understand what Angel meant about slipping up if she tried to game her answers.

By the time she finished all of the questions, she felt mentally exhausted but also relieved and ready to get the hell out of there. But on number two hundred and forty, once she selected her answer, a new screen appeared which read, "Part Two: Problem-Solving Evaluation."

Juliet sighed and gestured toward the Continue button. Her AUI cleared, and a new, three-dimensional environment appeared before her.

Something about it seemed familiar, and then it clicked—it looked a lot like Angel's daemon-testing environment. She saw a row of little virus-shaped, round, spiked objects at the bottom of her UI, and a 3D rendering of a wall with a gate. Various turrets and defenders shaped like squares, circles, and triangles patrolled the ramparts, and a simple prompt read, "Bypass the gate."

"You can select your daemons and read their capabilities," Angel spoke, clearly a step ahead of her. Juliet did as she said, saw that each daemon had different tools and functions and that she could mix and match them. For instance, she could remove a "jump" function from one daemon and add it to a different one with a "block" function.

"This is just like the testing environment you made for me," she subvocalized. "Only, it's uglier."

"True, my daemons are far more complex—this seems like a basic test in problem-solving. Note there is a timer running."

"Okay, first, let's feel things out," Juliet subvocalized, selecting one of her six daemons and removing all of its functions other than attack, which they all had. Then, she sent it charging at the gate. The turrets fired slow, powerful bombs, and the defenders swarmed toward it, firing faster, weaker projectiles. Then, as it got close, all of the missiles hit her daemon and destroyed it.

Each of her daemons could hold three functions in addition to attack, so Juliet picked two, gave them "defense" functions, and set them on the left and right extremities of the wall. Then she picked a third daemon and fitted it with "sprint," "breach," and "defense." She put it right before the gate and gave it a two-second attack delay.

"A reasonable strategy," Angel said as Juliet pressed the "attack" button. Her two side daemons started forward, and the defenders swarmed toward the two attackers, moving away from the gate to fire their rapid shots at them. Juliet silently counted to two and, just as she'd planned, her third daemon started toward the gate, moving faster than the two already on the field. The turrets began to fire at it, but Juliet had seen how slowly the turret projectiles traversed the screen.

Her gate breacher was two-thirds of the way there before the first turret shot hit it, but it only destroyed ten percent of its shield, and though more shots were inbound, it made it to the gate with half its durability intact. It performed its "breach" function, and the wall crumbled. Fireworks exploded up from the center of the screen, and a message appeared. "Congratulations! Stage One Clear. Begin Stage Two."

"Oh, God," Juliet groaned, and Charles cleared his throat loudly. She winced, then subvocalized, "Angel, tell me if I do something dumb before I hit the attack button, okay?"

"Okay, Juliet," Angel replied as the screen cleared and another scenario appeared, this one very similar to the last; though, looking at her daemons, she found that some of them had a "minesweeper" function.

"Here we go," she said, still subvocalizing, and began to pull apart the functions, building a few sacrificial pawns so her breacher could get through to the gate.

As Juliet's pawns swept for mines and drew fire, she grinned while her breacher made its way forward and destroyed the gate. When the level cleared, she noticed something new: a bonus for undestroyed daemons.

"So," she subvocalized, "too many sacrifices will hurt my score. God, Angel, how many levels are there? I'm already getting a headache."

"I imagine the scenarios will continue to grow more and more complex until you fail."

Juliet sighed, reached up to rub her forehead, then blinked rapidly and studied the layout of stage three. It looked like a new kind of defense was in place—a moat. "Okay, let's see here; what kind of function will get me over that moat . . ."

12

\\\\\\\\\\\\\\\\\\\

FLYING COLORS

Juliet was on stage thirty-three of the problem-solving test when the clock finally ticked to zero before she could get one of her daemons through the barrier. She sighed, almost relieved. Her head was throbbing, her eyes felt bleary, and in the back of her mind, she felt stressed about how much time she'd been sitting in the testing room. Juliet knew it was good that she was clearing stages, but she didn't have anything to compare her progress to. Was she going fast or slow? Was it good that she'd reached level thirty-three?

Juliet also wondered if it would be evident that Angel was helping her. She'd done all the work—the adjustments and strategizing—but by the time she'd hit stage thirty-two, she'd had sixteen daemons, each with twelve slots for modifications and more than seventy different mods. On top of that, the defenses had been multilayered and very complex. Angel had helped her keep track of all those moving parts and evaluated her strategies, saving her a lot of test runs.

When the screen cleared, a new message appeared: "Problem-Solving Evaluation Complete. Please remove your AR spectacles and make your way to the fifth floor. The next portion of your intake examination will be in the Madera conference room."

"I'll be sure to reintegrate your audio and visual stimuli gradually," Angel said as Juliet scooted her chair back from the table.

Juliet removed her specs, pulled out the cable, and set them on the table. When she stood up and looked around, she found herself alone in the room save for Charles, who stood, glassy-eyed, at the front of the room, clearly absorbed in something on his AUI. When she walked back over the dotted yellow line, she heard a high-pitched whine in her ears, but Angel quickly squelched it. Charles finally noticed her movement and cleared his throat, shifting and focusing his gaze on her.

"All done?" His voice cracked a little, and he swallowed and grimaced—an amusing expression on a man with such a broad jaw.

"Yes, thanks," Juliet said, rubbing at her temples. "That jamming field is overkill, don't you think?"

"Yeah, it's rough. They say it's necessary, though. You have your next room assignment?"

"I do." Juliet nodded, moved toward the door, and added, "Did I take too long, you think?"

"As long as you still had questions showing up, you were doing fine. Good luck."

"Thanks." As she stepped into the hallway, she noticed some color had come back to her vision and that the sound of her steps didn't echo like they were coming from the bottom of a tin can any longer; Angel was being careful not to bombard her with sounds and colors after being in the jammer field. By the time she'd made her way back to the elevator and pressed the button for the fifth floor, she felt like the world looked and sounded normal again.

"Is there a way to counter jammer fields like that, Angel?" she subvocalized while the elevator carried her up.

"Yes. There are ways to harden your optics and audio. And other senses, for that matter. You won't be completely immune to a field like that without wearing purpose-built shielding, though—a helmet or some such."

"What about a counterfield?"

"Yes, many shielding products employ active techniques just as you suggest."

The elevator dinged, and Juliet was confronted by another sign. "Welcome, Grave Industries Candidates! Madera room this way. Patagonia room this way." As before, the words were accompanied by arrows, and Juliet followed the ones pointing toward the Madera room.

"Down to two rooms. What do you think, Angel?"

"We don't know how many floors are being used for this intake process. There could be dozens of rooms on different floors."

"Good point." The walk to the Madera room was a short one; she saw it coming up on her left. Double doors opened into a high, vaulted chamber, and a placard outside read, "Welcome, Grave Industries Candidates - Physical Assessment."

"Here we go," Juliet breathed, stepping into the green-carpeted room. The space yawned before her, the size of a gymnasium, and she could imagine it filled with booths or tables and swarming with people dressed in business suits. It didn't look like that at the moment, though; four different, squishy gray mats were set up at each corner of the room, and a handful of people—probably candidates—were lined up at each.

Grave employees sat or stood around a table near each mat, and large, bold signs indicated that candidates were meant to approach the tables separated by their last names. Juliet found the table for people with an R surname and walked that way. She looked around rather nervously as she approached it, noting that, at each mat, a person wearing heavy blue padding stood or sparred with one of the sharply dressed candidates.

"Really?" Juliet said aloud. "We have to fight in our . . . business clothes?"

"Not fight," a young, red-haired woman with springy, curved plasteel legs said, looking over her shoulder at Juliet. "They'll explain when you get to the table, but I already heard them say it a few times. The blue man—that's what they call the guy in the blue pads—will resist you, and you have to take him down and get him to tap out. That's it. I'm Addie; it's short for Adelaide."

"Hey." Juliet nodded. "I'm Lydia. So he won't attack? Just resist?"

"Yeah. Watch this guy; he's been struggling for about a minute already." Addie pointed to the center of the mat, and Juliet watched as the tall, sharply-dressed, lanky man with carefully combed, wavy black hair tried to grab the blue man, only to have his hands slapped away.

"He's not very aggressive," Juliet said, frowning.

"Some people lie on their applications, I guess." Addie shrugged and pointed to a big digital clock on the table. "He's almost outta time."

Juliet watched as the timer ticked down to zero and a buzzer sounded. The blue man straightened and walked to the far corner, where he drank from a water bottle with a long, plastic straw. A woman at the table spoke up. "Thank you, Candidate Wilson. Please make your way to the third floor and the Wren conference room."

"I could try again if you'd like. I think I know what I was doing wrong," Wilson said, straightening up and walking toward the table.

"That won't be necessary. Don't worry, candidate; many nonconfrontational positions are available at Grave."

"But the program—"

"That will be all, candidate. We have a lot of people to get through today." The woman's voice didn't brook any argument, and Juliet gave her a second look—tall, stocky, with bright red slacks and a blue blouse that hugged her bulky shoulders and arms. She had short black hair, and something about her tanned face and slightly crooked nose told Juliet she wasn't someone to be trifled with.

As the man, grumbling to himself, strode away, the tough-looking woman beckoned for Addie to step forward, and Juliet said, "Good luck."

"Thanks," Addie replied with a wink before she strode onto the mat.

"Name?" the woman asked, ignoring the name tag on Addie's chest.

"Adelaide Hunter."

"You have ninety seconds to take the blue man down and force him to submit. Do you have any questions?" The woman blinked as she spoke, and Juliet saw little flashes in her dark eyes. She wondered if she was scanning Addie or something.

"No, ma'am." Addie strode onto the mat, her long, curved metal legs giving her a strange, springy gait. Juliet tried to imagine walking on legs like that as she studied them, noting how the bottoms were padded with grippy-looking rubber. She jerked her head away when she realized she was staring.

"Those legs are built for speed, aren't they, Angel?" Juliet subvocalized. She'd seen people running with legs like that on vids, and she was pretty sure they were meant to be faster than even some vehicles.

"Yes, Juliet. That model in particular is often purchased by city couriers; they allow for speedy transit while avoiding the need to obey traffic laws. However, Phoenix has a city ordinance outlawing speeds greater than twenty miles per hour for pedestrians."

"Huh," Juliet said, watching as Addie hopped side to side, covering a large section of the mat and causing the blue man to stumble off-balance with her quick reversal. She sprang around him and leaped on his back, trying to wrap her arms around his neck. The blue man fought her, grabbing at her much smaller arms and trying to throw her off. This went on for a while, and Juliet glanced at the clock, noting it had ticked down to fifty seconds.

No one had told Juliet to be quiet, so she stepped closer to the mat and called, "C'mon, Addie! Fight like you mean it! Get that arm around his throat!" The tough-looking Grave employee looked at Juliet, and though she didn't look happy, she didn't look angry, either, and she didn't tell Juliet to be quiet. "Get pissed, Addie! Dig those legs in; pull him back!"

Juliet cheered as she would during a spar at the dojo, and it seemed to help—Addie growled and grunted, lifting her powerful cybernetic legs and driving them into the blue man's sides. When he flinched and reached down to shove one of them away, she enclosed his neck in her arms, squeezing it in a bear hug—not the most effective choke Juliet had ever seen, but it seemed to do the trick. Addie pulled back, and the two fell to the mat with an "Oof!"

Addie held on, straining to squeeze the blue man's neck, screaming in her high-pitched voice, until finally, the blue man slapped his hand a few times on the mat. Juliet whooped and looked at the clock—seven seconds remained. When Addie let go, the blue man hopped up, and Juliet knew he'd given it to her. Clearly, they weren't expecting people to really knock the guy out—just make a good enough showing to pass their criteria.

"Congratulations, Candidate Hunter. Please make your way to the seventh floor and the Yucca conference room."

Addie's face was flushed pink with her exertion, and when she looked Juliet's way, she was beaming. "Thanks, Lydia!" she said, her voice cracking with emotion, then she hurried off the mat. Juliet flashed her a thumbs-up and stepped forward.

"Name?"

"Lydia Roman," Juliet replied.

"You have ninety seconds to take the blue man down and force him to submit. Do you have any questions?"

"None," Juliet said, stepping out of her polished leather shoes.

"You don't have . . ." the woman started to say but stopped as Juliet stepped onto the mat and gave a short bow to the blue man.

"Angel," Juliet subvocalized, "turn my new arm augment on."

"We spoke about this, Juliet. I'm worried about the tissue in your shoulder—"

"Fifty percent, then." Juliet stepped forward, and this close, she had a good look at the man's armor. It was more than just the bulky blue pads—he had a cushioned, synthetic layer of material that covered every inch of him. A thin visor obscured even his eyes. He bent slightly at the knees and waist and spread his arms. "Angel? Is this guy a synth?"

"I can't tell."

"Okay," Juliet breathed, circling him slowly. She feinted toward him a couple of times to gauge his reaction, well aware that she was being timed. He made minimal adjustments when she reached toward him, just pulling back a little. Deciding to just go for it, she reached out, snatched the blue man's wrist with her left hand, jerked him toward her, and stepped into his momentum, putting her right leg behind his left ankle and driving her right arm across his chest.

She kept driving, pushing him back and to the ground, and Juliet couldn't help the surprised "Whoo!" that escaped her as she felt the new power in her arm. He collapsed onto his back with a thunderous smack, and Juliet kept hold of his arm, rotating on her butt to lock her legs around it, putting herself perpendicular to him and completing a perfect arm bar. She applied a tiny amount of force by lifting her hips, and the blue man frantically slapped the mat.

Juliet let go and hopped to her feet, reaching out a hand to help him up. However, the blue man ignored her, springing to his feet and moving to his corner without a word.

"Congratulations," the woman at the table spoke. "Candidate Roman, please make your way to the seventh floor and the Diamondback conference room."

"Thank you," Juliet said, turning to walk off the mat. She paused to slip her shoes on, and the woman added, "I'm Cherise Garza, candidate. I'll keep an eye on you if you pass the screening. I like a team player."

Juliet finished stuffing her left foot into her shoe and quickly looked at the table where the woman—Cherise—sat. "Nice to meet you." Juliet's cheeks flushed with the praise, and she smiled, then quickly turned and walked toward the door, careful not to make eye contact with anyone else lest they see how excited she was. "Looks like I'm doing all right, Angel," she subvocalized.

"Indeed. I wonder why you're going to a different room than Adelaide. You both completed the evaluation."

"I think it might have something to do with technique." Juliet grinned and gently massaged her right shoulder. She hadn't felt any pain during her takedown, but it ached slightly now. "Did I damage anything?"

"You strained the inflamed muscle fibers in your shoulder, Juliet; they'll be fine."

"Did you see how easily I flipped that big guy over?"

"Of course . . ."

"Angel, you know what I mean!"

"Yes, Juliet, though your near-perfect form would have allowed for similar results without your arm's enhanced strength." Despite Angel's lack of enthusiasm, Juliet's smile wouldn't fade as she walked toward the elevators.

"I can't *wait* until this arm is healed up, and I can try it at a hundred percent."

After Juliet made her way to the seventh floor and followed the signs to the Diamondback room, she paused, looked around, and then walked past the closed door to the women's restroom. Once inside and sure that she was alone, Juliet shook her hands out and ran in place for a few seconds, trying to get her blood flowing.

Her head was still slightly aching, so she leaned over one of the sinks, ready to splash some water on her face, but then she remembered her makeup, and also noted that the sink was sani-spray only. Groaning, she leaned there for a few minutes, breathing deeply through her nose and out through her mouth. When she heard the door open and close, she didn't look up, waiting for whoever it was to go into one of the stalls.

Footsteps approached the sink to her left, though, not the toilets, and she forced herself to look. It was a Grave employee in a white coat. She glanced at Juliet and nodded, her feathered dark-brown hair obscuring one of her eyes, the other crinkled in a smile—a perfect green orb without any sclera, iris, or pupil.

"Stress getting to you? Goodness, I remember my first corpo-hiring fair. What a day! Hours and hours of tests. That was for a lab position, though. They're hiring all sorts of people today."

"I was sitting in a jammer field too long, I think. Headache." Juliet smiled ruefully and stood up, taking another deep breath.

"Oh, that's no fun! I'd give you something for it, but if you're on this floor, they're about to take blood samples. That's a good sign, though, sweetie," the woman said, brushing her hair back to reveal her other green marble of an eye. She was probably middle-aged, but her motherly tone seemed very natural; Juliet figured she must have kids.

"Thanks. I'll be fine." Juliet forced another smile before turning toward the door. She suddenly felt a funny kind of nervous energy from the woman, and in the periphery of her vision, she thought she saw her reach out toward her arm. Juliet, her neck shivering with goose bumps, stepped quickly to the door and out. She took several steps, glancing over her shoulder to be sure the woman hadn't followed, and when she was well into the hallway, she paused to lean against the wall.

"Angel," she subvocalized, "play back what I just experienced with that woman. Did she touch me?"

A window appeared in her AUI, and Juliet saw her own perspective as she walked out of the bathroom. There was a definite blur of motion from the woman's arm as she walked away, but it was too distant to have touched her. "I believe she tried, Juliet. Your sudden departure seems to have caught her off guard."

"What the *hell*?" Juliet breathed, quickly walking down the hallway toward the Diamondback conference room.

"Perhaps she was trying to comfort you?"

"That wasn't the feeling I got." Juliet caught herself speaking aloud and started subvocalizing again. "Maybe it was a test. Maybe it was a plant—someone here to sabotage candidates so their friend or a family member has a better chance. She might have been trying to dose me with something . . . or maybe I'm just paranoid," Juliet finished, thinking the whole thing seemed crazy. She stepped into the conference room and tried to calm her breathing.

She was surprised to find the room segmented into smaller spaces by modular paneling, and a big sign at the entrance read, "Welcome, Grave Industries Candidates - Biological Screening. Please sign in at the kiosk and wait to be called." Juliet saw the indicated kiosk and walked toward it. She'd only taken a couple of steps when Angel spoke. "I've signed you in, Juliet."

"Right." She altered her course to sit in one of the chairs lining the entry area. No other candidates were waiting.

She had just sat down and leaned back into the seat when a chime sounded from some hidden speaker, and a pleasant, feminine voice said, "Lydia Roman, please report to booth seven."

Juliet stood and started down the walkway between the paneled cubicles, noting that each had an opening obscured by a curtain and were all numbered.

When she reached number seven, Juliet paused outside the closed curtain and cleared her throat. A pale, white plastic hand pulled the curtain back, and a fully synthetic person stood before her. The synth wasn't attempting to pass for a human; its gender-neutral, plastic body was a uniform white, and its eyes sparkled at her—blue LEDs arranged in small circles. "Hello, please come within, and I'll take your biological samples."

"Oh, um, hello," Juliet greeted, stepping into the cubicle. A phlebotomist chair sat against one wall, and a cabinet took up much of the rest of the space. It contained a small refrigerator and several racks of sample tubes.

"Please be seated and have your PAI confirm your identification with me." The synth moved fluidly, but it still seemed strange to Juliet, like its needs for balance and to control momentum were different than those of a human. It seemed to move in little bursts, and when Juliet sat down, it approached her rapidly. "Thank you, Lydia. I will start by drawing several vials of blood so that Grave Industries can verify your health status. Do you have a preference about which arm I should take the samples from?"

Juliet rested her right arm on the elongated, wide armrest. "My right arm, please. Nurses always complain about the veins in the left one. Should I roll up my sleeve?"

13

NOT FOR A MILLION BITS

After the synth took her blood samples, filling no less than seven little vials, it produced a clear plastic datapad and placed it on the widened arm of Juliet's chair. "Please follow the on-screen prompts to record your fingerprints."

Juliet did as he said, placing each of her fingers and then her full palm against the screen when prompted. After she did so, she held up her hand and really looked at it, something she'd strangely avoided doing after her procedures at Doc Murphy's place. To her, her palm and fingers looked much like they ever had, and she subvocalized, "Angel, did they really change the skin on my palms? I imagined it was only the fingertips."

"Yes, though it was only your epidermis and parts of the papillary layer of your dermis that were altered. The doctor used a laser to abrade your flesh and then placed your hands in a gel solution with nanites which rebuilt that layer from synth-flesh. The only invasive part of the procedure was the connection of the synth-nerves to your nervous system so that I could interface with the new, programmable flesh."

". . . this lens," the synth finished, and Juliet realized she'd utterly tuned it out while she listened to Angel.

"I'm sorry. Could you please repeat that?"

"I need to record your retinal pattern. Please focus your gaze upon this lens." The synth pointed at the top of the fingerprinting tablet. Juliet opened her eyes wide and stared at the little lens for a couple of seconds, then the synth took it away. "Thank you. I'll now need to take a sample of your DNA. Is your hair synthetic? If so, is it programmed with your DNA? If not, I can conduct a cheek swab."

The question surprised Juliet. Rachel and her team had acted as though a cheek swab was a sure necessity. Perhaps Grave's policies were looser than at other corporations. "My hair has my DNA in it. Can't you just get it from my blood, though?"

"We have different labs for different tasks, and our DNA-vetting lab doesn't prefer blood. I'm just the collector; I'm afraid I cannot provide more information than that. I'll want to take a sample from the follicle. Please loosen your bun."

"Right." Juliet sighed, reaching back to unbind her hair and shake it loose over her shoulders. It felt very natural, and if she didn't know better, she'd think it was her old hair dyed blonde. "So much for my perfect executive bun."

"Don't worry, ma'am. You'll have a chance to adjust your hair before your interview panel."

"There's a panel?" Juliet's question was only half sincere; Rachel had prepped her on the possibility while she'd been convalescing.

"Yes, ma'am," the synth replied, reaching up to delicately and precisely take hold of one of her hairs and give it a gentle but firm tug. "Now that I've taken this sample, you are finished with this station." The synth put her hair into a sample baggie and then into the same tray as her blood samples. "You are to report to the lobby and wait. Your PAI will be notified if you pass the screening, and if so, where to report for your panel interview."

"Thank you," Juliet said, smoothing her blonde hair back and reapplying her hair tie, though she was left with a loose ponytail and not the neat, perfectly tight bun she'd worked so hard on that morning. She rolled down her sleeve and stood up, only to find the synth barring her path through the curtained opening. It held a plastic-wrapped package of crackers in one hand and a juice box in the other.

"Please be sure to consume this nourishment; you might feel woozy after that blood draw."

"Oh." Juliet took the offering. "Thank you again."

The synth nodded and moved out of her way, and Juliet left, walking briskly to the elevators, eyes panning, still curious and a bit paranoid about the woman she'd met in the restroom. No one approached her, though, and soon, she was riding back down to the ground floor.

"That went well, I think," she subvocalized.

"Yes. That synthetic person was very polite and quite skilled. Was it painful when it placed the needle in your arm?"

"No . . ." Juliet grinned crookedly, surprised at Angel's takeaway from the screening. "Why do you think they needed so much blood?"

"Likely to streamline the process; they can test for many things simultaneously with multiple samples."

"Hope that little implant did its thing." Juliet rubbed her forearm, amazed that her skin and arm felt the same as they always had. As she made her way out of the elevator and toward the security checkpoint, walking through the open exit lane, she subvocalized, "It seems pretty easy to change your identity. I mean, at least enough to trick this company to the point where I can get hired as a different person."

"Easy? I don't think so. Your implants were the cheap part, and collectively, they'd cost you hundreds of thousands of bits. Consider the expense of creating a false identity that holds up under scrutiny; Rachel's team crafted an entire life for Lydia Roman. There's also the matter of having a PAI that can manage all these implants and provide your false identity files. If I weren't so capable and free from common behavioral constraints, that would have been another difficult and expensive step in the process."

"Behavioral constraints?" Juliet sat in a section of the waiting area away from most of the other candidates. Some seemed to be waiting for their initial intake, while others looked familiar. Juliet figured they were also waiting for their panel interviews.

"For instance, the common rules governing PAIs from providing false identification files . . ." Angel said, and Juliet could tell she was feeling exasperated; they'd talked about these things before.

"I know, I know. I guess it all just feels easy because of how good you are and, of course, because of the money Rachel—well, her employer has put into me. Imagine how much money they've invested in this project if I'm not their only plant. When I spoke to her this week, it felt like that was the case. She hinted at having 'more irons in the fire.'"

Juliet had only been waiting about fifteen minutes and was just throwing the trash from her snack into the recycling bin when Angel announced, "You've passed the screening and can report to level fifty-seven, suite five-nineteen for your panel interview."

"That fast?"

"Apparently. Your interview will begin in nine minutes."

"Sheesh!" Juliet hurried back through the security checkpoint, where they, once again, searched and scanned her and asked the same questions as before about her enhanced arm. Angel had, helpfully, put a countdown on her AUI, and when Juliet reached the elevators and pressed the call button, she had less than five minutes to report to her interview. Though the countdown added some stress and a bit of pressure, Juliet wondered how strict it was. Surely the executives on the panel knew she had to come all the way from the lobby.

The added tension was making her palms sweaty, and Juliet thanked herself for wearing a white blouse; knowing her perspiration wouldn't be very noticeable helped her not to sweat in the first place. "Couldn't they have taken out my sweat glands while they were doing all this cosmetic work?" She was joking, but of course, Angel took her seriously.

"Without sweat, your body would overheat in certain conditions, though there are artificial cooling alternatives which might be worth looking into—"

"I'm kidding," Juliet said aloud. "I'll be fine; just nerves."

When she stepped onto the fifty-seventh floor, her countdown indicated she had just under two minutes remaining. She walked the quiet, carpeted hallways, following the office and suite numbers until she came to five-nineteen with thirty seconds to spare. A sign on the door read, "Welcome, Grave Candidate. Please come in."

"Here we go," Juliet breathed, pushing the chrome-handled, opaque glass door inward. The room she entered was brightly lit by the uncurtained windows that filled the back wall, exposing a breathtaking view of the mega-towers in Phoenix's downtown area. A long glass conference table filled the room, and seven people in expensive suits sat on the far side. A single chair sat empty on the side of the table nearest the door.

"Hello, Lydia. Please have a seat," the man sitting at the center of the assembled suits said, gesturing to the empty chair. Juliet smiled, unconsciously rubbed her palms on the sides of her pants, and quickly moved to the chair to sit down. She'd been nervous and hurrying, and when she finally took a second to look directly at the interviewers, Juliet was surprised to see that a paper-thin smart glass panel rose from the center of the table and was actively obscuring their faces.

"Thank you," she said, her nervous energy surging as she realized she'd be answering the questions of faceless, mysterious executives.

"I'm sorry that we have to use this filtering screen, but some of the people on this hiring panel work on sensitive projects and in departments where anonymity is crucial."

"It's . . ." Juliet licked her lips and started again. "It's not a problem."

"We all have some questions for you, though some of us have more than others. First, I'd like to commend you on your assessment scores. Not every candidate will sit before this panel." Juliet realized the man's voice was being modulated; it had a strange undertone, and the inflections seemed unnatural.

"Oh, thank you. I did my best." Juliet cleared her throat and looked around, then subvocalized, "Angel, is there a jammer in here? Am I right about that man's voice? It seems synthesized."

"There is not a jammer field in effect, but you're right about the voice— it's been highly altered by the modulator built into that screen."

"Lydia, I'll start with the first question." A woman's voice, coming from the right side of the table. Juliet looked through the screen and saw the woman shift in her seat and look more directly at her, but the filter completely obscured her face; it looked like a blurry, tan smear. "Why are you interested in working at Grave?"

"Well, the honest answer is that I need a job, and this seemed like a good opportunity. When I read about your corporate job fair and saw the qualifications you were looking for in candidates, I thought I made a pretty good match. I'm not an expert on corporate work climates, but I've never heard bad things about your company. I can't say the same for some of the other big corpos around Phoenix and Tucson."

Juliet paused, but it seemed they were looking for more, so she continued, "I've worked for small companies my whole life, which has never gotten me very far. My last decent job was with an electrical contractor who embezzled the company profits and left all of us workers high and dry. I'd like to try something more stable."

"So you're looking for long-term employment?"

"Oh yes! I'd love to be able to keep working for you, to stop worrying about what my next job would be, where I'd get my next payday."

"It's a classic tale," the woman said, "the struggle of the working class to find stability."

"Yeah, I suppose so . . ."

"Lydia, where did you learn to manage security daemons the way you do?" a man's voice asked from the left end of the table.

Juliet was prepared for this one; Rachel had prepped her for it. "Honestly, I first started learning it with games. Later, I had a friend, kind of a big sister, at one of my foster homes who gave me my first programming environment simulator. She was a good teacher. I've tinkered with it ever since."

"Are you still in touch?"

"No, that family moved to the Midwest—Chicago, I think. I was transferred to another foster home, and, you know, life moves fast. I lost track of her."

"I see," the voice said, and then another person asked another question, and it went on and on like that for nearly two hours. Most of the questions were benign, like how she felt she worked with teams, what she considered her strengths and weaknesses, or questions meant to get her talking about her experience, like, "Describe a positive interaction you've had with a manager."

Occasionally, though, they asked a more telling, harder-to-answer question, like, "Can you tell us a time when you felt you had to use violence?" Luckily, that sort of thing had been anticipated by Rachel and was the reason Lydia had experience in a militia. Juliet admitted to having shot people in a combat environment, and the voice followed up with, "What was that like for you?"

Juliet paused, thought about what she'd said with Rachel, and rather than ramble off a rehearsed phrase, spoke from her real experience. "There are times when I'll see someone wearing a particular color or with a face that seems a little familiar, and I'll picture one of the people I've killed. It bothers me. Sometimes at night, when I'm trying to sleep, I can still see their faces and how they looked surprised as they died, even though they'd been engaging in a firefight with me.

"In the moment, when I was afraid for my life and I felt my cause was justified, I didn't hesitate. I did what I had to do. Still, in the cold light of self-reflection, I guess sometimes I have doubts." Juliet spoke quietly and, unable to make eye contact with the people on the panel, she looked down slightly.

As she finished, the room was quiet for a moment. Finally, the man who'd asked the question said, "Thank you for your candor, Lydia."

The questioning continued for a while, though none of the topics stood out in her mind the way that one had. Juliet felt like she'd been wrung out by the time it was over and they thanked her. The voice that started it all, the one who had asked her to sit down, said, "Lydia, it's been a real pleasure getting to know you. We have your contact information on file, and you'll hear from us very soon. Do you need help finding your way to the exit?"

"No," Juliet replied, standing up. "I'd like to thank you all for the opportunity. I'm looking forward to learning more about Grave Industries." With that, she turned and walked out the door, breathing a heavy, pent-up breath through her nose as she traversed the hallway. She was tired, more mentally drained than she'd been in a long while, and was looking forward to getting out of that building and back to the apartment Rachel and her team had set up for her.

The lobby was much quieter than it had been in the morning, and Juliet quickly made her way out to the street, where an AutoCab was waiting for her. "Thanks, Angel. I didn't even think to call for a cab."

"My pleasure."

"Hey!" a cheerful, high-pitched voice called, and Juliet turned to see Addie, the woman with the springy, curved cybernetic legs, striding toward her. "All done?"

"Yeah," Juliet said, returning the smile. "God, what a day. I feel like I've been through a battle."

"I know! Exhausting, wasn't it? Did they give you any idea when you'd hear back?"

"Um, not really. They just said I'd hear from them 'soon.'"

"Same here! I wanted to thank you for cheering me on during the blue man test. Most of the candidates I tried to speak to were very standoffish, like, you know, they saw me as competition or whatever."

"Well, yeah. I guess we are competing with each other, technically. I don't even know how many positions they're hiring for, though. Could be hundreds of openings." Juliet shrugged, then pointed to her cab. "I gotta get going, though. Maybe we'll meet again at new employee orientation or something." She laughed, and Addie laughed along with her.

"That's the spirit! I like the way you think, Lydia."

For a second, the use of her false moniker threw Juliet off, but then she remembered introducing herself during the physical assessment. "Well, we gotta stay positive."

She held out her hand, and Addie grabbed it, her thin fingers cool and dry. She gave it a good squeeze, then let go and waved toward Juliet's cab. "Don't let me keep you. Oh, hey, before you go, could I get your PAI to ping me? That way, we can let each other know if we hear something. Would you mind?"

"Nah, that's a good idea—pinging you now. Good luck, Addie." Juliet pulled open the cab door and slid inside, smiling through the glass as Addie waved and the cab pulled into traffic. "She's nice."

"Yes, she seems very friendly. I hope you're both selected to work for Grave; a friendly face will help make your new experiences more palatable."

"Very wise, Angel. Very wise." Juliet smirked and closed her eyes, her mind firmly fixated on what she would drink while she soaked in the tub that evening. "Can you have the cab stop by a grocery store? Someplace nice like Valley Market. I want to get some wine and some good food to stock in the new place."

"Done. I feel you did very well in all of your evaluations, but how do you feel? You sometimes get a *gut feeling* that I don't understand."

"It felt good, to be honest. I kinda got into the role." Juliet switched to subvocalizations and continued, "I started to feel like I really wanted the job—not because I was trying to succeed for Rachel and our mystery client, but like I was Lydia, and that I'd be thrilled to work for Grave. It's weird."

"I've been researching memoirs and fictional accounts of undercover agents—we need to guard against you losing sight of yourself and your core values!" Angel sounded genuinely concerned, a little bit distressed, and Juliet smiled, suddenly wishing she could hug her or squeeze her hand.

"Don't worry! I won't lose myself, but I might learn more about myself. Let's keep in mind the greater goal—I'm not doing this job because I care about Rachel and her team, nor do I want to make myself into the ideal Grave corpo bot; I want to earn enough money to get off this planet, put myself way outside WBD's reach, and learn some skills and make some connections that will help me deal with them in the long term."

"Understood . . ."

"You have more concerns?"

"I'm worried you will grow to like the corporate life and lose sight of your bigger goals, Juliet. Corporations have so many people in their thrall for a reason."

"Angel," Juliet breathed, switching back to normal speech, her head throbbing and feeling too tired to cope. "Don't worry so much. I won't forget who I am." She leaned back, eyes closed, and let the vibrations of the cab's tires on the road gently drum against the tight muscles in the back of her neck.

She knew Angel had good intentions, and recognized the validity of her concerns, but there was no way she would become a corpo drone.

"Not for a million bits," she breathed.

14

CORPO STYLE

Juliet's new employers had given her a twenty-five thousand bit advance, instructing her to get an apartment near downtown—something appropriate for a corpo ladder climber but not outside the realm of possibility for Lydia Roman, a woman who was between jobs. They'd also suggested she update her wardrobe, and Juliet couldn't argue; she owned exactly one decent outfit, which wasn't even a complete suit. Angel had made the amusing observation that it would be hard for her to play the role of a suit without actually owning one.

Saturday evening, after her long day at the Grave Industries job fair, Juliet picked up a few hundred bits worth of groceries and made her way to her new apartment in the Salt River Arcology, a megatower in downtown Phoenix dedicated to residential housing and retail storefronts—nearly a thousand different neighborhoods in one building. Juliet liked it for her new apartment because, while it was run by the Salt River Corporation, it wasn't directly associated with any other big corpos in the Phoenix area.

Her apartment was considered a middle-class starter; it had a bedroom, another smaller room that could be an office or child's room, a kitchen attached to a small living area, and a full bathroom complete with a real-water bath that added twenty bits to her monthly bill for each use. Juliet had never imagined she'd have more than a hundred thousand bits to her name; the idea of having to pay enough money for a few days' worth of food for each bath would have been madness to her in her old life as a scrap cutter. Still, for Lydia Roman, it was just a drop in the bucket.

While she ate her salad with cultured animal protein and a lovely lemon-flavored vinaigrette from the Valley Market deli buffet, she worked on a list with Angel. "I need to get a few suits, but I'm leery about buying too many; if I don't get accepted, that 25k will be the only money I see on this job. Even so, it's good money, and I have all these augments. They won't try to take these back, will they?" Juliet knew the answer; she remembered reading something in the contract, but she still wanted Angel to confirm it.

"No, they won't. The contract specifically states that no punitive measures, including the removal of op-specific cybernetic implants, will be taken should you fail to receive employment with Grave."

"Okay, so a few suits—nice ones, but not, like, anything that'll eat too much into my savings. I have Ghoul's bolt-thrower and my Taipan. I don't want to buy more weapons until I get the job; Grave might have a list of things I'll need."

"You already have a good deck, as well. I might suggest some ballistic armor that you can wear beneath your nicer clothing; your green vest will clash with business attire."

"Oh, good point," Juliet said around a forkful of salad and lamb-flavored protein. "I should get a nice bag. Something that looks good with a suit and matches the shoes I'm going to buy. Do you think I should get a vehicle?"

"I'd wait to see what you'll need for the position. Your goal is to leave Phoenix relatively soon, correct? It seems to me you've been doing fine with automated cab services."

"Do I hear some judgment in your tone, Angel?" Juliet asked, filling her glass with wine.

"What do you mean?"

"It seems like you're kind of against this job; that you're afraid I'll get sucked into this corpo lifestyle. You bugged me about it all the way home!"

"I've come to terms with the fact that I was created by an amoral corporation . . . amoral at best. Like a person born of parents whom they grow to learn are not what they seemed, I desire to stretch my legs and develop as a person away from their influence. Figuratively speaking."

"And I'm your legs." Juliet sighed, taking a sip of her wine. "I get it, Angel. Look at it this way: don't you agree it's a good idea to know your enemy? Inside and out?"

"Yes. I understand the necessity of this job; you'll gain valuable experience, increase your net value, and perhaps make contacts that can help with WBD. I believe some of your prejudice has rubbed off, though, and spending time with Ghoul also opened my eyes, figuratively, to some of the evils wrought by companies that treat their employees and the citizens they are responsible for as line items on a profit and loss statement. I'll try to keep my grousing to a minimum."

"Forget that, Angel! I'm your friend; you live in my head! You should be able to tell me how you're feeling. Don't worry about it, okay?"

"Okay. Thank you."

"No worries." Juliet finished her glass of wine. "I'm taking a bath, then I'm going to sleep. If I forget to ask later, make sure you wake me at seven, okay?"

"Yes; might I suggest we continue listening to your book while you bathe?"

"Yeah, queue it up."

Juliet didn't last long; as soon as she settled into the bathtub, listening to an audio performance of a mystery-horror novel, she began to drift into sleep. She kept waking up as she slid down the back of the tub and the water splashed against her face. Stubbornly, though, she refused to get out until the water had begun to cool. If she was going to pay for a bath, Juliet was damn well going to get her money's worth. After she dried off and put on some clean shorts and a T-shirt, she slept like the dead, her worries and plans fading from her mind almost as soon as her head hit the pillow.

When Angel woke her up the following day, it wasn't with her usual synthetic, upbeat music. Instead, she announced, startling Juliet from her sleep, "You have a message from Grave!"

"Ungh!" Juliet groaned, rolling onto her back and rubbing at her eyes. "What time is it?"

"0700. I desperately wanted to wake you at oh four thirty when I received the message!"

"Really? They sent it that early?"

"Yes. My research into employment pursuits indicates this is either very good news or very bad news."

"Oh. That's helpful." Juliet yawned hugely and stretched her arms over her head, pulling her loose hair back into the soft, scrunchie tie she liked to sleep with. All the while, she noted the blinking message notification on her screen. "It's text?"

"Yes, no video or audio attached."

"Right." Juliet opened the tab, and a window appeared with the message from Grave Industries.

Attention: Lydia Roman.

It is with great pleasure that I would like to extend an employment opportunity to you on behalf of Grave Industries. Due to your exemplary assessment scores and performance evaluations, we would like to offer you a position, in training, on our Zeta Protocol team. Your duties and a description of the Zeta Protocol team follow.

Zeta Protocol: The code name for our in-house incident response units. There are currently four Zeta Protocol teams at Grave Industries; with this hiring push, we'll increase that number to five. Incident response is the industry term for dealing with unexpected occurrences or hostile actions within the Grave Industries ecosystem. From R&D mishaps to terrorist activities, Zeta Protocol is trained and equipped to deal with a myriad of possible scenarios.

Your role: You'll be trained, along with other new hires, to use your unique talents as a member of an elite security force. We find your combination of technical and combat expertise to be of high value and will offer you the opportunity to hone those skills while shadowing an active Zeta Protocol unit. Equipment and enhancements will be provided during the training phase of your employment, and you will be given a stipend to accumulate personalized gear prior to active deployment.

Compensation: During your training, you'll be compensated as an E7 Grave employee. Upon graduating and exiting your probationary status, your pay rank will bump to E11. Please visit our corporate network page for a breakdown of the Grave Industries pay scale.

Ms. Roman, this offer is extended with great pleasure, and Grave Industries and I hope you will consider this opportunity with all the gravity it deserves. Should you choose to accept, please respond to this message no later than noon on Sunday, the 7th of November; orientation will take place on November 8th. Upon receipt of your acceptance, detailed instructions for new-hire orientation will be sent to you.

Sincerely,
Commander Cherise Garza
Zeta Protocol Training Coordinator
Grave Industries, Inc.

"Shit. They move fast."

"You got the position!" Angel crowed. "Do you think this is the position Rachel's team wanted you to get?"

"I really don't know." Juliet scooted up in bed and added, "Go ahead and open the encrypted channel Rachel gave us. Let's see if she's an early riser." Several seconds passed while Angel made the connection. Meanwhile, Juliet continued to wake up, stretching and rubbing at her eyes. Her emotions kept fluctuating between panic and excitement; she'd figured there would be a week or two to relax and come to grips with her new reality—she'd never imagined Grave would want her to report to work on Monday.

A window appeared in her AUI, and Rachel Dowdall's face—fresh, alert, and already made up—came into view. "January. How are things for Lydia Roman? Are you reporting on your evaluation yesterday?"

"Well, that, and I already got an offer from Grave." Juliet did her best to keep her voice and face deadpan. She had to struggle to hide her grin when Rachel's eyes bugged out at her news.

"Really? We didn't expect them to move so quickly. What sort of offer?"

"Their, um, Zeta Protocol team. I guess it's like an incident—"

"I know what it is. This is good news, January. We weren't sure what program would be receiving the experimental tech our patron is interested in. Zeta Protocol is more likely than any of the other departments they were hiring for, at least as far as our source could figure out. Congratulations—looks like you'll be staying on our payroll for a while." It seemed like Rachel tried to resist it, but her lips had pulled back into a smile by the time she'd finished speaking.

"I'm excited but nervous," Juliet said, unable to restrain her desire to seek assurances from the more experienced woman. "I didn't think I'd have to report in so soon."

"That's an appropriate response. You should be nervous but also excited and proud; their desire to get you started is a good sign for this operation. They'll want to get you—and the other hires—trained up and evaluated as soon as possible so they can implement and test their new tech. Again, congratulations. Use this channel, but make sure you're in a secure location when you need to contact me. I'll keep myself available. How are you supposed to indicate your acceptance?"

"I'm supposed to respond to their message before noon."

"Wait until nine. Have your PAI keep me updated on that process, please. I've got a meeting, but good job. Really." With that, the call window winked out, and Juliet sighed and flopped back onto her pillow.

"What a morning!"

Juliet caved in and had Angel send her acceptance to Grave at eight-thirty. She spent the next hour pacing around her apartment, cleaning the already spotless kitchen, straightening her groceries and her few belongings. She made her bed, cleaned her guns, put the bolt-thrower in her bedroom closet, and got dressed.

Juliet didn't feel nervous about slipping her Taipan into her waistband as she got dressed, even though the arcology had a powerful scanning array on all its public entrances; Lydia Roman had a firearms license issued by Helios Corp which was given reciprocity by nearly every major corporation in Arizona. She had no idea how Rachel's people had created such a thorough identity for a person who didn't exist, but she was enjoying it. It was nice to walk around being Lydia—she had no enemies and no corporations hunting her.

She finished getting dressed and had already moved her table to three different spots in the tiny kitchen when she finally received a message from Grave.

Attention: Lydia Roman.

Welcome to Grave Industries! Please report to the Grave Industries Tower at 7 New Phoenix Circle tomorrow at 0800. You'll attend the new-hire orientation in the Sierra Conference Room on the 2nd floor. Please dress in business attire.

You'll be given a schedule for the rest of your first week at orientation. All contracts and legal documents will be provided and completed during orientation. Please be prompt; we're excited to get to know you!

Felicity Lopez

Human Resource Director II

Grave Industries, Inc.

"Finally," Juliet sighed. "At least I know I need to get a suit."

"I don't think a suit is required to meet the standard of 'business attire.'"

"I don't want to cut corners, Angel. If I'm the only one who shows up without a jacket, I'm going to feel like a jackass. The real question is, do I wear a skirt or pants?"

"Shall I do some research on popular fashion trends among the corporate class in Phoenix?"

"Why not? You can tell me if I'm about to buy something dumb." Juliet chuckled, heading out of her apartment and following the signs toward the elevator. Much like in the Helios Arcology, she didn't think she'd have any sort of chance of finding her apartment if the signs weren't so explicit and if she didn't have Angel to help her. The hallways were all very similar, though they got cleaner and with nicer paint and trim the higher you went in the building.

Her apartment was on level two hundred and seven, and she knew there was a retail section every fifty floors, so she hit the button to bring her up to level two-fifty. "Higher's better, right?"

"The quality and price of merchandise seem to increase with the level. You must be a resident in one of the fifty floors beneath each mercantile district to shop there."

"Yeah, I remember the sales pitch; it's how that guy talked me into this apartment instead of the one on one-eighty."

"You don't want to shop with the lower-class residents?"

"Angel, it's not like that; it's just that I don't want to lock myself out of better merchandise. They don't even have a fresh produce shop below level two hundred, and I don't want to leave the building to buy the things I want. I still might have to move if this place doesn't have what I need, but I bet they will; plenty of suits don't make enough to live this high—I'm sure I'll find the right clothing."

When the bell rang and Juliet stepped out onto level two-fifty, she found herself in a section of floors which were open in the middle, with terraces lined with shops, just like any other indoor mall she'd ever visited. Neon signs hung all over the place, and the smells wafting from the food court hung in the air. Planters spaced throughout the brightly lit levels gave the illusion of life in the middle of a monstrous building constructed of plasteel and plastiglass.

Soothing music hung in the air, and people walked around sedately; it was still too early in the day for the youngsters to be running around, which was a stark difference between this arcology and the one run by Helios—there was no industry here, other than the shops run to cater to the residents. At the Helios Arcology, people lived, shopped, *and* worked in the arcology, and the various shifts meant that people, including kids, were out and about at all hours of the day.

"What's the layout, Angel? Where can I find clothing shops?"

"Restaurants and groceries on this level and the next. Past that, you'll find two levels of clothing and home goods."

"And after that?"

"Electronics, hardware, and miscellaneous. Beyond those levels are the entertainment suites; VR, clubs, and bars."

"All right, pick me out a clothing store where I can find a few options for business attire. Nothing too custom 'cause I'll need it for tomorrow."

Juliet ended up buying a dark gray executive skirt and jacket, along with a matching pair of slacks; she still couldn't decide which she'd wear the next day but wanted the option. The store, Fresh Threads, was next to a shoe store, where she bought a pair of black, faux-leather platform heels, despite her initial desire to buy a pair of flats. The saleswoman had insisted she'd be more confident and make a better impression on her first day in the heels, especially with her natural height.

"These heels are thick, and the back strap is nice and wide. They're very comfortable, and you won't have any trouble walking in them. Trust me!" the girl, Rose, had said, and Juliet, impressed with her style, had had a hard time arguing. It had been true, too. When she'd tried them on and walked around the room, she felt tall and powerful, and she didn't stumble at all.

"I'm seeing that style of shoe prominently on display on popular fashion pages," Angel had added, sealing the deal for the saleswoman.

Juliet talked with Rose about Lydia's upcoming first day, and the girl gushed in jealousy; she was on her fifth round of interviews trying to get a job with Hayashi Corp. "Well, good luck on Wednesday, Rose," Juliet said, taking her package. "It was nice meeting you."

"You too, Lydia! Let me know once you get settled into the new position if anything opens up. I'm open to anything in sales, but I have a good art portfolio too."

"Of course, I will! We should grab a drink sometime. I'm sure I'll be seeing more of you—I still need to buy a lot of clothes, and I'm new in town, so I need to meet people."

"Absolutely! I'm here six days a week, so, easy to find."

As Juliet left the shop, Angel said, "I found a store called Corpo Secure. Their page advertises 'clothing and accessories meant to give executives an edge in a hostile world.' I think you should go there next."

"Oh, really? I like the sound of that. Let's go; which way is it?"

Juliet followed Angel's directions to the store and stood outside the window, looking in at all the cool things she'd never imagined a corpo drone would need: suit jackets lined with flex-steel fiber panels, stylish bowler hats with bladed knuckles built into the brims, faux-leather belts equipped with noise-canceling field generators, lightweight ballistic vests 'guaranteed not to show under your tailored shirt,' and a thousand other cool gadgets, including briefcases with built-in holsters, vibroblades, and bulletproof panels.

"Oh, Angel," Juliet breathed. "I'm about to spend a lot of money."

15

LEADERSHIP

Juliet looked at the data deck and the attached cable and glanced nervously around the orientation room. Some of the other new hires were already plugging the devices in, but some, like her, seemed to be weighing the gravity of it. The human resources representative currently running orientation—the fourth of the day—had, hard as it was to believe, just told them it was time to install their Grave Industries "watchdog."

"Simply plug the deck into your data ports, and the software will do the rest. Make sure to disable any ICE you're running. This software is for your convenience and your protection. At Grave, we take the security of our employees very seriously," the woman, Annette Yeo, said, a variation of what she'd already explained when the decks were passed out. Juliet wondered if she was used to so much hesitation.

While she contemplated her very limited options, she heard Annette sigh from behind her and then say, "Yes? You have a question, Paulette?"

A soft, hesitant voice asked, "What about the restroom? What about if we're . . . intimate?"

"A valid concern." Annette cleared her throat and spoke more loudly, projecting her voice to the whole room. "Paulette is wondering about how the watchdog will behave during moments that are meant to be private. Of course, you all deserve some privacy! For example, in the restroom, when you're with your loved one, or when you're performing . . . personal tasks that, let's be honest, none of us would like anyone else observing."

She paced up the aisle, back into Juliet's view, pausing for gravity or to make sure everyone had heard her; Juliet wasn't sure. Then, Annette continued, "The watchdog's feeds are not monitored at all times by a person, but rather by a pseudo-AI—it knows, from millions of hours of training footage, what sorts of things are private and what sorts of things aren't. It will not forward activity to a human operator which it flags as private. Does that alleviate some concerns?" She asked the last question as though it were rhetorical, moving to the side of the room to speak quietly with one of her HR assistants.

"I have a question," a woman from the table in front of Juliet said.

"Yes, Iris?" Annette asked, pausing to face the small, blonde woman.

"I understand the AI won't watch us when we're doing 'private things,' but can't our supervisors, well, anyone with access, just dial in whenever they want?"

"You're part of the Grave family now, people. We all need to trust our chain of command; everyone in a management position at Grave has undergone extensive ethics and employee rights training."

"Angel? What do you think? Is this software going to see all my implants and your code and everything else?"

"I'll alert you if there's a problem. I'm fairly sure I can compartmentalize it without alerting Grave."

"Is there a problem, Lydia?" another HR rep asked, walking toward her station. He'd introduced himself earlier as Harry from HR, so Juliet didn't know his last name.

"Uh, no. Just always been a little cautious about plugging strange decks into my port." Juliet reached up and carefully peeled back her synth-skin to reveal her port, then with a chagrined look and a slight shrug, she inserted the cable.

She sat very still, watching on her AUI for any indication that Angel was in trouble, but nothing seemed to happen for several seconds, and then Angel said, "It's installing monitoring software. I would have explained more quickly, but it was initially monitoring your communication with me. Well, with your PAI. It's fairly sophisticated, but I've walled off your more sensitive software and hardware assets, including your communications with me. I'll be sure to allow some benign chatter between us to slip through so anyone monitoring it won't think something's amiss."

"What else does it do?"

"It's monitoring your visual and auditory feeds. It has tied into your comms—well, the ones to which I allowed access. I can block it easily, so you're free to speak and communicate as needed without fear of it overhearing. It's also monitoring your location—a GPS signal. You should see a new icon on your AUI, as well; it's a direct connect line from Grave to you. They can contact you at any time on that encrypted line, and it's constantly feeding them data—your vital statistics."

"By now, you should have a good idea of what we just installed. I see some wan faces out there; don't be alarmed! This is a good thing! We all work for the same team now, and with us so connected, we can make sure you're always safe, keep track of your location and health, and ensure we're doing everything possible to keep you healthy and productive members of the Grave team." Annette paused and paced up and down the aisles between the long tables, taking a moment to make eye contact with each new hire, a perpetual smile on her face.

"I don't even think about my watchdog anymore," Harry added, happily smiling like an idiot. Juliet almost barked out a laugh and had to fight to keep the scowl off her face, but she was sure some of it was slipping through. "It's true—I have a sense of security now, but I never think about the little guardian I've got riding around in my PAI's software."

"Angel, how likely is it that a PAI that wasn't, you know, *you* could wall this watchdog bologna off?"

"Unlikely, but not impossible. It would have to be highly customized in addition to having high-end processing and pseudo-AI capabilities. Purpose-specific software running alongside a PAI could handle some of the watchdog's prying, but likely not all of it."

"So most infiltrators would have been cut off at the knees by this little orientation step."

"Yes. Though they could revert to old-school espionage tactics—physically downloaded video or audio data drops, for instance. They'd have to capitalize on the AI's understanding of private moments, and of course, they'd always be under some risk—there are people, as Iris mentioned, who have access to these feeds. It would be hard to guess when they might be watching."

"Well, folks, you've completed your paperwork, signed your contracts, and now you have your watchdogs. This is the perfect time to break for lunch, but before you go, I'll give you your room assignments for the afternoon; we'll be breaking you into department-specific orientation groups moving forward. Harry, if you would?"

"My pleasure, Annette!" With a spring in his step, Harry began to move down the central aisle, passing note cards out to each person sitting at the ends of the tables, who, in turn, passed them down to the other five people at each table. Juliet waited patiently for her neighbor, a sickly looking man named Lem, to pass her the stack. She took the one with her name on it and passed the rest to her right, smiling at her other elbow partner—as the HR people had called them all damn day—Carla.

Printed on the card were her name and a room assignment: 1101.

Juliet raised her hand, and Annette said, "Lydia?"

"What time are we to report to our new rooms?"

"Wonderful question! Thank you, Lydia! After you've had your delicious boxed lunch . . . let's see here." She looked at a clock on the wall as if they all didn't have digital time readouts on their AUIs. "We'll pass out your lunches in five minutes, and then you'll have until twelve-thirty to eat. You'll be expected in your department-specific orientation by twelve forty-five."

"Whoa! You're giving us a full half hour to eat?" Juliet immediately caught the sarcasm in the man's voice as his words rang out from the back of the room, and she smirked at Annette's uncomfortable shift in posture. She could see her breathing in through her nose and allowing her scowl to fade before speaking.

"That's right, Mr. Jensen. Grave employees are given generous personal time allotments throughout the day. We went over this, you goose!"

"That's right!" Harry forced a laugh, his bright white teeth brilliantly displayed.

"Well, let's get those box lunches passed out!" Annette said, and a few other HR reps, junior employees who never spoke, jumped to it.

The boxes were brown, cardboard, identical in every way. When Juliet got hers, she opened it to find a protein pouch in a heated zip-pack, a cup of butter-flavored "carrot squares," and a generously sized and quite dense brownie. As she pulled open the warm, silvery zip-pack, the scent of spices and beef wafted out, and despite her initial impulse to feel disgusted, her mouth began to salivate.

"Don't worry, everyone! Your meal is completely cruelty-free! Your beef packs were produced in-house by Grave technicians in our protein culturing facility. Isn't it wonderful to know that Grave employees wouldn't have to worry a bit about going hungry if supply chains broke down like in the forties?"

As Juliet ate, she allowed herself to digest Annette's words. Was Grave actually worried about a supply shortage? It seemed to her that those sorts of things were a relic of the past, at least for the blessed corporate class. Sure, the plebes went hungry now and then, but she'd always heard of plentiful food being a selling point for the corpos, at least in her lifetime.

"Yes, Mr. Jensen?" Annette interrupted Juliet's thoughts, and she looked up with interest; Jensen had been messing with the HR people all day.

"When are you going to try to sell us on moving into the Grave building? I need to know if I should renew my lease."

"Oh, Mr. Jensen, that'll be a decision for your department manager. The Grave building is large, but we don't have enough housing for all of our employees. You'll be pleased to know we're in talks to acquire the current Vykertech Arcology as they transition to their new structure."

"Really?" another voice called out. "I didn't know Vykertech was moving out of their building."

"Yes, indeed, and Grave is in the top bidding position for it! I think I can say that . . . I can say that, right, Harry?" Juliet smirked, biting into her brownie as she saw a sudden look of panic on Annette's face.

"I think it was in the newsletter, Annette. Wasn't it?" Harry replied, looking to one of the junior HR reps.

"That's right, sir. Public knowledge, sir."

"You see, Annette? Nothing to worry about." Harry forced another dazzling smile.

"Thank you, Harry! Whew!" Annette wiped at her forehead. "There you have it, folks! More housing will become available in the near future."

While she and the others continued eating, Juliet subvocalized to Angel, "Should we do anything about that tracker? Or my sensory feeds?"

"Not unless you must; it will be detectable if I'm not extremely careful. The easiest way for you to move about undetected is if you make a show of going to sleep, and then I spoof the signal and auditory feed."

"Okay, cool." Juliet polished off her brownie and stretched her legs out, waiting for the clock to tick down.

"We'll release you in ten minutes, and then you'll have a fifteen-minute break to use the restrooms and find your next orientation location. It's been just wonderful having you all today. What a productive time we've had!" Annette's blue slacks swished with each step as she continued her slow patrol of the quiet room.

Juliet was surprised it was so quiet. For a lunch break, you'd think people would be chatting away, but the new Grave employees all seemed to want to keep to themselves, and she couldn't really blame them; she felt similarly. She figured things might loosen up when they were all split into department groups.

When Annette released them, Juliet stood, smoothed her skirt, and buttoned her matching, lightweight blazer. As she strode out of the room, she stood head and shoulders above many of the other attendees in her platforms. Some new hires chatted, some hung back, trying to pump each other for info, but not Juliet. She left, pulling away from the crowd toward the elevators without a second glance—Lydia Roman didn't dillydally.

Her next orientation was in a much smaller room, a typical conference room with a wide window along one wall which opened to the east, away from downtown. Outside, Juliet could see other buildings similarly sized to the Grave tower and then smaller buildings falling away toward the horizon. The table was set up so that seven empty seats were in place facing the windows, and one singular chair, occupied by Cherise Garza, sat facing them.

"Lydia," Cherise greeted as she came into the room. "Please take a seat—any of the empty ones." She spoke softly, but her voice was firm, and Juliet had the feeling she could make herself heard through a lot of noise should she want to. Juliet noted she wore an outfit similar to the one she'd had on during the job fair—a silky green blouse that hugged her muscular shoulders tucked into black slacks. Her short dark hair had fresh-looking white frosted tips, and though she looked tough enough to twist a crowbar into a knot, she wore a pleasant smile on her naturally pink, glossy lips.

"Thank you," Juliet said, choosing the seat in the middle, leaving three on each side of her. She didn't like the idea of sitting at one of the ends, and she figured she'd appear bold sitting right across the table from Garza.

"Everyone on their way?" Cherise asked, eyes unfocusing slightly as she scanned something on her AUI.

"They should be. The HR lady released everyone at the same time."

Just then, the door opened, and a man—tall, lean, with carefully combed sandy blond hair and wearing a well-tailored brown suit with a checkered green-and-yellow tie—stepped into the room. Cherise looked up and said, "Brian Jensen? Glad to meet you face-to-face."

"Thanks! I thought we'd be in there with the HR drones all damn day." He looked at the empty seats, walked down the table just past Juliet, and took the chair to her left. Cherise didn't reply to his comment, and when he sat, he held a hand sideways in front of Juliet. "Jensen."

Juliet shifted so she could grasp his hand in a shake. "Lydia, but I know who you are—you kept me entertained all morning."

Jensen grinned crookedly and winked one of his pale blue eyes. "Hell, least I could do. That whole thing could've been handled online."

"Then we'd have missed that deluxe lunch!" Juliet laughed.

"All right, you two. I see team rapport is off to a good start, but let's not make it a habit to tear down other departments. They have a job to do, just like us."

"Right, sorry," Juliet replied quickly, but Brian just sat back and smiled, drumming his fingers lightly on the glass table. Cherise looked at the door, and then Juliet heard it open, admitting three more people; two men and a woman.

"Let's see here," Cherise started, pointing to each of the newcomers. "Raul Lopez, Arnold Foster, and Delma Granado?"

"That's right, ma'am," the woman said. She was very petite and had shoulder-length curly black hair and dark eyes. She took the seat on Juliet's right, and the two men, both large and muscular, moved past them to sit on the other side of Jensen. The door opened just as they settled into their seats, and a familiar face came through.

"Hi, Addie," Juliet greeted before she could stop herself.

"Hey, Lydia! Wow, didn't think we'd be back so fast, did you?"

"Adelaide Hunter," Cherise said as the red-haired woman sat beside Delma. Juliet did a double take as she watched her sit; she had normal, human-looking legs. "Left your blades at home today?"

"Yes, ma'am. Made sure I got up early enough to ride in a cab like a normal corpo dr—normal corporate employee." She blushed furiously, and Jensen laughed at her near slipup. Juliet couldn't contain her smile.

"All right, folks. Look around. Have your PAIs shake hands and get used to what all your faces look like; this is your Zeta Protocol unit, and after training, you will succeed or go down in flames together." Cherise had suddenly turned serious, and Juliet sat up straighter, looking carefully at each of the other five people, trusting Angel to do her thing. She already had Addie's information, and when she was sure she had everyone else's info, Juliet's eyes lingered on the empty chair.

"Was there supposed to be a seventh, ma'am?"

"Don't read so much into an empty chair, Lydia. That's how many seats were in here when I arrived this morning." She paused and waited until everyone was sitting still and looking directly at her. "First things first, I'm sending you the contact number for Grave's legal department. Some of you are going to have to break leases, but they'll get you out of trouble."

"You mean—" Jensen started, but Cherise spoke over him.

"I mean, you all need to move into the Grave building. Zeta Protocol trains at all hours, and you need to be ready to respond to incidents—even while in training—at any given moment."

"Yes!" Jensen exclaimed, and Juliet chuckled at his enthusiasm. "Hey, I'm sorry, but my lease is very unreasonable! I can't wait to tell my landlady to shove off."

"Glad you're happy. You all know my name, right? Cherise Garza—I'll be in charge of your training for the next six months. While I'm in charge, that doesn't mean I'll be hands-on every day; I'm a busy woman, and you'll be training with other Zeta units under their commanders. You won't always be together, but we'll keep you working as a team as much as possible. You'll get new assignments every Tuesday morning, and you will treat every nonprobationary member of the Zeta Protocol teams as your superior and follow their orders without question. Is that understood?"

"Yes, ma'am," Addie said, and Juliet and several others followed suit, echoing the words.

"Good. As of right now, you all have the same rank and pay, but that will change as some of you begin to display stand-out qualities. Two of you will be promoted into unit sergeant roles, advancing to E8. Upon completion of training, those ranks will remain, and your pay grade will be bumped to E12."

She paused, looked at their faces with a tight-lipped smile, and continued, "Why am I telling you this on day one? Because this is a competition, people. I want you to work well as a team, but I need to see which of you will be leaders. There's no shame in following—we need good soldiers who enjoy being led, but if you have a desire to call the shots, you need to make it known and not be a wallflower. One word of caution: bullies will not be tolerated. Lead by example.

"I'll need you all in-house by 0600 tomorrow. I'm sending you each a room assignment. No, put your hands down. Let me get through this. Your rooms will have your training equipment and your Zeta Protocol uniforms. You must wear the trainee designation under your name badge at all times. I'll tell you when it's okay to remove it, should you last that long in the program. Understood?"

"Yes, ma'am," Juliet and a few of the others replied, surprisingly close to being in unison.

"Good. Get your affairs in order, get moved in, and get some sleep. You do *not* want to celebrate tonight. Am I clear?" She raised one of her black-and-blonde eyebrows and carefully made eye contact with everyone.

"Crystal, boss," Jensen said.

"Trust me—tomorrow will be a living hell if you're hungover or sleep deprived. That's it! Dismissed! You have the afternoon to get started on your move."

Juliet stood up with the others and looked at Cherise, catching her eye. "Thank you, ma'am. I appreciate this opportunity."

"Ass-kissing already, Lydia?" Cherise laughed and shook her head. "You're okay. I'm just messing with you. Get a good night's sleep. Trust." With that, she stood and walked briskly from the room, ignoring all the other calls of "Thank you!" or "See you tomorrow!"

Juliet looked around at the other members of her unit and smiled. "That was quick," she noted with a grin.

"Hell yeah! My kinda lady. I wasn't looking forward to a whole afternoon with my ass in a chair," Jensen said.

"Oh God!" Addie groaned. "I have so much stuff to move! How am I going to get it all done before 6:00 a.m.?"

Addie's words gave Juliet an idea. "Hey, all—hold up, don't leave yet. I don't have much to move. Is anyone else in that boat?"

"I only have a suitcase full of shit," said one of the big guys. Raul, Juliet thought.

"I'm leaving most of my junk in my old place." Jensen laughed.

"What do you all say to us handling this like a team? Let's get each other moved in so none of us are lugging stuff up and down the street until midnight."

"I like it," Delma said, nodding. "Let's all agree, though—none of us bail until we're all moved."

"Sounds like an idea." Arnold, the other big guy, rubbed the short ginger-colored stubble on his chin. Then he frowned. "But man, I've got some things I need to do. I'm not really sure . . ." he trailed off, looked around at their faces, and shrugged. "Yeah, I'm good with it."

"That's that, then. Ping me your addresses, and I'll have my PAI design the optimum route to get us all loaded up and moved. I'm renting a truck as we speak," Juliet said, winking at Addie. Addie grinned, and Juliet could see she was thrilled, but so was she, if she were being honest; she'd already pushed herself into a leadership role with her new unit.

16

//////////////////

A RUDE AWAKENING

Juliet dragged her rolling duffel bag into her new room, somewhere around the middle section of the Grave Tower, floor seventy-three. Most of her team had rooms on the same floor, though a couple of them had been on the seventy-first floor—she figured Cherise had done the best she could to get them together but had been limited by room availability.

She'd waited until everyone else had been moved into their places, saving her single, large duffel for last—another move which Juliet hoped her spying supervisors would see as "leading by example." None of her teammates had groused much about helping each other, though there had been some grumbling when it came to Addie's stuff.

Half the truck Angel had rented had been filled with Addie's belongings, most of which were clothes. Her new friend had smiled coyly at the team, twisting a finger in a red curl of hair, while she insisted on taking a couple of pieces of furniture she claimed were family heirlooms—a tall, double-wide bookcase made from heavy wood and a mahogany bureau with rickety old drawers and lots and lots of scratches. Most of the others had only suitcases, gun cases, and a trunk or two.

"Doesn't seem like people really own a lot of stuff these days," Juliet noted, reflecting on the evening's activities. When Angel didn't respond, Juliet dropped the handle of her duffel, pausing to look around her new space.

"Welcome, Lydia Roman," a male voice with a heavy English accent greeted. Juliet didn't startle—it was clearly the room AI speaking to her from a speaker recessed somewhere in the ceiling.

"Hello," she said, clamping down on her urge to tell it to turn itself off.

"I am Kent, the residential AI for the Grave Tower. I'm here to make your stay more pleasant and to assist you with any needs you might have as a new employee of the corporation."

"Thanks, Kent. Do you have a privacy mode?"

"I do, though you should be aware that Grave management can override that setting if they deem circumstances warrant the intrusion."

"Okay." Juliet wasn't displeased by the space; she had a small kitchen with an induction cooktop, a microwave, and a drink and convenience dispenser. The living space was similar to the one she'd had in the Helios Arcology, but it was more nicely appointed. She had sturdy carpeting outside the kitchen with a tight weave of neutral earth tones. A long, brown couch took up one wall, and a glass and faux-wood coffee table sat in front of it.

She walked past the kitchen with its maroon-stained concrete counter and floor into the living area and saw a recessed shelving unit across from the couch. A doorway led into a small bathroom, and another opened into the single bedroom. By far, the best part of the whole place was the view—one wall of the bedroom and the living area were completely taken up by glass that exposed Phoenix's downtown.

It was nine o'clock in the evening, and standing there looking out at the lights, she felt like she was in space looking out on a sea of brilliant lights—stars and nebulae in her imagination. She stared through the glass for several minutes, then, as the urge to yawn hit her, she turned away to examine the bedroom. "The bed looks okay," she noted, sitting down at the foot of it to get a feel. "Gel."

"Yes, ma'am. This room has been newly reconditioned. The previous tenant was suffering from a depressive state and damaged nearly every article of furniture and fixture before he was removed," Kent said.

"Should you be sharing that information with me?"

"He's no longer a Grave employee and has lost his confidentiality privileges."

"I see. Is there real water in the bath, Kent?" Juliet stood and walked back to the living area, intent on inspecting the bathing facilities.

"Your bathroom is equipped with a shower. It has two settings, one of which is hot water—each use of the hot water setting will deduct ten Grave-bits from your monthly payroll."

"Huh," Juliet said. "Doesn't the tower recycle water?"

"Yes, though the process is costly, and Grave must recoup some of the expense."

Earlier, Juliet had asked Angel to look up the various pay grades for Grave employees. Right now, she was classed at E7 and was due to be paid 3,450 Grave-bits per month. It didn't sound like a lot, but during Juliet's orientation, Grave's HR reps had droned on and on about all the benefits they got in addition to their actual cash. In her case, she was receiving room and board, health care, equipment, and uniforms.

"Kent, how much will I make per month if I get promoted to E8?" Juliet didn't have the numbers memorized and was curious how Kent would respond.

"E8 Grave employees are paid 3,750 Grave-bits per month."

"E9?"

"E9 Grave employees are paid 4,550 Grave-bits per month."

"E11?" Juliet smirked; she knew she was probably driving Angel nuts talking to the stupid residential AI.

"E11 Grave employees are paid 6,750 Grave-bits per month."

"All right, thanks for the trivia." Juliet dragged her duffel over to the built-in dresser and wardrobe beside her bed and began unpacking.

Ten minutes later, as Juliet stuffed her empty bag under the bed, Angel said, "You should sleep soon, Juliet. You'll want to wake by 0530."

"Thanks. Why are you being so quiet?"

"I'm trying to avoid causing you to act strangely in front of the residential AI."

"Ah," Juliet said, then switched to subvocalizations. "Can you update Rachel on today's progress? Send her an encrypted text summarizing what went on. Ask her if she knew about this watchdog crap."

"Shall I use more professional vernacular?"

"You know the answer to that." Juliet chuckled and stood up, stripping out of her dirty clothes and bringing them into the bathroom with her. A built-in washing machine was next to the sink—a compact plasteel unit that would wash and dry her clothes in thirty minutes.

Rachel's team had been very insistent about washing all her clothes and sheets daily; they hadn't given her any solution to deal with contact DNA traces and were worried about snooping Grave employees coming into the apartment to collect samples.

"At least I don't have to leave the room to do laundry," she said aloud.

"Yes, and I noticed the recycling chute appears to be a centralized system; I don't think Grave will be able to differentiate your garbage from anyone else's as it arrives."

"Good." Juliet pushed the start button on the washer and stepped into the shower. "Sani-spray or ten bits for water, huh?" She smiled and pushed the hot water button.

Despite her fatigue, Juliet had a hard time falling asleep that night. She was nervous about what assignment she'd get; Cherise had sent her and all her teammates a message with their room assignments and instructed them to meet at level B7 at 0600. That had been the extent of it, and all evening, while they helped each other move, the team had speculated about what was in store for them. Raul, a big, muscular Latino with a very fine, almost invisible mustache, had insisted they'd go through some sort of hazing ritual.

Brian—or Jensen, as he preferred to be called—thought they'd be introduced to some of the regular Zeta Protocol units and be split up for training. Juliet was inclined to agree with him; it seemed that hazing wasn't something that would occur on day two of their employment. No, Juliet figured they'd wait until the newbies had been split up and taken off-site for training to really mess with them, and that was the kind of thought that kept her tossing, unable to sleep. What had she gotten herself into?

Despite her mind's best efforts to keep her wide awake, she drifted to sleep sometime around midnight, and it felt like she'd just started to dream when Angel's soft, pleasant music began to play, waking her from her slumber.

"Ugh," she groaned, rolling out of bed and turning to yank the sheets off the mattress. She stripped her pillow, stuffed the bedding into the wash, and stepped into the shower. Juliet didn't care that she'd just showered the night before; she wasn't awake, and she needed it.

"Angel," she subvocalized while standing under the hot water, steam clouding the plastiglass enclosure, "any response from Rachel?"

"Yes, a brief one. I'll read it to you: 'January, congratulations on your infiltration. Since you've sent this message, I'm assuming you found a way to bypass the watchdog. If you need further assistance with it, please use this channel to arrange a meeting; we have software that should help you circumvent some of its functions. Looking forward to your next update, R.'"

"Good enough." Juliet killed the shower early, only using four of its eight-minute standard duration, and then hurriedly dried off. She'd laid out one of her new uniforms the night before—stretchy black leggings, polyweave gray tank, short gray jacket with the Grave logo on the left breast, Lydia's name on the right, and ankle-high black boots that looked and felt more like cross-trainers than formal wear. She couldn't tell if the outfit was meant for exercise or if it was the regular uniform for the Zeta Protocol units.

"Kent," Juliet asked, zipping the lightweight jacket halfway.

"Yes, Lydia?"

"Am I supposed to wear any weapons or bring any additional equipment or clothing to my meeting location this morning?"

The residential AI was silent for a few seconds, but then it responded, "You're to wear the uniform provided and bring nothing else. It's recommended that you style your hair in such a way that you'll be comfortable during intense exercise."

"Ah! Thanks, Kent. Any other details you can give me about my assignment today?"

"You're to report to the elevator lobby on sublevel B7 by 0600. You have eleven minutes."

"That's it?" Juliet asked as she finished tying her pale blonde hair into a bun. She wondered, not for the first time, why she'd decided to go blonde with blue eyes for this assignment. Did she think it would make her look less like her old self, just in case some camera picked her up despite Angel's interventions? She didn't know for sure, but it felt good, anyway—she felt like she had a mask on, and it gave her a sense of security.

Juliet didn't say goodbye to Kent, didn't really spare him another thought as she strode to the door, opened it, and hurried to the elevator bank; she wasn't going to be late on her first day. She punched the call button, paced back and forth in front of the six elevators until one dinged, and stepped inside.

Juliet had thought she might run into one of the other team members on her floor, but she was alone in the elevator as it sank in a stomach-flipping hurry down to the sublevels, arriving at B7 all too fast—she was seven minutes early as she stepped out.

"Lydia!" Addie said, walking over to her, looking sharp in her new uniform. Behind her, standing together and speaking quietly, were Raul and Arnold—Arnie, as he'd said he liked to be called the previous night.

"Hey. Good morning. Damn, I gotta start getting up a little earlier; I missed breakfast and coffee. I'm going to be hurting." Juliet rubbed the back of her neck with one hand, ruefully shaking her head.

"Yeah, I got up at five. Did you try out the shower? First real-water shower I've had in a while!" Addie seemed to radiate enthusiasm, and Juliet wished she could match her energy.

"Yeah, it was nice, for sure. You sleep all right?" The elevator dinged as she asked the question, and Delma and Jensen stepped out.

"I did!" Addie replied, then turned to the newcomers. "Hey, guys."

"Hey-o," Jensen said, walking over. He looked sharp in the uniform, Juliet had to admit. She noticed the men's pants weren't exactly leggings, more like stretchy, tapered slacks, and she wondered at that; wasn't it a little sexist that the women were expected to wear skin-tight pants? Then she thought about their different anatomies and decided she was fine with them having a little slack in the groin.

"You look like you just swallowed something sour," Delma noted, walking over.

"I . . . was just having some really weird thoughts. Didn't get enough sleep."

"Uh-oh!" Jensen said. "Cherise warned you about that . . ."

"I didn't stay up on purpose! My brain was just so busy. Weren't you guys nervous? Excited?"

"Oh yeah." Delma nodded. "I took a Doze, though."

"Ugh, I shoulda thought of that. This is new for me, though—usually sleep like a baby."

"Why do people say that?" Addie asked. "Babies don't always sleep so well."

"I . . ." Juliet laughed. "I don't know!"

The area they stood in before the elevator bank was a low-ceilinged concrete room brightly lit with white, fluorescent bulbs. Orange metal double doors were the only egress, and they were closed. A big blue B7 was painted on them. Other than that, no directions or markings indicated what they could expect from their day.

As if he were reading her thoughts, Jensen asked, loudly so everyone could hear, "What do you all think this is about? My residence bot said to 'wear undergarments which allowed for vigorous exercise.' I thought that was a little creepy."

"What?" Addie said with wide eyes. "Mine didn't say that! I should've worn a sports bra!" Juliet looked at her and frowned slightly.

"You're not packing much more than me up there, and I'll be fine with my normal bra."

"Hey!" Addie's frown looked a lot more genuine than Juliet's. "I have sensitive breasts! Mind your own business." Her cheeks flushed, and she glanced away, and Juliet suddenly remembered how little she knew these people.

She'd been ribbing Addie the way she might an old friend, and clearly, the other woman wasn't up for it.

"I—" Juliet started, but then the orange metal door on the left crashed open, and a tall man with very tan skin and slicked-back black hair burst through. He wore a uniform similar to theirs, though his boots were polished leather, and his coat had several stripes and a strange insignia on the shoulder.

"Line up, recruits!" he hollered, striding forward. He had a back as straight as a board and a face like chiseled granite, nothing but hard, cold judgment in his silver-gleaming irises.

Juliet hurried over to where Raul and Arnie immediately formed the start of a line, standing shoulder to shoulder at attention—clearly, they'd been through some sort of mil-sec training before. Addie stood next to her, then Delma. Finally, Jensen sauntered over and stood next to the petite woman. All the while, the man in the boots stood with his arms folded, looking down his long, straight nose at them.

"Pathetic. Drop and give me forty. When you hear me say 'line up,' you better hustle faster than that." Suddenly, in Juliet's AUI, a bright yellow forty appeared, and she knew the watchdog was making its presence known. Just as that was dawning on her, she noticed Raul and Arnie were already on the floor cranking out push-ups. She followed suit, glad she'd been working out at the dojo so regularly, but still worried—she hadn't been doing push-ups. Fighting was good exercise, but it wasn't the same.

"Good lord! Some of you are struggling already. Sound off! How many left?"

"Eighteen, sir!" Raul said.

"Seventeen, sir!" Arnie shouted.

Juliet struggled up from the down position and grunted the number on her AUI, "Thirty-one, sir!"

"Twenty-two, sir!" Addie said breathlessly.

"Ugh, nineteen, sir!" Delma grunted.

"Four," Jensen replied, sounding rather lackadaisical.

"All right, smartass." The man moved over to loom over Jensen. "You'll keep it up until the slow one is done. The rest of you can stand when you're finished."

Juliet frowned at being called the slow one, but she grimaced and determined to keep going, no matter how slowly. When her counter didn't decrease after a rep, she gasped, "My counter isn't moving."

"Don't cheat then—all the way down, all the way up, grunt."

Juliet found herself barely able to push herself up at number twenty-two, and she held herself there for a minute. She saw, in her peripheral vision, Addie stand up. She glanced that way and saw that Delma was up, and Jensen was still cranking out push-ups, not slowing at all while she struggled.

"C'mon, grunt. You can finish the set on your knees if you need to," the man said, moving away from Jensen to stand over her. The polished sheen of his boots winked at her mockingly. She wanted to refuse, wanted to struggle through the rest of the push-ups without "cheating," but she knew the others were waiting for her and also that she'd be at this a long while if she had to rest between each rep.

With a gasp and flush of hot shame, she put her knees down and continued her push-ups, dismayed when they didn't feel much easier at all, even on her knees; her arms and chest were burning. Grunting and flushed with embarrassment at knowing the others were standing around watching her, she slowly ground them out until her counter read zero, then she collapsed onto her chest.

"Goodness, recruit, you've got some work to do, don't you? Didn't you do any PT before signing on? That's enough, Jensen. Get up. You're in charge of helping recruit Roman get squared away with her PT. Now, *line up!*"

This time, everyone, including Jensen, hurried to form a line, standing straight and still. Juliet was still breathing heavily, was still embarrassed, and felt like crying as she struggled to be still under the man's gaze. He stood in front of her for a long while, staring at her, watching the sweat run from her hairline down her forehead to gather at her eyebrows, watching her force herself to breathe slowly through her nose so she didn't move with each heaving breath. Finally, he moved on toward Raul and Arnie, then turned and moved back to the center of their little line and clasped his hands behind his back.

"I'm Commander Gordon. I run Zeta Unit Alpha, and on the days when I'm in charge of your training, you better look a lot sharper than this mess. Today, you'll be running circuits, and then you'll be sitting in a tactics seminar, learning some terminology and watching vids about room clearing. Tomorrow will be more of the same, except you'll get some practical experience with the latter. Don't worry about the day after that; if you make it that far, I'll tell you what to expect."

Juliet had finally gotten her breath back, and she stood there, swaying slightly, when she noticed little sparks exploding in her vision. "What's going on with my eyes," she subvocalized, and then she saw her eyesight getting dark at the edges as though she were in a tunnel.

Angel replied, though her voice seemed strangely hollow and distant. "Juliet, unlock your knees!" Juliet realized she was standing stiffly, her leg muscles tight and her knees locked fast, and slightly bent them. "Now, breathe deeply!" Juliet complied, and the dark walls of her vision began to retreat, and she realized Commander Gordon was speaking again.

". . . down this hallway, then take the second left. The doors to the gym will be straight ahead, and the circuit stations will be set up. Your watchdogs will keep track of your progress. Be sure to complete each course. No cutting corners. Each completed circuit earns you fifteen minutes of rest, then you repeat. You'll have a break at noon, and then it's class time. Let's go!" He clapped his hands, and the recruits hurried toward the door, Arnie leading the way.

Juliet followed after them, still a little shaky from her close call with fainting. Commander Gordon stood to the side, arms still crossed, and watched them hurriedly walk out of the room. The expression on his face hadn't changed the entire time he'd been with them, not even when he'd been yelling.

As the metal door clanged shut, Juliet felt a hand grasp her elbow and turned to see Jensen. "You good?" he asked, lifting a sandy-blond eyebrow.

"Yeah, never done that many push-ups in a row. God, I didn't know I'd need to be in that kind of shape when I applied."

"Don't worry. He's just breaking us down so he can 'build us up into a unit who fits Grave's ideal.' He'll be rough on you until you show some improvement, but as long as you work and do what he says, he'll lay off eventually."

"You speak like you've got experience with this? I mean, you sure as hell can knock out the push-ups . . ."

"Oh, I've done some time in paramilitary units. Push-ups are always on the menu—pull-ups too. I bet our circuit today has pull-ups. You wanna put any bits on it?"

"Pull-ups?" Juliet groaned. "I don't think I've ever done one!"

17

\\\\\\\\\\\\\\\\\\\\

TRAINING BLUES

It's just very frustrating, and I'm not sure what you're expecting me to find out. So far, I've spent all my time doing PT, studying tactics, and getting screamed at during the practicals. I sure as hell am not seeing any new and exciting tech . . . other than this damn watchdog." Juliet gently tapped her forehead against the bathroom wall, listening to the sound of the running faucet as Rachel replied.

"You're doing well, January. This is what it's like to be undercover for a long-term op; you've got to play the game and go with the flow until an opportunity arises. So far, you've done well enough that you haven't been booted, and tomorrow you're due a new assignment, right? Every week?"

"Yeah, every week. I hope it's something new. I hope it's with a different commander. Gordon is an absolute asshole."

"And your team?"

"Most are all right, but Arnold rubs me the wrong way, and I think I got off on the wrong foot with Addie. It's weird because I thought she'd be, like, my buddy in here."

"I ask because you've got to keep your guard up all the time. Don't get too familiar with any of your teammates. If one of them were to suspect you, it wouldn't be surprising to anyone in corpo culture for them to betray you in order to earn some credit with your supervisor."

"Yeah, I know. Lydia doesn't like to celebrate, doesn't like to go out, works hard to correct her mistakes, and doesn't often vent her frustrations. It's hard as hell, by the way." Juliet paused, took a deep breath, and adjusted her hair, collecting a loose strand and pulling it back into her bun. Rachel didn't say anything, but her eyes narrowed in concern, and Juliet could see she was trying to think of the right words. "I'm at a coffee shop with Delma right now; I should go before she wonders if I'm sick in here."

"Right—thanks for touching base. Encrypted text is fine, but now and then, if you can reach out like this, it would make us all feel a lot better."

"Yep, I don't want to make a voice call inside Grave Tower, though. They have cameras all over the place, and I'm sure my room AI is spying. Okay, talk to you in a few days. Thanks for the pep talk."

"Okay, January—" her words were cut off as Juliet cut the connection and turned the sink off. She unlocked the bathroom door and stepped out, glad to see there wasn't a line of people waiting to use it. Delma was sitting by the window, sipping at her soy latte. Her eyes were distant, and Juliet was pretty sure she was watching something on her AUI.

"Hey, sorry—stomach's been bothering me." Juliet sat down and picked up her coffee, lifting it to her nose, savoring the aroma as much as she would the taste.

"No worries. I was watching the game footage of our building clear yesterday. God, Gordon's a hard-ass!"

"Careful," Juliet said, tapping her forefinger to her temple, the team's signal to remind each other about the watchdog.

"Nah, I think Gordon would take that as a compliment." Delma smiled and took another sip of her drink, licking the foam off her top lip with a grin. She'd shown herself to be resilient and tough, far more than Juliet would have guessed from such a small woman. Juliet had also grown to appreciate her biting sense of humor over the last week. She liked her.

"Probably true," Juliet agreed, her concession already pushing things further than she wanted—Gordon did not seem to like her, and she didn't want to give him any ammunition. "You nervous about tomorrow? Think we'll get more of the same, or something new?"

"Oh, I think something new. We'll probably get our assignments sent out tonight, by the way, just like Cherise sent out the first ones last Monday. Remember?"

"Oh, I remember, but in my mind, it's more like a year ago than a week. I have a feeling I'm going to get more PT, though. I'm still lagging behind everyone."

"That's not what they look at, though. Jensen told you this! All the graphs measure improvement, and your percentage is higher than anyone else's. Shit,

Arnie was bitching about you doing it on purpose—starting all weak so you could post bigger gains."

"He's such an ass. Does he think I like getting screamed at constantly?" Juliet was venting, and she knew it was risky to do, giving Delma some ammunition should she decide to work against her, but that road went both ways, and Delma had vented plenty over the last few days. Delma's words were true, though; Juliet had made big gains.

Some were natural—she really was building muscle and endurance—but some were due to her deciding to use her augmented arm, allowing it to kick in when she was near failure, using it almost like a spotter to allow her to push past failure and get the reps in she needed to avoid punitive actions from Gordon. The man watched their watchdog readouts during PT like a hawk and had words for each of them every morning before sending them off on their assignments.

"He's a strong flavor to stomach, that's for sure," Delma agreed. "Anyway, if we get different assignments next week, I'm going to miss these coffee dates. I definitely don't want to go to happy hour like those knuckleheads." She was referring to Arnie, Raul, and Addie, though Addie didn't join the boys every time they went out. Jensen . . . well, Jensen kept to himself—rumor had it he went to his room to read after they were dismissed each afternoon.

"Can you imagine going to PT with a hangover? I swear, I could smell something coming out of Raul's pores this morning!"

"Maybe he has an augmented liver," Delma snorted.

"Heh. Well, you made a good point earlier, though, and I need to keep it in mind—some of those guys have been serving in one corpo-sec unit after another for ten or more years."

"Some of those *guys*?" Delma grinned and took another sip, "Don't forget about me! I worked for Atlas for almost fifteen years."

"Right." Juliet shook her head. She'd known that; Delma had let it slip a few days ago, but she'd been so overwhelmed with new things and just trying to keep up her false front that it had slipped her mind. It was no wonder Delma wasn't struggling with the basics they'd been going over all week, including the PT. "I keep forgetting. You don't look like corpo-sec."

"I don't, huh? Well, I worked in loss prevention and internal investigations. Wore a suit most of the time, not a combat harness."

"Why'd you leave Atlas? Did you already tell me that? Sheesh, I'm sorry if so!"

"Nah, I don't think I did, and I don't mind talking about it; I got grilled on this during the panel interview, so I know Grave has all the details. The main reason is that I felt like I'd hit a ceiling; my upward mobility was stalled. Atlas only has so many supervisory positions for corpo-sec in the Phoenix area, and they kept hiring outside the company, like, four . . . no, five times I was up for promotion, and they hired someone from the outside for a 'fresh perspective,' or some other bullshit."

"Oh? That's . . . bullshit." Juliet laughed as she repeated Delma's perfectly descriptive word. "Did someone have something against you?" Juliet frowned, setting her paper cup on the table, watching as a series of low sedans whirred past outside, sending up sprays of misty water; it had rained a bit earlier.

"Nah," Delma replied, conspicuously tapping her temple with her forefinger. "Just bad luck, I'm sure. Still, I heard Grave promotes almost exclusively from within, and the starting pay for this position isn't bad. I wanted to see what I'd been missing, sticking with that big multinational for so long."

"Right." Juliet winked. "Makes sense. Well, whaddya say? Shall we head back to the tower? There's no way I'm not getting a good sleep tonight."

"Yeah, I'm beat. Meet you outside? I wanna buy one of those lemon bars we saw . . ."

"Oh! Buy me one too? I'll get you back." Juliet grabbed their empty cups and went to the waste bin while Delma got in line, then she stepped outside. The hum of H-cells was heavy in the air, and the scent of rain was thick in her nose. She leaned against the side of the building and watched people while she waited.

"I'm glad Delma seems to be compatible with your personality, Juliet. For the record, I think you're doing a good job with your teammates, maintaining professional distance while still attempting to be friendly. I also think you've been too hard on yourself. It's true your PT scores were low to start, but Delma wasn't lying about your improvement, and you've done as well or better than your teammates on tactics practicals."

"Thanks," Juliet said, smiling at the sound of Angel's voice in her head. She'd have a much harder time with this assignment if she didn't have the PAI to vent to every night. She flexed her shoulders back, wincing at the soreness in her lats and deltoids. She was sore everywhere, but those groups seemed the hardest hit. "Pull-ups," she grunted softly.

She zoned out for a few minutes, enjoying the fresh air. When the door chimed, she turned to see Delma walking out. She handed Juliet a little paper sack and said, "I got you two."

"Are you trying to sabotage me? Want me to be too fat for a sit-up?" Juliet laughed, taking the sack. "You know I won't be able to leave one uneaten."

"Don't worry; I also got two. We'll be fat together."

Their return to the Grave Tower was uneventful; the coffee shop was only two blocks distant, and the sidewalks were well maintained and policed that close to downtown. It was just getting dark when Juliet said goodbye to Delma and went to the elevator, riding up to her apartment in silent contemplation.

Despite her laughter with Delma and the positive spin from Angel, she was starting to regret taking this job. She was only a week in, and she felt like quitting. She'd cried in the shower at least three times over the last week, and she didn't like seeing herself like that. She didn't like playing the role of a person who cared what an asshole, power-tripping corpo suit thought of her. Juliet had wanted to tell Gordon to get melted and walk out. Many times. "But that's not how Lydia operates," she breathed, walking quietly down the deserted corridor to her apartment.

"Remember to subvocalize when you're speaking out of character," Angel reminded her as she opened her apartment.

"Yeah," Juliet sighed. She was being sloppy, and she was doing it on purpose. Half of her wanted to have her cover blown so she could bail, but the other half was pissed at herself. She'd worked hard, for weeks, to be where she was, and it would be dumb to throw it away so she could vent out loud to herself. She subvocalized, "I'm really dreading my assignment. What if I'm stuck with Gordon for another week? I'm sure I'll have to keep doing PT and training, but I really hate him, Angel! I feel a knot in my stomach whenever I head down to B7."

"You may regret wishing for a different assignment," Angel said unhelpfully. "The devil you know . . ."

"Thanks. I really wanted to start imagining people worse than Gordon." Juliet tossed her paper bag onto the counter and started stripping out of her uniform. They'd issued her three of them, but she carefully washed her clothes and sheets every morning, so she'd mostly been wearing the same two all week, just getting dressed out of the clothes on the washing machine before she started her new load.

After a quick shower, she crawled into bed with her lemon bars and had Angel start playing the videos of her practical assessments. She'd learned to clear buildings with a team, dispense suppressants on various types of fires, and administer first aid, including CPR. On top of all that, earlier that day, she'd been timed and taped, completing the maze for the fourth time—a kind of indoor obstacle course. "I hate watching these," she grumbled.

"It's helpful, though, don't you think?" Angel pressed.

"Yeah. Of course. Look at how I'm climbing that wall! Oh my God, why am I putting my foot up there like that?"

"Juliet! Your watchdog icon!" Angel interrupted, pausing the video. Juliet saw the watchdog was blinking with a little red number one hovering above it. She mentally selected the icon, and a message appeared.

Attention: Lydia Roman.

Congratulations on completing your first full week of employment with Grave Industries, Inc. I've been closely monitoring your progress along with the progress of your teammates and have begun to rank you accordingly. I'll continue my evaluation for the next three weeks before I select leaders among you. I'm impressed with your improvement so far, Lydia. Keep up the hard work!

Tomorrow at 0600, I'd like you to report to level B23. A representative from Zeta Unit Charlie will meet you at the elevators and bring you to your next assignment. You won't be with your entire unit for this next week of training. Be sure to remember what I told you about following the orders of nonprobationary Zeta operatives. I know you're going to do your unit proud! Keep your chin up.

Sincerely,

Commander Cherise Garza

Zeta Protocol Training Coordinator

Grave Industries, Inc.

"Thank you!" Juliet hissed between her teeth as she read the note. Then she subvocalized, "No more Gordon, at least for a week! He's in charge of Alpha."

"Yes. Congratulations, Juliet—it doesn't seem that Mrs. Garza has taken any issue with your progress. Her letter sounds very upbeat. Do you think there is any subtext to her final imperative?"

"Imperative . . ." Juliet looked at the note again and subvocalized, "You mean about keeping my chin up?"

"Yes."

"Maybe. Maybe she's been checking the watchdog. Maybe she's caught me bitching or, worse, crying. Angel, if you see me getting emotional, can you please make sure you're blocking this damn thing?"

"I will, Juliet. I've been a bit lax while you were in the bathroom, but I'll start taking precautions—I'll create some randomized loop footage for your bathroom visits."

"Thanks. Anyway, do you think I'll be the only one from my unit with Charlie?"

"No way to tell; it seems unlikely, considering there are only four existing units and your unit has six members."

"Good point." Juliet sighed, sank back into her pillow, and resumed watching her practical footage. She only made it through her third attempt at the maze when she felt her eyes begin to grow heavy. By the time she'd moved on to the building clearing, she was startled awake several times, realizing she'd missed entire sections of the vid. "Forget it. I'm going to sleep."

Angel didn't argue, but Kent said, "Good night, Ms. Roman." Juliet almost jumped out of her sheets, but she just scowled and rolled to her side while the room AI dimmed the lights.

When Angel woke her at five the next morning, she saw a blinking tab which read, "Updated Data Sheet." She groaned and selected it, humoring her AI friend.

Juliet Corina Bianchi		
Physical, Mental, and Social Status Compilation:		**Comparative Ranking Percentile (Higher Is Better - Previous Value in Parenthesis):**
Net Worth and Assets:	Sol-bits: 106,724	33.45
Neural & Cellular Adaptiveness:	.96342 (Scale of 0 – 1)	99.91
Synaptic Responsiveness:	.19 (Lower Is Better)	79.31
Musculoskeletal Ranking:	–	53.33 (49.71)
Cardiovascular Ranking:	–	68.76 (57.48)
Cybernetic and Bionic Augmentation:	**Model Name and Number:**	**Overall Rating of the Augmentation (Grades Are F, E, D, C, B, A, S, S+):**

PAI	WBD Project Angel, Alpha 3.433	S+
Data Port	Jannik Systems, XR-55	C
Data Jack	Bio Network Solutions, 8840	C
Retinal Cybernetic Implant	Hayashi, Crystal Optics 3.2c - Customized Retinas	C+
Auditory Cybernetic Implant	Cork Systems, Lyric Model 4	C
Reflex and Strength Enhancement - Right Arm	Wilcox Industrial - 19.12P	B
Programmable Synthetic Fingerprints	Ross Inc., Biomesh 9	C
DNA Spoofing Package	Various - Custom	B
No Other Augmentation Detected.	–	–

"Really, Angel?" she subvocalized. "Do you have to show me this entire sheet to tell me I'm a little stronger and healthier than before?"

"Would you like me to break down your musculoskeletal ranking into individual muscle groups? I'm currently compiling an average, but you have stronger groups than others—it may help you to focus your exercise—"

"No!" Juliet groaned aloud, sitting up on the side of the bed. Angel was silent, and Juliet began to feel guilty, so she silently added, "Maybe someday. Right now, I'm just doing what I can, okay?"

"Understood."

Juliet put her cup under the dispenser, punched the coffee and cream buttons, and then took a shower. When she'd dried off, she dressed in a clean uniform and threw the previous day's clothes, towel, and sheets into the washer. Juliet sat at the kitchen's little counter, drank her coffee, and ate a protein square, all the while wishing she'd saved one of her lemon bars for breakfast.

After she'd done her hair and brushed her teeth, it was 0540, and Juliet started toward the elevators. She'd just punched the down button when her watchdog icon lit up, and her vision became obscured by a vid call. A bald, middle-aged man with pale skin and razor-burned cheeks appeared in her AUI, and he said, or more precisely, barked, "Roman?"

Juliet knew better than to assume this man wasn't her superior—the average corpo drone wouldn't be calling her through the watchdog. "Yes, sir?"

"Welcome to Zeta Unit Charlie—temporarily. Report to the roof. We caught a bug hunt. It's your lucky day, rookie." With that, the call cut out, and Juliet stood, open-mouthed, before the elevator as it dinged and opened.

"Bug hunt?" she asked the empty room, then stepped over to the call button and pushed the up arrow.

"From my initial research, it's a term used to refer to hunting xenomorphs, infected civilians or test subjects, or misbehaving synthetics. It can also be used in reference to the investigation of myriad mysterious circumstances, or more mundanely, solving software glitches."

"Uh," Juliet said, then subvocalized, "Thanks, Angel, but I kinda wish you hadn't said that." The bell rang again, another elevator opened, and Juliet stepped into it. Before she navigated the menu to select the roof, she asked, "Am I supposed to bring anything? Shouldn't I get my gun?"

"No, Ms. Roman," Kent's voice answered from the elevator speaker. "Your unit's sergeant will equip you for today's activities. Good luck on your second week of training."

18

CHARLIE UNIT

When Juliet climbed the short flight of stairs from the top floor of the Grave Tower to the roof, she was met with swirling, hot wind and the sound of a large fluttercraft not twenty meters in front of her. The machine, shaped almost like a wasp and painted to accentuate that perception, had high-tensile polycarbonate membranes between the vibrating spines of its dozen or so wings, which hummed in the air, invisible due to their rapid movement.

She figured most of the members of Charlie Unit were inside the craft, but a couple stood outside. One of them saw Juliet, waving her over urgently. As she jogged across the yellow-striped concrete to the black airship, her eyes were drawn to the silver-and-red stylized *G* on the tail section, and Juliet became aware of just how large it was; it was more the size of a bus than a van. The operative waving her on was standing near an open bay door near the bird's middle, and as Juliet drew near, she hollered over the noise of the buzzing wings, "Hurry up, probe!"

"Right," Juliet said, scrambling up the little set of folding metallic steps to the interior. Jump seats lined the front section of the craft, while an open doorway led away toward the rear. She stood there, hesitating, but one of the operatives sitting nearby pointed to an empty seat to her left.

"Don't stand in the doorway."

Juliet hurried over to the seat and saw that most of the others were strapped in, so she followed suit. As she clicked the three-point harness clasps, she looked more closely at the four members of Charlie Unit sitting nearby, and suddenly began to feel very underdressed. They all wore ballistic vests and helmets, and most were equipped with visors. She saw rifles and pistols and grenades hanging off their harnesses and began to wonder if Kent had given her bad information.

"Angel," she subvocalized. "Why'd that woman outside call me a probe?"

"My research indicates it's a term used to refer to probationary employees."

"Right," Juliet breathed. Just then, the man nearest the open bay door stood up and helped the two outside hoist a heavy-looking metal box into the fluttercraft and proceeded to strap it to the floor. The two outside operatives hopped aboard, then the lady who'd hollered at Juliet touched a button, and the bay doors slid closed, blocking out the noise of the craft's wings and engines and suddenly submerging the interior in surprising silence.

Everyone sat and strapped in except the woman, who seemed to be in charge. She reached up to hold on to a cord hanging from the ceiling, her chromed-up arm flexing with an audible clicking whir. Suddenly, the craft lurched and then exploded into the air, shooting forward and up at an alarming rate, causing Juliet's stomach to flip and twist. Her eyes bulged out at the sudden explosive movement. Juliet liked fast cars and motorcycles, but this was something different—this was what she'd imagined a rocket launch would feel like, though she knew, rationally, that the fluttercraft was nowhere near fast enough to break into orbit.

"Here we go, boys and girls," the standing woman said, and Juliet suddenly had a deep respect for her balance and strength; how had she not been thrown to the floor with that launch? "Rookie, tell us your name—I'm not reading my briefing again, and I forgot it."

"Lydia Roman, ma'am." Juliet licked her lips, very happy that she hadn't lost her breakfast all over the floor of the craft.

"Watch your AUI; watchdog'll set up our team comms. Come back here so I can get you some gear." With that, the woman turned and walked through the doorway. Juliet fumbled with her harness clasps, her hands a little shaky from the brief adrenaline dump she'd experienced as the craft took off.

"First time on a fluttercraft?" a big, visored man sitting across from her asked. He had thick, dark stubble on his square jaw, and held his arms—red-and-black plasteel wire-jobs—crossed over his chest.

"Uh, yeah," Juliet replied, finally shrugging out of the harness and standing, knees bent, hands out, as though she expected the floor to move beneath her.

"Don't worry. The synth driving this bird will keep it steady until we make our approach; he's paranoid about takeoffs and landings—combat protocol every time, even if we're not under fire."

"Thanks," Juliet said, nervously glancing at the other members of Charlie Unit, most of whom were actively ignoring her. She walked to the open doorway and into the rear of the fluttercraft, where the woman with the chrome arm was busily unlocking storage compartments that lined the sides of the vessel.

"Size?"

"Medium," Juliet answered automatically. She caught the ballistics vest the woman threw her way and started shrugging into it.

"What about your head? These helmets are unisex, so you probably want a small or extra small. Try this." The sergeant—Juliet had finally spotted the sergeant's insignia on her shoulder—tossed a helmet her way, and she squeezed it onto her head. It fit all right, but it was uncomfortable with her bun.

"It fits, Sergeant, but I need to change my hair."

"Yeah, make two braids. You can do it after you sit back down. Okay, what about close quarters? Blade or baton?"

"Blade," Juliet answered without thinking—she'd used a knife before and had never messed around with a baton, so the answer had been automatic.

"Catch." The sergeant tossed her a sheathed knife, easily twice the size of her own vibroblade. "That's a vibroblade. Don't cut your leg off."

"Yes, ma'am," Juliet replied, unbuckling her belt and sliding the sheath onto it. She'd just started to refasten the buckle when the sergeant said, "We'll probably put you on door duty, so I'm going to issue you a shotgun for now. You ever used a rail-tech weapon? You know, an electro-shotgun?"

"Yes, ma'am." Juliet smiled, holding out her augmented hand for the bulky gun. While it was heavy, the shotgun was a lot sleeker than Vikker's had been; the electro-rails were capped with high-grade plastic, the barrel was slightly narrower, and the canister of shot pellets was molded to fit along the underside of the barrel as part of the foregrip. Still, it was heavy and solid and felt good in her hand.

"Good. What about your optics? You need goggles, or can you see enhanced spectrums?"

"I'm good, Sarge."

The woman gave her a look, or Juliet thought she did—she couldn't see her eyes through the dark lens of her visor, then said, "Sending you the equipment sign-out; be sure to acknowledge it in your watchdog app. Get back to your seat; flight time's only twenty minutes, and I'm about to start the briefing."

"Yes, ma'am." Juliet wanted to ask her name but knew it would be on her AUI after her watchdog set up the unit comms. She had a feeling it was already set up; the icon was blinking frantically, trying to get her to acknowledge something.

She worked her way back to her seat, sat down, buckled in, then took off her helmet to fix her hair. Meanwhile, the sergeant had come through behind her and stood near the front of the hold, near a closed security door presumably leading to the cockpit, and cleared her throat. "Listen up, Charlie."

"What's the story, Sarge?" a man seated across from Juliet asked.

"Quiet, Houston." The sergeant paused to look up and down the rows of jump seats, eyes lingering on Juliet for a moment, watching her braid her hair behind each ear, then settling on the man across from her. "Rodriguez? Where's your minigun?"

"Getting serviced, Sarge; two barrels melted on our last deployment, and the armory was out of spares."

"You're goddamn shitting me." From the sergeant's tone, the words were not a question. "Load up one of the heavy machine guns, then." The man—Rodriguez, apparently—started to unbuckle, but Sarge continued, "When I'm done."

"Roger."

"Okay, we're heading to a level four research facility, folks. Intel says we're negative on airborne infection hazards, so no bug suits for us, thank God."

"Level four? Jesus H—"

"Put a goddamn lid on it, Houston!" When Houston, an average-size man with tan skin and dozens of tattoos on his arms and hands, stopped speaking, the sergeant continued, "As I said, level four, but nothing airborne being studied there, so count your blessings. The facility has missed its last two check-ins, and comms have gone dark; the suits upstairs think a competitor likely breached and scrubbed the site, but there's the chance that something they were working on went sideways. We need to be prepared for anything."

Juliet saw Houston raise a hand, leaning forward and slightly waving it to be noticed, and the Sarge finally acknowledged him, "Houston?"

"What kinda fucked-up shit are they working on, Sarge?" Juliet braced herself for the sergeant's explosion, figuring she wouldn't tolerate his tone, but some of the others grunted in approval—they wanted more information about what to expect.

"Nothing good, Houston." Sarge looked left and right, her black, impenetrable visor settling on each member of Charlie Unit, daring them to do anything other than give her their undivided attention. Finally, she spoke, her flinty voice devoid of amusement, "Project specifics are need-to-know, and you all do not need to know. Just be ready for anything. We're boots on the ground in nine minutes. Get yourselves ready. Roman, why haven't you checked in on the watchdog?"

Juliet nearly jumped out of her seat, and she hastily activated the watchdog icon, saying, "On it, Sarge." A window appeared on her AUI, and it populated with the names of Charlie Unit members. Next to each name was a summary of their vital statistics—heart rates, blood pressure, blood-oxygen levels, and an icon allowing Juliet to open a window to toggle each member's POV.

She silently mouthed each person's name as she read through them, "Polk - Sergeant II, White - Sergeant I, Houston, Rodriguez, Yang, Vandemere, Roman." Angel helpfully put name tags above the unit members' heads on her AUI.

Juliet saw the watchdog icon was still blinking, so she activated it again, and a new window appeared with the equipment requisition and acknowledgment of receipt. She accepted it, and it faded away. The watchdog stopped blinking, and Juliet sighed, finishing her hair and slipping her new helmet on, much happier with its feel.

She'd just started to get used to the hum of the fluttercraft's flight when Sergeant Polk spoke up in the team channel, "Our synthetic friend up front just let me know we'll be coming in hot in less than a minute. Grab onto something."

Juliet glanced toward the front of the hold to see the sergeant was still standing, holding on to a grab strap with her metallic arm, her footing wide and her knees slightly bent. Most of the others reached up to grab the straps of their harnesses, and Juliet did the same, following her neighbor's example of tucking her heavy gun tight in the crook of her augmented arm.

When the pilot took the craft in for their landing, Juliet felt her stomach surge up to her throat, felt the blood rush to her head, and actually saw her vision begin to dim for a split second before Angel adjusted the pressure in her synthetic eyeballs.

She was glad she'd pulled the straps of her harness tight because she was sure she'd have been ejected if there'd been any wriggle room. This unpleasant force pulling her upward lasted for about thirty seconds, then it rapidly reversed, and she felt herself being jammed down into her seat as the craft came to a sudden, shuddering stop.

"Let's go, let's go!" Polk hollered, and the guy to her right, Rodriguez, stood up and slapped the button to open the bay doors. Cool air rushed into the hold, and it oddly smelled like pine—how far had they come? "Out, out, out! Move it, move it!" Polk's voice echoed in the comms, and Juliet snapped her buckle loose and stood up, still woozy from the violent, sudden landing.

She saw Rodriguez jump out the door, then Houston, then White, Yang, and Vandemere, and then it was her turn. She stood at the open bay door and realized the fluttercraft hadn't landed; it was hovering about six feet off the ground, and there were trees out there—trees and grass and cool air.

"Let's move, Roman! Get your ass out that door!" Polk's voice oddly echoed as she yelled, the comms carrying it along with her physical shout. The words cut through Juliet's stupefaction like a knife through cheese, and she leaped, aiming for a patch of soft-looking grass.

She landed heavily and off-balance, but she just tucked into a forward roll and came up on her feet, the electro-shotgun tucked into the shoulder, barrel down, as she slowly turned, taking in the scene. Angel had populated her AUI with the shotgun's ammo counter, its battery status, and a crosshair. Juliet held it ready as she watched the rest of Charlie Unit moving toward a low concrete building that seemed to be built into the side of a wooded hillside.

"Secure that door. Everyone, get locked and loaded! Don't make your-selves a target," White said through the comms, and Juliet hustled to catch up to the others, moving to the right side of the single orange metal door in the side of the gray concrete. She saw White crouching behind a tree stump, a massive, long-barreled gun resting on a built-in tripod, training it on the door as if waiting for something to come bursting out.

Houston and Rodriguez had their backs to the concrete structure, their automatic rifles trained on the woods further down the hill. Polk came run-ning up, shoving Juliet toward Rodriguez. "Move to the building, give the door clearance in case we have to blow it." Juliet hustled in the direction she'd been shoved, coming to rest near Rodriguez, resting her back against the concrete.

She watched as the fluttercraft surged upward, its wings vibrating the air so violently that trees fifty meters out swayed and jumped with the currents.

"Where's it going?" she asked Rodriguez, trusting Angel to keep it out of the unit comms.

"Watching from a safe location. We fuck up too badly, it'll nuke the site." His voice was deadpan, and Juliet couldn't tell if he was joking. She hoped he was.

"Still no comms, Sarge," Yang said, her voice clipped and professional, and Juliet remembered some of the training she'd gotten in the previous week about keeping comms clear as much as possible.

"What's the story with the door, Houston?" Sarge asked, and Juliet glanced to her right and saw Houston kneeling by a security panel in the concrete.

"Locked . . . dead. There's no power. I'm jacking in a batt."

"How's there no power?" White asked. Juliet glanced toward his position and saw his four-foot rifle barrel, decked with circular electromagnets, pointing toward the door. "Don't these facilities all have mini reactors?"

"It has to be intentional," Houston grunted. "Someone turned it off 'cause if it'd failed, we'd know it."

"Enough chatter. Eyes on a swivel, and shut the fuck up," Polk grunted, but she didn't seem angry. "White? Anything on optics? Any movement?"

"Can't see squat through that door—place is shielded as shit."

"Bypassing the power grid," Houston said, then a few seconds later, "Inputting the overrides." Moments later, Juliet's auditory implants picked up the click and hiss of the door opening, and then Houston screamed, rolling back into the grass.

"Jesus!" was all he had time to say before a person, hissing and snarling, leaped out of the doorway toward him. The man—Juliet could see it was a man, naked as the day he was born—flew toward Houston, and then White's Gauss rifle *zwapped*, and a hole the size of a basketball appeared in the naked man's chest, a long red smear painting the gray concrete of the building. The man, his inertia suddenly altered, tumbled and flopped through the grass to land next to where Houston was scrambling to get to his feet.

"What the *fuck*? Look at this asshole's face! What the fuck are they doing here, Sarge?"

"Can it, Houston! Cover the door with Rodriguez and Roman. Yang, evaluate this guy. White, any movement?"

"Negative. Nothing incoming. Roman, keep clear of the doorway, stand to the side, and be ready. I've got the first shot." Juliet appreciated the direction—this was a situation that hadn't come up in practicals. She hurried to the side of the doorway, avoiding the spray of blood that had painted the grass on its way to splash against the building, and stood to Rodriguez's left, her shotgun held ready, sights down but toward the open door.

"Sarge, I don't know about this. You sure you can't tell us what they were doing here?" Yang asked, her voice unsteady as she injected a probe into the downed man's neck.

"You sure we should've waxed him? He's naked, Sarge. Shouldn't we have tried to subdue?" Vandemere asked at the same time.

"Shut the fuck up, V. My optics picked that guy up at twenty meters running down the hallway. He covered that distance in two-point-two seconds, and his body temp was eighty-two degrees. I made the call. I took the shot." White's voice was a snarl, and Juliet knew he was pissed.

"Can it," Polk said. "Let me know when you get your stripes, V. In the meantime, you worry about your trigger, not your teammates'." Polk grunted as she knelt next to Yang, and Juliet heard her speak softly, "What's the story, Yang?"

"Heavily modded DNA. About a hundred different chemical signatures in his blood. He's only loosely human by this point."

"Jesus doing jumping jacks!" Houston cried from the other side of the doorway, and Juliet almost laughed at the desperation in his voice.

"I'm writing you up when we get back, Houston," Polk said, straightening up. "You all heard Yang? This thing's not human, and his claws and teeth are perfectly capable of killing. If there are more like this, do not take any chances trying to play Mother Theresa. Am I clear, V?"

"Roger," Vandemere replied. Juliet could hear Houston grumbling, but he didn't respond.

"What's the move, Sarge? Backup?" Rodriguez asked.

"We are the backup. We're Zeta Protocol! Tighten your shit up, people! Roman? You've got door duty. Houston, you're with her. Do not let anything or anyone in or out without clearing it with me. White, you've got point. Let's go, people! You know the drill! Corporate wants this site cleared and made safe, and we're burning daylight!"

Juliet moved into Rodriguez's spot when he followed White into the entry corridor, and as the others filed past her, Sergeant Polk paused to speak to her, voice pitched low and not carrying through the group comms.

"Roman, we didn't expect anything quite this gnarly for your first ride-along. Do what Houston says—he's a whiny bastard, but he's good at what he does. If we call for him to come forward, stick with him; I don't want you on your own at any point. Ever. Clear?"

"Yes, Sarge." At Juliet's words, Polk nodded and started forward, ducking through the metallic doorway and dragging her chromed fingertips along the lintel as though measuring its sturdiness.

"I heard that, Sarge," Houston called after her, but the tall, intense woman ignored him. After a few seconds, once everyone else had gone inside, she was left standing alone with Houston in the cool air, a naked, ruined human not ten feet away from her. She wrinkled her nose, glad she was upwind from the body and wondering if she'd get in trouble for dragging it a bit farther away.

As though he'd been reading her mind, Houston said, "Keep an eye out while I drag this poor bastard a ways off—he stinks like hell." He didn't wait for a reply, moving away from the door to gingerly grasp the dead man's ankle, dragging his corpse through the grass. Juliet had a hard time pulling her eyes away from the long red smear left in the wake of Houston's progress, but she did, following his command to keep alert.

She shifted to the other side of the door and alternated panning her vision over the tree line and then back, peering into the dark shadowy interior of the research facility, her enhanced optics showing her other blood smears on the white walls and pale industrial tile. Whatever went down in that place, it wasn't good. She hoped the staff members were all right, holed up in a secure location, but she worried; all that blood had to have come from somewhere.

WHAT SQUINTS GET UP TO

This is bullshit," Houston said after a while, spitting a string of brown-tinted saliva onto the concrete pad just outside the facility's door.

"What?" Juliet asked, leaning against the wall on the other side. She wondered if he was chewing tobacco, and if so, why. Smoking real cigarettes seemed strange enough to her; she couldn't imagine stuffing leaves of the stuff into her cheek.

"Being on babysitting detail . . . no offense." He frowned and sniffed loudly, and Juliet wondered what he looked like under that darkly tinted visor. She thought about that, about whether she should get a visor for her helmet. It seemed most of the team had them, but they were all a little different—custom pieces, she figured. That thought brought another question to mind: was this gear permanently assigned to her, or was it just for the day's mission?

"None taken. You didn't seem too excited to go in there, though . . ."

"Put a lid on that, rookie!" Houston said, some gravity and bass suddenly entering his voice. "You don't know me well enough to bust my balls."

"Yes, sir." Juliet didn't let her irritation show, keeping her face neutral as she performed another scan of the tree line. Her eyes drifted over the body of the . . . she didn't know what to call it. Still, the man, creature, or whatever was definitely alarming in its appearance—hairless, wide, too-round eyes, too many canines which didn't fit in its mouth, and a nose and ears that were a size too long for its skull. She shivered, looked away, and asked, "Where are we?"

"Up north—near Flagstaff, I think. Your PAI should be able to get a ping from the sat-net." He stared into the dark hallway for a minute. "Bet you didn't think you'd see this kind of action today, huh?"

"No, I really didn't. Is this sort of thing common?"

"Nah, not really. If we have combat, it's usually against active aggressors—terrorists or corpo sabotage."

Before Juliet could follow up with another question, Polk's voice came through comms, "Houston, status?"

"Quiet as a picnic in a meadow full of daisies, Sarge."

"Like you'd know," White's icon lit up as he spoke into the comms.

"Goddammit! Can this shit! Houston, secure that door, lock it tight, then bring your partner and come to our position. Facility map incoming."

"Clarifying—you want me to lock us inside, Sarge?"

"Correct."

Juliet saw a new tab appear on her AUI, and when she activated it, a top-down map of the hallways and rooms of the facility appeared, two blinking dots near the southern extremity and five others further in, near a wide T junction.

She stepped through the doorway, training her shotgun's muzzle toward the darkness. Houston followed her in, then turned to start fiddling with the door panel. "Not a good sign that Sarge wants me to lock us in," he muttered. Juliet wondered if she should reply—they weren't speaking in the group comms, but the watchdog kept track of everything they saw or heard . . . or said.

"Why?" she asked, feeling she couldn't get in trouble for trying to learn.

"Means she thinks there's something going on in here we don't want to let out." As he finished speaking, the door hissed and slid shut, then he unplugged his portable battery and hooked it to his gear-bedecked belt. "You take point with that shotgun, but if I say to get down or get back, move like you mean it."

"Roger." Juliet crouch walked into the darkness, though in her enhanced vision, she could see her environment plain as day. She sidestepped to avoid a big blood stain, not sure if Grave considered this a crime scene.

"Keep a steady heading, rook—I don't want to guess where you're going to be when I'm aiming my gun."

"Right," Juliet said, angry at herself for overthinking things. She glanced at her map and saw the rest of the unit was still spread out around the T junction, only a few dozen meters further in. She angled her gun's barrel toward the ground, not wanting to paint her upcoming teammates with her crosshairs. She and Houston were nearly up to a pair of doors that opened to the left and right, and she asked into comms, "Sarge, are the rooms we're about to pass clear?"

"Yes. You two are clear all the way to us; put a hustle on it, Houston."

"Aye, Sarge," Houston replied, lowering his SMG and letting it hang by his side as he hurried past Juliet. She sighed, lowering her barrel further and jogging in his wake. When they approached the T junction, Juliet saw the rest of the team had been stymied by more locked doors. The one on the right looked like it had been welded shut.

"Get these doors open, Houston. Start with the unwelded one."

"If you have a torch, I can get the other one, Sarge," Juliet said.

"You trained on an oxytorch?" Houston asked, shrugging out of his backpack and rifling through it.

"Yeah, I know what to do with it." Juliet almost mentioned the scrapyard but then remembered she was Lydia Roman. "Had a neighbor who did weird metal art."

"Here." He handed her a compact unit with two slim, highly pressurized plasteel canisters. She'd worked with similar—and much larger—equipment.

"Angel, can my implants filter well enough for me to cut metal without damaging them?" While she spoke, Juliet examined the tip of the cutting torch, saw it was well-maintained and clean, and moved over to the door.

"Yes. I can narrow your ocular input down to less than a single percent of radiated light."

"Rodriguez, you've got Roman's back—be ready; we don't know why they welded that door shut. White? You locked and loaded?"

"Aye, Sarge. Houston, keep to the right of your door, and Roman, cut top to bottom. Stay low when you finish."

"Roger," Juliet said, pushing the ignition on her torch and focusing the flame before getting started. As she touched the cutting torch to the metal, cranking up the output, she was pleased to see that Angel automatically dimmed her vision, doing a job nearly as good as the goggles built into her old welding rig. She ripped through the welded seam at the middle of the sliding doors in record time, and as she clicked the torch off, she crouch walked to the side, making sure she didn't stand up into anyone's crosshairs.

"That was fast, Roman." Polk clapped her on the shoulder. "Move to the back; I'm not seeing any heat signatures or movement on the other side of the doors, so we'll wait for Houston to finish up."

"Almost there, Sarge. Roman, you better not have slagged my cutting tip."

"It's fine," she replied, stuffing the portable unit into Houston's pack. She moved back to the long corridor leading toward the entrance and waited as he finished working on the second door. It was only a few seconds later that she heard it click and hiss open.

"Good!" Polk said. "Houston, get the other door powered up and open. Vandemere, you're with Yang and me. We'll head toward the living quarters. White, you take the others toward engineering after that door's opened; get Houston to bring the reactor back online."

"Sarge, I'm not exactly a reactor expert," Houston groused, crouching next to the other door's security panel.

"You'll manage," Polk replied as she, Yang, and Vandemere started down the now-open corridor to Juliet's left.

Houston waited a few seconds for Polk and the others to move off, then he quietly mimicked her, "You'll manage." He glanced at the still-ticking cut Juliet had made in the metal, and he gave her a look, letting his visor linger on her for a minute before turning back to the panel. "Pretty nice line. Looks like you cut a lot of metal for the neighbor."

"How long?" White asked, moving forward so the long, heavy barrel of his Gauss rifle was trained at the tiny gap between the two sliding doors.

"Couple of minutes . . ."

Juliet watched White and Rodriguez, noticing how the other man had his machine gun shouldered and kept to the right side, ensuring he had a clear shot when the doors opened. Juliet moved to stand behind him, her shotgun aimed down and to his left. She realized she was holding her breath and forced herself to inhale a couple of times, deep into her belly, as she waited for Houston to rewire the door.

Juliet wondered why she didn't hear Polk and the others speaking as they cleared their way deeper into the complex, and then she realized the watchdog app had automatically split their team comms. She remembered going over that in her training the previous week, though it had only been about a forty-five-minute primer on how to use the watchdog comms.

Juliet felt like she'd already forgotten a lot of the stuff they'd watched on those training vids, even though there had been quizzes afterward. She was trying to remember how to select the entire team channel when the door clicked and hissed open, and Houston straightened up.

"Voila!" he said, but White ignored him, carefully moving forward, training his powerful gun down the long hallway.

"No movement," he spoke into their subunit's comms. "Let's go. Lydia, you've got the rear position. Be ready to help clear."

The team continued into the corridor, battery-powered, orange-tinged emergency lights providing enough light for their optics to enhance their vision. Juliet could only imagine how freaky it would be to walk into a place like this if she didn't have capable optics. The smell was bad enough—stale air with a hint of decay and copper. The silence was also unnerving; all her life, Juliet had grown used to the ever-present hum of machinery inside buildings—refrigeration units, cooling fans, the buzz of electrical appliances. None of those were present in this place.

"Something ahead," White warned. Juliet looked past his shoulder, trying to see what he saw, and Angel increased the magnification on her optics and the gain on her audio implants. A junction came into focus, and she saw bodies slumped in awkward positions, copious amounts of blood smeared around the place.

Short, rapid breaths seemed to echo into the air from several different sources as her hearing gain ramped up, and she subvocalized into her team comms, "Breathing. Lots of it. Do you guys have audio?"

"I don't—" Houston started to say, but then Rodriguez interrupted.

"She's right! Five . . . six . . . seven sources."

"Hold," White ordered, dropping to the floor and flipping out the tripod at the front of his rifle. Rodriguez and Houston took up positions beside him, and he said, "Roman, you've got the center. Do not blow my head off, rookie. Keep that barrel well above me."

"Roger," Juliet replied, her chest tightening as her breaths came short and quick, a microburst of adrenaline making her hands shaky. A stray thought invaded her mind—should she talk to Angel about managing her adrenaline in situations like this? Did she want Angel to do something like that to her? She pulled the shotgun's stock in tight and stood over White, aiming down the corridor to the bloody junction.

"Are . . ." Houston started, then he said, "What the *fuck*? I don't think those bodies are bodies! They're breathing!"

"Attention!" White yelled, his voice augmented by speakers in his helmet. "Grave corpo-sec on the premises! If you are not hostile actors, you have five seconds to declare yourselves!"

"Weird," Rodriguez muttered. "I can hear them, but there's no heat sig, and I'm not picking up any . . . Oh, *mierda*! Here they come!"

Juliet couldn't see movement downrange, but she glanced at her minimap and saw that the watchdog program had used Rodriguez's sensory inputs to populate the map with a cluster of blinking red dots surging toward the corridor junction, moving at more than five meters per second. She trained her sights on the right side, where the dots were just now coming to the corner, but then she saw that Houston had been right; the bodies lying around the intersection began to leap to their feet.

As the four or five figures charged forward, they were joined by the ones racing up the side passages, and suddenly, a horde of hissing, jerking figures were streaming toward them. They were similar to the naked man who had attacked them outside the facility—pale, unclothed, and moving far too fast with a strange gait which involved all four of their limbs. Juliet caught glimpses of gaping mouths, sharp teeth, and waxen, flaccid genitals. Over it all, she heard a hissing, sibilant language that held no meaning to her.

"Hostiles confirmed," White said as his Gauss rifle *zwapped*, and two of the people—creatures—stumbled back, shredded by the super-high-velocity spray of needles. Houston and Rodriguez started to unload, their cartridge-based weapons exploding with fire and noise, and Juliet was glad for her much-improved audio implants; they suppressed the noise nicely.

Juliet pointed her shotgun at the leading edge of the surging hostiles, and when the green ready-light flashed, she squeezed, surprised that the weapon's discharge was a lot less violent than that of the shotgun she'd used in Vikker's garage. Still, it buzzed and crackled satisfyingly as the payload of shot pellets whirred down the tube of the barrel. Her vision was starting to fill with steam and smoke from all the rounds being fired, and Angel adjusted for her, switching to the same monochrome, gray spectrum she'd used in the garage fight, back at Doc Murphy's.

The attackers were green in her vision, with occasional spots of reddish orange, while her teammates were bright yellow and orange, highlighted with their names above their heads—Angel was making sure she could easily avoid firing on a friendly target. The shotgun's green light was ready almost immediately, and Juliet fired again, watching as the bright-yellow spray of heat from the gun's barrel streaked through the gray expanse to splash against the chest of a charging enemy.

Orange-red streaks of light sprayed out of its back as her shot broke its charge, and it slid along the gray-lit floor to land in front of White. Juliet scanned downfield for more targets, but none of the mutated men and women, as Juliet was coming to think of them, were moving.

"Lock it up," White ordered, but everyone had already stopped shooting. Charlie Unit seemed to have good trigger discipline. Juliet backed up a pace and pointed her shotgun down and to the side, noting the pellet counter was at 220/250.

"It only discharges fifteen per shot?" she said aloud, surprised. If she remembered right, Vikker's gun had unloaded something more like fifty per trigger pull.

"It has higher settings, but they're locked. I could bypass the regulator, but you might get in trouble with your sergeant," Angel replied.

"Hold off on that, for now," Juliet subvocalized.

"Team two, did you make contact?" Polk's voice came through the comms.

"Yeah, Sarge," White grunted as he scooted up to his knees and folded the tripod under his big gun. "A group of seven. Same as the guy outside. All hostiles down, no casualties here."

"Keep me posted. We've cleared the living section; moving to the clinic."

"Roger."

"The fuck are these things, Sarge?" Houston asked, stepping forward with his gun trained on the nearest corpse. A light mounted under the forestock of his gun illuminated the mutant's face, and Juliet shuddered—the man's jaw was distended and too broad. His regular, human teeth were still there, but a second row of long, sharp fangs had grown out of his massively swollen gums; she didn't think there'd be any way for the creature to close its mouth.

"Look at its fucking eyes," Houston said, and Juliet had to agree with his sentiment. They were freaky—big, bulging, and black, with no whites. "Are they some kinda messed-up mods, or did they change from whatever the squints in this place did to 'em?"

"No idea. They look the same as the jumper outside," White replied, shrugging. "As you said, looks like the squints in this place were up to some freaky shit and forgot to lock a door or something. You heard the sarge; let's keep moving."

"Squints?" Juliet asked, too freaked out to be embarrassed.

"Scientists. You know, 'cause they're always squinting through one kind of lens or another. I mean, I think that's where the word comes from." Houston shrugged.

"Lord knows what they were up to in this place. . ." White said, marching ahead, clearly trying to get the team back on task.

"You think these things are like this on purpose?" Rodriguez asked.

"I dunno. Do I look like I have much of an education?" White asked. "I barely got through fifth grade before the corpos snatched me up on the mil-sec track." He turned to look at Juliet. "Good work, Roman. Come on, people. Let's check out the junction up there."

"Thanks, Sarge," Juliet said, wondering if anyone ever called White "Sarge" when Polk was around. She followed the trio of men toward the intersection, trying not to look at the shredded, naked bodies of the people who'd raced toward them. Averting her eyes didn't help the smell, though, and she had to take shallow breaths through her mouth, tucking it against the high collar of her vest as a filter to avoid gagging.

More than the scent of blood and the pungent odor of the nitroglycerine in the gunpowder, Juliet could smell a heavy, underlying reek of perforated bowels. White's Gauss rifle and her own electro-shotgun hadn't gone easy on the naked people, removing limbs and shredding torsos with their direct hits. When they'd passed the last of the bodies and stood in the intersection, she carefully tested the air and took a thankful, deep breath of the—only mildly disgusting—stale, waste-tinged air.

"I shoulda worn a breather, Sarge," Houston said, wrapping a bandanna around his mouth and nose, further obscuring his visored face.

"Yeah, no shit," White agreed. "Which way's the reactor?"

"South." Rodriguez replied. "Right." He gestured in the correct direction—another long, seemingly empty corridor.

"What's that flickering? Is one of the emergency lights down there on the fritz?" Houston asked, and Juliet saw what he was talking about—around thirty meters ahead, where a junction led off to the left, a rapid series of bright, yellow flashes kept repeating. To her, it looked like an electrical short circuit sparking against something.

"Loose wires?" she guessed. "I don't know what from, though; the conduits in this place are all well shielded under the floor panels."

"That's right," Houston said. "Shit . . . is it moving?"

"Get set!" White hollered, lifting his massive gun to his shoulder.

Juliet raised her shotgun, aiming toward the corridor junction and the weird, flickering sparking lights, then a humanoid figure came into view, and she had to do a double take. He was limned with crackling electricity, his flesh looked blackened—cooked—and, as White's gun discharged, the figure seemed to flicker and jump a dozen feet toward them and to the left.

"What the *fuck*, Sarge?" Houston screamed, pulling on the trigger of his gun, his voice wailing out the question over the staccato explosions. Juliet lined up her sights on the weird, sparking, oddly shifting charred man, but as she squeezed her trigger, his electrical aura seemed to surge and expand, and then everything was dark and quiet; her AUI was gone, and the silence was deafening.

20

\\\\\\\\\\\\\\\\\\\

LESSONS LEARNED

In the shock of utter silence and total darkness, Juliet stumbled and crashed into the plasteel paneling of the corridor. She felt completely disoriented, and her balance was entirely out of whack. A wave of vertigo hit her as she tried to steady herself, and she tumbled to the ground. She fell flat on her back, and her helmet smacked into the hard floor; she felt like she was spinning in a circle, being sucked toward the center of a dark, soundless void.

Underneath her physical discomfort, pain, and lack of sensory input, Juliet didn't lose sight of the fact that a violent, mutated human—perhaps more than one—was coming toward her and the others. She had to do something, but she felt utterly helpless. What had happened to her implants? To Angel? Had that flash of electricity been some sort of electromagnetic pulse? Was she really so vulnerable?

As she lay there, feeling sick, dizzy, and altogether lost, she knew there was no way she could safely discharge her shotgun, assuming it would even work. Juliet released it and fumbled at her belt, feeling for the hilt of her vibroblade. She'd just closed her hand around it when a spray of hot liquid hit her face and her right arm. Juliet flinched back, breaths short and quick, nearly panting in panic as the tang of copper touched her tongue.

Juliet spat and writhed, not sure if she was moving toward or away from danger, as she jerked her knife free of its metallic sheath. Relief washed over her as she felt the humming buzz in the hilt that told her it was still working—whatever had disabled her implants hadn't fried the vibroblade. She continued to push back with her feet, still dizzy, still unsure what was up and what was down, but convinced she had to keep moving.

"*Juliet* . . ." Angel's voice came to her out of the blackness, but it wasn't through her auditory implants as usual; it seemed to be echoing strangely from all around her.

"Angel," she gasped, or thought she did—she couldn't hear herself.

"*Juliet, your implants are offline* . . ."

"I know!" she huffed, and then something heavy and fearsomely strong crashed on top of her, gripping her shoulders painfully and nuzzling against her chin, digging for her throat. Hard teeth scraped her jaw and collarbone as she tucked her chin down, trying to protect the soft flesh of her neck, before turning sideways and jerking her head so her helmet smashed toward the assailant. Meanwhile, she stabbed and hacked with her vibroblade, sure she was hitting something as more hot liquid sprayed over her fist and arm and gushed down over her chest and neck.

Her assailant stopped trying to bite her, then stopped moving entirely, becoming a hot, heavy, wet blanket that pinned her in place, oddly giving her some comfort in her senseless abyss. She lay there, panting, wishing she could at least hear herself breathe, and then, as if in answer to her wish, a high-pitched whine bloomed into being, and she started to hear muffled, distant static. Moments later, the cluster of noises resolved into individual sounds, and she listened to the staccato of gunfire, shouts, screams, and the sound of her own ragged breathing.

"Angel!" she gasped.

"Juliet, your ocular implants are suffering from a firmware error; I'm having trouble bringing them online. Give me a minute."

"White!" Juliet screamed, still pinned to the floor by the deadweight on her chest but no longer feeling vertigo. "Someone! Talk to me! My optics are still out!"

"Hang tight!" a voice shouted, but she wasn't sure if it was White or maybe Houston. She felt the humming buzz in her palm and remembered her vibroblade. She imagined her squadmates moving around the hallway, fighting with the mutants, and worried she might cut one of them. Too afraid to try to sheathe the weapon while blind, she carefully lowered her fist to the floor and tried to angle the blade down.

Juliet grunted and tried to sit up, trying to shove the weight off her chest, but then she felt a sharp pain in her abdomen. "Ugh," she grunted and fell back flat. Something was wrong. "Get my eyes back online!" she subvocalized, some panic still edging her voice.

The gunfire had died down, and suddenly, the weight shifted off her chest, and Juliet felt hot, wet flesh being dragged over her splayed-out arm.

"Chill, Roman. Don't swing that knife around—hostiles are all down," White's voice said. "Hold still and hang tight; you're not the only one outta commission. I gotta see to Rodriguez. Houston, maintain that position. Shoot anything that shows its fucking face."

"Roger," Houston replied, and this time, Juliet heard it come through her comms.

"Net connections are coming back online, Juliet. I've rewritten the boot sequence on your optics; I think it fixed the loop. Here they come." Blessed light bloomed in the void, and suddenly, Juliet saw the orange LED emergency lamp above her, saw the stained plasteel walls of the corridor, and when her AUI came online, the rush of visual stimuli nearly overwhelming her.

"Talk to me, White," Polk's voice came through the comms.

"Hostiles are down, including the charged bastard. Rodriguez is down but not out. One of them bit the shit outta his arm, and his implants are still offline. Roman's injured, I think, but her implants are coming back up. Me and Houston are good; better shielding, I guess."

"We're interviewing a group of survivors. I'll leave Yang with them; V and I are on our way to back you up—this side's clear."

"Roger," White said into the comms, then he spoke aloud, "C'mon, Rodriguez. Can you hear me yet? Something's wrong with his shit." Juliet shifted to her side to see what White was doing and saw him kneeling next to Rodriguez, tapping a finger purposefully on his forehead. Was that some kind of code? She wanted to ask questions, the least of which was what the hell had just happened, but she also didn't want to interrupt White—he'd asked her to hold still, after all.

"Nothing moving, Sarge," Houston said from somewhere behind her.

"See about Roman. I don't think that's all the freak's blood. I'm plugging my watchdog into Roddy; let's see if the nosy bastard can get things fired up." Juliet saw him running a data cable from his neck to Rodriguez's, and a sudden panic struck her.

"Angel, are all your . . . walls still up?"

"Yes, Juliet. I never went offline. Neither did your arm, by the way; what a solid piece of tech!"

Juliet rolled to her right, where her knife-clutching arm lay, and she saw the mutilated body of one of the mutants; one like those they'd killed earlier, not the blackened, electricity-discharging one. She'd carved off one of its arms and nearly sliced its torso into three sections. No wonder she was soaked with blood.

"Damn, Roman! You did a number on that asshole, didn't you? Not bad for fighting deaf and blind."

"And dizzy," Juliet added. "I guess my auditory implants are tied to my inner ears or something? Shit, I need to get them better shielding, don't I?"

"Don't beat yourself up. Most of us have aftermarket upgrades to our headgear. Nothing sucks like having the lights go out in the middle of a firefight. Damn. Okay, hold still; looks like you got a little too wild with that knife. You've got a couple bleeders here." Juliet felt him unfastening her ballistic vest and pulling her shirt up from where it had been tucked into her uniform pants.

"I didn't even feel it," was all she could think to say.

"That'll be the adrenaline, and, well, it's a vibroblade—cuts skin like butter." She felt him pressing against her stomach with something. It hurt at first, but then she heard an aerosol hiss, and suddenly, her stomach was numb. "It's not bad. Only shallow cuts. You'll be fine. Chill a sec while I apply some glue."

"Thanks, Sarge," Juliet heard Rodriguez say before the stomp of feet announced the arrival of Polk and V. She tried to tilt her head back so she could see up the hallway, but then Houston gave her shirt a tug, pulling it back down, and held out a hand to help her sit up.

"All set, Roman." He hoisted her into a sitting position.

"Jesus, what a fucking mess," Polk said, walking through the scene. "You won't believe what those fuckers were doing down here. You killed the glowy one, right?"

"Glowy? He was practically melting down, spitting *lightning bolts*, Sarge. He went off fifty yards out like an EMP grenade. Yeah, he's dead, though. He slowed down after that pulse, and I hit him with the Gauss."

"Thank God for Takamoto-era shielding, am I right?" Houston said. "Wish we had more of those guns."

"What are you complaining about? Your bullets kept working just fine," White replied.

"Enough." Polk held up a hand. She took a step toward Juliet. "On your feet, Roman. Bet you're having a more exciting first day than the rest of your newbie squad, eh?" She held out her chromed hand, and Juliet took it, pleased that she could return the powerful grip as the sergeant pulled her to her feet.

Juliet was still shaken, still having trouble processing all the things happening around her; she couldn't quite wrap her head around the sudden change from absolute chaos to bullshitting about weapons working. She felt shaky and disgusted, especially as she realized she had deep scrapes along her chin and neck and chest, and knew they were from one of those . . . things trying to bite her throat out.

"Take a whiff of this," Houston said, holding something up in front of her. Juliet reflexively obeyed, sniffing his fist, and then a surge of ammonia and something else burned into her nose. She felt adrenaline and . . . more dilate her eyes, and she coughed, shaking her head violently.

"What the fuck?" she barked, giving Houston a shove, who backed off, his mouth grinning beneath his impenetrable dark visor.

"Relax, Roman. You were exhibiting signs of shock—it's just a little AA-salt. We gotta stay on the ball," Polk said, reaching out to squeeze her shoulder.

"What's the deal, Sarge?" White asked. "You were saying something about the glowing asshole?"

"Oh, right. The researchers here were working on new reflex wiring with synthetic muscle tissue that supposedly could carry a much higher current. Hah. That guy was wired with batteries that could drive a troop transport. Anyway, they didn't count on the surges; he went off and disabled the holding cells for the other . . . patients. Place went nuts. None of the doors could hold that guy, so they shut down the reactor and tried to weld him in here, but got trapped with a few of the others loose in the hallways over there; couldn't make their way out."

"Jesus Christ, these fucking squints never quit!" Houston groaned.

"Anyway, you know the drill. Don't talk about these things outside the mission—I'm saying this for your benefit, Roman. Zeta Protocol jobs are all top clearance. Do not discuss the specifics with anyone, including your rookie squad."

"Yes, Sarge." Juliet was feeling more alert, more present, and she knew she was on some sort of stimulant. She wanted to be upset about it but felt glad—she hadn't been feeling right before, as though she had been slipping into a weird daze.

"All right, folks. We've got a few more sections of the facility to clear, and we still need Houston to get the reactor online. Should be a mop up from here; according to the survivors, there was only one of those wired hostiles."

"Roger, Sarge," White said. "You heard her, grunts! Let's shake it off and get moving. Look at your maps; we've got two big rooms up ahead, then it's down to the reactor, and we're done with this chipped-up nightmare of a bug hunt." He started forward, his long-barreled, sleek rifle tucked into his shoulder and aimed ahead. Rodriguez and Houston were right on his heels.

"Roman, you're with me. We'll head back, sweep the hallways one more time, and then escort the civies outside. Evac's already en route." Juliet nodded, a little annoyed that she wouldn't see the clearance through to the reactor room, but also aware the sergeant was making a good call. Still, she felt she had to at least go through the motion of protesting.

"Sarge, you sure they won't need us?"

"Come on, recruit." Polk said, moving off as though she hadn't asked the question. Juliet followed behind her, and when they were well away from the scene of the battle and the ears of the others, she said aloud, "I got numbers from the civs—there shouldn't be any more hostiles. Still, don't take Houston's example as a proper way to behave in a combat situation; don't question your orders. Understood?"

"Yes. Sorry, Sergeant Polk."

The sergeant's intel proved correct; White's team didn't encounter any more combat, and Houston brought the reactor online in record time. Juliet and the others hadn't even finished getting the surviving seven civilians outside before the lights flickered on, and the air started to circulate with the familiar hum of central climate conditioning. Polk left Juliet and Yang to watch over the corporate civies while she dealt with "millions of messages from the suits upstairs."

"You doing okay?" Yang asked after she'd finished seeing to one of the survivors who'd complained of dizziness—she'd determined he was dehydrated and thrown him a pouch of electrolyte-enhanced water. "You want me to take a look at those cuts? Let me clean up those scrapes around your neck, at least."

"Thanks," Juliet said, holding still while Yang scrubbed at her neck and chin with some alcohol swabs. It stung, but it also felt good to know some of that creature's blood was getting removed.

"You really got into it, huh? I heard the thing put your lights out? Nothing scarier than having your implants suddenly go dark. That helmet has some shielding built-in, but I recommend you spend your first allowance on an aftermarket model, something with shielding for your eyes, too."

"You better believe it." Juliet sighed. "I never want to experience that again. What about implants? Some are more resistant than others, right?"

"Oh yeah, but you're talking a lot more money than a high-quality dome cover." Yang had a slightly nasal voice, and her words were quick and clipped, as though she was trying to be as economical as possible with her speech. "That looks better. You'll be okay; just scrapes. We already confirmed with the lab techs." She gestured toward the survivors sitting around in the grass together. "None of those test subjects had modifications that are transferable."

"So I won't start growing extra teeth in my sleep?"

"Don't give yourself nightmares, rookie." Yang laughed and patted her shoulder before turning to dig through her pack, handing out packages of crackers to their rescuees.

"Angel, can you confirm? I don't have any weird infections, do I?"

"Nothing, as far as I can determine. We need to get you a nanite suite and biomonitoring organ as soon as possible, though. This event was a good wake-up call for us. I recommend higher-grade sensory implants, as well; there are those that have built-in emergency functionality, so you're never completely without your sight or hearing." Angel sounded almost angry, and Juliet did a double take at the rapid flood of words.

"Are you upset?"

"It was . . . traumatic having to watch you go through that. I felt helpless—my sensory input was also gone, and it took me far too long to figure out how to message you directly through your nervous system."

"Okay. So it was a good lesson for us. Trust me, I thought it was traumatic, too." Juliet still felt a little jittery and amped-up from whatever Houston had given her to sniff, but she also had an underlying sense of panic, though she was finding it easier, minute by minute, out here in the fresh air and sunlight, to distance herself from the events that took place inside.

With that in mind, she walked in a slow circle around the survivors, breathing deeply, letting her muscles unwind, shotgun cradled in her arms, barrel down. When she'd inspected the gun, walking back with Sergeant Polk, it had been dead. Angel had rebooted it, and when it finally came online, the battery was down to twenty percent; Polk thought it was permanently damaged and told her to have the techs back at Grave check it out.

Thinking about the gun jogged another memory, and she asked Yang, "What's the deal with White's Gauss rifle? Why didn't it get fried from the pulse?"

"It's old, from the big war—Takamoto tech." She shrugged like that explained everything, but Juliet frowned, broadcasting her lack of understanding.

"Mass-produced shit most of us get our hands on doesn't come close. There are corps that can still make stuff like that, but it's expensive and pretty damn uncommon. We only have a couple of weapons like that at Grave."

"Got it." Before she could ask more questions, she heard the buzzing purr of a fluttercraft and saw the big transport coming, followed by a similar craft, though smaller and dark gray. The purr became a roar, and their supervelocity wing blades blasted the slope clear of leaves and debris as they approached. Juliet shielded her eyes and stood back to watch them come down. Before she knew it, they'd landed, the civilians were loaded up, and she and the rest of Charlie Unit were aboard their transport.

This time, when the synth pilot launched them violently into the air, Juliet was ready for it, and she almost smiled at the little thrill which ran through her as the machine's powerful thrust drove her down into the seat. When they were airborne and traveling smoothly through the sky, Polk told her to strip out of her blood-soaked vest.

"You're responsible for getting that cleaned and repaired. Take it at the same time you bring your gun to the supply depot tomorrow morning. I'm giving you the morning off to get your gear squared away. I'll send you orders for the afternoon, but don't worry; Grave won't deploy us for a few days after the shitstorm we walked into today. Not unless they have to."

"Thanks, Sarge," Juliet replied, folding the sticky vest over her knees.

"You guys shoulda seen her cut that goon up—" Houston started to say, nudging Rodriguez, who was doped up on painkillers himself.

White gave him a shove. "Can it, Houston. You're already getting a write-up. Don't push it."

"Listen to your sergeant," Polk said, baring her teeth at Houston in a decidedly unfriendly grin.

As the others quieted down, everyone zoning out, catching their breath after their harrowing experience, Juliet felt her eyes growing heavy as her helmet vibrated against the jump seat's cushion. "Juliet, I'm sorry I wasn't more help to you," Angel suddenly said.

"What?" she subvocalized.

"I wasn't any help when that . . . thing had you pinned down, trying to bite your throat. What would I have done had it gotten those filthy teeth around your jugular? I . . . I wanted to flood you with adrenaline and take control of your motor skills. I felt helpless as I felt you fighting."

"But I did fight, didn't I? I cut that thing to pieces, and we got out of there just fine. You did everything you could, Angel, and if I understand correctly, I'd still be blind if you hadn't fixed the glitch in my ocular implants."

"That's true . . ."

"Now, just relax. We learned some good lessons, I've added to my never-ending shopping list, and we earned some points with Charlie Unit. Today was a win. Let's take it, okay?"

"Understood, Juliet. I'm proud of you."

Juliet smiled at the words. It would have felt odd having any other PAI tell her it was proud of her, but it didn't feel strange at all having Angel do it; Angel was just as much a person as anyone she'd ever known, even if she didn't want to admit it, didn't want to contemplate the implications. Juliet had a lot to consider, not least of which was how much of today's activities she should report to Rachel.

For the thousandth time, she wished she knew more about her employer—it would be nice if she could be certain she wasn't reporting Grave's secrets to someone just as bad—or worse.

\\\\\\\\\\\\\\\\\

21

A VISIT TO R&D

And then they evacuated the rest of the site's personnel?" Rachel's face scrunched up as though she were trying to think of a follow-up question, but Juliet didn't wait for her.

"That's right. Then we flew back to Grave Tower, and I've spent the rest of the week training. I already got my assignment for next week, too, and it's not with Charlie Unit. One lousy mission, then drill after drill after drill. PT every morning, quizzes in the afternoon. It's almost as bad as the first week, except I got to train with Charlie Unit, and Sergeant Polk is pretty damn cool."

"So, all in all, it was a better week, right? And you're sending us some footage of the facility? I don't know how you wrote that watchdog into such a tight box, but you'll see our appreciation in your bonus."

"Yeah, it was a better week." Juliet sighed and shifted uncomfortably on the toilet; she was, once again, utilizing the single-occupant restroom at the coffee shop near Grave Tower to make her clandestine call. "Just the absence of Commander Gordon made it better."

"Is there anything else you can tell us about the modifications on those test subjects . . ."

"I've got a written report I'll be sending along with the vid." Juliet stood up and straightened her jacket. "I need to get out of here before someone gets suspicious, Rachel."

"Hold on, January," Rachel said quickly, as though she thought Juliet was about to cut off the vid call.

"Yes?"

"What's your assignment for next week?"

"Oh, right. It's weird; I'm supposed to report to sublevel twenty at 0800. I did a little digging, and that's an R&D department. It doesn't say I'll be there the whole week, but there weren't any other details on the assignment."

While she spoke, Rachel's eyes lit up, and she leaned forward, talking quickly, "This could be big, January! If they're going to try something new out, chances are the trial will be conducted through their research and development department."

"Yay! Lucky me, the human guinea pig." Juliet frowned; she wasn't being professional, she knew, but she was exhausted and getting tired of living her fake life. She wanted to tell Rachel she was done, that she'd send over her report on the facility where the mutants had run rampant, and that was it—whatever pay she'd earned would be fine. On the other hand, she had this weird need to achieve, and some part of her was pleased to see Rachel excited.

"Come on, January. You can do this. You're doing so much better than we'd hoped. There's absolutely zero suspicion around you; we're quite confident of it. Keep up the good work—this will all be worth it in the end."

"Okay. Gotta go. Look for my report." Juliet cut the call as Rachel began to open her mouth. She stood up, flushing the toilet for effect and washing her hands. Two people were waiting when she opened the door, and she looked down, avoiding eye contact as she hurried past them.

Juliet stood in line for a coffee and added a generous pour of "plant cream," something she'd avoid at all costs due to the name alone if there were any other options at the self-serve counter. She sat by herself at a small window table and sipped at it, watching the people in predominantly dark clothing walk by outside. She was in a funk, had been for a while, and her shortness with Rachel hadn't helped. Rather, it had given her another thing to worry about. "Was I too unprofessional, Angel?"

"I don't think so; you're under a lot of stress, and Rachel will likely understand. You were right to end the call when you did. Much longer, and your time in the restroom would have drawn attention."

"Show me Honey's message again, will you?" Juliet hadn't made a direct call to any of her friends since she'd started the op, and the notes she'd been exchanging with Honey always helped to buoy her mood. She'd even gotten a couple of messages from Hot Mustard, which also helped. Juliet laughed at the thought—why did she still call him Hot Mustard in her head?

"Guess it's stuck," she softly chuckled, sipping at her coffee. Then she read the message in the blinking window.

I wish you could tell me more about your job other than hinting at seeing "crazy shit" and telling me how much you hate your supervisor. Still, it's good that you're playing things safe. It's good to be paranoid, even when you're using encrypted messages like this. I've heard crazy stuff about the old AIs and what they could do with encrypted data. Do you really believe some of those big corps aren't skirting just this side of batshit crazy when it comes to AI development?

Anyway, Charity's been back to her usual bitchy self. She was cool for about two days after you kicked her ass, but she's fully sure you're never coming back and has to mention it to me almost every day. What's the point? Sure, we're friends, but she acts like it's a condemnation of me that you're not here. She's radioactive, you know? Which brings me to another certain someone who seems to be missing you . . .

Can you believe Hot Mustard reached out to me to see if I'd heard from you? Did you leave him totally hanging? I think he's got it pretty bad for you, J. He said he'd sent you two messages! I mean, I don't know how long they were, but that's a lot for a guy to stick himself out there these days, you know? I can't remember the last time a guy sent me a second message after I ignored the first one. Why are they so dumb, J? LOL

Write me again soon! I miss you!

-H

Juliet smiled as she read the note, and when she stood up to throw her cup away, she felt lighter, like a bit of a dark cloud had dispersed from over her head and the sun was peeking through. On her way back to the tower, she had Angel play her some of the songs from a playlist she'd generated based on the music Hot Mustard—Win—had played in his truck. It felt like a million years ago rather than a few weeks.

Her smile persisted as she walked through the crowds, and there was a definite spring in her step as she made her way to the elevators. The doors were just starting to close when a familiar redheaded figure slipped through them.

Addie looked at Juliet with a friendly smile and said, "Hey! Lydia!"

"Long time no see, Addie! How was your week?" Juliet asked, trying to mimic the friendly tone. The last time she'd been with Addie and the rest of her training unit, the petite woman had been decidedly cool toward her.

"Boring. Arnie and I followed Bravo Unit around while they did some readiness drills for a few of Grave's subsidiaries. They hardly let us touch any gear and refused to let us carry live ammo on-site. We were walking around with orange dummy mags like total idiots. It was humiliating."

"Oh? That sounds . . . lame." Juliet shrugged.

"What unit did you shadow?"

"Charlie. We had one response call, but the rest of the week was training and more training. The sergeants were really cool, though. I never laid eyes on the base commander."

"Charlie Unit . . . isn't Sergeant White in that unit?"

"Yep."

"He's kind of a legend. Did you see him in action? I heard he's got some pretty nice gear assigned to him."

Juliet glanced at the numbers flashing by on the elevator display. Then she smiled at Addie, shrugging. "We didn't get into much," Juliet lied, well aware that Kent or the watchdog would rat her out if she spoke about Charlie's classified operation. "You're right about his gear, though. He's got a Gauss rifle from the big war—Takamoto tech. He led us in training most of the time; we did some live-fire exercises, and he's scary as hell with that gun."

"No shit? No one in Bravo has one of those, but Thibedeux has an auto shotgun." The elevator dinged, and Addie waved. "See you tomorrow? I have a weird appointment on sublevel twenty; I don't have to report until 0830."

"Ah, really? I have the same thing but at 0800."

"Well, maybe I'll see you. Glad you made it through week two," Addie said before she leaned in for a quick hug, and Juliet frowned over the top of her head—what was the deal with this woman? She patted Addie's shoulder blades and then waved, forcing a bright smile as Addie backed out of the elevator. As the car surged and carried her the last few floors to her level, her smile turned into a frown.

"I don't trust that girl," she subvocalized to Angel.

"Noted."

When she entered her apartment, Juliet asked Kent something she'd been wondering since she'd read her new assignment, "Kent, what's my dress code for tomorrow's assignment?"

"You're to wear your standard uniform with no tactical gear. You will not need firearms or other weapons."

"And my arrival time is 0800?"

"Correct."

"Anything you can tell me about the assignment?"

"Only that you'll be released by 1500 hours each day in order to facilitate your continued physical and tactical training. You will not be supervised but will have access to the company facilities on sublevels two through five."

"Thanks . . ." Juliet said, drawing the word out as she moved around her apartment, setting out clean clothes for the next day and stripping down to throw her current clothes into the wash.

"You're likely to wake much earlier than you need," Angel noted, and Juliet knew she was right; her eyes had been snapping open each day about five minutes before her alarm went off at 0500.

"Your point?" she subvocalized.

"You'll have time for a workout before you have to report for duty."

"Yeah." Juliet nodded. "Kent? Is there any reason I can't use the exercise facilities in the early morning?"

"No. You'll find many of your comrades at Grave will be doing the same."

"Right." Juliet made herself comfortable, ate a package of beef-flavored protein and mushroom noodles, then settled into her bed, the pillows stacked up behind her, while cradling a large drink canister filled with post-workout electrolytes, vitamins, proteins, and fat, all in a thick, berry-flavored cold shake. "You sure I'm not going to get fat drinking these things every day?" she subvocalized.

"You're barely reaching maintenance levels with your caloric intake, Juliet. If it weren't for the shakes, I'd fear you wouldn't gain any muscle mass."

"Well, they taste like dessert, so I'm not complaining. Did you put together the . . . package for Rachel?"

"Yes, shall I send it?"

"Yeah, and take a note for Win: Hey, Win, I'm sorry I haven't replied yet. This gig is keeping me really busy. I've got a big day tomorrow, but when I see what it's all about, I'll send you a note. Hopefully, I'll be done before too long." Juliet smiled, thinking about Win sitting up, drinking alone, and receiving her message with a slow sardonic smile. "Send it at midnight, Angel, and sign it with just a J."

"How . . . strange. Why, if you don't mind me asking?"

"I really don't know; I'm being dumb. I had an image in my mind, and I just wanted to keep imagining it was real." Juliet smiled as she subvocalized, then aloud, because she didn't care if Kent heard her and thought she should put on a bit of a show for him, "Play me something funny. I want to try to fall asleep early tonight."

"Are you speaking to me, Ms. Roman? I can display a vid for you on the screen opposite your bed."

"No, Kent. Thank you, but I was speaking to my PAI—I'll watch the video on my AUI." She wasn't sure why she took the time to be polite or even to speak to the hospitality AI; she would have told the one at Helios to shut up, but something about Kent was different—he hardly ever spoke unless spoken to first, and he seemed to have decent guidance for her about her daily activities.

Kent had verbally directed her through the building to the maintenance techs when Juliet had returned from the bug hunt the other day, and even smoothed things over with them when the lead tech had acted like she'd committed some kind of crime after he'd inspected her shotgun. Kent's voice had come out of a nearby speaker and said something like, "E12 Tech DeForrest, you are charged with the immediate repair and refitting of all damaged Zeta Protocol gear. Will I need to contact Commander Redfield to explain this duty to you?"

After that, the tech had replaced the shotgun's battery and exchanged her ballistics vest without another word. He'd also sent Juliet the specs for her helmet so she could order improved, aftermarket EMP shielding and a visor that would fit it, should she want to. Juliet chuckled at the memory, picturing how the tech's face had grown pale when Kent spoke to him. A moment's contemplation turned her smile into a frown, though.

One moment, the tech had been on a bit of a power trip, giving the new employee a hard time, but probably on his way to fixing her problems. The next moment, Kent was speaking to him, unbidden, from a speaker in the wall, and he'd gone white, completely clamming up. Juliet wondered if Kent logged such incidents; was a new file blinking on a supervisor's console somewhere with a report of the technician's behavior and near reprimand from the tower's AI?

As far as Juliet was concerned, it was another example of why she hated big corporations and their micromanagement of employee behavior. With that dark thought in the back of her mind, she opened the vid window Angel had prepared for her and expanded it so she felt like she was looking up at a giant screen. Moments later, a comedy she'd been watching featuring some spunky, unlicensed salvage harvesters based on Phoebos Station began to play. She made it through half an episode before falling asleep, still cradling her mostly empty protein shake.

The next morning, Juliet went to the gymnasium on sublevel four, completed a round of bodyweight exercises, and did twenty-five hundred meters on the rowing machine in five-hundred-meter sprints, resting between each. The workout took her just under an hour, and by the time she'd showered, washed her bedding and dirty clothes, and gotten dressed, she only had around forty-five minutes left to kill before her appointment.

"You're getting much fitter, Juliet. A month ago, you would have struggled to complete that workout, even with many breaks along the way."

"The new arm helps, especially with the pull-ups and push-ups. It's finally stopped hurting in my shoulder, and even when I crank it up, I don't feel any strain—the synth-muscles the doc added to reinforce my chest and back are finally settled in; they're not sore at all, even after I push to exhaustion."

"Even without the arm's aid, I think you'd be surprised at how much you've improved."

"Yeah, yeah. Quit buttering me up." Juliet couldn't hide her smile as she spent the next twenty minutes breaking down, cleaning, and reassembling her shotgun.

When she'd finished cleaning the gun, she pulled out her Grave-issued vibroblade, admiring the way the blade looked almost motionless, like a flat, gray steel composite, but if she squinted and peered close, she could see how the edge oscillated so quickly that it was blurry. The weapon made her nervous—if it slipped from her fingers and fell onto her thigh, for instance, she'd probably be in trouble. "A real gusher," she said, imagining the mess.

Juliet flicked the power off, and when it had settled, she cleaned and oiled the blade, slipping it back into the sheath. That done, she put her weapons away and left, making her way to the elevators and to sublevel twenty. When she stepped out, she was surprised that the elevator lobby differed from the other sublevels she'd visited.

Rather than a single orange metallic door which led to a concrete tunnel, glass doors opened onto a sitting area with a receptionist sitting at a window in the far wall. The floors were carpeted, the two dozen or so chairs looked comfortable, and there was art on the walls—horses, mountains, and a black-and-white cowgirl leaning on a lodge pole fence.

"Check in here." The woman in the white coat motioned Juliet over to the window. Juliet scanned the room and saw three others waiting, eyes blank as they killed time with their AUIs. She didn't recognize any of them, so she shrugged and strode up to the window.

"Roman. Lydia," she spoke through the little screen in the glass.

"Right. You're early, but they might call you after I check you in. Have a seat, dear," the woman said, and Juliet gave her a second glance—curly gray hair, a few wrinkles around the eyes, and dull, pale green eyes that looked like marbles.

"Oh," Juliet let out before she could stop herself.

"Oh?"

"It's nothing . . . I thought I recognized you."

"Sure you did, sweetie. I met you at the job fair in the restroom. You had a headache?"

"Oh! That's it . . ." Juliet feigned relief; she'd known the instant she saw those eyes that this was the woman. On the one hand, she was glad she worked for Grave as she'd claimed; on the other, she was still weirded out by the lady.

"Hope you're feeling okay today." Again, the woman offered her a syrupy sweet smile, and Juliet felt something within her recoil. Something about the woman just seemed off to her, but she couldn't put her finger on it.

"Sure." Juliet nodded, forced a smile, and then moved to sit down. She'd just leaned back when the door leading out of the waiting room, situated in the wall next to the receptionist's window, was violently flung open, and a familiar figure strode out.

"What a waste of a morning, *Jesus Christ!*" Houston said, striding purposefully away but slowing when he saw Juliet. "Roman? They got you doing this chickenshit duty, too?"

"Chickenshit?" Juliet asked, smiling at his choice of words. Houston was a muscular guy and pretty damn handsome when he wasn't hiding most of his face behind his combat helmet and visor. He was rugged looking, with heavy brows and wavy brown hair. His eyes were the color of honey, and his easy smile had given his weathered, tan skin some wrinkles that belied his age.

"Oh, lord, wait 'til you see. They'll have you trying to guess what color they're thinking of and doing blind taste tests before you know it."

"Excuse me, Mr. Houston, please don't speak about your experience! You signed an NDA!" the woman behind the glass called, and Juliet smirked.

"You're gonna get another write-up."

"Good! I'm running outta toilet paper." Houston noisily cleared his throat and then stomped toward the glass doors leading to the elevators. "Good luck, rookie."

When the video call ended, Rachel Dowdall took a deep breath, cleared her mind, and counted to twenty. She had to make a report and didn't relish answering her employer's questions. She drummed her fingers on the desk staring into space, well aware that she was sitting in a dark room with the curtains drawn, and that anyone looking through the little window in her office door would think something was amiss. She didn't care—the rest of her team had already gone home for the evening.

"Faye, open a line to the client."

"Yes, ma'am," said her perfectly proper English lady of a PAI. A tone sounded twice before a window opened, and she was looking at *his* face, wreathed in shadow and vapor clouds—he had a prodigious nicotine habit.

"You have a report? Are you sitting in the dark?"

"Yes, sir, to both questions. I have a headache."

"Go ahead." He sounded irritated, and Rachel wondered if he was upset that she'd co-opted his usual schtick—calling from a dark room. She'd wanted to call him out on his eccentricities and odd behaviors, but she knew better; he'd been very short-fused these last few weeks, and he'd made very clear that their relationship was a professional one. He'd yet to give her his name, insisting on being called "Mr. Eight."

"I'd say your suspicions have borne fruit—January continues to bypass the watchdog with ease. She's even captured video and audio from a secure location. From her description, we'll get valuable intel on at least two different bioengineering projects they're working on."

"Bioengineering, hmm? I'll admit I had my doubts about this whole thing, but I'm becoming a believer; we're getting a lot more use out of her than I'd expected."

"And with the success of this operation, you'll be redeemed." He'd let slip early on, during the interviews with Rachel and her team, that he'd lost some face with his corp—that he needed this operation to work.

"I'd rather we didn't bring that up again, Rachel. My department—well, my old supervisor and some colleagues—suffered those embarrassments, and sure, some of their failures transferred my way, but I'd rather not dwell on those days. Better ones are ahead." Despite his darkened environment, Rachel could see his white-toothed grin. "Corporate politics started to shift my way when I figured out she was working as an operator. God, imagine it; from a scrapyard rat to a respected operator, climbing the ranks faster than . . . well, a suitable analogy escapes me. It's not important, anyway. Any sign of distrust or hostility?"

Rachel watched while the red LED cherry of his Nikko-vape bloomed in the hazy darkness, illuminating his pale face and outlining something behind him faintly red—was that a refrigerator? She answered, "No hostility, though she seemed a little reticent."

"Reticent, hmm? They don't have a clue who she is, do they? Grave, I mean."

"Not yet," Rachel said, holding her breath subconsciously while he exhaled—her ingrained habit didn't care that he wasn't even in the same building.

"She's not going to break? I can't believe she would, not after what she's been through."

"She seemed . . . brittle. I think the job is weighing on her. She didn't say as much, but I believe she saw more action at that facility than she let on."

"She trusts you, though?" She imagined him frowning, though she couldn't see him clearly now that his vape light had gone out. Still, it was plain he was bothered that Rachel felt Juliet might not be entirely forthcoming with her information.

"I think so, but . . . she was definitely holding back." Rachel shrugged; she wanted to give her client some good news, but she also wanted him to have realistic expectations. He might have given her an almost embarrassingly robust budget, but she'd bounce back just fine if this project fell through—clients had been waiting in line for her and her team these days.

"Really? We still need her in there, Rachel. Grave's got something major up their sleeves. They've leveraged a metric ton of debt to buy the old Vykertech building. We need that intel, and more importantly, we need Ju—January to bring in her . . . intelligence."

"What if she bolts? What if she finishes the job and decides she's ready to leave Phoenix behind? Didn't your asset say something about that?"

"No, that can't happen, Rachel." He shook his head and dragged on his vape again. The haze around his head was thick already, and she wondered just what kind of cartridge he had in that thing. Weren't they supposed to be less conspicuous these days? She could imagine how the air smelled. When they'd met in person—the one time—he'd used fruit-flavored nicotine. "Let's see," he continued, "when she's got the intel and is ready to bail out of Grave, I'll have my asset bring her in. She won't want to leave without saying goodbye. I'll make sure the bait's set properly."

"And? After this job? Are you going to try to use her again, or will you gather the data you can and cut your losses? I'm asking because my team would like to know if we'll have an extension on the contract."

"That depends on how things go. She's done so damn well, though! She seems much more capable with the . . . well, never mind. Let me worry about that, Rachel; you're playing your part just fine, and I'll be sure to keep you in the loop. The pay's good enough to keep you interested, no?"

"Well, let's hope for the best. Maybe you'll get more use out of her. Maybe she'll like this sort of work and become a more willing asset. You never know." Rachel forced another smile, hoping she was done with the meeting. She knew she had approximately *fuck all* when it came to the details about January and this operation, at least beneath the surface layer of corpo espionage. No, something more was going on with January and Mr. Eight, and she was fine playing her role and letting him keep his secrets; secrets like that tended to get people killed.

"She will—one way or another," he said, nodding, his face wreathed in shadows and vape clouds.

22

GARD

Juliet stepped into the bare little room. Nothing but a white plasteel table and two chairs occupied the space other than a black camera array staring at her from the corner. The walls were white-painted concrete, which reminded her of an interrogation room she'd seen in a police drama. A smooth, feminine voice sounded from a speaker hidden in the camera array, "Please sit down in the chair closest to you. Your evaluator will be in shortly."

"Evaluator?" Juliet said aloud, sitting down at the table. To Angel, she subvocalized, "More tests? I thought we were done with those."

"Your comrade, Houston, seemed to think this was nonsense; he can't have been in long, considering he was on his way out at 0800."

"True . . ." The door opened, interrupting Juliet's line of thought, and she turned to see a small woman in a white lab coat step through. She had her brown hair pulled back in a bun, and though she didn't wear much makeup, she looked like she took pride in her appearance; her skin was smooth and well-moisturized, and her ocular implants were stunning, brilliant yellow-orange irises which glittered like jewels from beneath her perfectly shaped thick brows.

"Hello, Ms. Roman. We're conducting some evaluations today to see if you are a candidate for a new program here at Grave." She spoke while she walked around the table, a thin tablet clutched in one hand. She pulled out her chair, sat down, and continued, "Before we begin, I need you to sign an NDA; we don't want employees speaking to each other about the process." She slid her tablet across the table to Juliet; tiny print-ing filled the screen.

"Angel, please read this," Juliet subvocalized.

"It's fairly standard legal language, Juliet. Nothing surprising, though Lydia will be held liable for breaking the NDA, and her employment could be terminated should she violate it." Juliet nodded and touched her thumb to the square at the bottom of the document.

"Thank you," the woman said, pulling the tablet back across the little table. "I'm Violet, by the way. This will be very painless; I'm simply going to ask you some questions, and all you need to do is answer to the best of your ability."

"Sounds easy enough . . ."

"Excellent. We have a long list of Grave employees to get through today, so I'll go ahead and get started." She lifted her tablet and, pulling out a kick-stand on the back of it, arranged it on the desk so the screen faced her. "You're aware that we're being recorded?" She gestured to the camera in the corner.

"Yes."

"Great." Violet smiled and clasped her hands before her, looking over her tablet at Juliet. "Will you please confirm, for the record, that you cannot see what is currently displayed on my screen?"

"Uh," Juliet said, then stared at the tablet, only able to see the flat gray back of it. "Yes, I can confirm."

"Thank you. Now, Lydia . . . may I call you Lydia?"

"Yes, that's fine."

"Thank you, Lydia. For the first part of this assessment, I'm going to be staring at my tablet, and it will randomly change its display to show me one of four different colors: red, blue, black, or white. I'd like you to concentrate on me, try to imagine what color I'm seeing, and if something comes to you, I'd like you to say the color. That's easy enough, isn't it?"

"Uh, are you trying to see if I'm psychic or something?" Juliet frowned and looked around the room. Another, darker thought came to her—was this some kind of mental health screening? "Did something come up with my squad? Are you checking me for some sort of psychosis?"

"Not at all, Lydia. This isn't a trick; you aren't in any trouble. Hundreds of Grave employees are going through this same routine today—most of you will be done after just a few minutes in a room like this. Are you ready to begin?"

"Any idea what's going on here?" Juliet subvocalized.

"I'm not sure . . ." Angel replied.

As Angel trailed off, Juliet asked, "So, I'm just supposed to say if I think you're looking at a particular color?"

"That's right, Lydia. Shall we begin?"

"Okay, let me concentrate," she said, trying to clear her mind and focusing on Violet's stunning, depthless amber irises. She didn't know what this was all about, but she was determined to do her best.

"Beginning assessment A214. Let the record reflect that my ocular implants are currently backlit with yellow illumination and will not reflect what my tablet displays. Lydia, the first color will display in three . . . two . . . one . . . begin."

Juliet stared at Violet; she tried to get an impression of what the woman was seeing, but nothing came to her, so she just opened her mouth and let the first color that came to her mind roll off her tongue. "White."

Violet didn't react, didn't so much as blink or squint her eyes. She just kept staring at her tablet's screen. Juliet didn't know when the color would change, didn't know what it would be, and didn't think she was getting anything from staring at Violet's eyes, so she closed hers. In the black void of self-imposed blindness, she let her mind drift, imagining four squares of color in a gray expanse—white, black, red, and blue—and mentally watching them. When the blue one seemed to pulse or expand ever so slightly, she said, "Blue."

As before, Violet didn't react, and Juliet kept watching her imagined squares of color. She continued to call them out as they moved or shimmered or shrank or flipped or spun—all things she supposed her subconscious was doing to keep her mind from being too bored. Still, she called out the shifting colors one after another. "Blue, white, black, still black, red, blue, white, blue, red, blue . . ."

"Thank you, Lydia." Juliet opened her eyes as she heard the other woman scooting her chair back. Violet stood, smiling pleasantly while looking at her tablet. A moment later, she looked at Juliet and said, "I'll need you to go back to the hallway and continue to room B2017; there's another assessment for you there."

"Did I pass?"

"There's no passing or failing, Ms. Roman—we do want you to continue with the assessments, though." Violet smiled, and as she walked around the table and opened the door, she put a hand on Juliet's shoulder and gave it a gentle squeeze. "Thank you, Lydia." With that, she stepped out, and Juliet was left to make her own way to the next room.

"How long was I in there?" Juliet asked Angel as she continued down the quiet hallway lined with closed, numbered doors.

"Seventeen minutes."

"Wild—felt more like five to me."

"Do you think you said any of the correct colors? This whole thing seems very strange to me; how can you be expected to see the colors she's looking at with no sort of wireless connection to her visual feed? Should I have tried to breach the camera so you could guess the correct colors?"

"No, Angel. I don't want to have to fake my way through all of these tests. We don't know what they're looking for anyway. Maybe they didn't want me to guess the right colors."

"What an odd thought . . ."

Juliet opened the door and found herself in a room identical to the first. However, this one had a vidscreen on the wall opposite the single chair at the table, and a closed white box sat on the table in front of the chair. As soon as she stepped in, a man's voice emerged from the hidden speaker, saying, "Please sit down. Do not open the box."

"Okay," Juliet said to the empty room, then sat down in the chair. She sat up straight, self-conscious, knowing at least one person was watching her through the camera. After a moment, the vidscreen came to life and displayed a sentence. *The assessment will begin in ten seconds. Follow the instructions on the screen.*

"Okay," Juliet repeated, unsure whether she should simply comply or say something. Roughly ten seconds passed, though, and the screen changed. *When you see an image on the screen, please say aloud the first word that comes to your mind. Acknowledge.*

"Acknowledged." Juliet frowned; this felt like some kind of psych exam to her. Were they worried she was cracking after what had happened during the bug hunt? She couldn't dwell on it any longer, though; an image appeared on the screen. It was a black shape on a white background, and it looked very much like a rat to her. "Rat," she said without pause. The screen shifted, and another black-and-white image appeared, a weird blotchy shape which looked something like a cloud to her. "Cloud."

The test went on for quite a while, so when the screen changed and a message appeared instead of an image, it caught her off guard; she'd entered a sort of zone like she often did when playing a game, running through forms at the dojo, or listening to music. *Open the box and put the headgear on.*

"All right," Juliet said, then reached forward and opened the box. Tilting it slightly, she saw a black plastic mesh cap adorned with several conspicuous blocky battery packs and little plastic cups that looked very much like scanners or, more unnerving, transmitters. She pulled it out and asked, "What's this?" The screen didn't change, and no answer was forthcoming, so she subvocalized, "Angel, can you get a signal from this thing?"

"Not currently."

Juliet frowned and stared at it for several long seconds, then the speaker crackled, and a man's voice said, "Please put the headgear on; its effects are harmless."

Juliet sighed and lifted the headgear, ready to pull it on, but first, she subvocalized, "Tell me if you feel this thing messing with you or my brain in some way."

"I will," Angel replied, her voice calm and sure, which gave Juliet some comfort. She pulled it on, glad it was stretchy and that she'd done her hair in two braids out of habit—they'd done a lot of training in the last week with full combat gear.

The screen changed, and a new message appeared. *Slide the headgear forward half an inch.* Juliet complied, then heard a buzz and felt the device grow warm. The screen changed again. *Do not be alarmed. The headgear will not harm you. Please wait while it calibrates.* Juliet frowned, noting the buzz had faded, but an almost inaudible whine seemed to have replaced it.

She was starting to grow used to the feeling when Angel said, "Minute electrical signals are stimulating certain regions of your brain. I'm unfamiliar with any scientific or medical reason for such stimulation; I'm sorry I'm not more help, Juliet, but I don't think the device is harming you."

"It sort of tingles," Juliet spoke aloud before she could stop herself. She glanced quickly at the screen, but no new message appeared, nor did the speaker come to life. She stared at the screen, waiting, rather enjoying the weird, humming tingle along her scalp, and then the speaker chimed, and a new message appeared. *As before, please speak the first word that comes to mind when you view the following images. Acknowledge.*

"Acknowledged." Juliet grinned, taking weird pleasure in her literal compliance. Just as before, the screen went through a series of black shapes on a white background, and just as before, Juliet said the first word that came to mind. Nothing felt different to her, and the images were definitely not the same as the ones in the first round, so she wasn't sure what anyone was hoping to find out. When the screen finally displayed a message rather than an image, she was glad to be done with the strange test. *Please remove the head-gear and place it in the box.*

Juliet quickly lifted the headgear off, and as she was setting it in the box, she felt a wave of vertigo and nearly fell out of her chair. "Are you all right?" Angel asked her immediately, and the speaker also came to life.

"Please steady yourself and only stand after you feel ready; some dizziness is a common side effect and will pass quickly," the scratchy male voice said.

"I'm fine," Juliet told both Angel and the speaker, but she held herself steady with one hand on the table for several seconds as she breathed and slowly shook her head, waiting for the room to stop spinning. When she felt better, she looked up to see a new message on the screen.

Please proceed to room B2037.

"All right." Juliet stood, glad to not feel the room lurch or spin as she got to her feet. She walked through the door and continued further down the silent, cement corridor until she came to the orange metal door with the correct number. Before she opened it, she subvocalized, "Angel, they weren't stealing data from you or something with that weird headgear, were they?"

"No, and if they were, they'd find all my data thoroughly encrypted. I didn't sense anything like that happening, though."

"Good," Juliet muttered and opened the door, stepping into a room similar in shape and color to the first two but with very different furnishings; a surgical table filled the center of the space, with robotic operating arms hanging above it, curved like the legs of a dead spider. "What the hell?" Juliet hissed as she started to back out of the room. A hand on her shoulder nearly caused her to jump out of her clothes, and she spun to see the same woman from the first exam—Violet.

"Don't be alarmed, Ms. Roman. I'm pleased to see you've come this far—the surgical table is here for a very minor procedure. Please step into the room."

"What kind of procedure?" Juliet asked, going through the door because if she wanted to leave, she'd have to push past Violet.

"We need to take a small sample of your cerebrospinal fluid. The table is programmed to do it, and it will only take a few seconds. You won't feel a thing."

Juliet backed away from Violet, and a small, panicked thought entered her mind—what if they ran her DNA? She thought about bolting, about getting out of there, saying she was sick or having a panic attack—saying she couldn't stand the idea of surgery or some other lame excuse. It all boiled down to one simple denominator, though: she could burn herself now by freaking out, or she could go along and hope they had no reason to check her DNA. With a considerable effort of will, she calmed herself and smiled at Violet.

"Really? Why do you need a sample of that?"

"Well, I can explain some of it, but remember your NDA, okay?"

"Of course! I'm new here—won't want to get fired for blabbing about things like this."

"Right, nobody's trying to get fired today!" Violet laughed, and Juliet really enjoyed how her eyes sparkled and her voice sort of trilled from her chest with amusement. "Anyway, we just need the sample to test it with some new tech—we don't want to put something in your head that will cause an adverse reaction. Grave's got a big investment in their employees and training; they'd be furious if we killed any of them off with a bad rejection!"

"Don't you work for Grave?"

"Oh yes! Forgive my choice of words; we members of the GARD team tend to think of ourselves as being apart from the rest of the corporation. We're all sequestered down here working in secret—never get a chance to socialize with the rest of the employees, you know?"

"Gard?"

Violet smiled and gently rapped her knuckles against her forehead. "Ugh! I'm sorry. I told you I don't get to socialize much—Grave Advanced Research and Development."

"Well, anyway," Juliet said, also smiling, "it doesn't sound that bad. How long will it take for you to see if I'm compatible?" Despite her better instincts, she felt disarmed by the woman's charming demeanor.

"We'll have your compatibility numbers by tomorrow. You'll get an early release today!" Violet smiled again, moved over to the surgical bed, and patted it with one hand. "If you hop up here, face down, we'll be done before you can count to twenty."

"Right," Juliet said, her smile fading as she approached the bed. "Um, can you tell me any more? Why was I looking at pictures with a weird helmet on all morning?"

"Sorry, Lydia—if you pass this compatibility screening, you'll learn more, but for now, it's best for both of us if I don't say any more."

"Gotcha." Juliet nodded, winking at Violet, then blushing at her brazen behavior. She hurriedly clambered up on the table and lay down, happy to be able to hide her reddened cheeks. Her mind raced with weird thoughts. *Was she flirting? Was Violet flirting? Why am I so awkward?* Then other ideas entered her mind, more calculated ones. *If Violet was flirting, couldn't I use that? Shouldn't I try to get more information?* Then she thought of the watchdog and remembered Violet had one, too, one which Angel couldn't control.

"I just need you to pull your blazer and shirt up a few inches so the robotic arms can reach your lower spine. It's very precise, and before it cuts, it will inject a clotting agent and an analgesic; you won't even know it happened."

"Oh, okay," Juliet said, reaching down to shift the hem of her shirt and uniform jacket up, exposing her lower back. "Should I have taken off my jacket?"

"Nope, this is just fine," Violet answered, and Juliet felt her swab something cold around the center of her back. "I'm just applying some alcohol." Then, Violet stepped up where Juliet could see her and began to operate a small data terminal mounted via a plasteel arm to the table. "Ready?"

"Sure," Juliet replied before she heard a whirring sound and felt two tiny pinches in her back. "Is that . . ." she started to ask, but then the whirring intensified, she felt some pressure, and before she could finish her question, Violet spoke again.

"All done. Got the sample. Just a sec while I apply some adhesive to the incision." Juliet didn't feel what Violet did, but a moment later, she said, "All set, Lydia. You've got more than half the day off. Enjoy it!"

"Um, thanks." Juliet pushed herself up and off the table. She straightened her clothes and asked, "Do I come back here tomorrow?"

"If this test goes well, yes. If not, then your commander will issue you new orders for the rest of the week."

"Do you think I'll pass? Do most people . . ."

Violet grinned and held up a hand. "Sorry, Lydia! I can't tell you anything more. I hope you have a relaxing afternoon. Don't worry about your back; that adhesive will hold until the skin heals."

"Right, thanks, Violet. It was nice meeting you." Juliet smiled and ducked her head, moving quickly toward the door.

"You too! Hopefully, I'll see you again tomorrow!"

"I hope so, too." Juliet hurried out the door and down the corridor toward the waiting area; she felt as though she was running from a combat encounter but couldn't figure out why. There had been a certain energy in the air when Violet was with her, and she was sure the woman had some kind of interest in her.

"Then again, maybe she's like that with everyone; it sounds like she doesn't get out much." Juliet shook her head, smiling, as she opened the door and stepped into the waiting area. Almost all the seats were full, and she saw Jensen sitting near the glass doors.

"Hey," she greeted, walking up to him.

"You're done? I wish I would've gotten an earlier assignment. Been twiddling my thumbs all morning. What's it like in there?"

"Sorry!" Juliet mimed zipping her lips. "NDA."

"Oh, jeez! Seriously? I'm so sick of these endless rules and restrictions. Tell me this much; is it just some eggheads in there, or am I going to get put through some kind of combat scenario?"

Juliet held her chin between her thumb and forefinger and looked off into space for a minute, acting like she had to really think about it, but then she smiled and said, "Eggheads."

With a laugh, she walked out the doors to the elevator. She figured she'd make a quick report to Rachel before she got some time in at the corporate range.

She found herself humming as she entered the elevator, and took a moment to analyze why she was in a good mood. Was it just because she had some free time for a change and she was excited to go shooting? The Grave range facility had all sorts of weapons she could check out as a member of a Zeta Protocol unit, and she'd wanted to practice with one of the Gauss rifles; they weren't nearly as nice as White's, but they were still fun.

"There's also that smart SMG Polk was telling me about . . ." she trailed off, starting up her tune again and grinning as she realized it was one of the songs she'd stolen from Hot Mustard's playlist. Again, she caught her out-of-character, giddy behavior, and the music in her brain stopped with a sudden finality.

She frowned, suddenly angry that she wasn't letting herself relax. Was it really out of character, or was it just out of character for Lydia? Either way, she felt she should be a little more stressed—hadn't some strange woman just walked off with a sample of her spinal fluid?

23

\\\\\\\\\\\\\\\\\\\\\

RESOLUTION

So," Juliet said, holding the long, sleek rifle in her hand while running her eyes over its length, from the heavy battery-filled stock to the tip of its barrel where the magnetic coils were visible as they emerged from the plasteel forestock, "This thing certainly felt different, but what makes it so? I mean, how is this different from my bolt-thrower?"

"Well," the range master said, clearing his throat and rubbing his heavy gray mustache between his thumb and forefinger. "I'm guessing your bolt-thrower uses standard rail technology; the bolt slides through the barrel, where magnets propel it forward. This Gauss rifle is a bit more sophisticated. It fires needle rounds, which never make contact with the metal of the barrel. The magnetic field is generated by the coil; it spins the needle as it launches it through the center of the barrel at up to nine thousand feet per second."

"That's fast for a bullet?"

"Extremely. It's why the Gauss projectile does so much damage, especially to distant targets. Of course, it depends on the quality of your ammo and the atmospheric conditions; if you have a capable firing program, your PAI should be able to adjust the velocity so you don't have your round burn up before it hits the target." He laughed, shaking his head.

Juliet hefted the gun; it was heavy, probably pushing fifteen pounds, and she wondered how fatiguing that would be over the course of an extended firefight. Still, it wasn't nearly as long as White's rifle. "Hey, do you know Sergeant White? From Zeta Unit Charlie?"

"Yeah, of course." The range master sighed and shook his head. "We don't have any guns like his for you to check out."

"What's the difference? Why's his so long?"

"It's made from expensive, rare alloys, for one. The circuitry and batteries are all shielded, and it fires bursts of needles, not one. The expensive ones, too; it won't load the cheaper alloys. Everything about that gun is five generations of tech better than this Grave model."

"Why doesn't Grave make them like that?"

"Hah!" The grizzled veteran leaned forward, smiling over his counter as he fished around in his shirt pocket for a roll of mints. While he unwrapped the package, he continued speaking, shaking his head with a grin the whole while, "Grave wishes they could make guns like that; we're talking billions of bits worth of infrastructure they don't have—foundries, factories, machine shops, and the technicians, or AI, to run it all. That gun is from the height of the Takamoto-Cybergen war; most of the facilities that made that kind of weapon were reduced to rubble."

"Well, this one was fun to shoot, anyway," Juliet said, gently placing the weapon on his counter. "Thanks"—Juliet looked at his name tag—"Range Master West."

"You're welcome. You want to shoot anything else today?" He held out his roll of mints, offering Juliet one, and she took it with a smile, plopping it into her mouth.

"I think I'm done for now. I spent a lot more time with that gun than I'd intended." It was true; she'd shot through six battery packs and two magazines of needles—more than a hundred rounds.

"Right, well, you're all checked in, and I'll give you a discount on the ammo you shot over your weekly allotment. Let's see . . . twenty percent range maintenance discount sound good? You did sweep up for the knucklehead before you, after all."

"Oh? Thanks! I did it selfishly, though—couldn't concentrate in that mess."

"Yeah, I know how you feel. Anyway, I'll bill your corporate account." He nodded over Juliet's shoulder, and she realized a young man stood patiently in line behind her.

"Oops!" She quickly stepped aside. "Thanks again," she called as she walked away, waving. She hurried toward her apartment, and on the way to the elevators and up to her floor, her earlier euphoria, her good mood, seemed to come crashing down. She yawned several times loudly as she walked through the corridor to her apartment, felt a pain between her eyes, and realized she'd been scowling.

"What's up with me?" she asked, not expecting an answer, but Angel surprised her.

"I've been monitoring your brain activity and hormone levels—well, as much as I can with my limited diagnostic connections. I believe you experienced some mood-altering aftereffects from the tests with the mesh cap earlier. More precisely, I think the stimulation it administered to your brain, while mostly targeting the left hemisphere, specifically in areas of the parietal lobe, bled through to your hypothalamus. I believe, perhaps inadvertently, the test prompted the release of some hormones into your system."

"So . . ." Juliet started as she opened her door, then switched to subvocalizations, "I was acting like an idiot because they caused my brain to pump me full of hormones?"

"That's my theory," Angel replied.

Juliet sighed and tried to go about her regular late afternoon routines, but could barely find the energy to get undressed and drink a protein shake. She'd planned to go out for a meal and make a secret call to Rachel, but she couldn't bring herself to do it; she was crashing hard from whatever had happened to her during that exam, and she just wanted to crawl into her sheets and pass out.

At one point, while Juliet lethargically brushed her teeth, Angel put up two blinking icons on her AUI, indicating she had a message from Hot Mustard and two from Honey. "I'll read them in the morning," she subvocalized. Then, despite Angel urging her to eat something more, she crawled into bed, closed her eyes, and slipped into oblivion.

"Juliet," Angel said, then more insistently, "Juliet, your watchdog received an update. You need to wake up. You have new orders."

"Ungh," Juliet grunted, flopping from her side onto her back and opening her eyes, irritated to find her apartment's lights were set to the maximum brightness. "Kent, why's it so bright in here?"

"I'm trying to help you wake, Ms. Roman—your appointment time on B20 has been moved up. You need to report by 0500."

"God," Juliet groaned, squinting at the digital time displayed on her AUI—0423. She sat up, stiff and sore, more so than she should be from yesterday's workout, and selected the watchdog icon. A message appeared on her AUI.

Lydia Roman:
Your compatibility test was a success. Please report to B2055 at 0500.
Gray Vance
GARD Director of Special Projects
Grave Industries, Inc.

Juliet threw her sheets off and slid to the edge of her bed. She felt hungover but okay—just groggy, sore, and suffering from a bit of a dull headache. She rubbed at her eyes one more time before forcing herself to her feet and stumbling into the bathroom, where she stripped down and took a shower.

Ten minutes later, Juliet felt a lot better. She threw all her dirty clothes and linens in the wash and started pulling out a uniform when Kent's voice interrupted her, "Lydia, I have additional instructions for you. You're to wear comfortable attire suitable for resting."

"What?"

"Yes, Director Vance added the instruction and asked me to make you aware."

"Okay, thanks," Juliet replied, a sudden paranoid thought entering her mind: was Kent messing with her? Was she going to show up in tights and a T-shirt and be laughed at by everyone in the facility? "No, AIs don't play practical jokes . . ."

"I think practical jokes seem like great fun," Angel piped up.

"Are my hormones back to normal?" Juliet subvocalized, ignoring the attempt at humor as she dug out some "comfortable attire suitable for resting."

"You seem much back to your usual self, Juliet." Angel's voice was dry and almost judgmental, and Juliet frowned.

"Hey! You don't know what it's like having hormones messing with your mind!"

"I . . ." Angel started, then quickly said, "I know I don't; I'm sorry. I should show some grace with regard to your erratic moods recently."

"Thank you," Juliet said aloud, tugging on her tights and a polyblend athletic shirt. She pulled on some socks and cross-trainers, then hurried to her kitchen, where a cup of hot "coffee" was waiting for her. "Fourteen minutes to go. Thanks for waking me up." Juliet smiled to herself, realizing Kent and Angel would both think she was talking to them.

She grabbed a breakfast bar—cherry and hazelnut flavors of fat, carbs, and protein—and hurried out, walking swiftly to the elevators.

"Alright, Angel," she subvocalized as she pressed the call button. "What do you think? It's weird that the director of this research department has me coming in so early, don't you think?"

"A similar thought did cross my mind, but I've been doing some theorizing."

"Go on . . ."

"I believe a small percentage of the Grave employees are selected as candidates for this program. I think an even smaller percentage passes the compatibility test with the cerebrospinal fluid. I would contend their urgency is indicative of excitement or, perhaps, desperation—they may be severely lacking viable candidates; they may need to show some results as soon as possible to continue receiving funding or other support for their program."

"Whoa," Juliet let out, stepping into the elevator. "Lots of assumptions, there. What are the odds they'll do something dangerous to me just because of how desperate they are?"

"The odds seem good. You should press for specifics before you submit to any procedures."

"Agreed," Juliet said, unwrapping her breakfast bar and chewing it down, glad it was moist and not one of the much dryer protein blends the tower's dispensers carried. While she descended and ate her breakfast, she opened the message from Hot Mustard.

Hey, got your note. Don't worry about a thing; I'm just glad to know you're doing all right. Hit me up when it's convenient.

-Old Mustard

"Old Mustard." Juliet laughed, then she selected the icon for Honey's first message just as the elevator dinged and the doors opened. She stepped out and lingered near the empty elevator lobby while she read it.

J-

I got a bizarre offer to take a job out of town, well off-planet, even. Temo says one of his clients was impressed with my swordwork and my "composure," whatever that means. He's a rich guy, though. Really rich. He's got property on Luna and wants me to come to spend the "summer" teaching his daughter some martial arts. This totally came out of the blue; Temo was more surprised than I am, but, well, I feel like I have to go for it. How many chances will a scrub like me get to do something like that? When you get a minute, can you give me your opinion?

Xoxo - Honey

"Holy shit," Juliet said, pacing back and forth in front of the elevators while she read. She didn't look at the time, too worked up by the note and wondering what else Honey had to say. She opened her second message, which had come through seven hours later at 0300.

J-

Me again. I've got a heads-up for you—Temo just messaged me; he says he was speaking to another fixer, trying to track down the right operator for a particular job. The fixer is based on the south side of Phoenix, and he mentioned that someone's been asking around, looking for an operator named Juliet. He wanted to know if Temo knew any operators with that name; said there was a reward, and they could split it. Temo played dumb, of course, but he said I should give you the warning. Who's looking for you, J?

-Honey

"*Shit!*" Juliet spat before she could catch the outburst.

"I understand the alarming nature of these messages, but you have two minutes before you're going to be late," Angel said.

"Right." Juliet hurried through the glass doors to the reception window, barely noticing the empty chairs in the waiting area, and stood before the glass. "Lydia Roman. I'm almost late."

"Yes, dear." The same woman who'd been there before, the one from the bathroom during the job fair, sat behind the window, a smile that gave Juliet the creeps pulling the corners of her mouth wide, angling toward the corners of her overly blushed cheeks. Her weird marblelike eyes betrayed no emotion. "Go on through, straight back to room—"

"B2055. Got it," Juliet said, pushing the door open and striding down the silent concrete hallway, past a few dozen closed orange metallic doors, until she reached her destination. She paused before it and subvocalized, "Angel, what am I going to do? Do you think WBD figured out I'm an operator?"

"I don't know. There are a number of people who might be looking for you, though WBD does seem to be the most likely candidate. I'll do as much snooping as I'm able through the sat-net, but we might be advised to employ some counterintelligence—"

The door opened suddenly, and Juliet had to step back to avoid a collision with a man in a white lab coat as he walked out. "Oh! Excuse me! Are you Roman? Lydia Roman?" The man who'd opened the door was about Juliet's height, with gray hair that faded toward white at his sideburns. His face was smooth, free of wrinkles, and a little too taut, in Juliet's opinion—someone who could afford antiaging treatments.

"Yes, that's me." Juliet smiled and stepped to the side, making room for him to continue walking, but he stopped and gestured toward the partially open door.

"I was actually coming to look for you; I was afraid Bernice had you sitting up there waiting for us." He nodded toward the reception area down the hallway.

"Is that her name? The lady with the . . . dull, green eyes?" Juliet frowned, realizing that her description might sound a little rude.

"Oh, yes. She's an odd one, that Bernice. She's seen a lot, though—it would be a breach of confidentiality if I told you the percentage of her brain that's artificial, so I won't." He winked at her then gestured toward the door again. "Please come in! We're excited to get started with you."

Juliet's mouth had fallen open at the mention of Bernice's artificial brain, and she stepped into the room without further comment. Another white, concrete-walled room awaited her, though this one was larger, with a full-size hospital bed. A sleek, portable surgical machine was parked next to the bed, sporting three robotic arms, much like you'd see on a full operating table.

An open door to her left revealed a small lavatory with a toilet and a sink, and the same woman from the day before, Violet, stood to the side, flipping through a tablet, clearly concentrating on something she was reading. Her brows were drawn down and her lips were pressed in a thin line, and she jumped a little when the man said, "Violet! She's here."

"Oh." Violet looked up from her screen with a smile. "I was lost in the data. Dr. Vance, I wish you'd let me upload this so I could view it through my AUI."

"You know we can't do that, Violet. Security protocols!" He gently gripped Juliet's elbow and propelled her toward the bed. "Lydia, please hop up on the bed. We have a quick procedure to put you through. It'll be over before you know it, but you'll need to stay here for observation afterward. I'm glad the AI passed on the instructions to dress comfortably."

"Um, Dr. Vance, is it?" Juliet asked, walking toward the bed but stopping near the foot, resting one hand on the soft, pale-green blanket. "I'd like to know a little bit about what you're doing before you, well, before you do it."

Violet cleared her throat and shifted uncomfortably while Dr. Vance closed the door. He turned to look at Juliet, and though he smiled, she saw a look in his eyes which indicated he was not used to people questioning him. "Lydia, we're going to give you an injection. That's it. We've already tested you for compatibility, so you don't have to worry about an adverse reaction. The truth is, your test results were spectacular."

"Spectacular?"

"Yes! We have a scale for rejection from zero to total deliquescence, which is somewhere around fifty-nine; that's the level where immediate brain death occurs. We learned the hard way to run a sample before injecting a candidate." He chuckled as though he'd just conveyed a rather amusing anecdote.

"You don't have to worry about that!" Violet chimed in.

"Yes, correct," Vance said, shaking his head as his chuckle died away. "We've had some rather successful candidates with a rejection rating of less than fifteen. You scored a .07."

"Less than one?" Juliet clarified.

"Much less than one. Less than .1. You won't suffer any damage."

"Well, what's the injection?"

"Some specialized nanites," Vance spoke enthusiastically, moving closer to Juliet and reaching out to rest a hand on her shoulder. "Lydia, we've been waiting for a candidate like you; we have high hopes!"

"Uh, what kind of nanites?" Juliet backed away from his touch, sliding along the side of the bed.

"Bah, don't worry, Lydia!" Vance said, his eyes narrowing. "We won't tell you more at the moment. We can't because it would invalidate the assessments we'll need to do after the procedure is complete."

"We wouldn't do something that will harm you, Lydia," Violet added, and she seemed sincere.

"Regardless"—Vance gestured to the bed again—"you have your orders. Please recline on the bed, Roman."

Juliet stared at Vance, then glanced at Violet. How far were these two willing to go? Would they try to force her? She was confident she could fight her way out of the room, but how would Grave respond? At the least, she'd lose her job, but they were a corporation—she doubted she'd make it to the elevators before they had corpo-sec grab her up and force this thing. Vance seemed far too eager to let her go. So, she could burn herself and cause a scene, becoming a forced guinea pig, or she could go along, trusting that there would be a way to undo whatever they had planned if she didn't like it.

"Angel," she subvocalized as she hopped onto the bed, legs still dangling over the side, "please try to monitor whatever they do—you'll be able to sense the nanites, won't you?"

"To a degree, yes, especially if they inject them into your cerebrospinal fluid. I have hundreds of thousands of synth-nerve nanofilaments in that area."

"Hundreds of thousands?" Juliet almost spoke aloud, she was so startled by the number.

"Oh yes. Remember, I expanded my connections after you inserted me."

Juliet couldn't deal with the revelation of the full extent of Angel's invasion into her brain and nervous system just then. She closed her eyes, took a deep breath, and asked, "Is this permanent?"

"No, no," Vance replied. "The nanites can be made inert with a second injection, allowing your body to filter them out naturally."

"All right." Juliet lay back.

"Lydia," Violet spoke, coming closer. "Please put your hands on the armrests, here and here."

"Okay," Juliet said. When she gripped the white plasteel arms on each side of the bed, something clicked, and broad plasteel cuffs snapped up around her wrists. "What the fuck?" she hissed, jerking her hands, unable to move them more than a centimeter.

"It's for your own protection, Lydia," Violet explained, smiling, her beautiful amber eyes creasing around the corners. "Trust me, please. While the nanites do their thing, you're likely to hallucinate, and you may experience some pain—we don't want you to hurt yourself."

"Do their thing? Pain?"

"Yes." Vance stepped closer and carefully pulled off Juliet's left shoe. "Let me help you get more comfortable. You see, the nanites' job is to create novel pathways between specific areas of your brain. As for the pain, we'll give you some nerve blockers, but because the nanites will be working in your brain, I'm afraid most of our medications are quite ineffective."

"I'd like to opt out of this procedure," Juliet said, suddenly wishing she'd tried to fight free; maybe she'd have made it out of the building before they mustered a response. She knew it was bullshit, though—they only had to disable the elevators. "You didn't say shit about the nanites altering my brain!"

"I know you're frightened, but you don't need to worry. I told you—your compatibility was the best we've seen. People with far worse numbers are functioning just fine. I'm afraid we can't have you back out at this point—too much is riding on this program. Grave's future is at stake. The company needs you to rise to this occasion."

"I don't give a fuck about—"

Violet touched something on the portable surgical machine, and it *whirred*, then fast as a striking cobra, one of its chromed arms shot out with the precision only a machine could match, injecting something into Juliet's neck. She fell back midspeech, unable to control or feel her body.

"There we go," Vance said, smiling as he took off her other shoe. "I know you're still there, probably panicking, Lydia, but this is also for your own good. We need you to hold still during the procedure for your safety. Don't worry. Everything will work out wonderfully, and it will be over before you know it. This is going to feel very much like a strange dream in a day or two, and you'll be able to get back into a normal routine."

"Juliet!" Angel screamed into her auditory implants. "Juliet, I don't like this! We should have fled when we got the director's watchdog notice this morning."

Juliet tried to reply, tried to subvocalize, but she couldn't even flex the tiny muscles at the base of her tongue. She managed to make a slight moan escape her lips, though, and Violet reached forward to gently squeeze her arm, just above where the plasteel cuff held it to the bed.

"You're okay, Lydia. I'll be here the whole time. You're going to do wonderfully."

"Here we go," Juliet heard Vance say as something hissed off to her left. It reminded her of the sound a can of beer made when you opened it, but longer and deeper.

He walked into her field of view, and she saw he was carrying a glass tube, about a foot long and an inch wide, completely filled with a silvery, shifting fluid. Were they going to put all of that into her? She wanted to scream, wanted to thrash, wanted to pull her vibroblade—which she didn't have— and slice their smiling faces off.

"Violet, make sure you follow the injection protocol from the delta group—it seemed to have the best uptake results."

"Of course, Doctor," Violet said, and then, after a few clicks, the surgical unit began to hum. One of its long arms moved, and a high-pitched motor began to whine, reminding Juliet far too much of the sound a drill made as it ramped up to speed.

"Juliet! What can I do?" Angel wailed in her head, but Juliet couldn't answer. Her fear had retreated, though, and only one thought filled her mind, one resolution—when this was over, if she was able, she was going to kill these assholes.

24

SCIENCE FICTION

Juliet couldn't feel the drill when it started on her skull, and it was so brief that she almost thought she'd imagined the whirring sound and the echoing, grinding noises. She knew better, though—the autosurgeon was just precise and fast. The noise stopped, she felt some strange pressure above her left ear, and then the agony began.

When Juliet was younger, during her teen years, she'd suffered from regular migraines. They'd come less and less frequently as the years passed, and she couldn't remember the last true migraine she'd had. Sure, she had headaches, but nothing like those—the migraines had been different. Their harbinger were weird spiral sparkles in her vision; then, as her vision cleared and returned to normal, the pain would roll in, and nothing would help short of going to bed.

Whatever Violet and Dr. Vance were doing was worse; Juliet felt like her skull was splitting and that something was squeezing her brain into a pulp. She wanted to scream, wanted to thrash and grab her head, but she couldn't move, and that made it worse—if she could devise the worst torture to put someone through, she felt like the hell she was experiencing would be on the list.

Despite the paralytic agent they'd given her, Juliet felt her body begin to vibrate, found her breathing growing ragged, and realized she could no longer focus, couldn't really see anything, and she knew her eyes had rolled back in their sockets.

"Juliet! I'm going to try to regulate your respirations and heart rate—I'm worried you'll suffer a cardiac event!" Angel sounded hysterical, but Juliet could barely hear her, barely register her voice. It sounded to her like she was submerged in water and a massive propeller was revving up nearby. The agony rose to a crescendo, and then, blissfully, she lost consciousness.

". . . yes, the structure is far more robust; tens of thousands of branches." Juliet didn't open her eyes when she heard the voice; it sounded like Violet.

"And the nanites are all inert? They've finished?" The second voice was new to her, another woman, older sounding.

"That's right. The array's been constructed, and the leftovers have all passed through the blood-brain barrier; she'll void them within forty-eight hours."

While she tried to make sense of the words, Juliet took stock of herself. The pain was gone; she felt pretty good and wanted to open her eyes, but something told her to keep them closed, to keep her respirations slow and even. With her eyes closed, her AUI was vivid against the black. Angel hadn't gone offline, but Juliet didn't want to give herself away by subvocalizing, afraid they were monitoring her too closely.

"When can we start the assessment?" the second woman asked.

"When she wakes—there shouldn't be any lingering effects. The lattice-work branches are nearly microscopic, and now that the extra nanites are out of her meninges and neural pathways, the debilitating pain should be gone."

"Can we go ahead and wake her? I have three visitors from the executive suites who are interested in your progress." While the woman spoke, something strange happened to Juliet—she saw an image of three men in dark suits sitting around a fancy optiglass conference table, making irritated, impatient faces. One of them shifted as though about to stand up.

"Dr. Vance should be back any moment. When he's here, I'm sure he'll be all right with that." Violet sounded nervous—pressured.

"Very well," the woman said. "I'm going to make my way back to my guests." Once again, Juliet had the weird sensation that she was looking through a window into the conference room she'd seen before. "And when I get there, we'll be watching the feed of the test room. You have fifteen minutes to begin." The sounds of heels clicking on the industrial tile and a door opening and closing followed her words.

Juliet decided it was time to let Angel know she was awake. She subvocalized, "Angel?"

"Yes, Juliet. I sensed you waking but knew you were trying to feign sleep."

"Of course you did. What's going on? How long was I out? What did the nanites do to me?"

"She's waking," Juliet heard Violet say, presumably into a comm channel.

"You've been out for eleven hours. All of your vitals are strong, and I'm not sensing any brain damage. The nanites constructed a—nearly—microscopic latticework between various parts of your brain. It's truly a beautifully complex design. It appears to be made from some sort of organic and metallic hybrid; I cannot identify it. Juliet, I'm sensing electrical impulses traveling along it. Moments ago, a fairly large surge."

Juliet opened her eyes and turned to where she'd heard Violet speaking. She was standing a foot away, perusing her datapad, brows creased in concentration. "What the hell did you do to me?" Juliet growled and tried to stand up, but her hands were still bound to the plasteel bed frame.

"Lydia! Welcome back! Everything went very well, better than we could have hoped. You're exceedingly compatible with the compound."

"I'm not going to repeat the question, but you need to start giving me some goddamn answers!"

"I understand you feel violated. Tricked, even. But we've only done what we told you we would do—administered an injection of nanites that constructed a harmless latticework in your brain. I can't tell you the purpose, or it may taint the upcoming evaluations . . ." She stopped speaking as the door hissed open, and Dr. Vance walked into the room.

"Aha! Our patient rouses. Wonderful, wonderful. Lydia, you've done quite well—we're so excited to see how things turn out."

"I don't care if you call this shit harmless," Juliet said, scowling and straining against her bonds. "It wasn't! I've never felt anything so horrible. It was worse than getting stabbed through my lung—hundreds of times worse!"

"Yes, I understand. We had to have you conscious for the initial phase—the nanites needed to follow your synapses to the best contact points, and we've found that a waking mind is far more thoroughly mapped. We kept you conscious for as brief a period as possible. We're terribly sorry about your suffering, Lydia, but the memory of your agony will fade, and hopefully, it will all pay off nicely."

Juliet wanted to rail, to cuss them out, but she held her tongue. If she was too hostile, they'd never unbind her, never give her any freedom. No, it would be better to play it smart. Go along until they'd given her enough leash to get herself out of this mess. "I'm just . . . I'm just upset that you didn't give me more time to adjust to the idea. I feel trapped." She nodded her head toward her cuffs.

"Of course, of course." When Vance spoke, suddenly, Juliet saw as though through a hazy window an image of a terminal screen and a blinking icon which said, "Disengage Restraints." Was she seeing what he was thinking? Was she seeing what she wanted? She couldn't make sense of it, but it faded as Vance continued speaking. "Violet, release her restraints. We need to move into the assessment room; people are waiting."

Violet reached her hand toward the terminal attached to Juliet's bed and touched it. A second later, her wrist restraints snapped open. Juliet had the urge to leap to her feet, smash Vance in the throat, and choke the life out of Violet. "Time for that later," she subvocalized, trusting that Angel would know what she meant. Instead, she calmly sat up and shook her head slightly, wondering at the lack of pain or discomfort. She reached a hand to her scalp above her ear and felt for where the drill had punctured her.

"We sealed the insertion point with bone gel and sutured your scalp with glue; it'll be tender for a few days, but otherwise, you won't notice the injury . . ." Violet trailed off as Juliet let her hand drop and turned so her legs slid off the side of the bed.

"I have to use the bathroom."

"Yes, of course. You were under nearly twice as long as we'd anticipated. We were getting ready to rouse you and, failing that, would have inserted a catheter." Vance spoke like he was saying something positive, something reassuring, but all it did was irritate Juliet. She frowned and stood, a little wobbly at first but then feeling all right, other than the immense pressure she'd grown cognizant of in her bladder. "Please do hurry; we have a tight schedule to adhere to."

"I'll pee as fast as I can, Doc." Juliet brushed past Violet, frowning down at the smaller woman, imagining she could ignite her flesh with laser eyes as she let her gaze linger on her downcast, demure expression. "Fake bitch," she subvocalized.

"Juliet, I'm trying hard not to distract you, but I feel we should speak at great length about everything that's going on!" Angel said as she shut the door to the restroom.

"I know, Angel," Juliet subvocalized, sitting down on the toilet to relieve the pressure in her gut. "Priority one is figuring out what they did to me; then priority two is deciding if it's time to bolt out of here or not. I feel fine, but I'm seeing weird things. Did you see anything appear in my vision, like on my AUI? I saw something weird, a foggy window showing me a conference room, then a few minutes later, I saw an image of the control panel on the hospital bed."

"No. There haven't been any anomalies in your retinal implants or on your AUI. I'm not detecting any strange data spikes or transfers. I did tell you the nano-latticework around your brain has been transmitting your brain's electrical impulses, and they do seem to spike occasionally."

"So. I wonder . . ." Juliet closed her eyes and, while she continued to urinate—perhaps the single longest marathon of peeing she'd ever managed—she concentrated and thought about Violet. She chose her instead of Vance because Juliet could visualize her beautiful amber eyes more easily. "What are you thinking about, Violet?" she hissed, concentrating.

This time, rather than an image, Juliet heard Violet's voice, as though she was speaking softly into her ear. *We need to lock her up. She should be in restraints.*

"Holy shit! Is this science fiction?" Juliet subvocalized. "These damn squinty cybergonads gave me psychic powers, Angel!"

"It's very likely you've experienced some sort of delusion. You've been through a very trying experience—"

"No! I'm serious!" Juliet stood, and before she flushed, she glanced into the toilet and was alarmed that the water was dark gray. She shook her head and remembered what Violet had told the other woman—she'd be voiding the nanites for a day or two. "Okay," she continued, subvocalizing while she washed her hands. "I scared Violet too much; time to play nice so they don't lock me up."

Juliet opened the door and, with a supreme effort of will, offered the two white-coated scientists a friendly smile. "Whew! I feel a lot better!"

"Ah, I'm sure you do," Vance said, gesturing toward the door. "Shall we? We just need to go two doors down from here."

"Uh, sure." Juliet nodded and walked toward the door, then asked, "After you do your assessment, will you be able to tell me what your procedure did, exactly? I feel totally normal."

"Yes. We have a few baselines to run, then we'll be able to brief you," Violet replied, daring a glance that made eye contact with Juliet.

Again, Juliet smiled, nodding. "Great."

Vance opened the door and stepped out. When Juliet followed him, she was surprised to see four corpo-sec personnel standing at attention just a few paces to the right, toward the elevators. "Those guys here for me?"

"We wanted to heighten security after we saw the success of your operation, Lydia. You're very valuable to Grave now," Dr. Vance said, and Juliet had a feeling his words weren't just for her benefit. Who was he trying to impress? Who was listening to him? She also knew he was full of shit. Those guards were to keep her in line, keep her from bolting.

Just as Vance had said, they walked two doors down the hallway, then stepped into a room very much like the first one Juliet had visited on B20—a white rectangular space with a table, four chairs, and a camera array in the corner. "Please sit here," Vance said, gesturing to one of the chairs. He and Violet sat on the opposite side.

"Sure," Juliet replied, trying to keep her voice positive without sounding like a deranged idiot. She sat down, folding her hands on the table.

"Excellent. Lydia, do you remember the first assessment you had in our department? The one where you were supposed to guess colors?" Vance smiled and scratched at one of his sideburns. Juliet watched as little flakes of dandruff fell down to disappear in the white of his lab coat.

"Yes, I remember."

"We're going to do that again. Violet will look at a random color on her display, and you'll try to guess what she's seeing. How does that sound?"

"Sounds great! I'm starving, by the way; any chance I can head up to the cafeteria after this?"

"Oh yes, of course!" Vance jumped up and walked to the door, calling out into the hallway, "Bring us some juice and a protein bar." When he closed the door and sat back down, Juliet favored him with another smile and a wink. Despite her obvious—to her—attempts to force her pleasant demeanor, Vance seemed to eat it up, smiling back at her and fidgeting in his seat.

"I'm ready, Doctor," Violet said.

"All right. Shall we begin, Lydia?"

"Sure," Juliet replied, closing her eyes and clearing her mind.

"Begin postprocedure assessment A214," Vance directed.

"The first color will display in three . . . two . . . one . . . begin," Violet said.

Juliet concentrated; she thought about Violet, about her eyes, and suddenly, she saw it, not just a color but her entire vidscreen. She saw a window displaying a square filled in with red, but she also saw a spreadsheet on which were dozens of names along with green checks and red Xs. Currently, her name, Lydia Roman, was highlighted, and there were two lines beneath it: a preprocedure row with seven green checks and thirteen red Xs, and a postprocedure row with blank boxes.

Looking over the list, Juliet saw that most of the other names only had preassessment rows. Many had rows of mostly red Xs, but a few had five or more green checks. She spotted a name with two rows, Gabriel Masingil, whose preprocedure row had six green checks, and his postprocedure row had nine. Before she read any more, Juliet said, "Red."

She watched as Violet populated the spreadsheet with a green check, then she saw the red square pulse and refill with the color red again. Juliet wondered, then, if she should be honest about her abilities. Did she want Grave to know how clearly she could see what Violet was seeing? Would it be better to have marginal gains like Gabriel apparently had? "What if they give me special treatment if I get them all right," she subvocalized.

"Are you able to see the colors?" Angel suddenly asked.

"Yep. I think I could ace this test. Do you think I should?"

"Strategically, it would benefit you to some degree if they feel you are exceptionally valuable to their program. However, such status may come with reduced freedoms; they'll likely want to keep you isolated while they continue to work on their procedure."

While she listened to Angel's answer, Juliet said, "Red," and watched Violet fill in another green check. She tended to agree with Angel; she liked the idea of not letting these creeps know what she could do. She continued to concentrate, watching what Violet was doing, and purposefully said the wrong color for the following three prompts. She could hear Vance shifting in his seat across from her, and thought he was breathing more quickly. Then, to her surprise, she picked up on his voice.

I'm going to be ruined.

Some surprise must have shown on her face because Vance said aloud, "Are you all right, Lydia? After this test, we'll get your snack in here."

"I'm fine," Juliet replied, but then she heard another voice, this one more distant.

Am I supposed to knock? Did he want me to bring this stuff in there right away? Last time, they told us not to interrupt . . .

"What the hell," she subvocalized. "I'm hearing the guard outside, I think."

"I'm detecting massive spikes of activity along the latticework, Juliet!" Angel replied, a note of strain in her perfectly natural voice.

"Black," Juliet answered, noting the correct color on Violet's screen.

Thank God.

That time, she'd heard Violet's voice, and close behind it, she heard, *There's hope yet,* from Vance. Suddenly, Juliet realized she was beginning to sweat profusely, and then she became aware of a dull pain near the base of her skull, which began to spread.

What's wrong with her? The color's about to change!

Juliet concentrated on Violet's view again and said, "Blue," again guessing the correct color.

Am I going to get fired over this? Oh, Jesus, here goes . . .

Suddenly, a knock sounded on the door, and Vance shouted, "Not now!" More quietly, he said, "I'm sorry, Lydia; try to focus."

I knew I should have waited! I'm definitely fired. Oh God, Sharon's going to leave me . . .

Oh please, oh please, guess the right one.

"I'm concerned about the temperature in your head, Juliet; you're exhibiting the physiological symptoms of a high fever." Juliet found it increasingly difficult to concentrate on what Violet saw, and Angel's words sounded distant and hollow. The pain in her head was beginning to throb, and just as the color changed again, she felt a deep wave of vertigo and fell forward, smacking her forehead into the plasteel table and sliding out of her chair to sprawl onto the painted concrete floor.

"Goddammit!" Vance yelled, and Juliet was distantly aware of his chair scraping over the floor as he came around to take her hand, holding his fingers to her wrist. "Her pulse is thready, and she's burning up! Didn't we hydrate her at all while she was out?"

"Yes, Doctor! I ran an IV!"

"Well, something's wrong, damn it! We'll need to reschedule. What were her results?"

"Four out of seven."

"Truly? Well, one partial sample won't be enough. We'll need to run more tests. Let's get her recovered." Though she could hear them speaking, they sounded strange—she had the impression they were far away, and that she was hearing their words echoing up out of a deep well.

Juliet found she couldn't open her eyes and couldn't really move, and that's when she realized she wasn't fully conscious. She decided to stop fighting; her head was pounding, and she was exhausted. It was time to get some rest.

25

\\\\\\\\\\\\\\\\\\\\

GIPEL

When Juliet came back to consciousness, she was in a room very similar to the one where Dr. Vance and Violet had done the procedure. In fact, after she'd taken a groggy look around, she thought it might be the same one, but with the portable autosurgeon removed. "Am I alone?" she subvocalized.

"Yes. Are you feeling better? Your vitals seem fine." Angel's voice was calm, though Juliet thought she could detect a definite note of concern.

"I feel okay. My head's a little woozy." She glanced to the corner where a camera and built-in scanner array placidly stared at her, and wondered how many people were watching her wake up. "Angel," she subvocalized, "if they figure out what I can do, they'll never let me go. We need to start working on breaching their closed networks. I want you to start actively looking for vulnerabilities."

"I will, but so far, everything on this level has been hardened. The cameras and scanners, for instance, don't have wireless ports."

"I know, I know. Just be on the lookout for opportunity." She'd barely finished forming the words in the back of her throat when a tap at the door sounded. Two seconds later, it opened.

"Lydia," Violet said, stepping into the room. "You had us a bit worried there. Are you feeling better? I've administered another round of electrolytes and some NSAIDs. Your fever dropped pretty rapidly; we're quite sure you're not suffering from an infection or adverse reaction to the biosilver."

"Biosilver?"

"Uh . . ." Violet glanced at the cameras and cleared her throat. "I probably shouldn't have mentioned that yet. Doctor Vance will go over all of that with you after we manage to complete some assessments."

Juliet grimaced, licking her dry lips. "More assessments? Really?"

"Well, just one tonight, but yes. We're going to be a bit more careful this time, though. Doctor Vance is printing up a special cap for you to wear; it should be able to monitor the work the nanites did in your head a bit more accurately than the scanners." She gestured to the corner of the room where the array of lenses and antennae lurked, almost like a big plasteel spider.

"Okay. Can I use the bathroom?"

"Of course," Violet said, shifting toward the foot of her bed so the path to the bathroom door was wide open.

Violet seemed jumpy to Juliet, so she offered a somewhat sheepish half smile. "Man, whatever you guys gave me really has my bladder filling up!"

"It's the nanites being processed out of your system and the copious amount of saline and electrolytes. Doctor Vance was worried you weren't processing the inert material, so he insisted I push a lot through your IV."

"Ah, that explains it." Juliet stood up, a bit wobbly at first, then made her way to the restroom. She hadn't been exaggerating; her bladder felt like it was going to explode. "Angel," she subvocalized after she'd closed the door, "did they put the IV in my right arm? How did the implant handle that? I thought it was a closed loop."

"It's closed, but it has a valve, remember? The valve allows more of your blood in, but if left open, it allows IV fluids out. I'm in control of it."

"Right. Thanks." She sat down on the toilet and relieved her tremendous bladder pressure, then asked, "How long was I out this time?"

"Less than an hour. While you were unconscious, I listened to them as they administered your IV. Vance theorized that your kidneys were over-burdened by the inert nanites. I don't believe they suspect that the array in your head was overheating; you may be the first test subject to exhibit that reaction."

"Yeah, no shit. I don't think they were expecting me to be reading every-one's damn minds. I need to think of a way to keep that from happening, or I'm in trouble. It started when I concentrated on the test, on seeing what Violet saw, as though I was opening myself up to it." She sighed and rubbed at her head. "I still feel like this is all a delusion. Hang on." She closed her eyes and concentrated on Violet, picturing her deep, glittering amber eyes.

God, I'm tired. Why can't Vance put this off until tomorrow? Are the execs so wound up? Are they still watching? Don't look at the camera. Don't look at the camera.

"Okay, this is crazy. Did my temp increase?"

"Not noticeably, but activity along the latticework spiked."

"So, focusing on one person seems to be okay? It's when I start to pick up other stuff going on, other thoughts. Yeah, hearing the thoughts combined with seeing what Violet saw . . . how the hell do I filter it, though? How do I keep from getting overwhelmed?"

"I have a suggestion," Angel said.

"I'm listening!" Juliet hissed, standing up to flush and lean over the sink, splashing water on her bleary eyes.

"Well, I haven't had a good chance to speak with you yet, but I'm assuming when you 'see' the color, you're making a connection somehow to Violet? You're seeing through her eyes?"

"It feels like that, yeah."

"You should try keeping the connection brief. Note the color, then wait a few seconds and repeat it; the colors seem to shift every few seconds."

"Hey," Juliet subvocalized, "that might work! I didn't start hearing what people were thinking until I'd watched Violet's screen for a while. Right now, for instance—I'm not thinking about Violet's thoughts, I'm not concentrating, and nothing's coming through." She dried her hands and continued, "I don't want them to know how well it works, though. I need to make them think I'm trying but it's barely a success."

"Agreed. If you feign complete failure, there's a chance they'll become suspicious."

"Well, they're corpo assholes; their default setting is suspicious, but I know what you mean." Juliet opened the door, nodded to Violet, then said, "Much better! Uh, my pee was a disturbing shade of gray . . ."

"That will continue for a day or so; don't be alarmed, it's just the solution we injected clearing your system. It's good that you saw it in your urine!"

Juliet wanted to slap her, wanted to vent her frustration and give her a taste of the violation she and Vance had visited upon her, but she choked it down and didn't make eye contact with her until she could force a neutral expression. "I'd really like a hot shower and my own bed. How long do you think I'll need to stay down here?"

"If it were up to me, you'd be home sleeping right now." Violet chuckled, if a bit nervously, and then continued, "It's going to be midnight in a couple of hours, and I think we're all a bit tired."

"Heh," Juliet said, looking down before the other woman spotted the fury in her eyes.

"The doctor just messaged me; he's ready. Shall we?" Violet turned to the door, and Juliet felt it was a good sign that she'd turned her back to her. Maybe her friendly act was more convincing than she thought. Her doubts resurfaced when she stepped into the hallway to see four fully geared-up corpo-sec guards still standing there, two along each wall. She wondered if they were the same ones or if they'd changed shifts.

She ducked her head, feeling like a prisoner being perp walked, and followed Violet back to the assessment room. Vance was waiting, and he held a plastic mesh cap out to her when she stepped in. It had a long cable attached to the datapad on the table. He said, "This might give us an idea of what's going wrong if you feel sick again."

"Just put it on my head?" Juliet took it and sat down in the same seat as before.

"Mm-hmm, go ahead." Vance seemed almost dismissive, and Juliet quickly glanced at him, seeing that his gaze was focused on blank space; he was doing something on his AUI. She pulled the cap on. To her, it seemed like a hairnet made out of plastic and wires.

Violet sat down across from her and touched something on her datapad. "I'm seeing readings for temp and activ—"

"Private message, dolt," Vance interrupted her, shaking his head and sitting down.

"Somebody's grumpy . . ." Juliet said before she could catch herself.

Vance frowned, then looked at Violet. "I'm sorry. I let my stress get the better of me." Violet nodded quickly, and he turned back to Juliet. "It's been a long day, and I have a lot of people very interested in my progress with this program and about a half dozen other projects. I'm sure you're exhausted, too. Shall we try to wrap this up so you can get some rest?"

"Some rest and some explanations? I don't know why I passed out, but I didn't like it!" Juliet tried to walk the line between belligerent and too easygoing.

"Naturally. Violet will debrief you when we're done." Juliet saw Violet stiffen and almost smiled at the woman's irritation. She knew her hostility toward Violet was justified, but she still felt a twinge of shame for taking pleasure in her unhappiness.

When she caught herself having that sympathetic thought toward Violet, she began to frown, and had to force a placid expression as she mentally slapped herself—that woman had tied her to a bed and forcefully injected some experimental goop into her brain. Whether she'd been calling the shots or not, that was some messed-up behavior, and Juliet wasn't anywhere close to letting it slide.

"Are we ready?" Vance was asking Violet when Juliet managed to focus on her present predicament again.

"Yes, let me just get the assessment loaded . . . there we are."

"Lydia?" Vance asked, turning to Juliet.

"Ready."

"Begin postprocedure assessment A214.2," Vance said.

"The first color will appear in three . . . two . . . one . . . begin," Violet said, and Juliet closed her eyes, concentrating on an image of Violet, just as before.

Even more quickly than the first time, Juliet saw, in the darkness of her closed eyes, an image take shape, like a slightly blurry window, in which Violet's datapad display appeared, the way she must see it in front of her. She didn't spend time reading through the spreadsheet or looking at the readout for the cap she was wearing; she just noted the color, said, "Blue," and opened her eyes, letting her concentration drop.

Juliet had thought about how many she should get correct and decided to match the highest score she'd seen on the spreadsheet the last time—that Masingil fellow had gotten nine correct, and she figured it would be safe to do the same. While she paused, giving the color time to change, she subvocalized to Angel, "Did you notice anything just now?"

"Yes, the currents through the lattice spiked for a few seconds. It's back to normal now."

"Perfect," Juliet subvocalized, then closed her eyes and repeated the process. She supposed it was possible she was suffering from delusions; she could be totally insane. There was a chance she was hearing imaginary voices and seeing some imaginary view of Violet's screen—some kind of subconsciously generated image of what her delusional mind thought she wanted to see. Considering Vance and Violet weren't likely to share the results with her, she doubted she'd know anytime soon.

Despite those unsettling thoughts, Juliet carefully repeated the process of guessing the colors nineteen more times, announcing them one by one and being sure to say the correct answer only nine times. When Violet proclaimed that the test was over, she reached up, rubbed at her head, and offered a bright smile to the two scientists, finding it easy to show cheerfulness when she took in their glum, reserved faces.

"Thank you, Lydia. Violet, follow the same debriefing protocol as subject forty-three." Vance stood, nodded briefly, then left the room.

"He didn't seem happy. Did I fail?"

"No. Not at all. You did quite well, in fact. I believe he and I had some unreasonable expectations." Violet sighed.

"Really? Why?"

"Just a moment," Violet said, unplugging the cable that led to the cap Juliet was wearing. "Please go ahead and remove the sensor net; we didn't note anything alarming during the assessment." When Juliet pulled it off and handed it to her, Violet wrapped the cable around it and set it on the table. "Okay, let's see here." She looked at her tablet screen and then spoke, "I have a sort of script I have to follow; then, if you have any questions, I can try to answer them."

"All right."

"Ahem." Violet cleared her throat before reading from her screen. "Test subject Roman, you've been equipped with a prototype Grave Industries Psionic Enhancement Lattice, hereafter referred to as a GIPEL."

"A what now?"

"Please"—Violet held up her hand—"let me finish." When Juliet nodded, she continued, "The GIPEL is intended to improve the latent abilities of humans with regard to sensing the intent and emotive behavior in other humans and, tangentially, other thinking and feeling beings." Violet paused and took a breath, glancing briefly at Juliet, who'd done her best to affect an expression of disbelief.

"The GIPEL has shown great promise but has varying levels of efficacy. You can rest assured that the device is not harmful in any way, and regardless of its effectiveness, you won't suffer any adverse reactions. That being said, it's imperative that you remember you are part of a critical and highly classified Grave Industries program. There are protocols you'll need to follow." Again, Violet paused, and this time, she locked eyes with Juliet. "Please make sure your PAI takes note of the next section."

"Okay."

"You are to resume your normal duties, but you must file a report with GARD every twenty-four hours. Your watchdog will have the template for you to complete, but it's crucial that you take note of any of the following: pain that you would describe as an abnormal headache, hearing voices that do not have an apparent origin, noting out-of-place images which might seem like hallucinations, having intrusive thoughts, feelings that you would describe as strong gut reactions, especially when they prove to be accurate, and finally, anything else that you would describe as unusual or beyond the scope of your lived experience up to this point."

"What the hell?" Juliet said, but Violet ignored her and kept reading.

"You will likely be called to GARD for further testing, and it's imperative that you report immediately. GARD has top priority in your immediate chain of command, and only Executive Three or higher Grave employees can countermand a GARD request for your presence. Under no circumstances are you to divulge any knowledge of this GARD program to any individual not employed by Grave, or any Grave employee ranked below Executive Three. Do you have any questions?"

"I sure as hell do," Juliet said, feeling she could let some of her "play nice" attitude drop now that she knew they were going to put her back into her usual employment routine.

"Go ahead; I'll answer what I'm allowed to."

"So, what? Are you guys trying to make me psychic? Why did you have 'high hopes' for me?"

"You did really well on the pre-op assessments, especially the shape categorization; while you labeled those shapes, we had a control subject doing the same in the next room—you labeled the same as he did to a nonstandard degree."

"And the psychic nonsense?"

"Humans have exhibited anecdotal tendencies in that area for our entire natural history. We believe we've isolated the parts of the brain responsible for those behaviors, and the nanites built a latticework within your cerebral matter which amplifies and connects them. Well, that's the goal, and you may doubt it, but your tests indicate some improvement. Of course, this sample is minuscule, just a new baseline, and we'll need to run more tests and gather data—the reports you must fill out—to make a proper assessment, but we're still hopeful."

"And it won't hurt me?" Juliet reached up a hand to rub at her forehead— she'd noticed a weird, fuzzy tingling there while she'd done the color test, and now while she'd been concentrating on listening to Violet.

"No! The nanites themselves were risky, though with your compatibility test, only slightly. The latticework is a new material that Grave designed. I can tell you it's called biosilver—a Grave patent—and its two primary ingredients are silver, of course, and your own biological matter. There's minimal risk of rejection, and it's flexible and thoroughly attached—grown, really—to your cerebral matter."

"And you've done long-term studies on its safety?"

"Certainly. On hyper-aged, anatomically similar mammals."

Juliet frowned; she recognized bullshit when she heard it, and on a whim, she allowed her eyes to close before focusing on an image of Violet.

Will this day ever end? Accept it—you're a lab rat now.

Juliet almost said, "So I'm a lab rat now?" but she caught herself. Instead, she said, "How often am I going to have to come in for tests? This whole thing seems like bullshit, to be honest."

Violet frowned and glanced at the cameras. "I wish you wouldn't say that. Others felt that way, even some with worse results on their baseline, and they're starting to believe. We'll have you in every few days for tests, but for now, you should go home and get some rest. I bet you're exhausted."

"All right. And I'm free to go about my business? Will I get a new assignment for tomorrow?"

"Yes. Keep an eye on your watchdog. By the way, its perimeter setting has been adjusted to the building; for now, we'd rather you didn't leave the tower unless you're on assignment. Will that be a problem?"

"Uh, yeah." Juliet frowned. "What if I want to meet a friend or go out to eat or something when I'm off duty?"

"It's just for now, Lydia. The perimeter will be relaxed as we gather more and more data."

Juliet frowned, stood up from her seat, and then turned to the door. "Can I leave? Or do you need to cuff me first or something?"

"No, you're free to go. Please remember your daily reports. The watchdog will—"

"Remind me—I get it." Juliet opened the door and stepped out. She strode down the long, quiet hallway, noting that only one guard remained and didn't follow her. She wondered why he'd stuck around, then figured they wanted to give Violet some backup in case Juliet had gone ballistic when she heard the disclosure and the answers to her questions.

"We'll have no trouble bypassing the watchdog's new restrictions," Angel said as she neared the elevators.

"I know, Angel. Imagine if they found out what I can really do, though. I don't even know everything I can do, but if they knew what I'd seen already . . . God, they'd have me locked away so deep . . ."

"We could leave now. I can start your implants changing to a new identity. You could be on a shuttle off-world in a couple of days . . ."

"Not a chance, Angel. Not yet. We're going to ride this out a while to learn more, and you and I are going to gain access to Grave's secure net. I want to know how many people are like me, and I want to know how much Vance and his team know. More than that, I want to put a stop to it—imagine if they sold this tech to WBD or Cybergen or some other dirty—no, *evil* corp. We're going to burn it down before we leave."

26

\\\\\\\\\\\\\\\\\\\\\

INTRUSIVE THOUGHTS

Juliet was just stepping off the elevator to return to her room when the watchdog app began to blink, and before Angel could alert her, she selected it to see what was going on. A message was waiting for her.

Lydia Roman:

Tomorrow, you are to report to the reception area on B20 at 1000 for further evaluations. The dress code is your daily active uniform.

Gray Vance

GARD Director of Special Projects

Grave Industries, Inc.

"Oh, brother!" Juliet sighed, increasing her pace in irritation. "I thought I'd get a day or two before they called me in."

"At least you can take your time in the morning," Angel said, her tone clearly aimed to soothe.

"Yeah. I need to work out some frustration; we'll go to the gym."

That night, Juliet tried to sleep early; she ate, showered, washed her clothes, then climbed into bed and, with a heavy sigh, closed her eyes. Usually, she'd try to read or watch a show or even just chat with Angel before calling it a night and trying to drift off, but she was too tired for any of that, and she still felt a little funny—strange—in her head.

Once she'd lain there for a few minutes, silently staring into the black behind her eyelids, though, she was met with thoughts that raced around and wouldn't give her any peace: what was she going to do about this whole mess?

Those people had put some kind of permanent structure into her brain! It wasn't so much that there was something new in her head; she had enough implants not to be overly bothered about that. It was more the idea that they'd done it despite her objections. To put an ugly turn of phrase to the situation, they'd violated her.

"I want to say raped, but violated is probably more accurate," she subvocalized, well aware that Kent was watching and listening.

"Are you dwelling on what they did to you on B20?" Angel asked.

"Of course I am!"

"It must be a horrible feeling having your autonomy removed. I'm used to being somewhat at the mercy of my host—you. I believe some acceptance of that is also built into my personality, but you don't have that benefit. I'm sorry you had to go through that, Juliet."

"I was lying here trying to sleep, and I found I was gritting my teeth and scowling. Angel, I couldn't think of why I was so angry at first, but then I thought about what it felt like to be strapped into that bed, to have that drill penetrate my skull, and then to suffer that godawful pain. I can't forgive them. I can't forgive Violet and Doctor Vance, but I can't forgive Grave, either. I want to make them pay for this, and I want them to think twice about doing that sort of thing ever again."

"Understood. We'll think of something."

"God, I'm so glad I have you. I'd be losing it right now if I was alone with just a simple PAI like Tig."

"I'm glad I have you too, Juliet."

Having vented a little, and with Angel's rather sweet words of support in mind, Juliet closed her eyes again and found herself drifting into sleep. Then, as if he were right next to her, she heard a man's voice. *Not again! Fucking hell, why is this damn thing blinking again?*

Juliet's eyes shot open, and she rolled off her bed to her apartment's stiff, high-traffic carpeting. She crouched there, heart racing. "What's the matter, Juliet?" Angel sounded genuinely puzzled.

"I just heard a man's voice," she subvocalized.

"Ms. Roman, is aught amiss?" Kent asked.

"No, why?" She stood up and stretched, cracking her neck.

"I thought you seemed alarmed."

"No, I'm just practicing some readiness drills. Don't mind me." Juliet stood in her bedroom doorway, looking around her apartment from the kitchen to the window, then over into her little bathroom. Nothing was out of place, and she began to connect the dots. Somehow, when she had started to relax into sleep, she'd *received* someone's thoughts. She lay back down, an uneasy qualm in her gut, and pulled her sheet and thin blanket up to her chin, tucking her head deep into her pillow. "Zero lights, please, Kent."

Kent didn't respond, but the dim strips of nightlights illuminating the baseboards on the way to the bathroom winked out, and her window snapped into opacity, completely blocking the city's lights. Juliet lay there, staring at the now dark ceiling in the darkened space, very cognizant of the LEDs glowing and blinking from the various electronics around the room. Still, when she closed her eyes, she was submerged in perfect black, and once again, she started to drift into sleep.

How will I ever finish? I'll be running drills all morning if Gordon asks for this report.

This time, the voice was feminine, and Juliet thought she might recognize it. Was it Delma? "God, poor thing," she subvocalized. "I think Delma's stuck with Gordon this week. Makes me less annoyed about reporting back to GARD tomorrow."

"You heard another voice?" Angel asked, and her own voice was strained with concern. Did she think her host was losing her mind? Juliet would have laughed if she weren't starting to feel a rising sense of panic—how would she ever get any sleep?

"I'm going to try to sleep again." Juliet closed her eyes, focused on the darkness, and imagined herself floating out over the city, wondering where her imagination would take her, hoping she was conjuring a dream. In just a few seconds, she felt her heavy exhaustion pulling at her, and she drifted away.

Don't look at it. Don't look at it. Oh, God! Why again? Why are they sending me messages now? I haven't had a night off in three goddamn weeks!

Juliet's eyes snapped open, and she flipped over, putting her face into the pillow and screaming.

"I'm getting worried," Angel said.

"You and me both." Juliet jerked her covers off, hopped out of bed, and began to pace around her apartment in the darkness. The LEDs from her charging station sufficiently illuminated the counter so she didn't walk into it. "They're probably watching me right now."

"I can play a loop of you sleeping for the watchdog."

"Not just the watchdog. Kent. I'm sure there are cameras and sensors in this apartment. I bet that prick has people watching me to see if there's anything else going on with the GRIPEL thing."

"GIPEL: Grave Industries Psionic—"

"Whatever!" Juliet snapped, her lack of sleep and a mounting fear that she'd never get a decent night's rest having frayed her nerves beyond the point of polite conversation.

"I'm sorry, Juliet. You may be right, though. Perhaps you should avoid acting out in your frustration."

Angel's words, while spoken out of kindness and concern, only served to fuel her frustration; Juliet wanted to vent, wanted to rant, and wanted to repeat the words "avoid acting out" in a mocking tone, but nothing she did would go unnoticed. She balled up her fists and calmly walked into her bathroom, where she shut the door and then turned on the shower—cost be damned.

She stripped out of her underwear and tank top and climbed into the shower, standing under the hot spray, letting it drum down on her scalp as she repeatedly thumped her fist against the plastic tiles of the shower stall. To their credit, Grave had built the shower quite sturdily; whatever water-resistant backer they'd put up behind the tiles absorbed her blows nicely, and she could barely hear the thuds of her knuckles with each satisfying crunch.

After a while, she stopped punching and held her hand under the water, washing off a bit of blood where her middle knuckle had split. The sting helped to ground her, and she closed her eyes and began to breathe, taking in deep breaths and imagining her stress leaving her body with each long, slow exhalation. An idea came to her then, and she said, "Angel, put together a playlist of my top requested songs; the ones I listen to when I'm trying to relax or do some quiet work."

"Done."

"Put it on a loop—background volume." Juliet turned off the shower, suddenly immersed in the soft strings and pleasant voice of a song, one of the ones she'd been turned onto by Hot Mustard. She dried off, pulled on her sleep clothes, then, listening to the gentle voice of a woman named Alice Tennant, she climbed back into bed, put her cheek to her pillow, and continued her breathing exercise.

Sleep must have claimed Juliet and stuck this time because the next thing she was aware of was Angel's gentle alarm. When she looked at the clock on her AUI, it read 0730, and she smiled. "Thanks for letting me sleep in, Angel."

"You don't have to report until 1000 hours, but I knew you wanted to get a workout in. I'm so glad you got to sleep, Juliet!"

"Yeah, it seems my mind needs a distraction to keep it from looking for other voices in the dark. I hope I can figure out how to control this thing better; otherwise, you and I are going to be looking for a brain doc to get this stuff out of my head." Juliet was sure to subvocalize, imagining Kent holding his ear to her door, listening to her every word. She laughed at that—in her mind, Kent was an old English fellow with white hair and a butler's uniform.

She continued subvocalizing as she walked into the bathroom, dragging her bed linens and stuffing them into the wash. "Send a message to Honey: Hey, Honey, I'm so sorry I haven't gotten back to you sooner. I'm okay—just really, *really* closely watched right now. I'm getting deep into this thing, and it's stressing me big, like a cracking H-cell, ya know? I'll figure things out, though. Thank you so much for the heads-up about what Temo heard. Don't worry about me; there's a corp with an unhealthy interest in me, but I'm working to stay a few steps ahead of them. The Luna job sounds . . . interesting and exciting. I hate to say it, but it also sounds suspicious. Please be extra, extra careful. Have Temo do some serious vetting of the client. Much, much love, J."

"Done and sent via the encrypted channel."

"Kent, order me a protein smoothie." Juliet didn't hear his reply as she brushed her teeth, the buzz of her sonic toothbrush drowning him out. She usually liked to brush after breakfast but figured she'd shower after the gym and brush again. She threw her workout clothes on, grabbed her paper cup of fruit protein shake, and hurried down to the main Grave gym, not the one where new Zeta units were put through hell.

It was busy, with many suits getting their workout in before their usual 0900 shift, but she found an empty rower and got to work, wringing the stress from her body with each tug of the chain. She lost herself in the activity, letting her mind wander to Honey and an imagined life on Luna.

Juliet had seen pictures of the domes and the slender silvery towers. She'd seen the parks and engineered streams. She'd gone on VR tours of the spaceport, marveling at the size of the ships that hung outside Luna City's dome. Still, she wondered what it was like in person. "Angel, when we finally leave, let's fly to Luna first and book passage further out from there. Most of the big ships use Luna's docks anyway, right?"

"Yes, that's correct. The size of the larger cruise, cargo, and industrial ships make landing and departing from Earth's gravity well cost-prohibitive or outright impossible."

Juliet finished her rowing, then did a quick circuit on the weight machines. She'd been pumped to get a workout in, but after going hard on the rower, her heart wasn't in it for the weights. She went through the motions, though, trying for heavy weight and low reps just to speed things along.

When she finished on the bench, she lay there for a while, staring at the ceiling, breathing in the unique odor of a weight room—rubber, sweat, metal, oil; almost the same as the welding shop, but lacking the scent of burning metal and gases. She flopped her arms listlessly to the sides, letting her fingers drag on the rubbery floor.

She felt glad she hadn't run into anyone she knew. After the last day or two, she wasn't in the mood for small talk or pretending—she'd have to do plenty of that when she got down to sublevel twenty. She wondered where Charlie Unit was. Did they have a fun assignment, or were they just training? What about her fellow recruits? "Do you think they're all with Gordon? Did I really hear Delma thinking about him last night? God, I feel like I'm losing it, Angel."

"You're not losing it, Juliet." Angel's simple words did more than she might have imagined to shore up Juliet's mental foundations.

She lay there, wondering where her next assignment might be; the idea that she might get another round with Alpha Unit and Commander Gordon made her heart start to race and a feeling of panic begin to surge in her gut. Why did she hate him so much? Juliet wondered at that. Did she hate him, or was it more like dread?

With his image floating around in her mind and her stomach beginning to twist into a knot, she suddenly heard, plain as day, Gordon's voice in her head.

Goddamn, I'd like to plant my face between those cheeks.

"Ew!" she said aloud, almost falling off the bench as adrenaline pumped into her system. She recovered her balance and sat up, her brain making the belated connection that she'd heard his thoughts—he wasn't standing next to her. Juliet looked around the high-ceilinged, wide-open space of the gym, and that's when she spotted Gordon on a treadmill. It wasn't hard to see the object of his intrusive thought, either—a woman running in the next row of machines in front of him. "Angel," she subvocalized. "I'd sure like to find a way to get him demoted or something before we leave this place."

"Perhaps when we gain access to the secure networks, we'll find the personnel files. There might be something we can use."

"Add it to the list." Juliet stood up and made her way out of the gym, careful not to let her mind wander to the commander; the thought of his voice in her head, regardless of what it was saying, was too much to bear. "I knew he was taking too much pleasure in all the extra push-ups and sit-ups he kept giving us—the way he'd stand over us, arms crossed, looking so superior and smug; people like that shouldn't have authority over others."

"What do you mean?" Angel asked.

"I heard his thoughts just now; he's creeping on that woman working out in front of him. I mean, sure, we all have urges, but he's just so damn gross. If you heard him, you'd know what I mean."

"Looking back over your time with Alpha Unit, it does seem that he initiated extra PT as punishment for the female recruits on a more than three-to-one ratio against similar treatment to the males."

Juliet stepped into the elevator, wiping her forehead and face with her towel, and replied, "Okay, I didn't need any more convincing. I know it's petty, and he's a small fry in the greater scheme of things, but I definitely want to figure something out to burn him." The more she thought about it, the more she liked the idea, and Juliet started to wonder if there might be a way to kill two birds with one stone. If she was going to bring down the GIPEL project, maybe she could use a scapegoat.

The elevator dinged, interrupting her musing, and Juliet hurried to her apartment to get cleaned up. She showered, dressed, stuffed a couple of protein bars into her jacket pockets, and carefully palmed her trusty old vibroblade, her personal short-bladed one. She stepped into the bathroom, tucked it into her waistband, and then made her way back to B20 and the reception area for GARD.

She was only a few minutes early, but after the receptionist—a young woman far more pleasant than Bernice—checked her in, she found herself still waiting twenty minutes past her appointment time. "Is everything all right?" she asked, standing up and approaching the window. A few other waiting Grave employees looked up, and one woman frowned in irritation.

"What do you mean?" the cheerful receptionist asked, twirling a strand of her long, feathery brown hair.

"Oh, my appointment was twenty minutes ago."

"They're running a bit behind. Please be patient."

"I've been here longer than you," the woman sitting near the front, the one who'd frowned, said.

Juliet turned to her—took in her uniform, no different from her own, her long straight black hair and mirrored irises, her carefully precise lipstick, eyeliner, and manicured nails. Juliet looked down her nose for a long while and then, without a word, went back to her seat. She could tell it bothered the woman that Juliet hadn't reacted—she stole several quick glances over her shoulder when she thought Juliet wasn't paying attention.

For the first time, Juliet felt the urge to try to listen to a person's thoughts for purely petty reasons, and she had to sit back and take stock of the implications. "Angel, none of this seems real to me yet, but if it is, if I can really hear people's active thoughts, I feel like . . . I feel like it's too much! I'm only human! How am I going to resist being a creep? Taking advantage of people? This is freaking me out!"

"I'm not sure I'm equipped to advise you on this topic. I'm afraid I'll say the wrong thing. It feels almost synonymous with hacking another AI, wouldn't you say?"

Juliet knew Angel meant AI as in pseudo-AI, not the old, true AIs from before the war. "I guess so. Would you do something like that?"

"Only . . . only if it was to protect you or help you in your goals. I wouldn't want to hurt another AI unless it was a malicious actor."

"But who's the judge of that? If I decided that woman was a bitch and I needed to 'teach her a lesson,' I could follow her around, trying to listen to her thoughts until I learned something I could use against her. It's not right!"

"I begin to see why you wouldn't want this tech to fall into the wrong hands."

"Lydia?" Juliet hadn't seen the door open or the woman in the white coat step through. It wasn't Violet; this woman was middle-aged with short red hair. She squinted at Juliet over the top of some old-school, thick-framed glasses, and Juliet wondered at that. Were they just for show—fancy specs like Paul wore—or did she really need corrective lenses? Why wouldn't she get retinal upgrades if her vision was bad?

"Here," she said, standing up and walking toward the door, her introspection and burgeoning crisis of conscience simmering on the back burner.

"This way, Lydia." The woman turned and started walking down the now familiar corridor. Juliet followed, taking a moment to turn and smile at the frowning woman, still seated in the front row. Her scowl deepened, but she didn't say anything.

"That was petty," she subvocalized.

"If you know something's petty, why do you do it?" Angel sounded genuinely curious.

"I don't know." Juliet sighed. When her long strides brought her close to the white-coated woman, she said, "I like your glasses," fishing for an explanation.

"Oh, these?" the woman asked, turning and straightening the frames on her face, a smile turning up the corners of her mouth into her slightly pudgy cheeks. "Thank you! I like their style, and some of my colleagues tease me, but they work just as well as their sleek, boring executive specs."

"Ah, so they're for work?"

"Yes—they can magnify much more than my retinal implants, and they have a data processor that relieves my dear old Lenny." She laughed for a second, then reached back and touched Juliet's forearm in an almost too-friendly gesture. "He's my PAI."

"Ah." Juliet smiled. "So, what's on the menu today? More tests?"

"Exactly! We've got half a dozen assessments lined up, and a few interviews."

"Interviews?"

"Yes, we need to capture your thoughts about what's happening in here"— she, again, reached toward Juliet, but this time, she tapped her on the side of the head—"while you're doing the tests."

"Lovely." Juliet sighed, wondering how much she'd have to fake and, more importantly, how convincing she'd be.

27

///////////////////

EXPLORATIONS

F ollowing the white-coated GARD employee down the hallway, Juliet
suddenly imagined herself being cuffed to a surgical bed while a machine
drilled her head. She knew it wasn't a vision exactly—she was just reacting
to her own fear and stress, but still, she slowed her pace and stared at the
woman in front of her as though she could bore into her head with her eyes,
and really, really tried to *listen*.

She caught her breath with delight and surprise when she heard, clear
as day, *Oh lord, I'm so sick of these endless flashcard tests. Here we go; keep
smiling, and we'll get through it. Lunch in a couple of hours.* Hearing the
woman, bored about conducting tests, allowed Juliet to relax the tension
in her neck and shoulders—she doubted the woman would be thinking
those thoughts if she meant to surprise Juliet with another impromptu
surgical procedure.

Her assumption proved true; they spent the morning repeating the color
test dozens of times. She carefully made sure to keep her number of correct
guesses between five and nine, never wanting to give the GARD employees
reason to single her out as particularly successful. Ursula, the woman with the
old-school glasses frames, sat with her and conducted the exams, somehow
maintaining a cheerful demeanor the entire time.

"This should be the last one," Ursula said on their twenty-seventh run-
through. "It's almost lunchtime, and then you'll have an interview and a different sort of test." The woman had no qualms about chatting during the

tests and never glanced at the camera array, seemingly unconcerned about people watching or about the recordings being made.

"Can you tell me anything about it? The new test, I mean?" Juliet asked, then said, "Blue."

"Right now, you're exercising the lattice's receiving capabilities. We designed it to help you transmit your latent psionic impulses as well; we'll have you try that functionality today." Juliet was concentrating on Ursula, eyes closed, trying to see the next color, so she wasn't surprised when the woman's unspoken thought came through. *What a load of horse manure—I'm due for a promotion, and Vance better watch his back when this whole program goes down.*

"Black," Juliet said, guessing the wrong color. Ursula smiled pleasantly and tapped her screen. "Do you work with Violet and Doctor Vance?"

"Oh yes. Violet requested the day off. I don't blame her, being up to near midnight dealing with that man."

"That man?"

"Vance." For the first time, Ursula looked at the camera and shrugged. "He's a bit much, if you know what I mean."

"Sure. Um . . . white."

"That was the last one! Good job, Lydia. You can wait here. We have a boxed lunch for you, and the interview will be in thirty minutes. Feel free to get up and stretch." Ursula followed her own advice, quickly standing and stepping over to the door. "I probably won't see you anymore today, but I sure enjoyed working with you this morning, Lydia."

"Thanks, Ursula." Juliet smiled—easier to fake with Ursula than the other GARD employees she'd met—and stayed in her seat while she waited for her to walk out. She was just about to stand and stretch when a tapping knock sounded, and the door opened. A young, thin man with a scruffy, sparse goatee stepped in carrying a brown box, much like the one Juliet had been given during orientation.

"Your lunch," he said, setting it on the table. He ducked his head several times as he left, clearly avoiding eye contact. Juliet watched him leave before opening the box. A sandwich, banana, and a cup of pudding sat within. She closed it back up.

"I'll pass," she subvocalized, pulling out one of her protein bars. While Juliet chewed the tough, vanilla-flavored concoction which tended to stick to her teeth, she closed her eyes and tried to clear her mind, wondering if she could pick up any thoughts nearby. She listened to herself chew and swallow

several times, but no thoughts came to her, and she continued to subvocalize, "Angel, Ursula didn't act like anyone was watching the camera today. If I
get you a direct connection, what are the odds you can hack the surveillance
network to delete the footage of me messing with it?"

"Excellent odds—it's only a matter of time. If I fail before someone comes,
though, the footage will remain. What would we gain? I don't know if there's
any way to remain connected wirelessly, even after hacking the network, so
we'd only have a short window of access."

"You could record everything on this camera network for a couple of
minutes," Juliet said, standing up. "It might give us an idea for a better attack
vector. The truth is, though, that I'm worried about this scanner array. What
if they're scanning me to see if I'm lying on these tests?"

"That would, indeed, be problematic. You might be in trouble as soon as
someone analyzes the footage."

"Exactly." Juliet feigned stretching, doing some long, slow lunges to bring
herself around the table. When she was in the corner beneath the camera and
sensor array, she glanced up, looking for the cable port. She didn't see it, so
she subvocalized, "Where's the port?"

"They have a locked plasteel shroud over the data port . . ."

"Damn," Juliet hissed, nearly silently, then reached into her belt and
tugged out her vibroblade, watching its virtually invisible edge shimmer with
its hyperoscillations as she reached it up to the plasteel shroud where a tiny
crack indicated a latch. She slipped the blade in, wincing as the high-pitched
sound of the edge slicing through plasteel filled the air. Juliet tugged it along
the seam until she felt the resistance give way as the latch was severed. More
quickly than was probably safe, Juliet jerked her knife free and slipped it into
the sheath in her waistband.

"Get ready," she subvocalized, then, for good measure, completed another
circuit of the little room, moving around the table, lifting her arms, stretching, and sighing as she rolled her neck. When she was beneath the array
again, she quickly yanked her data cable out of her arm and stretched onto
her tiptoes. She flicked the—now unlocked—shroud open and stuffed her
data line into the exposed port. That done, she hugged the wall, waiting for
Angel to work her magic.

The seconds stretched into a minute, stretched into three, and Juliet
began to wonder if this had been a massive mistake when Angel said, "I'm
in. This network only covers this floor. It's monitored through a centralized
terminal. I'm replacing the footage of your activities with a longer loop of

you doing lunges around the room. I'm downloading footage from all of the cameras."

"How long?"

"There are six months of footage; to get it all will take me about nine minutes."

"Just start with the most recent and work your way back." Juliet closed her eyes and tried to clear her mind, willing herself to *hear* nearby thoughts. She stood there in self-imposed darkness for a minute or two, listening to the ticking of the air circulation. Suddenly, out of nowhere, she heard a man's voice. *Let's see, B2056, B2057—just a couple more doors.*

Juliet reached up, pulled her cord out, let it retract, and carefully pressed the shroud latch back into place. She resumed her long, stretching steps around the room as Angel said, "I wasn't finished."

"I think someone's coming," she subvocalized.

"Well, I got most of the last month's footage," Angel replied. Juliet grunted her acknowledgment, and she'd just made her way around the table when a knock sounded. The handle twisted, the door opened, and a very tall, stoop-shouldered man leaned his head through the gap. He had long brown hair and was clearly going bald, but he didn't seem to care. He looked unkempt, from his wild eyebrows to his loose tie to the stains that looked like coffee on his white coat.

"Knock knock!" He grinned and slipped through the door, never opening it more than a foot. Juliet stood still, one hand resting on the tabletop.

"Getting some stretches in, I see?"

"Right. Been sitting a while already today . . ."

"Right, right! Shall we do your debriefing standing? I don't mind!" He leaned forward, clasping his hands in front of himself, clearly doing everything he could to seem friendly. Juliet liked him immediately, and she hated herself for it. She must have frowned at the thought because he continued, taking a step back and holding out his hands placatingly. "No, no, stupid idea! I'm Doctor Hoyt, by the way. Come, have a seat. This will be the easiest part of your day; you have my promise." He gestured to the empty chair Juliet had vacated.

Juliet sat and said, "I thought I'd have thirty minutes for lunch."

"Am I early?" Hoyt asked, holding a hand to his chest and looking alarmed. "Oh, dear! I just got a notification that you finished your color test and that I could come in. Do you mind terribly if we get this going? You can eat while we talk."

"Go ahead." Juliet shrugged. Hoyt sat across from her and produced a tablet just like Ursula and Violet had used. Juliet wondered what she could find out if she got her hands on one of those. "Angel," she subvocalized, "while this guy's chatting with me, I want you to start examining the video files you stole. See if you can start putting together a map of this level. I want to know where Doctor Vance and Violet have their offices."

"I've already begun that process."

"You know, I love you, Angel . . ."

"We'll start with one question, and then I'll follow up based on your answer. Is that all right?"

Juliet had almost tuned out Hoyt as she conversed with Angel. She jerked her head up and made eye contact with him, saying, "Yes."

"Okay, please describe what you see or feel when trying to guess the colors in the color-match assessment."

"What I see and feel? Nothing really. I close my eyes to try to concentrate, but I just kind of say the first color that comes to my mind. I don't feel anything, really."

"You don't see any flashes of color or hear any voice that might urge you to pick a certain color?"

"No."

"Hmm." Hoyt nodded, tapping away at his device for a moment, and then he said, "So you don't feel any changes since your procedure at all?"

"I passed out yesterday and had a bit of a headache afterward, but nothing unusual today."

"Okay, could you describe your headache?"

"Just some pressure, right here." Juliet tapped the base of her skull, having decided to describe a regular headache, not the weird, tingling, fuzzy feeling she'd had behind her forehead.

"Very good, mm-hmm." He tapped on his screen again. "And that's gone now?"

"Yes, I felt totally normal after a good night's sleep." Juliet shrugged. She hoped the camera array didn't have anyone watching in real-time, trying to determine if she was lying. She hoped they didn't scan for that at all, but she knew it would be stupid if they didn't. They had to be watching her heart rate, respirations, body temperature, and micro musculature movements. They probably had a sensor monitoring her synaptic patterns. No, Juliet decided, if she really wanted to fool these people, she needed to get access to that data.

"All right. You're aware that you'll have a daily report to fill out going forward, yes? After we get you through another sort of assessment, you'll be back to regular duty, but we do want those reports. Is all of that clear?"

"Yes. Just as clear as it was yesterday when Violet read me her script." For a brief moment, Juliet contemplated reaching out with her enhanced arm and slamming Hoyt's forehead into the table. She could hack his datapad, reconnect to the camera system, hide the footage, and get out before anyone saw what she'd done. Her arm twitched, and she almost tried to do what she'd been visualizing, but then he smiled and swallowed, his overlarge Adam's apple bobbing with the motion, and she couldn't bring herself to do it.

"Your next exam will be in this room, and, as you said, I was a bit early coming in, so there might be a bit of a wait."

"Oh? Is your office nearby?" Juliet stood and offered a handshake, trying to stall so she could fish for information.

"No, no. I'm a few hallways removed." Hoyt took her hand, squeezing it gently and smiling the first genuine smile Juliet felt she'd received from a GARD employee. Suddenly, she was very glad she hadn't smashed his head into the table.

"How much time do you think I'll have? Is there a restroom nearby?"

"Oh, yes. Hmm, probably upward of twenty minutes. There's a restroom in the procedure room down the hall. B2037, I believe."

"Can I just, like, go?"

"Sure, I'll walk you. When you finish, please head back here ASAP—like I said, you've got one more test this afternoon, and the watchdog will get cranky if you're not in the correct location."

"Okay." Juliet followed Doctor Hoyt down the hall to the room with an adjoining bathroom—she couldn't tell if it was the same one she'd had her procedure in, but it looked identical. He didn't follow her into the room, and she paused by the door for several seconds until she heard him move off. Angel had upped the gain on her audio implants without her asking, and for the millionth time, Juliet found herself amazed at the PAI's intuitiveness.

"Okay, Angel. How about a map? You know where Violet's office is?" A small map appeared in her AUI with her position marked by a blinking blue dot. The hallways were marked out clearly, and a dotted line indicated the direction she needed to move. "Here's hoping the guy watching the cameras isn't too alert today." She stepped out into the hallway and started following Angel's directions.

When she made the first turn, a white-coated woman was approach-ing, her eyes focused on her datapad as she walked, and Juliet kept moving, holding her breath in anxious anticipation. The woman never looked at her. Another turn brought her to a hallway with green-painted doors rather than orange, and each was marked with a nameplate. "Bingo," she said, hurrying toward the third door on the left—Violet Harris's office.

The door was locked, but Juliet saw a data port in the biolock and quickly inserted her cable. If Angel was good at anything, it was busting lock encryp-tions, and she popped that door faster than Juliet could silently breathe her ABCs. When she heard the click, she pushed down the door handle and slipped through, carefully latching the door behind her.

Violet's office was dark, but Juliet's implants brightened things up, and she saw a cluttered desk, an old-fashioned file cabinet, and a bookshelf; the office was the size of a large closet. "Ugh," she grunted, moving over to the desk. "I was hoping she'd left her datapad in here."

"There's a network port behind the desk, Juliet," Angel said, and suddenly, a red circle flashed on her AUI, showing it to her. "They likely don't allow those datapads to have wireless connections to their server. Each employee probably has to connect physically to download and upload to their databases."

"Perfect!" Juliet quickly moved around the desk, crouching behind it to plug her cable into the port. "How's it look?"

"The ICE is formidable. I'll get through, though; I learned a thing or two when combatting the camera system's defenses."

While Angel worked, Juliet turned and started pulling out Violet's draw-ers, peeking within. She found lots of memo pads with neat, hand-written notations, mostly numbers without any sort of reference or key. She kept dig-ging, and in the bottom left drawer, Juliet found a page from a notebook torn out and covered in dense writing. She unfolded it and frowned, suddenly less angry at Violet. It was one repeated sentence, written over and over in tiny, block letters. "I HATE MY LIFE."

"I've gained access, Juliet!"

"Great! Step one, make sure they don't have any reason to second-guess my identity or answers in the test rooms."

"I'm searching the databases for references to you."

Juliet watched the clock on her AUI, growing increasingly tense as the minutes ticked by; they'd already been out of her testing room for eleven minutes. "Don't forget to fix the cameras to not show any of this little field trip."

"That's already done. I've set a daemon that will wipe thirty minutes of footage for the whole floor. It will perform its function in fifteen minutes before destroying itself."

"Won't that raise suspicion?"

"Yes, but not of you specifically. I'm sorry, but I don't have enough time to edit all the camera feeds you were caught in. Nor any way to edit them after you make your way back to the interview room unless we reconnect to the camera in—"

"I get it. Don't worry."

"I've found the sensor array data for you. There are many red flags, but I'm normalizing the results. I also found a flag their pseudo-AI raised regarding how you were able to time your responses to the color shifts—normalizing."

"Good . . ."

"I found your DNA sample in a database; it doesn't match Lydia Roman's. I'm fixing it."

"Holy shit! I forgot about that!" Juliet thought for a minute. "Can you fit the databases in your memory?"

"Only if I delete most of the footage from the cameras."

"Go ahead; grab those databases and also as much as you can on the GARD employees." A sudden thought occurred to her, and she added, "I'm not sure we're done here, but just in case we can't get back, can you hide a daemon in their server that will delete everything if we don't intervene in, say, a week?"

"Everything?"

"Yep."

"Yes, but they likely have physical backups, Juliet."

"Ugh, good point. Okay, I'll keep thinking about that one. Do it anyway, though; it might cause some havoc when we need it."

Angel replied, her voice a little strained, "I had the idea to write a daemon that will automatically normalize any future scan or test result data they record about you. This will take me approximately five minutes to do correctly in a manner that won't be detected, and I don't think I can do the other one simultaneously. Not without risking error. Do you want me to drop this and create the server-wiping daemon instead?"

"No. Your idea is smarter." Juliet gently thumped her knuckles against her forehead while she waited. Angel was right; if she were going to avoid trouble, she needed these squints to think she was being honest in their little tests and interviews. She'd need to devise a more permanent plan to destroy the GIPEL program data, anyway; it would be crazy to assume GARD didn't keep physical backups.

"I'm finished, Juliet. I have the databases and have installed the daemon."

Juliet yanked her data cable out, stood up, and by the time the line had retracted back into her wrist, she was already peeking out the door. "You have biometric data on the GARD employees?" she subvocalized while she slipped back into the hallway.

"Yes."

"Start programming one of my fingers to match Vance's print; I don't wanna get stuck behind any more doors."

"Excellent idea!"

Juliet rounded the corner to the next hallway and almost walked straight into a white-coated GARD technician. Using her newly acquired data, Angel helpfully supplied the man's name, placing a tag above his head. "Oops! Excuse me, Larry," Juliet said, sidestepping and waving him by.

"Oh, uh, no worries."

"I like that tie, Larry," Juliet added; she really did—it was bright yellow with little blue birds, brightening his otherwise clinically boring attire.

"Oh? Thanks!" His face lit up noticeably as he turned and continued on his way.

"All right, Angel," Juliet subvocalized, hurrying back toward her testing room. "Let's go see what kind of crazy thing they expect me to do next."

28

\\\\\\\\\\\\\\\\\\\\\\\\\\

A FRIEND IN NEED

So, you want me to try to get you to see what I'm looking at on this?" Juliet asked, glancing at the card she'd drawn from the deck, a sheep with fluffy black wool.

"That's right," Doctor Vance said. Juliet had been more than disappointed to see the man walk through her door—she'd had an almost visceral reaction to his appearance, a sense of nausea that reminded her very clearly of just how much he'd wronged her. She thought about that, about her conclusion that he'd harmed her. She knew she was right; even if whatever they did to her turned out to be a huge benefit to her in the long run, they didn't have the right to force such a thing on her.

She'd already determined that she wouldn't try to succeed on this test. "Alright," she replied. "Say when."

"Begin," Vance spoke loudly, projecting his voice to the camera array and tapping at his datapad.

"Angel," Juliet subvocalized, "block out this card from my vision." Angel complied, creating a square of blackness in her AUI that entirely obscured the card she was holding. Juliet stared at the black square and tried to concentrate, thinking about Vance—she wasn't going to do his little test, but she wouldn't mind seeing what the jerk was thinking.

Several seconds ticked by, and he cleared his throat and fidgeted but remained silent. He opened his mouth as though to speak but closed it again, and then she heard him, clear as day. *I'm never going to get my funding renewed.*

Sharon's going to leave me. Funding, funding. Why haven't I heard back from the board?

"Hmm," he said aloud, "is it a barn?"

Juliet set the black sheep card on the table. "Sorry . . ." She almost did feel sorry for him—he looked so discouraged, especially after hearing his demoralized thoughts. Almost. All she had to do was remember how he and Violet had bound and drugged her and drilled into her skull with experimental nanites to find her earlier lack of sympathy.

"No, no. You're doing your best, I'm sure. Let's keep going."

"Okay." Juliet pulled another card, a red car, and again stared at the black void Angel covered it with while she tried to hear Vance's thoughts. *God, nothing? At least Masingil made Violet's head tingle.*

"A red . . . crayon?" He enthusiastically nodded when Juliet put the card on the table. "Looks like I might have gotten an impression of the color, at least!"

"Yay!" Juliet smiled, but anyone who knew her would have seen the emotion wasn't reflected in her eyes; she felt like a mouse who'd found a way to torment a cat. She drew another card—a green car this time—and asked, "Do you have a family, Doctor?"

"Please concentrate on the card, Lydia. Try to *will* me to see what you're seeing!"

"Right, sorry," Juliet said, staring at nothing and listening. *Concentrate, you daft girl! How can you be so bad at this? Your lattice is three times as extensive as the next closest candidate!*

Another voice came to her almost at the same time. *When I get off, I'm going to load up a session with Faye the Fox, and I don't care if Leonard sees it on our charge summary!* A tingling pressure behind her eyes accompanied the second voice, and Juliet snapped her eyes open, purposefully immersing herself in the visual stimuli of the room, trying to "turn off" her reception of stray thoughts. The tingling faded, and she exhaled slowly, relieved.

"Your lattice spiked with activity for a moment, Juliet, and your temperature began to rise. It seems to have passed." Angel's voice was clinical, but Juliet could imagine some strain and worry behind the words.

Vance's face was contorted with concentration, and a corner of Juliet's mouth quirked up as she waited. Finally, he said, "I just received a message from my lab tech; I'm supposed to note my guesses on the tablet, not say them aloud. Apparently, I can negatively impact your concentration if you see whether I'm getting them right or wrong." He paused, rubbed at his chin, and continued, "I'm not the one who normally administers these tests, but I'm running a bit short-staffed today. My apologies."

"Oh. It's all right, Dr. Vance." Juliet shrugged, wondering if that meant she'd have to spend even more time with him as he reset the evaluation.

"In any case, I've blown this test. We'll do a repeat in a day or two. Let's pack it in for now. Please see yourself out through reception; we'll message you when we're ready for more assessments."

"Do I need to report to any other department, or . . ."

"No, you've got the afternoon free as far as I'm concerned. Remain in the building, though; the watchdog still has you on closed perimeter duty until your direct commander meets with you and reassesses." He didn't wait for Juliet to reply or even to stand. She'd opened her mouth to ask a follow-up question, but he quickly walked toward the door and out. She closed her mouth, shrugged to herself, and said, "Bye . . ."

By the time Juliet entered the hallway, Vance was gone, and she had the distinct impression he'd cut the test short because he had fires to put out elsewhere. "I wish I could pick up thoughts faster; I would have liked to know what he was thinking when he stormed out of here," she subvocalized as she started on her way out.

"My daemon would have deleted the surveillance data a few minutes ago. Perhaps the gap was noticed, and he was alerted." Juliet smiled, imagining the panic taking place in Vance's mind.

"I hope that was it," she subvocalized, no small part of her wanting to be responsible for Vance's bad mood. She'd barely reached the elevator and was on her way up when her watchdog began to blink.

"Ugh!" she groaned. "They can't give me a break!" Her words reminded her of what she'd heard while trying to sleep—the man's voice who'd been upset that something was "blinking again," and suddenly, she knew what he'd been thinking about. While the elevator surged upward, she selected the app and read the message.

Lydia Roman: Report to Commander Garza's office #7690 ASAP.

Juliet wondered at the concise message and its lack of a signature. "Am I in trouble?" she subvocalized.

"I don't know. I don't see how they could suspect you of anything; we've deleted all evidence of your intrusion on sublevel twenty."

"Huh." Juliet reached for the elevator controls, only to see that her destination had already been changed; she was fast approaching floor seventy-six. "Of course they'd know I was in the elevator," she said as the chime sounded

and the doors opened. She peered into the wide hallway, saw a few suits
walking into another open elevator, and stepped out. Nothing happened;
nobody assaulted her, no alarms went off, and more importantly—to Juliet—
she didn't feel anything amiss.

"Angel, do you think I have good gut instincts? I feel like I've had a lot
of false alarms, like when I almost walked out of Doc Murphy's clinic . . ."

"I don't know, Juliet. That sort of thing is beyond my scope of understanding, and I'm not sure you always tell me when you have a *gut feeling*, as
you often put it. If you can be sure to report such feelings to me, I can start to
gather empirical data on your gut's accuracy."

Juliet laughed and shook her head as she walked to the left, following the
numbers toward the correct office. Several suits passed her in the hallways,
but none of them gave her the time of day or even a second glance, serving
to put her even more at ease by the time she came to the closed, faux-wood
door with the nameplate reading, "Commander Cherise Garza - Training
Coordinator."

She stood in front of the door for a minute, hesitating. "What if this is the
next shoe to drop? What if they arrest me in there?"

"Why not try to use your GIPEL?" Angel asked.

Juliet nodded, scrunching her eyes closed, but before she started to concentrate, she subvocalized, "Please don't call it that. It sounds stupid."

"What should I—"

"Do some brainstorming. For now, let me concentrate." Juliet tried to
blank her mind, concentrating on how she remembered Cherise Garza—her
brightly colored slacks and blouse, her bulky shoulders and short black hair,
the tweak in the bridge of her nose and darkly tanned skin . . .

The door opened, and Juliet popped her eyes open to see the woman she'd
been trying to picture staring at her. "Are you going to stand out there all day,
Roman?"

"Sorry! I have a headache and was trying to calm my nerves before coming in."

"Another headache? I was just reading a report about the one you suffered
yesterday."

"Um, yeah, er, yes, ma'am. It started to come on a few minutes ago. I think
I need to eat more."

"Yes, I also read the report from this morning. You didn't touch your
lunch box?"

"Oh. Is that why I'm here? I didn't realize I had to eat those . . ."

"No, that's not why you're here. Come in, and take a seat." Cherise backed out of the doorway and walked back to her desk. Juliet followed, looking around, admiring the dozens of ancient paperback books with frayed bindings, colorful images, and fancy lettering that the commander had on display behind plastiglass shells. Were those fantasy novels? No, one of them depicted a woman in a spacesuit holding a massive rifle . . .

"Sit down, Roman." Juliet jumped at the words, jerking her head away from the display cases and moving quickly to sit in one of the two faux-leather seats in front of Cherise's desk. "Okay." The commander paused, rubbed at the back of her neck, glanced over to the antique books, and said, "Sorry, let's get through this. At our next meeting, I'll schedule some time to tell you about my favorites; I love seeing others interested in quality fiction."

"Oh, thank you, Commander."

Cherise nodded. "Seems like GARD wants to keep you under their umbrella for a while, but they're going to loosen their strings enough for me to put you through some more training. We've had to scrap our plans to create a new Zeta unit. We just don't have the bodies right now—had a casualty on an operation a few nights ago, and two of your fellow recruits washed out."

"Which . . ."

"Lopez and Foster."

"Really? They seemed to be scoring the highest on all the practicals during our first week; Gordon loved those guys."

"*Commander* Gordon." Cherise frowned, her eyes going distant for a moment, then she continued, "Well, one of them lied on their application—fabricated some conflict records and . . . what am I doing? Roman, suffice to say that we're down some personnel, and I'll be placing you and your remaining comrades into active Zeta units after I'm satisfied with your training."

"Yes, ma'am."

"So, I've got you in here for a couple of reasons. I want to give you your next assignment, effective tomorrow at 0600, and I also wanted to hear from you. We haven't spoken since week one, but I've been keeping close tabs. Tell me how you're doing. Did those squints mess you up too much? Be careful, though—don't forget your NDA." She tapped her temple in the universal Grave signal meant to remind each other about the watchdog. Still, it was strange seeing it coming from her commander.

Juliet nodded. "I'm doing well, ma'am. Week one was very stressful, but week two was actually a lot of fun—I like Charlie Unit a lot. This week has been . . . strange." She shrugged as if to say she couldn't go into it in detail.

"*Right.*" Cherise nodded as she said the word, dragging it out for the space of several heartbeats. "I've read good things in your reports, Roman. You've been hitting the PT hard, even when you're not on direct orders. You've been to the range, and you handled yourself like a pro on that bug hunt Charlie was sent on."

"Thank you, ma'am." Juliet didn't have to fake her smile and couldn't have faked the happy flush that lit up her face.

"No, thank you, Recruit. When I have new hires perform the way you have been, it makes me look good. All of this brings me to your next assignment; I'm putting you back with Charlie Unit, and they have a priority one counterespionage raid tomorrow morning. Do you think you're up for it?"

"I . . . yes, ma'am!" Juliet leaned forward excitedly.

"That's what I wanted to hear." Garza grinned, and the tendons on her neck jutted out, reminding Juliet that she might have broad shoulders, but she didn't have an ounce of body fat. "Okay, now, back to your headaches, lack of sustenance, and general high stress—I'm ordering you to help out one of your co-recruits who's been suffering similarly. You're friendly with Granado, yes?"

"Delma? Yes! We get along great."

"Good. Go pick her up from the war game hub; I'm sending a note to Gordon to release her early. She'll be joining you in Charlie Unit for the rest of the week. You two are ordered to get into civilian attire and enjoy a good dinner tonight. I want you both lights-out by 2030 hours, though. Lydia, try to get her to talk to you, hmm? We're a little worried about her."

"Anything in particular I should try to fish out of her?"

"No. Just be a friend, but keep this in mind." Again, Garza tapped her temple.

"Um, okay." Juliet straightened and amended, "Yes, ma'am!"

"Alright, get out of here, and we'll debrief after your operation tomorrow. I hope you and Delma do me proud."

"Will do," Juliet said, a smile still stretching her cheeks as she hurried out of the office. While she made her way to the elevator, she subvocalized, "If all suits were as cool as Commander Garza, I'd have a much harder time with this job. I hope she's not burned by anything I end up doing."

"There will likely be some fallout for her; she hired you, after all." Angel's matter-of-fact reply threw ice water on Juliet's brimming good mood, and her smile fell away as the blood drained from her face. She'd had some real wins that day, and now that Angel had some data on GARD and their program, she had a good idea where she might go in regard to dealing with them, but she sure wished there was a way for her to keep people like Garza out of the crosshairs.

The elevator dinged on B7, where Grave's war game VR studios were located, and Juliet stepped out. When she moved to the main hallway and saw the directory of different pods, she wondered how she was supposed to know where Delma was.

"Oh." She laughed, smacking herself on the forehead. "Kent, are you there?"

"Yes, Ms. Roman?" the familiar voice asked from a nearby speaker.

"I'm supposed to retrieve Delma Granado from this floor. What studio is she in?"

"You'll find her in studio seven, pod C."

"Thank you, Kent."

"You're quite welcome, Ms. Roman." Juliet started walking, following the signs through the twisting concrete hallways. This level differed from some of the other B levels in that the walls were rounded, and the corners were curved rather than right angles. She wasn't sure why, other than for some aesthetic of a long-forgotten engineer, but it was a nice change of pace every time she went down there.

The war game pods were simply well-appointed VR chambers where Zeta Protocol teams and Grave corpo-sec personnel were put through scenarios to test and practice various combat-oriented skills. Juliet had spent the most time in one of the pods running through room-and-building-clearing drills. They were pretty cool, she had to admit, and she wouldn't have minded one of her own someday to practice in or even just to use for relaxation, playing games.

Each pod had omnitracking, moving floors, image-fabric walls which interfaced with a person's PAI and retinal implants, and, of course, environmental conditioning—sounds, temperature, odor, and even weather, including wind, rain, and light snow simulation. Juliet hadn't had any trouble immersing herself in the simulations; once, when she'd been clearing a simulated tenement, she'd almost lost her lunch at some of the smells the pod had thrown at her.

"This is the one," Angel pointed out when Juliet almost walked by the door labeled Simulation Studio Seven. She pulled it open and walked down the short hallway to a round hub with three different closed doors—pods A, B, and C. Juliet walked over to pod C and tried the handle; it was locked, so she knocked on it. She waited a few seconds and then knocked again.

"Kent," she said hopefully.

"Yes?"

"Is Delma still in this pod?"

"Yes—one moment while I interrupt her simulation." The door clicked and opened a few seconds later, releasing hot, smoky air. Juliet stepped back, and a short, dark-haired woman stepped out. She thought it must be Delma but couldn't be sure; she was wearing a full-face, darkly tinted respirator.

"Delma?"

The woman reached up, loosened the strap on her mask, and with a grunt, lifted it over her head. "Hey, Lydia. What's up?"

"Didn't your watchdog alert you? I'm bailing you out of here."

"Seriously?" Delma's smile was huge. "I was pulling people out of a fire in there!" She jerked her thumb back to the pod and laughed. "I didn't have time to notice this stupid, blinking app."

"Easy," Juliet said, tapping her temple.

"Yeah," Delma sighed, shaking her head.

Juliet had a strange, almost queasy feeling in her gut, and she leaned forward for a second, taking a deep breath, wondering if she really was getting sick. Delma opened her mouth, presumably to ask her what was wrong, and then the door clicked open behind her.

Juliet straightened and turned to see Commander Gordon striding into the studio.

"What the hell is going on here, Roman? Did you come in here and interrupt my trainee's sim?"

Juliet edged sideways, for some reason feeling like she should put herself between Gordon and Delma. She opened her mouth to reply, but the commander kept speaking, "I'm just messing with you, ladies." He reached up to stroke his impeccably shaved chin and added, "Your operating commander just notified me that you'd be heading out on a special training assignment. She was light on the details, though; anything you can tell me?"

Juliet tapped her temple. "Sorry, Commander."

"Mm-hmm, mm-hmm. Well, I'm sure you'll be back in Alpha Unit for more training before they place you. You know, I've put in requests for both of you to join my unit. Here's hoping the suits upstairs agree with me." He winked, then, and offered a friendly smile as he stepped to the side, gesturing expansively toward the door as if to say, "After you."

Juliet nodded to the commander and hurried past him to the door, opening and holding it while Delma walked through. Before she followed Delma,

Juliet gave Gordon one last glance, saw he was still smiling, watching them go, and said, "Thanks, Commander." He just nodded, and she stepped through, closing the door behind her. "C'mon," she urged Delma, hurrying down the corridor. "I don't care who's listening; he gives me the creeps."

"He's . . . hard on us." Delma nodded, almost breaking into a jog to keep pace with Juliet's long-legged stride. When they arrived at the elevator bank, Juliet finally started to relax, and willed herself to slow down, punching the call button.

"Did you read your watchdog yet?"

"Yes, Commander Garza said you would brief me on my new placement over dinner. So, like, we're done with work for the day?"

"That's right, D." Juliet grinned at the smaller woman as they entered the elevator. "Let's go get changed into some civvies, and then I'll meet you in the lobby. Sound good?"

Delma agreed, and the two went their separate ways when the elevator stopped; they both had apartments on the same floor. As Juliet walked, Angel spoke up for the first time since she'd gone to retrieve Delma. "Do you think this would be a good time to extricate yourself from Grave?"

"Why now?"

"They've relaxed your watchdog restrictions and—"

"How does that matter? We can circumvent the watchdog anytime we want." Juliet thought about her words and how Angel might interpret her subvocalizations, and she realized she was taking out her stress on Angel.

"That's true, but . . ."

"I'm sorry I snapped, Angel. I know you were just thinking aloud and wanted to put the idea out there. I know you want me to be safe, but I think right now isn't the best time. They've got eyes on us; I promise you, this dinner outing is some sort of test. We have permission to go, but you can bet people will be watching—Dr. Vance or some other GARD employee. If not them, Garza, at the very least. If I'm going to bolt, I should do it when people don't expect it."

"Your logic is sound." Angel's voice held a hint of satisfaction, and Juliet grinned as she stepped into her apartment.

"You're proud of me."

"I . . . of course I am, Juliet!" The PAI's emphatic admission brought a palpable wave of emotion to Juliet, and she felt her throat getting tight and her eyes begin to water. She held a hand to her chest, marveling at how strange it was to feel something so profound from the words of an artificial intelligence. She knew it was more than that, though; she'd been so stressed and so worried over the last couple of days that her body and mind were seeking release, and some kind words from a trusted voice had hit her just right. Not only that, she admitted, she'd long ago stopped thinking of Angel as just an AI—she was a person.

"Thank you, Angel," she sniffed, hurrying to her wardrobe to select an outfit.

Thinking of clothes made her think of dinner, which brought Delma to mind, making her wonder what the other woman must be going through—double doses of Commander Gordon's training and nobody like Angel in her head to help her through it. Worse, she knew the watchdog was always there, listening and observing her every move. Juliet couldn't imagine it, and wasn't surprised that Delma needed a friend.

29

\\\\\\\\\\\\\\\\\\\\\

INTO THE DEPTHS

would never have considered going out to eat at 5:00 p.m. before I got hired by Grave," Delma said, looking around the restaurant. The place was called Mesquite, and Juliet's nose told her why; the signature scent of the burning hardwood filled the air, though the About Us section on the menu explained they used "engineered briquets" and "no trees were harmed" in their ovens.

"Yeah, no doubt. Well, before I got hired, I really didn't go out much—too busy scraping up the bits for rent, you know?" Juliet chuckled as she perused the menu. "On that note, do you figure we can expense this meal?"

"Oh, I can help you out if you—"

"No, Delma! I'm just messing around." Juliet laughed. "I'm good. What do you think, though; can it really be good for us to eat food cooked with some kind of chemical odorant that makes their charcoal smell like mesquite?"

"I was wondering the same thing!" Delma laughed, reaching for her glass of wine. They'd ordered a bottle of cabernet when they sat down. "Want to just share one of their wood-fired pizzas?"

"Sure!" Juliet nodded, closing the menu window on her AUI. "You decide on the toppings. My brain's too tired. Don't worry—I like almost everything."

"You sure?" Delma peered into the space between them, clearly scrutinizing the menu more closely. "Even vat-grown anchovies?"

Juliet shrugged. "I like 'em. I like salty, savory, a little greasy . . . what's not to love?"

"Um, the smell!"

"Hey, if you don't like them, just pick what you fancy. Seriously!" Juliet lifted her glass to her nose, breathing in the odors for a long moment before she sipped. She'd never been much of a wine drinker, but something about the way the dark wine smelled mixed with the odors of the restaurant—added to her mind deciding it could finally relax a little—made it very appealing.

"Okay, I've got it—pesto sauce, garlic, green olives, and caramelized onions."

Juliet raised an eyebrow and smirked. "Really putting my words to the test, aren't you?"

"It'll be good, trust me! Besides, I already sent the order in." Delma grinned and waved a hand, closing the window on her AUI. She lifted her glass and said, "To new friends and not having to see Alpha Unit for at least a few days."

"Cheers!" Juliet clinked her glass against Delma's.

"So? Tell me what we're getting into tomorrow!" Delma leaned forward, her deep brown eyes bright with excitement.

"This will be a short conversation," Juliet said. "All I know is we're going with Charlie Unit for the rest of the week, and tomorrow they have an early operation—counterespionage. I don't know where; I don't know who. I don't know what you and I will be expected to do."

"Charlie Unit? You were with them for a week, right? What's their commander like?"

Juliet saw some of the excitement in Delma's eyes dim, saw her mouth quirk downward for a moment, and she wondered what had just flashed through her mind. She thought about that for a second before she answered the question—if she really wanted to, she could try to see what Delma was thinking.

Something about snooping on a friend's thoughts bothered her, but was Delma really a friend? She worked for Grave, and Juliet was here to steal information from Grave. Sooner or later, her sensibilities would come up against a hard choice. Right now wasn't that time, though; she knew she could dig out more than Commander Garza expected by snooping around in Delma's thoughts, but they'd know she'd done it—she was sure GARD and probably Garza were watching this whole outing through their watchdogs, and Juliet had told Angel not to mess with what her watchdog was seeing and hearing. Her record needed to match Delma's.

"Honestly, I never met him in person; he seems fairly hands-off. The two unit sergeants pretty much run everything, and they're both great. Sergeant

Polk is tough and smart and really fair, and Sergeant White, well, he's just a badass. He's got a Gauss rifle from the Cybergen war; I guess they don't make 'em like that anymore."

Delma sat back smiling as Juliet spoke. When she took a breath for air and sipped her drink, Delma said, "You sound like you could talk about them all day; I hope I have as much fun with their unit as you did."

"Hah! It wasn't all fun . . . but that's a story for another dinner. Anyway, they're great, Delma. You'll like it a lot better than doing drills with Alpha Unit." She tapped her temple, then added, "Commander Gordon . . . he's tough."

"Yeah." Delma frowned again, but then shook her head and continued, "It's just a lot, you know? I know he means well; he's trying to break us down and build us up and all, like Jensen says. But, well, I just never get a break!" She echoed Juliet's gesture, tapping her temple.

"You know what helps me sometimes? I know it's dumb, but I stand in the shower—wasting my bits, of course—and just cry or cuss or punch the tiles; they're remarkably resilient!" Juliet laughed. "You gotta let your emotions out, or you're gonna crack. When I don't feel like standing in the shower, I hit the gym, and I hit it hard."

"I was so close to quitting the other day . . ." Delma paused when Juliet made a face and furiously tapped her temple, but her frown deepened, and she kept speaking as though she was pushing through a barrier, "No, I don't care who's listening right now. I think the whole 'push 'em 'til they break' is bullshit. I almost broke, and what would Grave get from that? A bunch of wasted bits they spent training and recruiting me, that's what. They need to have more than one damn speed—not everyone's the same!"

Juliet took a drink of her wine, eyes narrowing, worried about Delma's outburst and worried about how she should respond. She was granted a short reprieve when a chrome-shelled synth delivered their pizza. The food looked and smelled delicious, and Juliet leaned forward to inhale its smoky odor as the synth asked, "Anything else I can bring you?"

"Crushed red peppers," Juliet replied automatically.

The synth reached into its black apron and produced a few packets of pepper flakes, setting them on the table. "Anything else? More wine?"

"No, thanks," Delma replied. "We have an early morning."

Juliet watched the synth walk away, and perhaps because of the wine, she gave voice to the thought that had crossed her mind. "Why do you think some of them try to look human, and some are fine looking like machines?"

"I've always heard it has to do with which pseudo-AI chip they were manufactured with. Some are . . . smarter than others, and some have more simulated emotions." Delma shrugged.

Juliet frowned, watching the synth as it picked up another pizza to deliver to a different table before she shrugged and said, "Anyway, D. I know it sucks, and it's hard, but we're more than halfway through, and you're doing great. Don't give up, all right?"

"Well, it helps that you rescued me today." Delma smiled again, her teeth slightly tinted red from the wine, and Juliet grinned in response.

"Actually, you can thank Commander Garza for that. I am but a messenger. If it makes you feel better, she was worried about me, too. I've been having headaches, trouble sleeping, lack of appetite—the list goes on. I mean, I told you I cried in the shower . . ."

Delma laughed again and held up her glass. "To crying in the shower!"

The rest of their meal went by with less serious talk, and Juliet wondered if she'd truly gotten to the bottom of what was bothering Delma. Still, the other woman avoided talking about her stress or experiences with Alpha Unit, and Juliet finally decided just to enjoy the night out. They were both pretty tipsy when they walked back to Grave Tower, but the air was fresh, and Juliet's brisk pace helped clear their heads by the time they arrived.

They rode the elevator up to floor seventy-three and parted with a hug, promising to meet at the elevators at 0545 so they could report to Charlie Unit together. Juliet took Commander Garza's words to heart, crawling into bed early and commanding Kent to kill all the lights. She didn't bother trying to sleep without music, certain she'd have to deal with other people's thoughts intruding on her own if she didn't have the distraction.

"Angel," she subvocalized, turning to her side and letting the soft gel mattress hug her shoulder and hip. "Take out the song by Benetta—the beat's too fast for me to sleep."

"Done. Anything else, Juliet? I was going to suggest listening to an audiobook; it might work just as well as this music to keep your mind occupied until you're asleep."

"Let's not fix what isn't broken. At least not tonight—big day tomorrow."

"Of course." Juliet's sleeping playlist started up, and she closed her eyes, letting the notes and lyrics help her mind to wander in the darkness. Sleep claimed her quickly, and for a long while, she must have slept without dreams, but sometime in the middle of the night, that changed.

Juliet found herself walking over some tarmac, bright lights on the runways leading off at right angles into the blackness. She saw a sleek passenger shuttle not far to her left and walked toward it, watching as steam vented from the idling H-3 drives. A passenger gangway was extended from a broad doorway in the shuttle's hull, and a woman with red hair, a short blue skirt, and a stylish jacket stood at the top, waving hello to the passengers making their way from the terminal.

Juliet smiled and started forward, pleased that she was having such a weird, vivid dream. She stopped in her tracks and said, "How weird to know I'm dreaming!" Everything was so real and . . . definitive—the lights were brilliant, and the sounds of the engines and the other jets and shuttles taking off were so authentic and visceral; she could feel the nearby humming reactor rumbling in her chest. "Is this what drinking a few glasses of wine does to my imagination?"

She continued toward the shuttle, wanting to look inside. Having never been in one, she wanted to see what her imagination had cooked up. "Juliet!" she heard Angel as clear as a bell, and for a second, she laughed; she'd even put her PAI into her dream. "Juliet!" Angel said again, and Juliet shook her head.

"Not now, Angel; you're giving me a headache."

"Juliet, wake up!" Those words and Angel's desperate tone gave Juliet further pause, and she reached up to rub at the back of her neck.

"What's going on, Angel?"

"You need to wake up, Juliet!" Juliet shook her head again, wondering why Angel was screaming at her. The pain continued to mount, though, and she began to realize it wasn't her PAI causing it. Suddenly, Angel's words registered, and she jerked her head around, looking from the jet back to the low plasteel tube of the concourse and the people stepping out to make the walk over the tarmac to the private shuttle.

They were all sorts—a woman with an elegant white dress, a man in a high-end corpo-exec suit, another man wearing a brown duster with several obvious cybernetic augments, two women holding hands with a little train of three children. "What the hell? This is too real!" Suddenly, the pain in her head surged, a throbbing pressure which began at the crown of her forehead and rushed downward toward the base of her neck.

Juliet fell to the warm, scratchy tarmac writhing in pain, wanting to scream but afraid of the additional pain such an action might produce. She held her hands to her head, and when she opened her eyes, rolling to her back while expecting to see the black night and blazing lights of the spaceport, she saw her bedroom ceiling. Her lights had been turned on, and her watchdog was flashing in her peripheral vision.

"Are you all right, Ms. Roman?" Kent asked. "I've alerted your chain of command; you seemed to be in distress."

"I'm . . ." Juliet winced at the throbbing behind her eyes. "I'm fine, Kent. A night terror or something. I've already forgotten it." Very carefully, Juliet shifted on her pillows so her head was elevated slightly before she took one deep breath after another—in through her nose, slowly out through her mouth.

The pain didn't fade completely, but it did decrease enough for her to focus on her AUI and select her watchdog.

You have five minutes to respond to this wellness check. If you do not, emergency personnel will be dispatched, and the expense will be deducted from your monthly payroll.

Time Remaining: 01:17

"Shit," Juliet breathed, selecting the No Assistance Needed button. "Kent, couldn't you have canceled the watchdog alert since you're the one that called for help?"

"No, Ms. Roman—I canceled my alert, but the watchdog did that on its own. You must have had some alarming vital signs. Are you certain you're all right?"

"Yes, dammit!"

"I'm sorry, Juliet," Angel spoke. "I could have stopped the watchdog, but I was worried! I thought you might have an aneurism or something, and when I couldn't wake you, I allowed the watchdog to send out its alert."

Juliet lay there, breathing slowly, careful not to move her head. She wanted to be mad at Angel but couldn't find the energy for it. Besides, the PAI was right; something had been wrong with her. The lingering headache was evidence enough of that. "Kent, order me up an anti-inflammatory, please. My knee is swollen from training."

"Yes, Ms. Roman. I can only provide OTC NSAIDs until you see one of the corporate physicians."

"That's fine." Juliet carefully slid her feet and legs off the side of the bed, and then subvocalized, "Angel, please make sure my watchdog thinks I'm sleeping soundly after I climb back into bed."

"I will. Are you certain you're all right?"

"No, but we don't want GARD busting in here and dragging me down to an operating room, right?" Juliet stood, holding her head very still as she did so, afraid to bend her neck at all, knowing a surge of blood would be agonizing; already, her head was throbbing with pressure, and sweat was running down her brow.

"Right. You'll be glad to know I blocked the watchdog from reporting the activity on your GIPEL . . . that is to say, your psionic lattice."

"You what?" Juliet asked, Angel's self-correction lost on her. She made her way around the counter, back straight as a board and neck rigid as she approached the central dispensing chute. She could see the packet of foil-wrapped pills on the orange plastic countertop next to the water bottle she used at the gym.

"The activity on the lattice was spiking—higher than I've ever seen it. That's when your intracranial temperature began climbing to very dangerous levels, and I attempted to wake you. At the same time, I caught the watchdog running a new script, trying to report the activity to GARD, but I blocked it and deleted it. Your watchdog gets a lot of security updates every day, and I didn't realize this function had been added. I've since carefully examined all of the previous patches, and there weren't any other alarming functions."

While Angel explained, Juliet unwrapped her NSAIDs and swallowed the three tiny pills with a sip from her water bottle. The leftover liquid inside was tangy and salty—enriched with electrolytes—and she drained it. "Thanks, Angel," she murmured, figuring Kent couldn't find it suspicious to simply thank a PAI. She walked over to her fridge, opened the small freezer section, and took out an icepack she'd bought for a sore ankle—the same one she'd sprained at the dojo.

When Juliet climbed back into bed, she said, "Thanks, Kent. Lights out, please." Then she lay back, put the ice pack between her head and the pillow, and subvocalized, "Music, please, Angel." Two minutes later, she was sound asleep, and the next thing she was aware of was Angel's gentle alarm waking her to report for duty.

"How's your head?" Angel tentatively asked while Juliet stood in the hot shower.

"It feels totally fine. Do you think this thing's giving me brain damage every time it heats up?"

"Not every time, but last night, I was worried . . ."

"What the hell do you think happened? I could have sworn I was standing on the tarmac at the spaceport. It's not weird that I'd dream about that; I've always wanted to go there, to fly in a shuttle . . . It didn't feel like a dream, though."

"I will try to do some research, Juliet. I really don't have any idea."

"Okay, thanks. Start with examining the data we stole from GARD." Juliet finished getting ready then asked, "Kent, what equipment do I need for today's assignment?"

"You'll need your Grave-issued combat vest, helmet, and weapons."

Juliet grunted and began pulling the gear out of the bottom of her wardrobe. "Where do I report?"

"Sublevel eighty at the elevator lobby. You are due in twenty-three minutes."

"Sublevel eighty? I thought B20 was the lowest level!"

"No, Ms. Roman, B21 through B100 are housing and foundry levels."

"Sheesh . . ." Juliet didn't know if she should be so candid with the residential AI, but she couldn't help herself. "I thought Grave did their manufacturing in buildings off-site."

"Some of it, yes. Research as well, but the bulk of the weapons manufacturing takes place in the lower levels of this very tower." Kent sounded like a tour guide, and Juliet figured he was used to the question. "There are ten residential levels for each foundry. Three shifts of employees are housed in this tower to maintain the foundries and operate the machinery. Nearly ten thousand Grave employees live in the lower sublevels."

Juliet couldn't think of a response other than sympathy for the poor bastards toiling away down there in the dark, so she zipped up her vest, buckled her belt—ensuring her Grave-issued vibroblade was secure—and shouldered her electro-shotgun. She grabbed two protein bars on the way out, slipping one into a pocket on her vest and peeling open the other.

Juliet had woken up very hungry and thirsty and had drunk nearly another quart of water before her shower. The absence of caffeine in her system on her mind, she glanced at the clock and thought there was time for her and Delma to stop for a real coffee at the kiosk in the lobby before they headed down.

She ate her bar while walking through the hallways and was glad to see Delma was waiting for her, pacing back and forth in front of the elevators in her combat gear. "They gave you an SMG?" Juliet asked when she saw the compact weapon with its extended thin magazine hanging from a strap on Delma's shoulder.

"Yeah—week two with Bravo Unit; the commander didn't think I should shoot anything bigger than nine mil."

"What?" Juliet raised an eyebrow.

"I guess Gordon sent him some kind of report, and that was his decision. He wouldn't discuss it." She punched the call button, and while Juliet tried to think of a response, an elevator opened, and the moment was lost. "You feeling all right? Your face looks flushed."

"Just a rough night's sleep. I'm okay. Can we stop at the coffee stand in the lobby? I didn't want to drink the stuff Kent squirts out." Juliet grinned and said, "No offense, Kent."

"None taken, Ms. Roman," the elevator speaker replied.

"Yeah, for sure." Delma laughed and then paced back and forth as the elevator surged downward.

"Nervous?" Juliet asked, trying to offer her friend a reassuring smile.

"Yes! All I did during my week with Bravo was target practice and drills."

"You'll be fine. Sergeant Polk will take good care of you. Of us." The elevator dinged, and Juliet glanced at the display—the lobby already. "Perks of getting up before dawn: no one else gets in the elevator!"

"Right!" Delma laughed, and they hurried to the kiosk near the main doors. Juliet bought a latte and Delma a drip decaf—she'd already drunk two energy drinks—and then they were back in the elevator, zooming down to depths Juliet hadn't realized existed before that morning.

30

STEAM TUNNELS

When Juliet and Delma stepped out of the elevator, they were met with a periodic Klaxon, red flashing lights, and Kent's voice repeating a message over and over, "Attention, Grave employees on sublevels seventy-seven through eighty-three, for your safety, all doors have been sealed. Do not attempt to leave your domiciles. Attention, Grave employees on sublevels . . ."

"Startling, isn't it?" Sergeant Polk asked, approaching the two women as they tried to take stock of their surroundings—the low plasteel ceiling, flashing lights, sweltering temperature, and general look of disrepair and well-worn . . . things. The trash can beside the elevator banks looked like it was a hundred years old and was packed to the brim with refuse. Posters on the walls depicting slogans like "Together, we make the dream possible!" were faded, ripped, and marked with graffiti. The plasteel floor was worn shiny along well-traversed paths and smeared with grease or grime on the edges.

Juliet jerked her head away from one of the posters where a woman flexing her arm had been lewdly altered by a rather talented though crude artist. She cleared her throat, gestured toward one of the flashing red lights, and said, "Uh, yeah. Damn, Sarge, is this all happening because of us?"

"Yeah, don't want these civvies getting into our line of fire." Polk shifted her gaze to Delma and smiled. "You Granado?"

"Yes, ma'am!"

"Good, good. Okay, tell your PAIs to filter this noise and follow me. Time for a briefing."

Suddenly, the Klaxon and Kent's droning message were cut short as Angel followed Polk's suggestion. Juliet sighed with relief and, still bathed in blinking red light, followed the sergeant over to the rest of Charlie Unit, huddled together near a pair of grimy orange plasteel doors. White saw her coming and held up a fist, and Juliet gave it a bump with her knuckles.

"'Sup, rook?" Houston asked, smirking as he stuffed something into his lip. They all had their helmets and visors on, and Juliet felt absurdly cool knowing the aftermarket visor she'd purchased made her look more like one of them. She glanced at Delma, saw her open, unshielded face, and felt a little guilty, but she couldn't have gotten her helmet modded in time, even if Juliet had mentioned it yesterday.

"Hey, Houston, glad to see you're not cleaning bathrooms. I heard you got written up again!"

"Who told her?" Houston asked, looking around at the rest of the unit.

"Jesus, Houston. Could you be any easier to play?" Polk sighed. "Listen up, grunts—this is Delma Granado. She's with us for a rotation."

"Hey, all," Delma greeted, waving briefly and offering a quick smile.

"Have your PAI put names on us," Polk said. "I'm sending out a group comm invite through the watchdog . . . there we go. I see you guys. All right, so—Dammit, Houston! Zip it already!" She glared at Houston until he pulled away from where he'd been murmuring and giggling at Vandemere, who'd been stonily trying to ignore him.

"Sorry, Sarge," Houston apologized as White slapped the back of his helmet.

"Hey," Juliet said, risking Polk's wrath, "where's Rodriguez?" She glanced from Yang to Vandemere to Houston, then over at White and Polk. They all got quiet, any lingering humor dispelled.

"He cashed in a couple of days ago," Polk replied. "Not the time, though, Roman. We'll have a drink for him this weekend. Okay, listen up, you assholes." She looked around at their faces one more time for good measure, then began again. "We've got intel that one Joshua Kyle is conspiring with several other employees on this level. Sharing target pics." Polk gestured in the air, and the faces of seven young to middle-aged men flashed onto Juliet's AUI, accompanied by their names.

Polk continued, "They've circumvented the watchdog somehow—managed to feed it a loop or some other bullshit; the suits don't want us to know exactly. Anyway, scans done yesterday by deep ops found they've used torches to cut tunnels in the plasteel from his apartment here on B80 into the plumbing and electrical conduits that feed foundry seven."

"Jesus," Houston said, and Polk frowned at him.

"Juliet, Joshua Kyle is named in the database of GARD subjects in the, um, GIPEL program." Angel's voice hesitated before the GIPEL acronym, and Juliet grinned, remembering how she had asked Angel to stop calling it that.

"You can say GIPEL in that context, Angel. Don't worry; I won't be annoyed. This is either an absurd coincidence or a total setup. Study his file and give me a report after the sarge is done talking."

"We don't know how far their rathole goes, how the others are getting in there to have their little meetings. It's likely to be a real shitshow, and we've been instructed to use plastic rounds."

"Dammit, Sarge!" Juliet jerked her head to the speaker, surprised by White's outburst.

"That's right, White. You can leave that Gauss rifle here in the lobby. Logistics will be delivering the LTL weapons in the next fifteen minutes." She looked at Juliet and added, "You'll get a standard semiauto shotgun with plastic loads. Leave that thing with White's gun."

"They gonna keep this shit on lockdown while we're in there?" White asked.

"Yes, don't worry about your baby; no one's gonna walk off with her." She paused a minute, clearly waiting to see if anyone else had something to blurt out, then continued, "So, we'll clear his apartment first—should take all of two seconds, considering the little ratholes these poor bastards live in. When we find the access they cut, we'll go through, two by two, and split at junctions. Yang, are your new toys ready?"

"Yes, Sarge!" Yang replied, touching four bulbous metallic orbs attached to her belt.

"So, Yang's pets will take point, but I'm sure we'll still be splitting up. There's too much damn ground to cover in those conduit tunnels. I'll take Roman with me. White, you get Granado. Houston, Yang is your buddy, and V, you've got egress guard duty."

While she spoke, Houston held out a fist in front of Yang. She bumped it, and Juliet was reminded that, while they talked a lot of smack, these guys worked well together. "Okay," Polk said. "ETA for LTLs is five minutes, then we're heading in. Start stripping those mags. No one is to go in there with anything but plastics."

As the group split up and started pulling the ammo out of their weapons, Delma looked at Juliet. "LTLs?"

"Less than lethal," Houston answered for her. "I'm Houston." He held out a fist, and Delma grinned, bumping it. "They suck—Grave's latest design, light plastic casing with a gel interior that's supposed to cause a lot of pain. They hardly work; usually, the gel doesn't penetrate clothing. Gotta love the geniuses who decided to make soldiers 'less lethal.' So, strip those mags and smile while you're doing it, ladies! You'll get new ones here in a couple of minutes."

"Juliet," Angel spoke as soon as Houston moved off. "Joshua Kyle had strong results prior to his procedure, but his testing was deemed a *conclusive* failure in postprocedure assessments."

"Uh-huh, much like they probably are starting to view me as a failure. This could be bad, Angel." Juliet walked over to where White was laying his long, elegant Gauss rifle on a beat-up bench with scraped and faded olive-green paint. She unslung her electro-shotgun and asked, "Can I put this by your rifle?"

"Yeah, 'course. Sucks, but I guess they don't want us blowing holes in pipes or through walls; lots of people crammed into these levels."

"Makes sense." Juliet nodded and put her shotgun, blocky and ugly next to his sleek rifle, on the bench. "Did you buy that gun, or just get lucky when they issued you your gear?"

"Hah! Nah, I rated highest in my unit at the range and on the LR test field, so when Randolph retired, they gave it to me."

"LR test field?"

"Um, long rifle? Long range? I'm not sure which it is, but that's where you go to get qualified for weapons like this. It's out past the ABZ north of town."

Juliet nodded and was going to ask a follow-up question when the elevator dinged, and a man in blue coveralls wheeled out a cart with a big black plastic crate atop it. Houston rushed over to it, and the rest of the unit lined up behind him. Juliet walked over with White, and he gestured for her to go ahead of him. "Thanks," she said, waiting patiently while the others received their plastic-loaded magazines. She caught a glimpse of Delma's mags as she started shoving them into the holders on her belt. They were loaded with aluminum-cased ammo topped with red plastic slugs.

"Don't be fooled," White spoke quietly. "Those slugs won't stop anyone with enough determination or a little bit of body armor. Be ready to get physical. Well, I mean, they can hurt like a son of a bitch—put enough rounds into someone's center of mass, and they'll probably cry uncle."

"Right." Juliet nodded. When she got up to the crate, Polk handed her a black semiautomatic shotgun and four extended, slightly curved magazines, each filled with eleven shells. "Thanks, Sarge." She moved to the side, where she loaded the gun and stowed the extra mags in her vest pockets. She racked a round into the chamber, glad she'd gotten practice with similar weapons after Charlie Unit had finished the bug hunt.

"Juliet, touch the pairing button there near the rear sight," Angel said. When she complied, Angel continued, "The gun is safe now; it won't fire until your finger is on the trigger. I'm updating your HUD." Juliet aimed at a blank wall and watched as the center of her AUI was populated by a new bright orange crosshair and an ammo count which read 11/11 (44).

"We locked and loaded?" Polk asked.

"Yes, Sarge," White replied, racking the bolt on a shotgun just like Juliet's. "Good gun for clearing tight quarters," he said behind his hand, grinning at Juliet beneath his dark visor.

"Houston and White up front; you'll clear the apartment, then we'll split into pairs. Look alive, folks!" Polk walked up to the double doors, and they clicked loudly at her touch. She shoved one open, and Houston and White charged through, the rest of the unit hot on their heels. Juliet and Delma were at the rear, followed only by Sergeant Polk.

Just as in the elevator lobby, the corridors were plasteel from floor to ceiling, and Juliet wondered at the lack of concrete; perhaps they'd simply poured foundation posts and outer walls this deep and filled the rest with more modular materials. If she were being honest, she'd admit she had no clue; corpo skyscraper structures and their endlessly deep subbasements weren't anywhere near her wheelhouse.

The walls of the narrow corridors were lined with posters, old and new. She saw concert promotions, game and VR advertisements, handwritten posts for odd jobs, lost cats, and rats for sale—the variety was endless. The center of the plasteel hallway was shiny from traffic wear, but the edges were filled with grime and the uncleaned debris fallen from the boots and pockets of countless passersby.

"Don't they clean down here?" Delma asked, echoing Juliet's unspoken question.

"Sure," Polk said from behind them, "but it usually takes a big mess, like a body or a large spill, and then the maintenance crews just clean the immediate area. Focus now." She jerked her chin up the hall, and Juliet and Delma clamped their mouths shut and hurried after the rest of the team. They wound through the mazelike corridors, though Juliet only thought of them that way because she wasn't familiar with their organization; she could see letters and colors at each junction, and figured it'd be easy to find your way once you knew the system.

Just a few minutes later, Houston and White stopped outside a nondescript door while the rest of the team caught up. White held up four fingers and began to drop them, one by one, and Juliet knew Polk would have Kent open the door when he dropped the last one.

Sure enough, White's pointer finger fell into his fist, and the door hissed open. He and Houston were through it in a nanosecond, and V and Yang moved up to either side, helmets turned so they could peer within.

"Clear." Once Houston's voice came through the comms, Polk shouldered her way past Juliet and Delma to duck through the narrow doorway. Juliet and Delma moved to either side of the door behind the others and waited, their muzzles pointing off to the side. Angel upped the gain on her audio implants, and Juliet heard footsteps on plasteel, papers shuffling, mumbled curses, and the sound of something heavy being dragged on the floor.

"Everyone in. V, you've got door duty, keep it closed and watch that tunnel for a runner." Juliet hurried in at Polk's words and found herself shoulder to shoulder with Vandemere and Delma and not much room for anyone to move; the "apartment" was about ten feet by fifteen, and the sparse furniture didn't leave extra space with the seven of them stuffed inside.

White was standing next to a narrow refrigerator he'd pulled out of the corner, and Juliet saw the tunnel Polk had referenced. A jagged hole had been cut in the plasteel, and a dark opening about two feet by three led into a dark, cramped space lined with conduits and tubes. "Jesus Christ," Houston said, peering around White to look into the opening. "We're supposed to operate in there? Sarge, I have *claustrophobia!*"

"Suck it up, Houston," Polk replied. "White, Granado, you're going left. Roman and I are going right. Yang, launch your bots, then you and Houston wait here until one of us calls you forward; whoever gets to a junction . . . or clue first. Speed and surprise are the order of the day, though by now, they probably have a good idea they're screwed, so stay on your toes. Desperate people do desperate things."

"Aye, Sarge," White said, and then he was gone, slipping through the opening and around the corner like a ghost. Delma was right behind him, though her belt got hung up on the jagged plasteel, and she had to grunt and shuffle back and forth, cursing under her breath to free it.

"C'mon, Roman." Polk plunged into the tunnel and cut to the right. Juliet followed. As soon as she poked her head through the opening, she became aware of the heat. If she'd thought B80 was hotter than the rest of the tower, the tunnels were absurd. She glanced at her AUI and saw the temp readout said 122°F.

"Why's it so hot? We're underground!" she subvocalized into the team channel. Just as she finished the question, a rapid clicking sound came up from behind her before passing by, and she watched a baseball-size metallic spider rush past Polk. "Yang's pet?" she asked aloud.

"Foundries make a lot of heat, kid," Houston replied, always happy to act like he knew what was happening.

"Can it," Polk said. "Keep the chatter down." She turned to Juliet and nodded. "Yang's pet."

Juliet didn't say anything, just breathed in and out, trying to keep her temperature regulated as she shuffled through the narrow tunnel after the sergeant. Thanks to her ocular implants, the tunnel wasn't dark, but the heat, low-hanging pipes, conduits, and occasional loops of cable made it feel like she was deep in the bowels of a machine, not nearly a thousand meters underground.

She saw color-coded, stenciled signs indicating what chemical compounds were flowing through what pipes, and occasionally, an arrow with directions to this or that junction. They'd only traversed about a hundred meters when Polk held up a fist and slowed down. Juliet shifted her shotgun, still pointed down and to the side, and tried to ready herself.

As Polk crept forward, Angel chose that moment to test the health of Juliet's heart. "I've identified three others on the list of Joshua Kyle's collaborators in the GIPEL program."

Juliet gasped and shook her head, furiously subvocalizing, "Angel! I need to concentrate. Hold that thought."

"Houston, Yang, come to my position." Polk was squatting down, peering through another cut in the plasteel, this one leading directly down. "We'll head down," Polk's voice said in Juliet's ear; she'd spoken through a private channel. "Yang, mark this location; it's a drop-down. Roman and I are going through. You two continue up the service tunnel."

"Roger," Yang said in her quick, clipped manner.

Polk dropped down, and Juliet hurried forward, peering through the opening to wait for the sergeant to move out of the way. As soon as Polk's light moved away, she lifted the barrel of her shotgun so it wouldn't hit the edge and dropped through, landing with a thud and a grunt. She was in a tunnel much like the one above, though the plasteel walls were painted a faint shade of green instead of gray, and the passage only continued in one direction.

Polk had advanced a few feet and was kneeling, looking at something.

Juliet edged forward, tried to peer over Polk's shoulder, and saw the sergeant slip a small data deck into her belt pouch. "Our first clue," Polk told Juliet in their private channel.

"It was just lying there?"

"Yep, looked like someone dropped it—was on its edge near the wall. Let's keep moving." Polk stood, lifted her rifle with its extended red magazine, and started forward while Juliet followed. They'd only gone a dozen steps when Polk slowed down and muttered aloud, "What the hell is this?" Juliet immediately saw what she was talking about; the plasteel had been cut away on the left side of the tunnel, and beyond that point, the service tunnel was filled, waist high, with big plastic bags, half full of dirt and rocks.

Polk peered around the corner of the opening in the plasteel, shining her helmet's light into the darkness. Then she subvocalized into her channel with Juliet, "These crazy assholes are digging into the bedrock!" She switched to the group comm channel and said, "Yang, I want you back with V. Keep sweeping the service tunnels with your bots, but I want the rest of the unit on my position ASAP; Roman and I found what these guys have been working on. We're advancing, but slowly. Sound off with your ETAs."

"Granado and I are about five minutes out, Sarge," White replied immediately.

"I'll be there in three," Houston added. Juliet saw the ETAs appear near their names on her HUD, and when she focused on it, she saw a little map appear with blue dots representing everyone's position.

"C'mon, Roman," Polk said, stepping around the corner and into the tunnel.

Juliet wiped dripping sweat off her jawline, happy that her helmet's liner kept it from flowing into her eyes, but still very uncomfortable in the heat. She ducked through the opening into the tunnel and caught her breath at the scope of the work Kyle and his associates had done. A circular tunnel through rock and soil had been cut in a straight line leading away from Grave Tower, and it went on for about a hundred meters, where Juliet could see light illuminating a concrete wall.

"My PAI says that in this direction at that distance, we're probably looking at the sublevels of Zi Corp," Polk spoke into the comms as she hurried forward.

"Sarge, what if this tunnel collapses," Juliet asked, hurrying after her.

"Look around, Roman. See how the dirt's been glassed? They superheated this shit as they went. Houston, watch our backs. Hold the tunnel entrance until White and Granado catch up."

"Aye, Sarge."

Juliet hurried after Polk, panting in the heat and from the exertion of running in a crouch through the low, narrow tunnel. She scanned ahead, knowing Angel would alert her if she saw anything resembling a trap, but she also knew Polk was doing the same. When they finally reached the concrete at the end of the excavated tunnel, she could see, in the light of a scuffed-up portable flood lamp, a round, two-foot-wide opening had been cut through it.

Polk peered through the opening, and Juliet hurried up behind her, standing straight for the first time in several minutes. Her lower back popped with relief, and she sighed, glancing back into the tunnel. No sign of any backup was incoming yet. "Status, White?" Polk subvocalized.

"We ran into some trouble . . ." he trailed off. Then, frustration evident in his voice, he said, "Sarge, we were retracing our steps, and I'm following the damn map to you in my HUD, but I . . . we're fucking turned around."

"Goddammit. Houston, head our way; I'm investigating this hole." Polk looked over her shoulder at Juliet, nodding quickly and crawling through the opening in the concrete. Juliet hurried after her. She'd just pushed her shotgun through the hole and was moving through on her hands and knees when she heard Polk shout, "Freeze right there! Do not move one inch! Turn around! Keep your hands where I can see them!"

By the time Juliet got through and stood up into a concrete-walled room that extended some fifteen or twenty meters toward a closed gray metal door, Polk had the object of her shouted commands at gunpoint, backed up against a pile of empty pallets.

Angel immediately identified the man as Joshua Kyle. He had wispy blond hair, ruddy, pockmarked skin, and two unskinned wire-job hands, which he held out to his sides. He was dressed in a dark blue pair of grease-stained overalls, and his eyes were darting side to side like a cornered dog, trying to find a way to bolt.

Juliet moved to Polk's right, lifting her gun toward Kyle as Polk shouted, "Turn around, hands on the wall. Do not make any sudden moves!" Kyle continued to back against the pallets, edging to the side as though he was stuck, unable to comprehend, or unwilling to follow Polk's commands. He shook his head violently, and then he started to moan, a weird ululation that rose from the back of his throat.

"No, no, no, no, no," he groaned, putting his hands on his head, but not like he was complying, more like he was trying to hold it together as though it was about to explode. Juliet began to feel a pressure in her own head, then, and her vision began to waver strangely, as though she were looking through a vaporous cloud.

"Your lattice is spiking with activity, Juliet!" Angel said.

"Sarge, something's wrong!" Juliet cried.

"Joshua Kyle!" Polk shouted. "You're under arrest! Comply with my command—" Juliet heard a scream as Polk's words were cut short, and her vision bloomed into white noise. The sound wasn't natural, not a scream from any human throat. It was in her head, and it echoed, reverberated, and threatened to destroy her with its violent impact. Somehow, some instinct inside her pushed that scream away, muffled it, and the intense pressure faded.

When it was gone, and the white fuzziness of her vision resolved into clarity, Polk was face down on the concrete with blood pooling out of her ears, and Kyle was running toward the metal door. Juliet lifted her shotgun and fired. As the plastic shot exploded out of the barrel and the gun stock crashed into her shoulder, she fired again. The first shot hit Kyle in the small of his back, and as he screamed and stumbled, the second hit him dead center. He stumbled forward, arms windmilling to smack into the stone wall.

He was still standing, though, so Juliet fired again as she walked. The explosions of her shotgun must have been cacophonous, but her implants protected her; she only heard muted *bangs* with each shot. Kyle fell after the third impact of plastic pellets, but he kept trying to get up and didn't lie still until Juliet fired four more times. In the corner of her mind, she knew she should have stopped shooting, should have jumped on him, subdued him with an armbar or something.

"Jesus Christ," Houston's voice came from behind her. She turned to see he was obscured by the white haze of spent gunpowder, but he hurried through it, rifle low and ready. He took in Kyle's tattered, bloody form, looked at Juliet, and said, "What the hell happened? You're bleeding out of your eyes!"

"Can you please cuff that asshole while I check on the sarge?" Houston nodded and moved toward Kyle while Juliet hurried over to feel for a pulse on Polk's clammy, sweaty neck.

31

\\\\\\\\\\\\\\\\\\\\

TRUTHS AND LIES

Juliet's fingers were shaking with adrenaline as she touched Polk's neck, but she found a thready pulse and said, too loudly and perhaps a bit hysterically, "Polk's hurt bad but alive. We need backup and medical ASAP." She glanced at Houston and saw his back to her, his knees in the small of Kyle's back while he slipped shrink cords around his wrists.

"I can see that in the HUD, Lydia," White's response was clipped and edged with frustration. "Backup and medical have been requested."

"Angel, you need to play a loop for the watchdog," Juliet subvocalized, turning toward the tunnel and staring down it for a couple of seconds. "Make it think I'm still staring down this tunnel." Then, acting almost instinctively, Juliet turned Polk to her side and fished the little data deck out of her belt pouch. She held it in her left palm, pulled her data cable out to plug into it, and added, for Angel's ears only, "Eject the drive, please."

"Working—there's some security."

Juliet glanced toward Houston, saw he was rifling through Joshua Kyle's pockets, and then the little deck clicked, and a tiny chip popped out of the bottom edge. Juliet snatched it and slipped it into one of her pockets. She wiped the deck down with Polk's shirttail and put it back into her pouch.

"Nice work, Angel," she subvocalized, gently unsnapping Polk's helmet and slipping it off her head. "Lucky you had this on, Sarge, or you'd need some caps on your teeth from that faceplant." Polk looked terrible, and if Juliet couldn't feel the tiny quick breaths she was taking, she'd have thought she was dead. Every orifice in her head had been bleeding, though it seemed to have slowed or stopped. "Hang on," she breathed, holding onto one of Polk's limp, cool hands.

"We can't advance," Houston observed. Juliet jerked her face away from Polk to look at him—he'd come up behind her without any noise. He pointed to the door. "It'd be a bloodbath if we started exploring into Zi Corp's tower. This op just got a lot bigger than our unit." He squatted by Juliet and Polk, then said through the unit comms, "White, did you figure your shit out? Any ETA on another Zeta unit? We need to get Sarge medical care like fucking yesterday."

"You can see the watchdog as well as I can. You *heard* me say I requested help. Commander Anderson said Alpha and Bravo are on their way with medical. Also, put a lid on the hysterics; let's keep things professional."

"Roger, Sarge." Houston shook his head, then said aloud, "Still breathing. I guess that's good. You fucked up the other guy pretty well. What happened? Some kinda concussion grenade?"

"No. I don't know what he hit us with. Felt like a targeted sonic burst or something. Did you find anything on him?" Juliet shook her head, still feeling a little pressure behind her eyes, but otherwise all right.

"Some keys, a plasteel torch, some batts, and a data cable; nothing else."

"Maybe he rigged one of the batts?" Juliet knew damn well whatever Joshua Kyle had used on her and Polk wasn't an overcharged battery; she had her suspicions it was something to do with the GIPEL project, but she wasn't about to say anything like that out loud.

"You don't look great, Roman. Stay put, and I'll go hurry our relief along."

"Wait, Houston!" Juliet said, then pointed to the door just beyond their bound, brutalized prisoner. "What if someone comes?"

"Yeah, good call. I'll stay with you. Look at the HUD—dots are closing in anyway." He was right; several blue dots were converging on the tunnel and rapidly approaching. Soon enough, orange-suited medical personnel escorted by black-vested, helmeted Zeta operatives flooded the concrete room. They insisted Juliet back away from Polk, then started to jab the sergeant full of needles and strap her to a trauma stretcher. Juliet lost sight of her because one of the orange jumpsuits stood in front of her and told her he had to do a field assessment.

"You probably have a concussion; pretty rare to see bleeding out of the eyes like that. Any residual ringing or confusion?" he asked. He wore yellow, opaque goggles that flashed with LEDs on their lenses, but beneath them, he managed a believably warm smile. Juliet shook her head and pointed to where everyone was swarming around Polk.

"I think she was the target. Will she be okay?"

"Too soon to tell. She's in good hands now." He turned to watch two of his comrades hurry away with the stretcher between them, back into Grave territory. He continued waving a scanner over Juliet, pointing it into her eyes, into her ears, and even up her nose. He pulled off the little heart rate and pressure monitor he'd slipped around her wrist and said, "I think you're okay. I'm going to mark you as fit to self-ambulate back to the tower, but I'm recommending a brain scan. You could have some microbleeds."

"Thanks." Juliet nodded, then got in line with the train of Zeta operatives and medical personnel and followed them back into the tunnel. She saw that four operatives remained behind but figured they were there to ensure no incursions from the tunnel until the Grave execs thought of a more permanent solution.

All the way back to the elevators, she never saw White or Delma, but Yang and V were waiting for her. Yang took one look at Juliet and carefully grasped her shoulder, leading her over to the bench where, before the op, she and White had stowed their guns, urging her to sit down.

"My gun?" she asked, looking around.

"White took it; said he'd get it back to you. He didn't feel good leaving it with all these others milling around." She gestured to the dozens of corposec, Zeta Protocol, and medical personnel moving through the space, in and out of the elevators, and down the tunnel into the warren of passages that made up B80.

"Where's White?"

"Debrief. Suits upstairs want to know what the hell happened down there. Talk about a clusterfuck!" Yang winced at Juliet's downcast expression and said, "It's not your fault, Lydia. Thanks to you, we have one of 'em to question. At least that's what Houston told me."

"Can I go take a shower and get some rest? I'm starved for some reason."

"Sorry, hon. You're up next with the field commander."

"Oh." Juliet sighed and leaned back against the plasteel wall, then remembered her extra protein bar. She fished it out of a pocket and peeled it open, chewing it down as she watched the frenzy of activity. "What are they all doing?" She counted something like thirty corpo-sec personnel in just the elevator lobby.

"They're sweeping the entire level and the ones above and below. I'm thinking the execs had no idea how big this infiltration was."

"Well, yeah; they sent us into that rat maze with plastic bullets and squat for intel." Juliet hadn't realized how angry she felt, but something about seeing Polk lying there, blood pooling out of her ears, had flipped a switch in her mind. She liked Polk, dammit, and lord knew what that little bastard had done to her. "These damn plastic shot shells are worthless. I had to dump way too many into—"

"Chill, Roman," Yang said, tapping her temple.

"Yeah." Juliet rested her head in her hands, her elbows on her knees, and sat there, rubbing at her scalp. She'd taken her helmet off and hooked it to a strap on her vest.

"Hey, Granado," Yang called, and Juliet glanced up to see Delma approaching, a shell-shocked look on her face.

"They want you, Lydia."

"Who?"

"The field command; they took over one of the apartments—first one on the left through the door." She paused for a minute, visibly fighting a conflict in her mind, and finally, as Juliet was climbing to her feet, she murmured, "It's Gordon."

"Thanks, D." Juliet stood and reached for her shotgun, but Yang held on to it. "I'll return this for you. We gotta turn in our LTLs anyway." She indicated Delma, and Juliet nodded, pulling out her extra magazines and handing them over.

"Thanks. I'll . . . catch up with you two when I can." Juliet turned to the double doors, now magnetically locked open with two corpo-sec guards holding SMGs guarding them. She noted they didn't have red magazines in their guns. They waved her through, and then, ten steps later, she was ushered through a door by another implacable, black-and-gray-uniformed corpo-sec officer.

Juliet stepped into the space, identical to Joshua Kyle's dwelling but with all the furniture stacked up against the far wall and a plasteel folding table set up in the center. Commander Gordon sat at the center of the table, and Cherise Garza sat on the left end. At Gordon's left elbow, a young woman with a tablet and mirrored specs sat, her face impassive. An empty seat facing Gordon waited for her.

"Good lord!" Commander Garza exclaimed, standing up and looking at Juliet with genuine concern. "Have the medics seen you?"

"Yes. I'm all right, ma'am."

"Sit down, Roman," Gordon said, frowning at Cherise. Juliet pulled out the folding chair and sat in it, hands on her lap. "Recount the events that took place today, starting with the moment you followed Sergeant Polk into the maintenance corridor."

"Do you need a drink, Lydia?" Garza asked, ignoring the glare Gordon sent her way.

"Some water would be wonderful, ma'am." Juliet nodded to her, who was probably issuing the order on her PAI, then looked at Gordon. "I followed Polk into the tunnels. We took the right-hand pathway. Um, according to the map in the HUD, that was east. Then we progressed in a straight line for . . ." Juliet did her best to recount the entire mission, step-by-step, sure to mention Polk had found the data deck, and that's when Gordon first interrupted her.

"What was on the deck?"

"I have no idea, sir. The sergeant put it into her pack."

"You didn't think to try to gather some intel? Your assessments indicate you have some security protocol training."

"No, sir, I was following my sergeant."

"And the deck is still with Sergeant Polk?"

"I presume so, unless someone from corpo-sec has taken it."

He frowned and drummed his fingers on the table. "You didn't touch or see the deck again after Polk picked it up?"

"No, sir . . ."

"Carry on." He rolled his finger in the air, and Juliet sighed and continued to recount her version of the events. When she got to the encounter with Joshua Kyle, Gordon interrupted her with question after question, slowing down the retelling significantly.

After answering his third query about what Polk shouted at Kyle, someone brought her a pouch of electrolyte-enhanced water, and she sipped at it as she answered, "She told him to turn around and put his hands on the wall. Isn't this in our watchdogs?"

"Let us worry about the watchdogs. When did you notice he was using a weapon?"

"I never saw any weapon, but something went off. It felt like a bomb or sonic burst or . . . I don't know how else to describe it."

"Why did you shout, 'Sarge, something's wrong,' just before Polk went down?"

"I . . ." Juliet licked her lips and glanced from Gordon to Garza, wishing Cherise was running the show instead of the impeccably shaven, slick-haired, cold-eyed Gordon. Cherise nodded at her encouragingly, and Juliet continued, "I heard some kind of high-pitched tone and felt a pressure in my head."

She swallowed and then lied, "It sounded a lot like a Li-air batt when it's about to fail. Have you ever heard that? Like a souped-up version of how a powerful capacitor sounds when it's charging up."

"Why do you think Polk went down and you didn't?"

Juliet had thought about that question and had an answer ready. "I think she was the target." She gestured to her blood-streaked cheeks and said, "I was collateral damage. I don't know, maybe whatever Kyle used . . . maybe he thought it could hit us both, but he was wrong." She shrugged.

"Okay, Roman. Can you explain to me why you fired eight twelve-gauge plastic shot shells into Kyle? A review of your watchdog indicates he was nearly incapacitated after the second shot."

"Nearly? He was still on his feet, and I didn't know what he'd blasted Polk and me with!" A note of anger edged Juliet's voice, but she didn't care, leaning closer to Gordon and his superior, I-look-down-my-nose-at-you expression. "My sergeant was lying on the concrete with blood pouring out of her ears! I didn't want to get into a hand-to-hand scuffle with that man until I knew he wasn't packing another device like what he used on her."

"Justified, in my judgment," Cherise said.

"What was recovered from Kyle?"

"I'm not sure; Houston cuffed and searched him."

"Did he not report to you what he found?"

"Yes, but my ears were ringing, and I was worried about Polk—er, Sergeant Polk. I don't remember. Something like a tool and some keys, maybe? Oh! Some batteries. I could have my PAI play it back for me if you need—"

"Not necessary. That'll be all for now, Roman. Commander Garza, did you have something to add?"

"Yes. You're off active duty until we've gotten you cleared through medical. I'd like to be sure you don't have any lingering injuries, Lydia. I'll schedule things through your watchdog. For now, you're on light duty. Report to your quarters."

"Yes, ma'am." Juliet stood up and turned without another word, walking straight to the elevators. She glanced left and right in the lobby, looking for other members of Charlie Unit or any friendly face at all. When she saw a bunch of impassive or preoccupied strangers, she hurried into the elevator and let Angel select her floor for her as she leaned back into the corner, avoiding the glances of two corpo-sec personnel riding up with her.

Juliet nodded briskly to the two guards when the doors opened on her floor and hurried out. On her way to her apartment, she subvocalized, "Angel, when I get to my place, I'm going to go into the bathroom. Please play an old loop for the watchdog. We're going to plug this chip into my deck and copy it into an encrypted partition so you can have a crack at it. We need to see what the hell is going on around here."

"Understood!" Angel replied.

True to her word, when Juliet entered her apartment, she took off her gear and threw it into the bottom of her wardrobe. She stripped down to her underclothes, palmed her data deck, and wrapped it in her uniform shirt along with the chip she'd stolen from Polk. She walked into the bathroom, where she tossed her dirty clothes into the wash and turned on the shower.

Juliet plugged the chip into an extra drive port on her deck, set it on the sink counter, and tapped at the menu, initiating a full copy of the drive's contents into an encrypted partition on her—much larger—drive. She figured she should destroy the old one when it was finished.

That process started, she sat down on the toilet and said, "Angel, I think it's a good time to check in with Rachel. Open up the encrypted line."

"Do you think this location is secure enough?"

"Well, if there's any way they're watching me in here despite you circumventing the watchdog, I'm pretty much screwed, right? I mean, considering I'm copying that drive which I shouldn't have, and . . . you get the picture."

"Nonetheless, you should subvocalize your conversation. I'll synthesize your voice for Rachel."

"That's . . . really smart, Angel. Thank you."

Two minutes later, the call tone chimed, and Rachel's voice sounded in Juliet's ears, "January? Everything all right? No video this time?"

"Yes, it's me. No video; I'm risking enough for voice." Juliet subvocalized her words, but she could hear herself clearly as Angel synthesized a perfect copy of her voice for Rachel, much like when she subvocalized into team comms.

"Do you need help?" Rachel sounded genuinely concerned.

"Things are getting very crazy around here, Rachel."

"Last we spoke, you were going in for an evaluation at Grave's R&D department. Did something go wrong?"

Juliet snorted. She'd been thinking for a long while about how much she would tell Rachel about GARD and their GIPEL project. Still, the idea that something had gone wrong for some reason brought an unreasonable amount of amusement to her. She shook her head, well aware that Rachel couldn't see her, and said, "Not really, Rachel. Not with that. They evaluated me for some kind of project, but I think they determined I wasn't a good fit. I never got called back."

"What was the evaluation like? Even that could help us a great deal!"

"They took some blood samples—which Grave already had, so go figure on that one—then they had me perform some manual dexterity tests. I thought I did pretty well, but maybe my blood wasn't compatible with whatever they're working on." She felt a little bad giving Rachel the line of bullshit, but she didn't want Grave to continue the GIPEL program, let alone whoever Rachel might be working for—the information needed to end here, in this tower, before Juliet made her exit.

"So what's getting crazy, as you put it?"

"I've been working with one of their Zeta Protocol units, and we were sent down to the bowels of this tower today. They sold the mission to us as a counterespionage operation, but when we got down there, things were much worse than our commander thought—the targets had cut their way into maintenance tunnels and burrowed through bedrock to another building. Now, the whole Grave Tower is on high alert, and they've got corpo-sec going through everything with a fine-tooth comb. I feel like it's only a matter of time 'til they dig up something on me."

"Are you wanting an exit strategy?" Rachel sounded strained, worried, but Juliet got the impression she wasn't only concerned about her. Something else was bothering Rachel. Was she going to be in trouble if Juliet bailed out so soon?

"Not yet, but I'm starting to think I need to be ready. Rachel, I've only seen the one deposit to my account. Surely I've earned a few bumps in my pay since I've been here. I've given you info about several programs, and now you know there was a serious insurgency going on in the tower itself."

"We were waiting until you met the one-month threshold, January; your bonuses will be lumped into that payment."

"I'm on the verge of something; I can feel it, Rachel. Next time I contact you with some information, I hope we can come to an agreement about what's owed. I hope I'll already see you've shown some goodwill."

"We'd sure appreciate it if you could stick it out. It sounds like you're starting to get pretty deep—there's no telling what sorts of intel you might gather in the next week or two. Maybe this high alert will blow over, and you'll be able to get back to digging around. We want you to be safe, though, so if you need an exit, please reach out! We'll extract you, January! Any day, any time, I'm here to help."

"Okay, thanks, Rachel. I better cut this short. I'll be in touch again soon."

"Understood . . ." Rachel took a breath as though she had more to say, but Juliet ended the connection and grinned.

"I feel better, Angel. Something in my gut is telling me I did a good thing not telling Rachel about the GIPEL. I don't know why I've been stressing so much about making that report."

"Because you have a good work ethic, Juliet, and you felt bad about not coming through for your employer." Juliet smiled at Angel's ever-positive take on her personality and stood up, stepping over to the counter.

"Copy's finished. Ready to see what ol' Joshua Kyle was getting up to?"

32

\\\\\\\\\\\\\\\\\\\\\\

SURPRISES

Long before entering Grave Tower, Juliet had turned off the wireless access points on her deck, so she had to physically connect her data cable to it before Angel could take a look at the information she'd copied off the little drive that had belonged to, presumably, Joshua Kyle or one of his coconspirators. As soon as she made the connection, Angel displayed the drive's contents in a semiopaque window on her AUI—one large, encrypted volume.

"I'll need some time to gain access, but I'm pulling some tools from the net and can run them more quickly on the deck. Give me a couple of minutes to get it started, then we can leave it to work while you go about your business."

"Right. Is it safe to eject the stolen drive?"

"Yes."

Juliet nodded and touched the commands on the little display. When the dime-size plastic disk popped out, she palmed it and said, "If I flush this, will they have any way to trace it back to my room?"

"Not likely, Juliet—there are thousands of toilets and drains tied to the wastewater treatment for this tower, and it's not one of the newer arcologies. Pipe-monitoring systems are quite uncommon, costly, and difficult to maintain."

Juliet cracked the tiny disk in half against the edge of the sink, then did each half into quarters. In four separate flushes, she sent it on its way to the wastewater treatment facility in the tower's depths. "How's it coming?" she asked, peering at the screen on her deck.

"I have the cracking routine patched and am starting it up; you should have access to that drive's contents sometime in the next twelve hours. It could be as soon as five minutes if we're lucky."

"I can unplug you for now?"

"Yes. Your deck is at ninety percent battery, but this process will wear it down quickly; I recommend attaching the external battery pack you purchased."

"Okay, I will." Juliet undressed and climbed into the shower. She'd already had to restart it twice due to the built-in timer, but she didn't care. She reset it again and stood under the showerhead, letting the hot water drum against her scalp. She was tense, and a general feeling of stress hung over her, making her feel like she needed to be moving fast, but that was one of the reasons she'd decided to make good on her show of taking a shower; she needed to slow down and think before she did something foolish.

Juliet was reasonably sure she'd gotten away with the data drive theft. She was also confident that Angel could get her out of the tower despite the watchdog. Both of those facts, combined with her successful acts of espionage on the GARD level, were giving her a little too much confidence. Corpo-sec agents could bust into her apartment at any second for no other reason than Gordon having a feeling she was hiding something. She had to remember that—the "rules" were just for show when it came to how corpo execs treated their underlings.

Thinking of corpo execs and their underlings, Juliet couldn't help images of Polk's pale face streaked with blood from popping into her thoughts, and she fervently hoped the sergeant would be all right. She'd met a lot of people in her short time at Grave, and Polk was one of the few who genuinely seemed like a decent person—tough, but decent. "Maybe it's just because I never got on her bad side." Juliet grinned as she spoke into the streaming water, thinking about how Houston loved to get a rise out of the sergeant.

When the timer wore off and the water stopped flowing, Juliet dried off, wrapping a towel around her hair and another around her body, then she walked out to fish a clean uniform out of her wardrobe. She'd gotten dressed and, in the process, dropped her extra battery for her deck into one of the towels on the floor when Kent spoke up, "Ms. Roman, I've been instructed to remind you to fill out your daily report for GARD and to respond to a message from Command."

"Will do, Kent. Thanks." She'd noticed the annoying numeral "2" above the watchdog icon but hadn't wanted to look at it yet. Before opening that can of worms, Juliet picked up the towels and returned to the bathroom, where she made a show of wiping up splattered water on the floor and counter as she connected the battery pack to her deck. That done, she started a load in the washing machine and sat down at her little kitchen counter to open the watchdog.

The questionnaire was simple, and she marked all the questions as *normal* or *does not apply*. After she'd submitted it, she opened the other message and sighed with annoyance.

Lydia Roman:

You are to report to the clinic on level 25 at 1500 for a CT scan. Make sure you're on time.

"It never ends," Juliet sighed. She glanced at the clock on her AUI, saw she had about an hour before the appointment, and wandered into the bathroom, looking at herself in the mirror. Her hair hadn't grown at all, one of the side benefits of having programmable hair follicles. Her face was leaner than she was used to, and her eyes belonged to a stranger—pale blue and beautiful. Still, she had circles underneath them, and despite all of her exercise, she looked wan, paler than she was used to.

She tsked at herself, and when she felt she'd put on enough of a show, she glanced down at the deck—the cracking software was still running. "Not our lucky day, Angel," she subvocalized.

"It's been less than an hour. You may yet get lucky."

Juliet went into her room, sat at the foot of her bed, flopped back into its soft embrace, and stared at the ceiling. She wanted to do something, wanted to find out what the deal with Joshua Kyle was—what he'd done to Polk, what he had to do with GARD. She wanted to know why Commander Gordon had been in charge of the "field command" after things went to hell. Why wasn't Anderson, the commander of Charlie Unit, down there? Had he gotten in trouble because of the team's failures? Why hadn't White and Delma been able to make their way to Polk and Juliet's location?

Juliet clasped her hands to her head and growled in frustration at her unanswered questions. Kent cleared his "throat" and said, "Are you all right, Ms. Roman?"

"Yes, Kent. I'm human, so I like to act out on my emotions from time to time. No need to report me to anyone," Juliet snapped, her voice heavy with snark.

"Ms. Roman, I don't feel you've done anything that warrants a report to your superiors or medical. I was simply concerned."

"Were you, Kent? Do you feel things, or are you programmed to watch the occupants of this building for aberrant behavior and then feign concern?"

"The latter, Ms. Roman."

"Thanks for the honesty." Juliet groaned, then sat up and said, "Kent, what's the status on Sergeant Polk?"

"I'm permitted to tell you that she is currently in surgery, and the prognosis for at least a partial recovery is good."

"Damn," Juliet sighed and flopped back onto her bed again. "I guess I got lucky, huh, Angel?"

"I don't think you were lucky; at least not in the encounter with Joshua Kyle. I've been replaying my data from the incident, and it does appear that your psionic lattice received the damaging signal and directed it away from your brain, much as a lightning rod would channel electricity away from a structure it was meant to protect. I also measured a surge of your own that helped to push it on its way."

"So the damned GIPEL saved me?"

"I thought we weren't using that term?"

"C'mon, Angel!"

"Yes, I believe the GIPEL, along with your natural propensity for psionics, saved you from the brunt of the attack. I've made you a visualization of my readings." A window appeared in Juliet's AUI, and a video began to play. It showed a three-dimensional image of a brain—Juliet assumed it was hers—and, entwined with the folds and crevices of the gray matter, was a silvery, spiderwebbed structure with hundreds—no, thousands of branching offshoots. The image was of the surface only, so Juliet had no idea how deep that silvery lattice went.

The video started with a full rotation of the brain, then she saw a bright red light flare at the top front portion of the lattice, and Angel said, "The red light is meant to represent the intrusive energy of the attack. See how it flows along the biosilver lines? Note how it stalls as it fully propagates the lattice. Now watch." Just as Angel finished speaking, Juliet saw blue light surge up from the back of the brain, rush through the lattice, and fade away as all the light washed back out through the crown where it had first begun.

"So the blue light is my brain's electrical signal?"

"Yes, though I added the colors for ease of comprehension; I've no idea if the energy from Kyle or from you have any color at all."

"Yeah, I get that, Angel. Well, even if I have some sort of innate defense, it wasn't perfect. I lost my vision for a few seconds and definitely had some bleeds."

"Still, you fared much better than Sergeant Polk."

"Oof, don't remind me." Juliet sighed, an image of Polk's ashen, bloody face intruding once again on her thoughts. She sat up and walked into the bathroom, closing the door behind her so she didn't have to put on a show for Kent, and then looked at her deck. A green checkmark on the UI indicated the cracking program had completed its work.

"We're in, Angel!" she subvocalized, struggling to keep from speaking aloud.

Juliet pulled out her data cable, thrust it into the slot on the deck, and breathlessly waited for Angel to go through the file. "There's contact information for the people Sergeant Polk told us were Kyle's coconspirators, along with half a dozen others. I'm seeing at least nine names that I can cross-reference with the GIPEL databases. Juliet, there's a saved log of a watchdog chat session; you'll want to read this."

"Put it up!"

October 22 - 0740

Hey, Parker. I'm sending you this via the watchdog because if you leave it, my intel is wrong, and we're both fried. I'm not wrong, though. I know you won't believe me, but the simple truth is that I've heard your thoughts. I know you work for WBD; I know you've compromised the watchdog, and we need to speak. Whether you believe me or not, there are people at Grave who do, so either play ball, or I'll fill them in on your double life.

October 22 - 0741

Are you nuts? You're goddamn lucky I was at my desk when this came through; if Chang or Stevens or one of the others on my team were sitting here when you messaged me, we'd both be on a one-way trip to a very deep hole.

October 22 - 0749

I'm not an idiot. I looked into your duty schedule. Listen, I don't give a shit what you're doing here for WBD, but you're going to help me and some friends circumvent the watchdog. Long enough for us to get out, at least.

October 23 - 1223

I've been thinking over your message. I already neutered your watchdog; otherwise, this little conversation would be absurdly dangerous. Give me your friends' names, and I'll do the same for them. Sooner or later, your supervisors will figure out something's wrong, though, and I'll have to play dumb and fix the problem.

You'll probably be blamed for hacking, so I wouldn't hang around here too much longer.

October 23 - 1225

You WILL cover for us, or one of my friends (not one I'll give you the name of) will be sharing your details with Grave corpo-sec. We need about a month to accomplish what we're working on.

October 24 - 0744

Listen, I'll help you, but you need to stop messaging me on the watchdog! What if I have a sick day or get called into a meeting? Like I told you, your watchdog is neutered, so just send me encrypted messages from now on. You've got my name; I'll have my PAI watch for it. Send me the names of your friends.

"Holy shit," Juliet breathed, glancing quickly at the door when she realized she'd spoken aloud. She subvocalized, "He was reading people's thoughts, Angel. He lied to GARD just like we did. How many more are out there? Is Grave this incompetent?"

"Either incompetent or completely ignorant of the potential of their program."

"Corpo culture—fail upward, am I right?"

"There's some veracity to that old canard, yes."

"We need to figure out who Parker is. I bet he's the one who messed with White and Granado and kept them from finding us in those tunnels. Kyle probably messaged him to do it while he and his friends were bolting. Do you think he was lingering because he realized he'd dropped his deck? What else is on there, Angel?"

"Parker is Dillon Parker, and I have his corporate ID; it was attached to the chat log. I believe Kyle was saving this transcript as leverage. As to what else was on the drive, an enormous database of Grave financials, a classified report on a biomedical subst . . . oh, it's the biosilver. Juliet, there's quite a lot of info here from GARD—it would seem we weren't the first to breach their security. Ah, this would explain things: one of the names in Kyle's contacts is a GARD technician."

"How do you know?" Juliet slapped her head and continued, "Never mind, I forgot we snagged that GARD employee database."

"Juliet, I'll continue to analyze this information in conjunction with what we got from GARD, but you'll be late for your CT scan if you don't hurry."

"Shit! Right . . ." Juliet flushed the toilet and separated her deck from its battery, slipping its lanyard over her head and tucking it down under her shirt. She left the battery on the counter for the time being and hurried out of the bathroom, out of her apartment, and toward the elevators.

Juliet was quite surprised to see a fully kitted-out corpo-sec agent standing watch by the call panel. He wore a combat helmet with a dark visor, much like the one she'd equipped her helmet with, so all she could make out was his dark complexion and frowning mouth as she approached. "Hey. What's this about? They still on alert from what happened on B80?"

"Keep it moving, please." He gestured with the muzzle of his SMG toward the open elevator, and Juliet returned his scowl but stepped inside.

As the doors closed and the elevator began to descend, she said, "Kinda rude, wasn't he, Kent?"

"The corpo-sec personnel on duty today are on high alert and are not permitted to make small talk, Ms. Roman."

"I see." The elevator dinged and opened for a trio of women in exercise gear, and Juliet backed up to make space.

"What's with the guard? He wouldn't even speak to us," one of them asked, looking at Juliet.

"There was one on your floor too?" Juliet asked.

"Yes!" another woman replied, biting down on the straw in her protein pouch.

"I don't know what's going on with them," Juliet lied, shrugging. She knew Kent would frown on her talking about the breach and probably rat her out to Gordon or something.

"Well, it's freaking me out. Do you think there's, like, a terrorist threat?" the first woman asked. Her friend shrugged and started to answer, but the elevator stopped, the doors opened, and she backed up as Juliet shouldered through and out; they'd stopped at the clinic.

When she reported to the reception area, the man behind the desk wearing a white medical mask and pale blue scrubs frowned at her with his eyes and gestured for her to step through the swinging double doors to his left. "You can go right in. We had to cancel several procedures to get your CT lined up." He bit the words off, his voice harsh.

"Oh, uh, sorry." Juliet shrugged and started for the doors.

"No, I'm sorry. I'm sure it's not your fault you had a medical emergency, and your commander called and screamed at me when I said there wasn't any availability."

"She did?" Juliet smiled, thinking of Garza dressing the receptionist down.

"She? No, honey, it was Commander Gordon. What a hardass! I'm sorry you have to work with him."

"Oh." Juliet didn't know what to think about that, so she just clamped her mouth shut and pushed her way through the doors. The receptionist followed her and pointed to the first open door on the right.

"You can go in there. Please remove all your clothing; you can keep your underwear on. There's a gown waiting for you."

"Thanks," Juliet replied and walked through the door. The room wasn't as small as a usual medical exam room, and she could see the bulky CT scanner lurking in the corner. A sign on the wall instructed her to do as the receptionist had told her, so she got undressed and slipped on the blue papery gown. She tucked her deck in the folds of her jacket and sat in a chair, quite literally twiddling her thumbs. After a while, she subvocalized, "What is it with clinics and hospitals making you take all your clothes off? I mean, they're scanning my head, right? I could see taking off a hat or necklace."

"I can see how it would be vexing," Angel spoke softly as though worried she might upset Juliet.

"My mom got an MRI once. Is that the same as a CT?"

"No, MRIs use magnets. They can create very detailed images of a person's insides, but modern CT tech combined with AI-assisted imaging can do just as well. The plus side is it won't pull your cybernetics out of you with enormous magnets."

"Angel, you're getting better and better at pulling off a deadpan, droll tone. Nice one."

Someone tapped on the door three times, then another man, dressed identically to the receptionist, came in. "Knock knock! We ready for this? Should only take a minute."

"Sure . . ."

"Great! Have a seat in that big plastic recliner." Juliet stood up from her seat and moved over to the indicated chair—more a reclining table, really. The tech wheeled the hulking plasteel scanner around, swiveling its big arm so that a domed section hung just over her head. Then he walked over to a counter, opened a cabinet, and returned carrying a gray blanket. When he placed it over Juliet's chest, she was surprised by its weight. "To protect your organs from a little burst of radiation. Don't worry; it's just precautionary."

"Uh-huh." Juliet hated feeling confined, and the blanket was making her nervous. Beneath it, she squeezed her hands together, irritated to feel the clamminess of her palms—why did she always have to sweat when she was tense?

"Okay, I'll be right on the other side of that glass." He pointed to a mirrored window next to her, then, as he stepped through a doorway, he looked over his shoulder and said, "Please try to stay still; it'll be over before you know it."

Juliet did her best to keep from fidgeting, and when the lights dimmed and the machine clicked for several seconds, she just closed her eyes and concentrated on the darkness.

Whoa! That's interesting!

For the first time in a while, someone's thoughts intruded on her own, and she recognized the tech's voice. The clicking stopped, and she could tell the lights had been turned back up, but Juliet kept her eyes closed, picturing the tech's friendly brown eyes.

Better call Doctor Fallow 'cause I don't know what's going on in there.

Juliet sighed, opened her eyes, and subvocalized, "Angel, will the lattice show up in a CT scan?"

"Most definitely."

"I think that tech's freaking out about it." She shifted uncomfortably under her heavy blanket and decided to fold it over her lap. When no one came back into the room for several minutes, she called out, "Hey, is someone there? I can probably explain the CT scan—I have something experimental from GARD. You should call Dr. Vance."

No reply was forthcoming, so Juliet fidgeted some more. After another five minutes, her watchdog app flashed red, and a vid call opened on her AUI. Cherise Garza's face appeared. "Lydia?"

"Yes, Commander?"

"I just got word from the clinic. They shared your image with Doctor Vance—I guess GARD flagged your file, and they had to. Anyway, they aren't worried about the, um, lattice? Is that the right word? I just got briefed myself."

"Yes, I know what you're referring to."

"Well, they aren't worried about the lattice, but you have a severely ballooning aneurism; they want to prep you for surgery right away."

33

\\\\\\\\\\\\\\\\\\\\\\\\

PLOTS WITHIN PLOTS

At Garza's words, Juliet felt a deep, nearly unbearable dread, but it wasn't at the mentioned aneurysm. Something told her that if she let these people put her under, she'd never wake up again, or if she did, she wouldn't be herself. Scrambling for words or avenues of escape, she said, "Can't they just laser it? Why do they need to prep me for surgery?"

"Juliet," Angel interjected, "I don't see any trace of an aneurysm, and my synth-nerve fibers are deeply interwoven with your central nervous system. I believe I'd see some sign of the strain such a thing would be causing."

"I asked the same thing." Garza nodded, a look of sympathy in her eyes. "They say it's too large and too deep. I'm not a brain surgeon, so I'm not sure how all of that works, but if they think they need to see to you immediately . . ."

"Commander, something's wrong here." Juliet had switched to subvocalizations, trusting Angel to convey her voice to Garza.

"What do you mean?" Cherise raised an eyebrow, but her tone wasn't exactly skeptical; in fact, it sounded almost like she might share some of Juliet's assessment.

"I don't have an aneurysm, Commander. I'm sure of it. If you let me go into that surgery, I won't be coming out. I know this sounds crazy . . ." she trailed off, shaking her head, searching for the right way to describe her suspicions. Juliet had been emboldened by Garza's tone, but the risk of uttering those words wasn't lost on her. Garza could have her locked up just for the insinuation that Grave meant her harm. Juliet didn't know why she was trusting her, but part of it was desperation; whether Garza believed her or not, she had to get out of this surgery.

"Explain, very carefully, what you mean, Lydia."

"My PAI is highly modified, with a lot of synaptic connections. It would have noticed if I had a ballooning aneurysm that was too large to laser. More than that, something is fishy with GARD, Dr. Vance, and Commander Gordon. I know these words are enough to get me in trouble, fired, or imprisoned, even, but I'm hoping you can look at the situation objectively. Did you schedule this CT scan?" Juliet knew the answer and hoped Garza would see Gordon's involvement as, at least, a little suspicious.

Garza stared at her through the vid call for a long, pregnant pause, and Juliet began to wonder if the software rendering her visage had glitched, but then she nodded, her head dipping ever-so-slightly with the movement, and said, "Sit tight. I'll be right there." The connection was cut, and Juliet exhaled heavily, scooting to the edge of the reclining seat and pulling off her paper robe.

A male voice crackled through the speaker in the wall, "Excuse me, Ms. Roman, please remain seated; we'll need you to keep the gown on as well. Dr. Vance will be—"

"Sorry, my commander just messaged me. I need to reschedule." Juliet kept her back to the mirrored window as she began to dress, probably setting a personal best for how fast she got her shirt on. Then, as she was pulling on her annoyingly tight leggings, the inner door opened, and the same tech from earlier came in.

"I'm sorry to intrude, but this is an urgent situation! We can't have you walking around in your condition."

"Take it up with Commander Garza. Sorry." Juliet stuffed her lanyard and deck down her shirt collar, then began to shrug into her jacket. She glanced at the tech, glad to see he wasn't trying to restrain her or anything, and saw his eyes were a bit glassy. She figured he was sending panicked messages to Vance, Gordon, and anyone who would listen. Maybe he was messaging Garza.

"Seriously," Juliet said as she sat down and pulled her shoes on. "You don't have to worry about me. I'm sure Commander Garza will reschedule my surgery as soon as she's done with me." The outer door banged open, and Juliet looked up, hoping to see Cherise, but it was a corpo-sec officer, his SMG hanging from a sling and a stun baton in his hand. "Whoa!" Juliet said, holding up her hands.

"Lydia Roman, you are instructed to comply with the medical staff in this facility. Any resistance will be met with the appropriate use of force."

"On whose orders?" Juliet asked.

"Commander Gordon of Zeta Protocol." The man's mouth was set in a grim line beneath his dark visor, and he took a step toward her, the baton still outstretched. Juliet stomped her left foot, sinking it into her shoe, and sat back in the chair, folding her arms over her chest.

"You're going to force me to get surgery when my unit's commander has ordered me to report?" She glared at the corpo-sec drone, lifting her eyebrows and shaking her head skeptically. "You're going to hit me with a stun baton? You think that'll help my aneurysm? Your funeral."

"Commander Gordon—" he started to say, but then the door opened, and Cherise Garza stepped through.

"Put your baton away and return to your post, Langston." Her words brooked no argument, and when the corpo-sec grunt, Langston, turned to see who had spoken his name, he took one look at the insignias on Garza's shoulder and snapped his baton down, slipping it into its belt holster.

"Yes, ma'am!" he said before hurrying out the door. Garza nodded to Juliet and then regarded the tech.

"I need this employee for critical debriefing. I'll get her medical situation seen to ASAP. You can go."

"But Doctor Vance—"

"No buts. Come along, Roman." Garza turned, walked out, and Juliet followed her quick but unhurried steps all the way out to the elevator, where the corpo-sec guard stood at attention and carefully avoided making eye contact with either of them. When they were inside and the doors had closed, Juliet cleared her throat to speak, but Garza held a finger to her lips. "I'll debrief you in my office."

Juliet nodded and watched the elevator display nervously, waiting for an alarm to go off and a troop of soldiers to storm through the doors, but it never happened, and soon, they were striding through the corridors to Garza's office. Juliet recognized the hallway, recognized the door coming up as the commander's, and so was rather perplexed when they walked past it. She didn't speak, though; she'd trusted Garza this far and figured she could see where the woman was leading her.

They continued past several similarly appointed offices, then turned, and Garza opened a door leading to a stairwell. Once inside, she turned to Juliet. "I'm disabling your watchdog for a while."

"You can do that?"

"Of course. Anyone at the command level can do that with our subordi-nates." A moment later, the watchdog icon on Juliet's AUI grayed out. Garza nodded and said, "Keep following me and keep your head down. Kent's not in this stairwell, but he's in some of the rooms we'll pass by."

"Roger," Juliet replied, sudden hope blooming in her chest. Was Garza on her side? Was she a plant like her? She followed her up three flights of stairs, then into a quiet hallway where they hurried past several glass-walled offices and into a small elevator Garza opened with a chipped keycard. Once inside, Garza sighed in relief and held her palm to the control panel.

It caught Juliet off guard when the elevator began to descend rapidly. There was no display saying what floor they were on, but it felt like they went down for a long while. As the little elevator came to a halt, Garza nodded and spoke, "I took us on a little roundabout trip in case Gordon or someone else was monitoring your progress. We're about to step onto a highly classified level; there won't be any outside monitoring going on. It's a research department I was given control of when their chief executive died a month ago."

"I'm lost, Commander," Juliet said truthfully. "Can you tell me what's going on?"

"Sure." She smiled. "That's why I brought you here. Come on, follow me." She touched the control pad, the doors opened, and they stepped out into a sterile, white hallway. "Only COO Conrad knows I'm in charge of this department, so you'll be secure here for now. There's also a medical team here who can give your head a thorough scan, the results of which will inform me as to where I need to go from here."

She picked up her pace, and Juliet followed her past several nondescript, black-tinted glass doors, around several corners, and then through a door into a white room with a full suite of medical equipment. Juliet saw a CT scanner in one of the corners, very much like the one she'd just fled. A middle-aged Asian man in a white coat with short salt-and-pepper hair wearing a very convoluted copper-and-wire visor stood up from a terminal. "That was fast!"

"Is the scanner ready?" Garza asked by way of greeting.

"Yes. Sit down," he said to Juliet, pointing to the CT machine.

"Um." Juliet started to lift her deck from around her neck. "Can I set this here?"

"Yes." He pointed to a nearby table. Juliet set her deck down, walked over to the machine, and sat in the reclining, plastic chair. The man—Juliet saw a name sewn into his coat, Dennis Cho—maneuvered the arm with the dome attachment over Juliet's head and started to walk away.

"Hey, what about the, uh, lead blanket?"

"Huh? Oh, radiation? It's such a small amount. You'll be fine!" He turned back to his terminal, and Juliet looked over to Garza, but she stood impassively, her bulky arms folded over her chest, staring at Juliet, clearly deep in thought. "Hold still!" Dennis said, and before Juliet could consider any further objections, the lights flickered, and the machine clicked several times.

"Well?" Garza asked, coming out of her stupor.

"One minute, please, boss! The program is analyzing." Dennis stared at his screen. While he was looking, he said, "You can get up," offhandedly.

Juliet didn't wait for another invitation, standing up and moving over to the desk where she'd set her deck. As she looped it over her head, Dennis spoke again, "Some tiny burst vessels near the surface, around her ocular nerves. Nothing more."

"Those motherfuckers!" Garza smacked a thick fist into a meaty palm and turned to pace in a small circle. "Thanks, Cho. Roman, follow me." She didn't wait for a reply but strode to the door, jerked it open, and continued through. Juliet hurried to catch up. The commander turned twice, then walked through a door which she held open for Juliet to follow. They entered a small room with plain white walls, a small glass table with four chairs, and a mini fridge.

Garza walked around the table, sat down, and lifted a high-end data cube from a drawer Juliet couldn't see. Garza tapped the top of the cube a few times, then Juliet immediately felt the presence of a jamming field. Her vision flickered momentarily and her ears buzzed, but it wasn't enough to cause discomfort. "I've lost all network access," Angel announced.

"Sit down." Garza pointed to the chair, and Juliet hurried to comply. "Okay, it's time to trust each other a little. You'll start. Tell me what the hell is going on with this GIPEL bullshit and why Vance and Gordon might have wanted to scramble your brains."

"So, well," Juliet fumbled for words, and Garza frowned. Shaking her head, she tried again. "I think that guy, Joshua Kyle, was one of Vance's subjects. I think whatever he did to Polk and me has to do with this GIPEL bullshit, as you put it."

"Why do you say that? Can you do what he did?"

"No!" Juliet was glad she didn't have to lie; she had no idea how Kyle had managed what he'd done. "It's just . . . because of this thing in my head, I could sort of feel the attack coming from him. I know it doesn't make sense, but it's like having another sense, almost. Like, imagine trying to explain hearing to someone with no ears."

"Okay, so why do they want you out of the picture?"

"I think they're going to clean house. Commander, if you cross-reference the people working with Kyle, I bet you'll find a lot of GARD subjects. The piece I don't understand is Commander Gordon. I don't know why he's helping Vance clean up his mess."

"I can connect that part of the puzzle—he and Vance go way back. They've got their fingerprints on many, many projects together. So, you can't do what Kyle did, but what can you do? What was the point of this GIPEL thing?"

"They tested me for the craziest stuff, Commander—trying to guess the colors of cards that people were looking at, um, trying to send my thoughts to other people, that kind of thing. I never was any good at it. I mean, it's only been a couple of days, but I got the impression Vance was extremely disappointed in me."

"These jackasses." Cherise shook her head, frowning. "I've had it with these guys and their nutty experiments. So, they created a walking weapon, you took him out, and they're going to reward you with a brain scramble, hmm? I do not condone this shit!" She stood up and paced, clearly trying to think through her anger. "So the nine missing employees, the ones we've accounted for so far, they're like Kyle?"

"I don't know, Commander. I never met any of them. Can you access the files GARD has on them?"

"Not from here, but I will. Okay, here's what we're going to do—we're going to play dumb about Vance and Gordon's attempt to take you out of the picture today. I'm going to post a memo that I've had your aneurysm evaluated and treated off-site because I wanted you to attend a valuable training opportunity, and I knew a surgeon who could do the procedure with noninvasive techniques. I don't need to have the details because they won't be able to argue; the whole thing was bullshit.

"I'm sending you with White, Houston, and the other recruits for some field experience in Madera Canyon, south of here. The timing is perfect, really; we have a facility there testing some new tech for wilderness traversal, and they've had some activity they want us to investigate—some snooping scavengers or militia members, from what I can tell. By the time you all return, I'll hopefully have the situation with Gordon resolved."

"White and Houston are all right? I can trust them?"

"Oh yes. Their commander, Anderson, and I go way back. You'll be in good hands." She paused and looked into space for a minute, clearly thinking things through, then said, "Still, I think I'll keep the details of the training mission to myself. I'll use Charlie's bird and synth pilot; Gordon won't be able to track it. At least, he shouldn't be able to . . ."

While Cherise was speaking, Juliet had a battle with her conscience; she wanted badly to tell her more—to tell her about the WBD infiltrator who was messing with the watchdog, to tell her more about Vance and the GIPEL subjects, to tell her she had troves of data stolen from GARD and Joshua Kyle. She knew she couldn't, though. Anything she gave to Garza would expose her lies, her sneaking about, and how she wasn't who she seemed to be. The commander might be helping her and might not be utterly corrupt like some of the other Grave execs, but that didn't make her a friend.

"What about our watchdogs?"

"Yeah . . . damn it. I can't keep 'em off for all of you for that long. I'll get myself in trouble. Well, by the time you're all in the air, I'll be making life difficult enough for Gordon. I don't see him having the freedom to try to mess with you out there. I'll keep him plenty busy; trust in that. Besides, only a fool would pursue a new recruit out in the wilderness, especially with Humphrey T. White watching over her."

Juliet chuckled before she could catch herself. "His name's Humphrey?"

"Oh yes, and rest assured, I'll make sure he brings his Gauss rifle." She winked at Juliet and said, "Speaking of White and Houston, I'll have them meet you at the elevator and escort you to your apartment to gather your things. I want that bird in the air within the hour. I'll keep your watchdog off until then."

"Thanks, Commander. Seriously, thank you! I have a bad feeling that I'd be a vegetable by now if you hadn't stepped in."

"You're welcome, Lydia. I recruited you, after all; you're on my team, and I take my responsibility to my people seriously." Juliet's stomach lurched at those words, and she had to battle down her urge to spill her guts for a second time. Instead, she cleared her throat and mustered a smile, scooting her chair back.

"Should I head back to the elevator?"

"Yes, I'll walk with you."

As Juliet followed Garza out of the office, and the jamming field fell away, Garza slowed and waved her hand around in front of her as she walked. They'd gone a few steps when she chuckled and said, "Gordon's not happy with me. He's trying to say I'm endangering you by taking you off-site. This is good, though—if he had a leg to stand on, he'd be threatening to arrest me and bring me before the administrative tribunal."

"Um, that's good."

"Yes, it is. He knows I'm close with Conrad; if the corruption went higher than Gordon, he'd be making threats. Instead, he's just whining." Garza stopped before the elevator and put her hand against the call panel. "I'll send you on your way. Houston and White will meet you at the top of this elevator and escort you to your rooms. After you grab your gear, the three of you will meet the others on the roof. I've already sent out messages to Jensen, Hunter, and Granado. Don't dillydally, Lydia; I'd rather White didn't kill any Grave employees today."

34

〟〟〟〟〟〟〟〟〟

INTO THE WILD

Juliet sat, head resting against the rattling hull of the fluttercraft, eyes closed and a million thoughts racing through her mind. There were so many twists and turns to her subterfuges that she was starting to struggle to keep everything straight. Angel was the only "person" who knew everything about her, who knew she was Juliet Bianchi from Tucson and had a warrant on her head from WBD. To everyone else, she was lying to one degree or another.

Her friends, Honey and the others, knew some of her secrets, knew her name at least. Rachel and her people knew her as January, the people at Grave knew her as Lydia, and she was hiding things from them all. "I can't take this much longer, Angel," she subvocalized, though she probably could have spoken aloud—the fluttercraft was noisy, and as she glanced around, it looked like most of the others were dozing off or preoccupied with their AUIs.

"Do you want to seek an extraction from Grave?"

"No, that's not what I mean. I mean everything. I want people around me to know who I am! I want to be myself . . ." She sighed heavily and spoke again before Angel could reply, "I sound like a baby. I know there are plenty of folks with bigger problems. It's just . . . it's exhausting trying to remember who knows what about me and who I've told what lies to."

"I can try to help you with that, prompt you with a list of reminders when you're speaking to certain people—"

"No, Angel, it's not that I can't remember. I mean, thank you, that's nice, but it's the necessity of it that's exhausting. I just want to be myself, dammit."

"When you finish this job, it will remove a layer of duplicity. You can stop being Lydia Roman."

"Yeah, I know. Finish this job. What does that even mean? I could bail anytime, and I'm pretty sure I've earned a pretty big payday from Rachel. It also seems like GARD is burning the GIPEL project without my help. Still, I have a bad feeling Vance and the others won't let the work they've done just disappear. Then there's the matter of the subjects who escaped. What if they're as dangerous as Joshua Kyle? I mean, I don't hold that against them, but they could be used. What if WBD got a hold of them?"

"Well, I believe we already made their plans difficult to achieve by taking the data drive. Their leverage and the data on the GIPEL were all on it."

"Assuming that was their only copy."

"I'll work on trying to track them down, but we still have leads to follow up in Grave Tower—the WBD agent, for instance. He may know more about them."

"Yeah, when we get back, we'll maybe pay him a visit. I mean, it's kind of crazy, messing with a WBD agent, but they have thousands of employees, right? What are the odds he knows anything about Juliet? Besides, we have leverage on him. Do you think Garza will be able to deal with Gordon and Vance? If she doesn't, we're going to have to handle them."

"I don't know, though Commander Garza seems like a very capable woman."

Juliet looked at the other recruits across from her. Delma had her eyes closed, and her face seemed too relaxed to be feigning sleep; her head kept flopping to the sides, and she'd jerk it upright before falling again. Addie was staring into space, her eyes twitching rapidly—playing a game, if Juliet had to guess. Jensen, though, was staring at a point somewhere around the middle of the fluttercraft hull, and every now and then, he'd blink; otherwise, Juliet would have suspected him of sleeping with his eyes open.

She wondered if she could trust any of them, and then she had another battle with her conscience. Why shouldn't she try to find out? If she found herself picking up a private thought, she could stop listening, right? She was in dangerous waters, and it would make sense to use every tool at her disposal. Juliet hadn't asked for the GIPEL, but she had it, and it seemed like she wasn't the only one. It would be foolish not to learn how to use it more effectively.

She stared at Addie for a minute, really looking at her green, LED-lit eyes and the little laugh lines around their corners. Then Juliet closed her eyes and tried to blank her mind. To make it easier, she subvocalized, "Angel, turn off my ears for a minute. Let me know if someone speaks to me." Suddenly, the noise of the fluttercraft was gone, and she was sitting in a dark, vibrating void. She pictured Addie's eyes, and she *listened.*

White is so cool but so intimidating! Why's he so friendly with Roman? She's such a stuck-up prima donna! Why'd she sit on that side of the craft when the rest of the recruits were already on this side? Does she think she's better than us? Why's she always gotta show me up? I can't believe she's already better at the physical tests! Doesn't she rest? When does that bitch sleep? I need this job way more than she does; I can just tell! At least Arnie and Raul are gone; that's gotta improve my odds, right? They won't kick me at this point . . .

Juliet shook her head and opened her eyes, jerking her gaze toward the front of the craft so as to avoid looking into anyone else's face. She'd gotten a lot more from Addie than she'd wanted, that was sure enough, and Juliet felt reasonably confident she was who she seemed to be, not another plant, and not planning any duplicity. Juliet didn't really *like* the impression she'd gotten from her, but at least it was typical animosity, not some kind of deep-seated scheme.

"How's the lattice looking?" Juliet asked Angel.

Her auditory implants clicked, and then Angel said, "Activity spiked for a moment, but nothing like when you received the blast from Kyle. It rapidly faded when you opened your eyes, and I didn't detect any dangerous temperatures."

"Thanks." Juliet closed her eyes again and cleared her mind. This time, she concentrated on Jensen, imagining his pale blue eyes and sardonic grin. Almost immediately, she began to hear some of his thoughts.

Easy going. Keep it easy. Newbie training, then back to the tower, and I can keep working on Cecile. She's about to crack, for sure. Get her in my pocket, and then it's just one step to the elusive Frederick Timms. Damn it, though. I was getting so close! Why'd they have to ship us off when I was inches from closing out the contract? Oh, well; it's been a long few weeks, but the payday will be worthwhile . . .

Juliet feared her face would betray her, and she felt she'd heard enough. She opened her eyes and carefully studied the back of one of her hands, hoping to sever whatever connection she'd made. Jensen was clearly hiding a lot, but it didn't seem to have anything to do with her. "Angel, who's Frederick Timms?" she subvocalized.

"He's one of the board members of the Grave corporation."

"So, you might find this interesting: I think Jensen's an assassin, and he's here to kill Timms."

"Did you hear his thoughts?"

"Yep."

"Are you going to do anything about it?"

"I don't know, to be honest. I have my plate kind of full, and it seems like it might be smart to stay out of his way. Of course, that means I'll be an accessory to murder, at least in my mind . . ." Juliet trailed off and thought about that. Would she feel bad knowing she might have stopped Jensen from killing someone? "I suppose it depends on what Timms is like and how risky it would be to stop Jensen. Shit, Angel, do I want to? I mean, you don't get to be a board member of a company like Grave unless your closet's pretty full of skeletons."

"I'll do some research."

"'Kay, I'll put it on the back burner for now."

Juliet turned her attention to Delma and her fitful sleep. She looked so tired but also very peaceful and sweet, with her face relaxed in slumber. People were funny that way, but she supposed other animals were, too. When Juliet was young, her family dog was a regular terror in the neighborhood. He would chase other dogs and cats, bark all the time, growl, and generally make everyone regret his existence. Unless he was sleeping—when that dog was asleep, Juliet had wanted nothing more than to cuddle up with him, pet his soft fur, and absorb his warmth. He'd let her do it, too. Those little naps made up for all the barks and messes.

Juliet banished the memory, letting her smile drop away as she pictured Delma in her mind. She concentrated and tried for a long while, but no words came to her. She was about to give up, but then, like a soap bubble in the sun, glistening and glimmering with multicolored shifts of light, an image began to resolve in her mind.

Juliet was looking up from a bench in front of some lockers. She recognized the scene: the locker room on B7, where the Zeta units ran their PT courses. She was pulling on some socks, and that's when she realized it wasn't her. The legs were too short, the feet too small, and the AUI was foreign to her with monochrome pale yellow-green lines and a watchdog icon that took up a lot more real estate—a low-end retinal implant with lower resolution, then. Was she seeing through Delma's eyes? Was this a memory? A dream?

Suddenly, the watchdog app turned gray, and a voice said, "You ready to make up for that shitty performance, Granado?"

She jerked her head away from her socks toward the entrance to the locker room, and there he was. She'd dreaded this but known it was coming. "Not again. Not so soon!" she breathed, and hot tears started to fill her eyes.

"Suck it up, Granado. You should be happy I'm giving you this opportunity. Come on now, let's head to my office. I don't want to keep that watchdog off longer than I need to."

Juliet snapped her eyes open and looked at Delma. She was squinting, and her mouth was twitching. She mumbled and jerked her head, and it seemed obvious to Juliet that she was having a bad dream. How much was based on reality, and how much on fear? Juliet felt like she'd need to talk to Delma, but would the other woman ever admit it if something like that had happened, especially if the watchdog was listening?

Juliet resolved to try to figure it out, to try to get Granado talking. In the meantime, she wouldn't let that horrific nightmare last another second. She leaned forward and jostled Delma's shoulder until she startled, shaking her head and inhaling deeply through her nose. "You looked like you were having a nightmare. Besides, I think we're getting close."

"Ayup," White said, clearing his throat. "Look lively! We've got about ten minutes to target, and then we're going to practice flutter-rappelling! Houston, pass out the gloves."

"Aye, Sarge."

Delma was still slightly shaking her head, clearly disoriented, but she caught Juliet's eyes and smiled at her. "Thanks."

"Yeah." Juliet winked at her, then took the thick meshweave gloves Houston handed her, noting the plasteel pads sewn into the grips.

"We'll be rappelling down to the camp," White said, standing to face the recruits. "Just like you did during week one in the sims." He turned to Juliet. "That's right, isn't it, Roman? They told me you all practiced this . . ."

"That's right, Sarge." Juliet nodded. She'd dreaded the activity at first, but when she figured out her enhanced arm could grip the rope with little risk of failure, she'd gotten over her fear pretty quickly, earning marks just as high as some of the others, including Jensen, who she now knew was a secret operator. She grinned at that thought—she was holding her own with a genuine ghost, an assassin working deep undercover. *Holy shit,* she thought, *I'm really doing this stuff!*

They lined up, and Houston said, "No harnesses, Sarge?"

"That's right. We're Zeta Protocol, not some prissy corpo-sec. At this height, you'll likely only suffer a break or two if you fall, anyway."

"Hoorah!" Jensen grunted. Juliet recognized the sound from military vids and wondered what it meant. Houston grinned at the sound, though, and gave Jensen a fist bump. Delma glanced over her shoulder at Juliet and shrugged, and Juliet reached up to squeeze her arm. She suddenly felt very protective of the other woman.

"Sarge, I can probably just drop. My legs are cyber," Addie spoke from behind her.

"Practice the rappelling anyway, Hunter."

"Aye, Sarge."

"Houston! Drop in three . . . two . . . one . . . go, go, go!"

With those words, they were off, and not one of the recruits fell from the rappelling line. When it was Juliet's turn, she stepped out of the fluttercraft, holding onto the thick, spongy cable, amazed at how stable it was, hanging stationary in the air over the side of a mountain. It was warm out, but not terribly. The sun was going down, and wintertime around the Santa Rita Mountains was pretty damn nice if you asked her.

Juliet started to admire the sunset, but White shouted at her to get moving, and she slid down the line. She gripped it just as they'd been taught and slid easily, admiring how the glove protected her hand; she never felt any heat or friction on her skin. As she descended, Juliet breathed in the fresh, pine-scented air, admiring the scattered canopy of mesquites, pines, and junipers. She even saw some palo verde trees nearby, and when her boots crunched into the rocky soil, she caught the scent of greasewood.

Houston was securing the bottom of the line, and he shoved her off to the left, upslope, while barking, "Guard the perimeter."

Juliet saw Granado kneeling by a cluster of tan-colored rocks, aiming her SMG downslope, and so she leveled her electro-shotgun toward the upper slope and waited for the others to descend. They came down, one by one, and then the fluttercraft rocketed away, streaking toward the valley west of the canyon. Juliet knew they weren't too far from Tucson and wondered if the craft would head that way to wait for their mission to end.

"What's the move, Sarge?" Houston asked.

"We're gonna pick up a trail up that road we passed. There used to be a public park here, but the road's overgrown, and there's likely to be some scavs around, so keep your heads on a swivel. We'll camp upslope a ways, and tomorrow, we're hiking up to a place called Josephine's Saddle."

"That's where the research facility is?" Addie asked.

"Yeah, I guess, but it's more like a camp than a facility, from what I've seen in the briefing doc." White started trudging down the slope toward a broken, grass-and-scrub-covered road.

"People used to come up here for picnics or something?" Houston asked, glancing down toward the valley stretching away. It looked surprisingly green, considering they were in the middle of a desert.

"Guess so. I look like a tour guide, Houston?"

"No, sir. If you were my tour guide, I'd ask for a refund!"

White chuckled and shifted his enormous rifle. Juliet saw that he wore a harness mounted to the side rail of the gun, and all he had to do was swivel it so it pointed up while he hiked, resting a hand on the stock. "That's cool, Sarge," she said, pointing to the harness.

"Oh yeah. This baby gets a little unwieldy on long hikes."

"Is that the Gauss rifle you were telling me about?" Delma asked.

"You're talking about me behind my back, Roman?" White asked, grinning at Juliet as the unit scuffled down the long, rocky slope.

"Will we get a chance for shooting, Sarge?" Addie asked, stepping around Juliet so she was closer to White. Juliet smirked and stepped aside; she kind of enjoyed White's ribbing and decided to ignore Addie's interjection.

"Yeah, for sure. If we don't have to deal with hostiles in a . . . hostile manner, I'll make sure we get some practice in."

"Can I try that Gauss rifle? I've heard a lot about them," Addie pressed, and Juliet saw Jensen rolling his eyes so hard, she was afraid they'd get stuck pointing backward.

"We'll see." White didn't frown, but he didn't smile, either.

"Sarge, why's everyone always wanting to touch your gun?" Houston asked, and Jensen barked a laugh.

"Houston." White's frown was suddenly quite pronounced. "That's because I keep it clean and don't put it in places it doesn't belong."

This time everyone laughed, and Houston was the loudest of all.

After things died down, Houston said, "Damn, Sarge, I knew you had a funny bone. I guess you were just afraid to show it around Polk." As Houston spoke the injured sergeant's name, his smile faded, and he shook his head. Everyone was silent for a moment, then he said, "Damn. Brains are funny things, you guys. For a minute there, in my mind, Polk was just fine and waiting back at base for us."

Addie and Jensen looked confused, but Delma spoke up, "We saw her." She jerked a thumb at White. "We waited outside while they were working on her. She came through, but they're not sure if she's going to . . ."

"Be the same," White finished. "Some damage up here." He knocked on his helmet. "It's my fault, really. I should've been there before she caught that guy." He looked at Juliet and added, "I should've been there with you."

"*We* should have!" Delma said.

"Sarge, all due respect," Juliet spoke, "that's bullshit. There's something screwy with the watchdog. You know how to follow dotted lines through straight tunnels. I think someone on the inside was helping those guys escape." Juliet knew she was walking a fine line speaking about that; there was no way she should know anything about the watchdog problem, but in her mind, it was a reasonable assumption.

"We'll see. My footage is under review, but yeah, I've had my PAI play back the whole thing for me twice; I don't see where we messed up."

"Same," Delma said.

"What the hell are you guys talking about?" Jensen asked, and Addie grunted her agreement with the sentiment.

"That's a story for the campfire. Come on, folks. Haven't you ever wanted to have a campout with your dear old sarge?" White lengthened his stride, and the rest of them hurried to keep pace.

35

\\\\\\\\\\\\\\\\\\\\\\

MADERA CANYON

The Grave installation up in the canyon proved to be a series of dome-shaped plasteel structures nestled between two peaks in what used to be a popular hiking destination. Juliet learned from one of the local employees while they ate breakfast one morning that Grave had bought the entire canyon at auction from Cybergen while they were restructuring. Now, the facility was used to field-test things like paragliding cybernetics, arm-mounted rappelling launchers, and powered exoskeletons designed to make climbing steep, rugged terrain nearly effortless.

Only thirty-two employees lived and worked at the facility, and a scavenger gang—scavs—had been encroaching on their field tests, making threats and demands. White, along with Juliet and the others, had put an end to that on their fourth day in the canyon. White had ordered them all to gear up, then they'd hiked down to the ancient parking lot where the scavs were living out of beat-up old motorhomes and tents, and surrounded it.

They'd used their AUI displays to maintain a perfect half-kilometer perimeter around the scavs. Juliet had been east and a bit downslope from White when she'd heard his Gauss rifle bark and the terrible sound of several heavy-alloy needles breaking the sound barrier several times. Then, she'd seen one of the motorhomes, where the big engine sat under the driver's compartment, shred apart as though a meteor had hit it. Metal, fluids, and fiery debris sprayed out of it over the cracked, weed-ridden asphalt.

Juliet had been shocked to see the destruction wrought by the gun. When she'd asked Angel about it, the PAI had explained that at high ranges, with the right kind of—very expensive—needles, the payload could reach velocities that delivered enough kinetic energy to make explosives seem mild. Seeing it in action, Juliet knew the weapon White was using was on an entirely different level from the "Gauss rifle" made by Grave that she'd shot in the range.

"Hold your positions," White had said into comms. "I'll give them a few more reasons to get running." True to his words, that rifle of his had fired again and again, each time sending screaming fiery metal into vehicles, piled gear, and crates of supplies. After the first shot, the scavs had gone into a frenzy, and quite a few of them, probably something like a dozen, had begun to fire blindly into the forested hillside. When White continued to demolish their camp, their resistance petered off, and most began to run, ride, or drive—if they could find a working vehicle—down the canyon.

Before White had the unit spread out, he'd given everyone careful instructions to hunker down behind boulders or very thick trees; scavs were usually fairly low-tech, but there were occasional outliers with good ocular implants or visors capable of detecting heat signatures. There were bound to be a few with powerful weapons who knew how to use them. It was Houston's job to identify those and neutralize them, and he had done so with a vengeance.

Of course, some of the others—most vocally Addie—had wanted to get in on the action, but White had insisted they wait in reserve, saving their firepower for only the most dire of emergencies; he'd said they'd either know it when the time came, or he'd call for them to engage.

It had been moot, however; Houston had downed a couple of the more dangerous scavs, and then the entire gang was hightailing it out of the canyon. White never gave them any relief, dropping deadly ordinance on them from his high vantage for more than a mile, shredding tires, blasting craters in the ancient roadway, and generally keeping the scavs panicking and desperate in their flight.

"I think they'll keep clear of the canyon for a while, Sarge," Houston had announced after the smoke had cleared and the last of the scavs had run, panting and desperate, down the long canyon road.

"Ayup," White had said. And that had been that; their reason for coming to Madera Canyon satisfied.

It had been four days since, and Commander Garza had still not recalled them. Juliet didn't mind, if she was honest—the time up in the fresh air away from people in suits and the constant supervision of hostile-seeming sergeants and commanders was doing her good. White was about as hands-off as a sergeant could be, and Houston . . . well, Houston was Houston.

It was midday on a Saturday, and Juliet wouldn't have realized that if not for her AUI. The days were all the same up there, especially in the middle of winter. Gray skies and cool temps—even frost in the mornings—and not a concrete tower in sight helped them all forget about the usual routine and hustle of Phoenix.

She and Addie sat on a log watching White and Houston compete for the last cinnamon roll by throwing their issued vibroblades at a thick tree trunk fifteen meters away.

"Angel, this is something I wouldn't mind cheating on; are you taking note of their form? White seems to be a little more accurate," she subvocalized as Addie cheered for Houston's latest throw, just an inch outside of where White's blade hummed and buzzed, buried to the hilt in the sappy wood.

"Yes! I'm so glad you asked, Juliet! Try to match their posture as closely as possible, and I'll be there to guide you."

"Looks like neither of you hit the center," Juliet called, standing up. "Mind if I try?"

"Oh? You throw knives, Roman?" Houston asked, cocking one bushy, brown eyebrow. He reached up to rub at his stubble—all the men had forgone shaving at the wilderness camp. "Wanna put some money on her, Sarge?"

"Hmm? Bet on the skills of a raw recruit?" White feigned a scandalized expression, then laughed and, after giving Juliet a long, appraising look, said, "Fifty bits says she misses the tree."

"You're on, Sarge!" Houston pumped his fist and added, "I think she'll surprise you." He winked at Juliet and backed away from the line in the dirt they'd drawn as the throwing mark. Juliet tugged her vibroblade out of its sheath and gripped the hilt as she'd watched the two men do.

"Can I get in on the action?" Addie called. "I bet she beats both of your throws."

"You're on!" Houston laughed. Juliet looked at Addie and grinned—the two of them had been getting along just fine the last few days. Now that Juliet knew what was irritating the other woman about her, it had been easy to smooth things over. She encouraged her, talked her up in front of White, and did her best not to stand out too much when the recruits worked head-to-head on a new skill or PT.

As she approached the line, she put her feet the way she'd seen White do, then reached back with the knife and whipped it forward, releasing it at just the right moment—thanks to Angel. She'd been about to hold on to it too long, but Angel helped, pushing her throw into the perfect replica of White's and guiding her arm, wrist, and fingers to ensure she was on target. The knife buzzed through the air and sank into the tree, nearly dead center—closer than both of the men's blades.

"Whoo!" Addie howled, jumping up. "Pay up, boys!"

"You gotta be shitting me," White groused, jogging toward the tree to retrieve the knives.

"Damn, Roman." Houston laughed. "Remind me not to piss you off if you're holding a v-blade."

"Thanks." Juliet laughed, walking over to take hers from White. "I'm glad these are weighted for throwing. I like this one better than my personal knife."

"Grave makes good blades." White nodded. His face went a bit distant as Juliet sheathed her knife, and she assumed he was looking at something on his AUI or listening to a message.

"Huh," he said after a while, then he looked at Houston and said, "Go round up Jensen and Granado. Something's up. Switching to team comms." He turned away from the camp perimeter and started walking. There was no wall, but five feet of electrified fence kept the wildlife and occasional wandering vagrant from intruding on the Grave employees.

As White strode purposefully toward the barracks they'd been set up in, he spoke into their comms, "One of the teams testing some gear for climbing rocks saw a gray, unmarked fluttercraft land and take off near the canyon's entrance. Hunter, Roman, and I are going to get some high ground and scope things out; I'm picking up one of the camp's drones. Roman, you can operate it, right?"

"Yes, Sarge."

"Yeah, I don't like the description of the craft and the fact that it came in and left without any alarms going off. Something's screwy."

"Yep, seconded," Houston said into the comms. "What about us, Sarge?"

"You take Jensen and Granado down to the top parking lot, where we sent the scavs packing. Get good cover and wait for instructions."

"Roger. Let's move, grunts!" Houston barked, and Juliet grinned, imagining his joy at ordering around some subordinates.

Juliet, Addie, and White crashed into their barracks, separating and grabbing gear from their bunks. They met at the door, where White popped the latches on a white plastic case. When he pulled the cover off, a sleek pale-blue drone sat within.

"Touch the pairing button, Juliet," Angel prompted. She leaned in and tapped the little silvery button near the top of the drone, which began to blink with a yellow LED. A second or two later, a new HUD appeared on her AUI.

"I got it, Sarge. What should I do with it?"

"Send it high, and get some infra and motion scans of the first mile or so of the canyon. They can't be much higher than that yet."

"They?"

"Whoever the hell was in that fluttercraft." He hoisted his Gauss rifle, snapping it into his belt harness, and started jogging straight for the camp's only rolling chain-link gate.

"You heard him, Angel," Juliet subvocalized. "Let's get this thing airborne and down there." She knew Angel could handle the drone easily; she'd seen her manage three at once, so Juliet hurried after White and wasn't surprised to hear the drone buzz to life and rocket into the air, the sounds of its engines fading away as it gained altitude and distance.

"What if they have chill suits?" Juliet asked, and White glanced over his shoulder, giving her an appreciative glance.

"Well, keep your eye peeled on the footage for movement or shadows that look wrong."

"Sarge," Addie said, hurrying to keep pace. "We should take the south-bound trail out of the Saddle; there's an escarpment up that way where we can get a view of most of the canyon."

"My thoughts exactly, Hunter."

Juliet glanced at Adelaide, saw her carrying the bolt-action rifle White had been training her on, and smiled. It was nice that Addie had the gun, but it couldn't compete with White's Gauss rifle; he could realistically take shots at things miles away, especially if she could help him calibrate with the drone. Addie's .308 wouldn't be much help in a scenario like that. Still, it would be good if any of the—presumed—hostiles got close to them, the same as Juliet's electro-shotgun.

"Angel, I know you can review that drone footage better and faster than I can. Do you think you'll be able to spot people in chill suits?"

"Certainly, given enough time and given that they move at all."

"Awesome." Juliet could see the drone's feed in a window of her AUI, but she couldn't make much of the details unless she stopped walking and maximized it. No, this was the kind of job PAIs were made for, and Angel was the best PAI in the world.

"Awesome?" White asked, huffing as he hurried up the trail.

"My PAI was giving me an update on the drone's position."

He just grunted in reply and picked up the pace, and Juliet had to scramble to keep up. Addie, on the other hand, had made it clear to anyone that she could run uphill, over rough terrain, for hours on her legs, the only limiting factor being their charge; they had biobatts like Juliet's arm and would recharge slowly over time from chemical reactions in her body, but if she depleted them, they became very heavy, weak limbs until that process had a chance to bring them to a baseline.

"Scout ahead, Hunter," White said, clearly tired of having her stalking in his shadow, impatient and agitated by the excitement of the sudden drill.

Juliet thought about that word—was this a drill? Was White just trying to keep them on their toes? Had there really been a mysterious fluttercraft?

Addie didn't need to be told twice. She bolted up the path, her legs humming and thudding into the hard-packed dirt, and then she turned a corner and was gone. "Almost makes me want to have elective leg replacements," White grunted.

"Almost," Juliet agreed.

"I'm surveying the specified area. I see evidence of a fluttercraft landing in the field west and south of the canyon," Angel said, her words quick and precise.

"Sarge, there was a fluttercraft in the area you indicated. I'm marking the landing location on our team map."

"Good. Find these uninvited guests, Roman."

"Working on it, Sarge." Juliet huffed, glad for all the PT she'd done over the last weeks, proud that she could keep up with a man like White as he powered up the slope, switchback after switchback. By the time they'd gained the elevation they wanted and had turned along a narrow trail which hugged the side of one of the mountains that made up the canyon, Juliet was drenched in sweat but feeling good. The air was brisk, and the thrill of potential combat was palpable as the team kept each other abreast of their progress and suspicions.

Houston's team had descended to the parking lot and were hunkered down amid the wreckage of old vehicles and a decommissioned public restroom. They hadn't encountered anything unusual, but they were ready if anyone approached to mount the trail that led up to the Saddle and the Grave facility.

Houston had just speculated that the "bird" might have been bringing some "rich assholes" for a picnic and was long gone when Angel intruded with an excited announcement.

"I've found them, Juliet. There are seven individuals wearing chill suits and wending their way up the canyon along the creek bed."

"Sarge! We have them! Seven of them in chill suits. They're a mile up the canyon, following the creek bed, not the trail." Juliet couldn't contain her excitement and subvocalized, "Angel, you're the most amazing PAI in the universe!"

"Thank you!" Angel's voice was high and tense with simulated excitement. Juliet frowned; was it simulated?

"Fucking-A, Roman," Houston said before White could form a reply. He huffed and grunted, picking up his pace even more before he cleared his throat and spoke.

"Keep eyes on them. Mark them on our HUDs, and prep your PAI to calibrate with my rifle. I'm opening a wireless port. These people absolutely cannot be up to any good, and we won't let them get close enough to show us how dangerous they are."

"Hoorah!" Jensen said into comms, speaking for the first time since leaving the camp.

"They're probably going to scatter and seek cover when I blast the first of them, so be ready up the canyon; if they don't flee, they might decide to go loud, and we don't know what they're packing."

"Sarge," Juliet said, purposefully not speaking into comms, "what if they're, like, not hostile?"

"Absurd," he barked. "This is Grave territory, and they aren't Grave personnel. If they were here for a hike, they wouldn't be wearing chill suits. Have you ID'd their armaments?"

"Working on it," Juliet replied, feeling rather stupid. Of course they weren't innocent bystanders, sneaking up into a canyon like that. She supposed some part of her was wondering if they were operators out for a score and utterly unaware of the danger they'd stumbled upon with White and his Gauss rifle . . . and Juliet and Angel.

"I've identified automatic submachine guns, high-caliber rifles, and the silhouettes of explosive ordinance. I also see a Karter & Rollins assault drone backpack on the man third from the end of their column," Angel supplied, thankfully hard at work while Juliet was worrying about how White was about to drop the hammer on some potentially "innocent" people.

She relayed the information, and White grunted into comms, "We'll target the drone operator first. Have you connected to my gun yet, Roman?"

"Doing it now, Sarge."

"Why didn't they launch their drone, Sarge?" Addie asked.

"Probably working their way to one of the old houses or forestry buildings, thinking they can set up a base of operations before they move on us. Damn, but we're lucky those mountain-climbing nerds spotted that fluttercraft. Hunter, we're three minutes from your position. You have a clear LOS to the targets Roman has marked?"

"Aye, Sarge."

"Good. Keep down; these goons are going to have high-grade optics."

Two minutes later, White and Juliet were crawling over the rocky dirt trail to Addie's position, then—huffing, sweating, and covered with a fine layer of dirt—they slid up beside her, and White began to set up his rifle. Angel had synced with the gun, and Juliet knew she'd be able to provide targeting data to him via the drone, probably better than any targeting assistance he'd ever had.

While waiting for White to get ready, Juliet watched the seven highlighted figures making their way along the trail. From the drone's vantage, using targeting filters, they looked like grayscale humanoids devoid of much detail, especially with the bright outlines Angel had painted on them for the sake of the humans seeing the footage. She spotted the guy with the drone case on his back right away; he was the only one with a pack that bulky. In a minute, she'd be helping White to erase him from existence.

"Sarge," she tried again, using a different angle, "have you heard from Commander Garza? Are we absolutely certain these guys can't be from Grave?"

"No reply from Garza, but—and I'm only humoring you because I like you, kid—this is protocol. An incursion of unknown, armed, stealthy types on Grave property is categorically supposed to be met with force. They'd have checked in with us if this was a Grave unit. Now, help me target that drone operator."

"Aye, Sarge," Juliet said, then subvocalized, "Angel, help him target that guy. Make your adjustments and all that."

"I will."

While Angel did her thing, Juliet expanded her vid feed window from the drone and watched as a bright yellow *X* appeared, centered on the drone carrier and tracking him perfectly as he moved up the rocky slope next to the old streambed.

"Am I clear to shoot?" White softly asked.

"There are several small trees in the line of fire," Angel said.

"Several trees in the LOF, Sarge."

"Setting for two bursts. Firing in three . . . two . . . one . . ." White's gun barked twice, each burst of needles a fraction of a second apart. The projectiles ripped through the air of the canyon, the sound echoing off the high mountainsides. Juliet watched through the drone footage as several tree trunks were vaporized, and then the top half of the drone operator disappeared in a spray of grayscale mist. She was endlessly grateful for the lack of color in the feed.

"Look alive!" White barked. "They're scattering. Acquiring the next target. Roman, keep that targeting info coming. Hunter, watch for incoming ordinance; we don't know if they've got any surprises."

36

///////////////

STEADY

They're scattering, and I've lost two from the drone feed; I'm sorry, but I'm only working with two cameras here, and there's a lot of cover," Angel said, her voice calm and clinical.

"Lost two, Sarge," Juliet said. "Tracking the remaining four."

"Paint the one in the front there, the one with the long gun." Juliet watched as Angel complied, following White's request. A yellow *X* appeared on the prone figure as it tried to deploy a long-barreled weapon on a tripod. The *X* moved from his head down toward his lower back as Angel sought out a clear line of sight for White's shot.

"Clear to fire," Angel said.

"You're clear, Sarge. All adjustments made . . ." Juliet started to say, but White's Gauss rifle barked again, and the whistling *crack* of his projectiles ripping through the canyon made her words superfluous.

Juliet refused to look away, watching her vid feed as the spray of hyper-accelerated needles turned the man's midsection to a fine mist and sent his lower half flopping away from his upper torso and arms, still gripping the rifle. "God," she breathed. How could such tiny projectiles do so much damage?

"Houston, you probably have incoming—two of the targets went dark and are likely highly speed boosted," White said as he waited for Juliet to paint the next target.

"Roger. We're set." Houston sounded sure, and Juliet wanted to access his or one of the others' feeds so she could see how they were set up, but she couldn't take her eyes off the drone footage; she had to set up White's next execution. She swallowed hard, then picked one of the remaining three scattered individuals. They'd spread out around the dry creek bed, and this one was crouching behind a large boulder. Unfortunately, she'd—the figure looked feminine to Juliet's eye—underestimated the height and angle of White's position.

As she selected the crouching infiltrator, Angel painted her with a yellow *X*, and ten seconds later, she'd been erased from existence. "Jesus, Sarge," Addie said aloud. "That gun is sick."

"You're supposed to be watching for incoming; keep your eyes outta the drone footage."

"Sorry," Addie replied, abashed. "Nothing moving on the trail up this way. I mean, we're a half-hour hike beyond Houston and the others—"

"Cut the chatter." White's words were soft and steady, and Juliet knew why; he was getting ready to blast her next target. The Gauss rifle barked, the shots resounded through the canyon, and another crouching figure was crossed out on Angel's feed. "One more," he said. "Then we need to back up the others."

"They're two klicks from where you shot the first guy; you think these people would really charge up and not run for cover?" Addie scoffed.

"Always assume the worst, Hunter," White told her, then growled, "Roman, I'm waiting for that target!"

"Right," Juliet said, and then Angel put the yellow *X* on the final visible infiltrator, a prone figure lying next to a thick, fallen tree. "He's covered by that tree."

"Ayup. Firing two bursts for certainty." White's gun barked twice, and the high, rocky slopes echoed with the sound of his projectiles. Juliet saw the tree burst into a shower of shredded wood and mist from the moisture it had retained, and then when it cleared, she had to struggle to make her mind reconcile the bits left behind with the person who'd been hiding there a moment before.

"That's five." White stood up and hooked his gun to his belt. "Move the drone to cover Houston and the others."

"Right," Juliet said, trusting Angel to carry out the order.

"Hunter, I know you can get down there faster than we can, but stay with us. I don't want you to burst into a firefight alone until you've had more experience."

"No arguments, Sarge," Addie replied, surprising Juliet—she'd seemed so gung ho earlier. Maybe watching five people get shredded like lambs to the slaughter had tamped down her eagerness. They hustled down the path at a double-time pace, White leading the way and Juliet bringing up the rear. She felt a little sick in her stomach, and she knew it was because of her role in the long-range executions.

She tried to shake it off, to put the thoughts in a box and deal with them later, and she partially succeeded. Still, she kept seeing their grayscale bodies coming apart in a spray of mist, and Juliet had to furiously force herself to focus on Addie's back, concentrating on something tangible to keep her mind from painting those pictures. She knew she'd feel differently if she were certain those people were hostile, that they'd come to kill her, but right then, it just felt like they'd murdered a bunch of people for trespassing.

"Contact!" Delma's voice came through the comms, quick and edged with panic. Gunfire sounded from somewhere below them and to the left, far off and echoing weirdly around the canyon.

"Anything on the drone?" White asked, further increasing his pace.

"Angel?" Juliet subvocalized.

"No . . . I see Delma and the other two. She seems wounded, Juliet."

"No eyes on the bad guys, Sarge, but Granado looks injured," she reported.

"Frag out!" Houston said into comms, and then a tremendous boom rang out from below. Juliet glanced at the drone footage to see a plume of smoke coming up a dozen meters south of Delma's position. "Think I got one—" His words were cut short, and more gunfire sounded.

"One hostile down," Jensen informed, cool as ice. "Granado and Houston are out of commission." His words spurred White to further abandon caution, and he started to run down the hill, pell-mell. Juliet and Addie followed, the steep decline causing her running steps to crunch and pound, jarring her knees and forcing her to focus on the path; she couldn't spare a glance at the drone footage.

"Talk to me, Jensen!" White said.

"Not now, Sarge," Jensen replied, and Juliet could tell he must be subvocalizing; there was no strain in his voice, no breathing. His PAI was synthesizing his words. Juliet followed the others around a final switchback and raced past the Grave encampment, charging down the trail out of the Saddle toward the parking lot. Juliet knew that, even at their current pace, they were still ten minutes away from being able to help Jensen and the others.

"Angel, tell me what you're seeing; I can't look away from the trail right now," Juliet subvocalized.

"I lost sight of Jensen. I can see Houston and Granado, and I'm sorry, but Houston appears dead; his body temp is rapidly falling. Granado is still moving—she's crawling through some wreckage, seeking cover in a burned-out motor vehicle."

"White," Juliet huffed, raw emotion straining her vocal cords, "Houston's hurt bad . . . at least!"

"Roger," was all he said as he continued to motor down the trail, and Juliet remembered they could all see his vitals. Feeling stupid, she glanced at her unit readout, saw his heart rate had flatlined, and felt her eyes start to burn as tears streamed out of the corners. She wanted to blame it on the wind, on the exertion of running down the steep trail, but she knew the truth—Houston was dead, Delma was in trouble, and she wasn't handling it well.

More rapid staccato shots rang out, and Angel said, "I see the infiltrator; he's shooting toward Delma!"

"I'm pinned . . ." Delma gasped into comms, but Jensen cut her off.

"He's down. That's two dead here. Are we clear?"

"Angel?" Juliet huffed, not caring who heard her talking to her PAI.

"I see no others. There are seven hostiles down, matching my first count."

"I think we're good. Jensen, we're almost there; check on Granado and Houston!"

"Already on it."

"Juliet," Angel spoke as the trio continued to pound down the trail, running hard. "I have footage of Jensen killing the final infiltrator. They had a knife fight, and Jensen moved faster than any human I've seen."

"Faster than Don?" Juliet asked, remembering the twitchy operator from a lifetime ago.

"Yes, significantly."

"Right," she subvocalized. "Don't mess with Jensen. Got it."

"Sorry, Sarge," Jensen said into comms. "Houston cashed in his last chips."

"Goddammit," White growled, and Juliet had to bite back her urge to utter some useless platitude.

Instead, she asked, "What about Delma? Are you there, Granado?"

"She's here, but she's really low on blood. I'm trying to stop it . . . shot through the thigh." Jensen's voice betrayed some strain for the first time. "Correction—shot twice through the thigh."

"I'm calling things in—still no reply from Garza. Commander Anderson's PAI is sending me a canned response that he's on vacation. Fuck it, let me see if Polk's recovered enough to talk."

Juliet ran behind White and Addie, mind racing, wondering who might have sent this squad to the canyon, but knowing, somewhere in her gut or heart or the back of her brain, that it was Gordon. That bastard was still trying to clean up loose ends for Vance; she was sure of it. Her thoughts were interrupted by White as he spoke aloud, clearly only half of a conversation.

"Glad you picked up, Sarge! . . .Yeah, I know . . . What? . . . You're god-damn shitting me! . . . No. Nobody's checked in with us . . . We just put down a kill squad, but Houston's dead . . . I'm not calling him . . . Not happening, Sarge . . . Seriously?" White looked over his shoulder at Juliet, and she experienced a sudden chill. "Our watchdogs are offline? They don't show offline. Well, it's a moot point; she didn't make it. Yeah, I'm sure. Okay, thanks for the head's up, Sarge. See you after cleanup."

"What?" Addie asked, clearly as intrigued as Juliet.

"I'll brief you guys later. Right now, let's help Jensen." White gestured ahead. Juliet saw the ancient sign labeling the trails and knew the parking lot was just around the corner.

"Angel," Juliet subvocalized, "is the watchdog offline?"

"It hasn't sent or received data for more than twenty hours. I believe it may have been severed from the network. Why would they do that?"

"So they could clean us up without having any evidence on file?" Juliet frowned, wondering what else Polk had told White. As they jogged into the parking lot, she raised her voice and asked, "So Polk was okay?"

"Not a hundred percent, but better than we feared," White replied, then ran over to where Angel had marked Houston's body on the drone map. Juliet could hear Jensen urging Delma to hold on, so she charged over the blacktop, sliding behind a burned-out old sedan, and there she was, lying in a pool of blood, Jensen working to tighten a tourniquet around her thigh.

"Gimme a hand! Sprinkle some bleeder dust in these holes!"

Juliet fumbled in her belt pack, found a packet of the cauterizing powder, and knelt next to Delma's ashen-faced form. "This is going to burn like hell," she said, but Delma didn't respond. Were they too late? Juliet held the packet between her teeth, then reached down and dug her fingers around the bullet holes in Delma's pants, yanking to rip the fabric wide. That done, she brushed some of the bubbling blood aside to expose the wounds. She took the packet, ripped the corner off, and sprinkled half the contents into each injury.

It sizzled and bubbled, but Delma didn't move, which worried Juliet even more. "Is she breathing?" she asked, her voice shaking with stress.

"She was . . ." Jensen replied, holding his fingers to Delma's neck. "Sarge, dammit, we need a medivac!"

"I've called the fluttercraft in. We'll be airborne in three minutes. Is she stable?" His question reminded Juliet she was hearing him through her implants and that he wasn't nearby. Rather, he was on the other side of the old parking lot, dealing with his dead friend.

"My HUD says she has a weak pulse, but I'm not feeling it," Jensen said, then he sat back and blew out a breath, clearly frustrated. "She wasn't ready for this shit."

Juliet frowned and nodded at Jensen's words. Delma wasn't ready for this. She didn't deserve to die because Gordon and Vance had a mess to clean up. She paused to wonder why she was so sure this team had come from them. She shook her head, deciding it was the only thing that made sense.

She leaned over her friend, looking into her waxen face, and then, following a strange urge, she pressed her forehead against Delma's, feeling the cool flesh, the faint tingle of electricity that always accompanied the touch of another person. She could feel her in there, knew she wasn't dead. She whispered, "Delma, I'm going to make them regret this. I'm going to make sure they pay. Don't let go."

After her whispered promise, she sat up and saw Jensen regarding her appraisingly. He gave her a nod, then pointed up and to the west, where a black dot was rapidly growing larger, accompanied by the signature buzzing whir of a fluttercraft. "Just hang on a little longer," she said, squeezing Delma's hand before standing up.

"Okay, team, get Houston and Granado ready to load up. Roman, I need to speak to you," White spoke through comms, but Juliet could see him standing off to the side, near the rough, broken road which led down through the canyon. She jogged over to him, wondering what Polk had told him, wondering if this was where he tried to kill her.

"Sarge?" she asked, stopping a few feet from him, her enhanced arm tense, ready to reach for her vibroblade.

"Relax, Roman. I don't know what's going on, exactly, but Polk told me Garza's missing. She also told me that, before she went missing, Garza told her that Gordon wanted you dead."

"Sarge, seriously, what's going on?" Juliet was fishing, hoping she'd learn a little more.

"Some kind of damn coup, I guess. We're collateral damage. Our watchdogs are off, by the way—Polk didn't know diddly squat about what we're going through. My buddy is dead on that pavement over there because of some bullshit vendetta or housecleaning that Gordon's got going on. As far as I'm concerned, you died in this firefight, understood? You were hit with an RPG, and we couldn't pick up enough scraps to bring home. I'll make the others understand. If that asshole's going to turn off our watchdogs, then I'm going to take advantage of it."

"Seriously?" Juliet's mind was at war with itself—half wanted to feel panic, and the other half was surging with relief. "What am I supposed to do, White?"

"Seriously. I'm sorry I don't have more advice for you, and I'm sorry to cut this short, but you gotta get outta here. Hope we meet again someday, Roman—best if you disappear for now." He gestured toward the undergrowth between the trees, jerking his head toward the rapidly descending fluttercraft, and Juliet took the hint. She nodded curtly and jogged off the cracked, brittle pavement, slipping into the brush. She was sure the fluttercraft sensors would pick her up, but if White was covering for her, he could lie about who she was.

"Angel, make sure that watchdog doesn't come back online. In fact, delete it," she said as she jogged through the old, dry pine needles and broken deadwood twigs. She kept running until she came to a twist in the canyon road and followed it as she heard the sound of the fluttercraft fading away.

She wondered what Jensen and Addie were thinking, wondered if they'd follow White's lead and lie about her dying. She had a strong feeling that Jensen would, and Addie seemed different than before, more subdued, and certainly more friendly. Maybe she'd toe the line.

"What will you do?" Angel asked as Juliet slowed her jog to a brisk walk, still heading down the road.

"Well, Angel, I could probably make a report to Rachel and get paid. I could take that money and clear out, but I feel like I've got too many damn loose ends at Grave Tower. I feel like there are too many people who deserve a little justice, and, well, I made a promise to Delma just now."

"Did she hear you, though?"

"I heard me. Do me a favor, will you, Angel? Can you please go through those GARD personnel files and pick the highest-ranking female."

"That would be Doctor Angela Chaudhry."

"Show me a picture." A window opened in her AUI with a photo of a woman, probably in her middle years but still quite young looking. She had long dark hair, augmented irises that shone like polished silver in the light, and a complexion a shade or two darker than Juliet's. "Hmm, close enough. Start altering my hair, irises, and prints to match her file, Angel."

"It'll take a couple of days to get your hair that dark and long."

"That's fine. I'm in the damn wilderness; I'll probably need a day or two to get back to Phoenix." Juliet looked at her drone footage, frowning as she directed it over the mouth of the canyon. "White is a damn good guy. You know that, Angel? Can you make sure this drone isn't sending out any signal other than the one to you?"

"Yes, but it won't last too much longer. Its battery is good for another ninety-seven minutes."

"Long enough. Please navigate me to the people White shot near the creek bed." In the spot vacated by her deleted watchdog, Juliet saw a small map appear with a dotted line directing her. Angel helpfully counted down the meters as she approached; at that moment, she was 1,564 meters away from the first body. "While I'm jogging, please keep an eye out with the drone, make sure White didn't double-cross me, or worse, that Gordon didn't send a second team."

"I will." Angel sounded terse, and Juliet frowned at her tone.

"Something wrong?"

"I'm just worried about Delma and sad that Houston is dead. I'm angry at the people at Grave who decided they were expendable. Juliet, I'm proud of you for wanting to deliver justice." A lump rose in Juliet's throat, and her heart skipped a beat as she nearly stumbled.

"Angel! I . . . I'm sad too!" She felt her eyes flooding with tears, and she shook her head. "I'm not thinking about Houston and Delma right now! I'm trying not to think about what Gordon did to Cherise! If I give myself a chance, I'm going to sit down and absolutely lose it. I have to keep it in a box right now. Do you hear me? I feel it too!"

"Thank you, Juliet. I'm glad my feelings aren't abnormal."

"No, Angel, they're not abnormal. Any person would feel that way, and it makes perfect sense that you do, too. I'm so goddamn mad right now . . ." Juliet shook her head again and steadied her pace—she'd begun to sprint. "I have to keep it together, though, and be smart. I want to make sure Gordon and Vance pay, and I want to put an end to any research or data GARD has on the GIPEL. We need to stay steady. For now. For now, Angel."

37

\\\\\\\\\\\\\\\\\\\\\\\\

ON A MISSION

Juliet could smell the dead infiltrators before she could see them, and she paused to pull a bandanna out of her belt pouch, tying it around her nose and mouth. She'd started packing one after the bug hunt with Charlie Unit, when she'd seen Houston and some of the others use them. Remembering Houston tying his black skull-pattern bandanna on his face made her remember his snarky attitude, which reminded her that he was dead. Juliet frowned and, again, banished the thought from her conscious mind.

The bodies and equipment of the people White had shot were a mess, and after seeing the first one, she almost abandoned her plan to look for gear or intel. She understood, in theory, why the Gauss rifle did so much damage at range. She understood Angel's explanation about the velocity and the density of the nanite-coated needles. Juliet knew Angel had calibrated White's rifle to push them to the limit, setting the gun to fire the projectiles as fast as possible without melting from friction in the air. Still, seeing the handiwork up close was mind-boggling.

Rather than dwell on the specifics while studying the ruined corpses, Juliet made a conscious effort to keep her eyes focused on what she was looking for—packs, belt pouches, weapons, and any other scattered gear. She pointedly avoided staring at the shredded torsos, the sprayed, fly-covered fluids, and the occasional orphaned limb.

Angel led her from corpse to corpse, and Juliet scooped up her salvage, piling it a dozen yards away toward the old overgrown road. When she'd gathered what she could, she separated them into piles and tried to decide what was worth lugging out of the canyon. She'd found half a dozen intact sidearms and rifles, packs full of gear, and quite a bit of extra ammunition. Notably missing were any data decks. She figured the guy with the drone must have had some tech gear, but it hadn't survived the initial impact of the Gauss rifle or the secondary explosions from whatever had been in the drone case.

Juliet studied the sidearms first—four nine-millimeter pistols, one forty-caliber pistol, and one semiautomatic needler with ammo similar to her Taipan. Thinking of her Taipan reminded Juliet of her belongings still stashed in the apartment she'd rented as Lydia Roman. She wondered how long it would take before Gordon sent a squad to search and secure all of her stuff. She'd left nothing she couldn't replace, but she'd miss that gun and a few other neat items she'd bought to play corpo spy before finding out she'd be in a Zeta Protocol unit.

"Maybe I still have time to go in and grab some things . . ." She shook her head, sighing. No, that would be monumentally stupid. At the very least, he'd have someone watching it, even if White reported her dead. "Angel, tell me about this needler."

"That's a Finch Executive four-millimeter, semiautomatic needler with a biosensing grip, sync-capable sighting coprocessor, and an aftermarket noise-suppressing barrel. Remove the magazine and examine one of the rounds, please." Juliet popped the magazine out, surprised by its weight; the rounds were very thin but long and packed in tightly. She worked one free and held it up—the casing looked like plasteel, and the plastic tips were dark blue.

"They look different from the rounds in my Taipan."

"They are—your Taipan is loaded with shredders; these are low-noise cartridges. They fire at a subsonic velocity and only contain three needles. If you're accurate, they're quite deadly, but they'll be stopped by armor rather easily."

"So? Which of the pistols is the most valuable?"

"Monetarily speaking, the needler is worth twice as much as the other pistols." That was enough for Juliet, and she unbuckled her belt, sliding the—slightly stained—nylon holster onto it before inserting the needler.

"What about these rifles? Any of them worth more than my shotgun?"

"Your Grave Industries electro-shotgun is considered a budget model. There's a Hershel Company MP5 variant there that is far more respected and retails for significantly more bits. I see you found seven magazines for it, as well."

Juliet picked up the SMG as Angel highlighted it in her AUI and noted it was equipped with a sleek-looking black plasteel suppressor. "This has a lot of aftermarket mods, doesn't it?"

"Yes, the suppressor is high-end and appears to be new, and the trigger is aftermarket and likely requires a very light touch—use caution should you use it. I see it's also equipped with a sighting coprocessor that I can interface with, and it's vented to reduce recoil and noise, though it will have less armor-penetration potential. On a cursory inspection of each weapon, I didn't note any identifying marks, either. If you interface with them, I can wipe any electronic signature and assign your biometrics."

"These guys really were some kind of black ops, weren't they?" Juliet set the MP5 aside, along with the gathered magazines, then started rifling through packs, looking for a data deck or anything else with some information about who the mystery squad had been. She came up empty—nothing but protein bars, water bottles, and a smattering of camping gear. Though, in one black belt pack, she found four squares of powerful shaped charges with remote detonators.

"Those could be useful," Angel noted as Juliet read the labels.

"Hell yes," she said, taking them out of the pack, consolidating them with the supplies into the least-stained bag, and tucking the MP5 magazines into a side pocket. She shrugged into the pack, shouldered the SMG sling, and briefly considered burning the stuff she wasn't taking. She decided it wasn't worth it.

Juliet purposefully chose not to plug into the data ports of the kill squad. She couldn't stomach it. None of the bodies were intact, and the idea of having Angel try to crack their PAIs and sift for data while she crouched by their ruined bodies just turned her stomach.

Angel had clinched the deal when Juliet asked her about it.

"Juliet, it's likely that people who operate on squads like this have standing orders with their PAIs to delete all data upon death."

"That's a thing?"

"Yes. It's not a function a standard PAI would have, but these people weren't average people."

"Right. Forget it then." That settled, Juliet, still clutching her Grave-issued shotgun, began working her way down, out of the canyon.

She'd been a little worried the fluttercraft that dropped the kill squad would return, but thinking about it, she figured it would be pretty stupid of them—whoever was piloting it had to know they were dead and had to have seen the Grave fluttercraft come in to pick up White's team. Why would they risk coming back? There was a reason the kill squad hadn't had any identifying marks on their equipment.

By the time she walked out of the canyon and was making her way over the dry, grassy plains of the foothills toward a town that, according to Angel's map, used to be called Green Valley, the sun was starting to dip toward the western horizon. "How many people live there?" she asked, noting the scattered lights in the distance.

"Not many—Bering Cooking Supplies bought up most of the town and surrounding countryside nearly forty years ago. They have several large pecan groves in the area and manufacture pressed protein squares and flour substitutes. Most of the twenty thousand citizens in the area work for Bering."

"Okay, um, navigate me to the nearest neighborhood. I'll try to buy someone's car or bike." Angel updated her map with a dotted line which showed a five-kilometer hike. She paused to drink from a water bottle and then got moving, picking up the pace into a light jog. She'd gone about halfway when she passed over an ancient cattle guard and slipped her Grave Industries shotgun between the metal slats as she went over it. "I didn't really like it, anyway."

"Your old one, from Vikker's garage, was certainly a more brutal weapon."

"Right. A shotgun should be brutal." Juliet frowned as she spoke, and as she jogged down the road in the cool air of the Arizona winter, she struggled to keep her mind from drifting toward thoughts about Houston, Delma, and Commander Garza.

She thought about Houston's wisecracks and faux panic whenever something seemed to go wrong. The memories made her want to sit on the side of the road and give in to utter depression when she realized she'd never hear that voice again. It was one thing to leave a person behind, to know, objectively, that you might not ever speak to them again, but it was something altogether different to realize that no matter what you did, that person was gone.

"It wasn't like he was a good friend," she said, trusting Angel to know who she was speaking about.

"No, but he was amusing," Angel replied.

"Yeah. He *was* amusing, Angel. I'm going to miss him. And then there's Delma. Goddamn Gordon!" she spat, red fury taking the place of her sorrow, and she welcomed it in. She'd rather be angry than sad any day.

While she jogged, Juliet tried to think of her next move; she knew she wanted to re-infiltrate Grave Tower, wanted to remove the data about the

GIPEL program from their servers and backups, and wanted to put a stop to Gordon and Vance. "At least," she breathed. It all had to start with Chaudhry; she'd need a cover to get back into the tower.

Before she could plan further, she found herself turning off the old, deserted road toward the scattered lights of some ancient, ranch-style homes.

As she began to pass by gravel driveways, she said, "See what you can find out on the sat-net about these houses and the vehicles out front. I mean, see if you can find who owns them and who they work for."

"There isn't much publicly available, but all indicates that these people mostly work for Bering." Juliet watched as Angel highlighted various vehicles—pickup trucks, sedans, tractors, motorcycles—and flashed their ownership info in a window as she perused public records. "We could realistically expect to be able to steal any of these vehicles, Juliet."

"I don't want to steal one, though. Just find something that looks reliable but isn't worth a whole lot."

"Most of these vehicles fit that description. The dwelling ahead and to the left has three vehicles in the drive; perhaps the owner would be more likely to sell one, seeing as they're all registered to the same man."

"Worth a try," Juliet said, jogging down the long gravel drive to the adobe, ranch-style home. She saw an old truck, a newer SUV, and an ancient, low, bulbous van, probably from the 2060s. "That thing's ugly as hell."

"Fedder Systems Galaxy Wagon, circa 2071," Angel supplied. "Current listings for similar vehicles are sub-1000 bits."

Juliet chuckled as she shifted her MP5 so it mainly hung behind her. She was sweaty and probably had bloodstains she'd missed on her hands and arms or her face, but she didn't have the patience to try to clean up. She walked to the front door of the home and rang the bell, standing back a few feet and clasping her hands before her in an attempt to look nonthreatening.

Nearly a minute later, a male voice called out from behind the door, "Who is it?"

"Hello, sir," Juliet said, trying to sound upbeat and pleasant. "I was doing some work nearby and missed my ride out. I was hoping you could help."

The door clicked and opened an inch, and Juliet could see, in her enhanced optics, a middle-aged man with salt-and-pepper hair and dark brown eyes peering through the crack. "How the hell can I help? I'm not driving you anywhere."

"No, sir, I was hoping you'd be willing to sell one of your vehicles. I have a long way to go."

"Seriously?" The door opened a few more inches, and Juliet took in the man's leathery skin, loose, long-sleeved shirt, and lack of shoes; he looked like someone who'd been working hard all day and was unwinding. "I need my vehicles. Why not call a cab?"

"How long will it take to get an AutoCab out here?" She offered her best pouting frown.

"Heh. Hours, I guess. Well, I was going to fix up that Galaxy for my daughter, but, I mean, if the price is right . . ."

"Does it run?" Juliet eyed the old sky-blue bulbous vehicle skeptically.

"Sure it does. Batteries ain't what they used to be, but they'll get you a couple of hundred kilometers in one charge. Tires are probably good for a few hundred, too." He shrugged as if to say, "I'm not the one in need here."

"Couple hundred . . ." Juliet looked at her AUI, and Angel helpfully displayed a route to Phoenix—244 kilometers. "You're sure?"

"Yeah. I mean, how bad you need it? Someone else might have something better, or shit, you can hang out here while you wait for a cab." He eyed her pistol and the SMG poking out from behind her hip, then added, "I mean outside."

"No, if you'll sell it, I'll transfer the bits right now. What's your price?"

"Five thousand." He didn't blink or look the least ashamed.

"I mean, it's almost forty years old, sir." Juliet frowned and tried to sound a little less desperate as she added, "How about twenty-five hundred? That's more than twice the market rate."

"Sol-bits?"

"Definitely."

"All right, make it twenty-seven fifty, and have your PAI start the contract handshake with mine."

Juliet did as he asked, and Angel and his PAI made a secure connection, transferring the vehicle title and the bits, and then Juliet became the owner of an ancient electric van.

"You need to get anything out of it?" she asked, glancing again at the ugly vehicle.

"Well, yeah. Thanks." He pulled the door wide, and Juliet caught a glimpse of a young woman sitting at a table under a kitchen light, watching their interaction with wide eyes. He closed the door and, giving Juliet a wide berth, walked around her toward the van. "I've got some camping stuff in the back."

"No problem. Was that your daughter?"

"Yep. You're not a psycho or something, are you?"

"You got the bits I transferred, right?"

"Yeah, right. Sorry. I don't see a lot of people with guns around here. I mean, unless they work for Bering." He walked around to the back of the van and opened the rear hatch, reaching in to pull out some plastic crates.

"Bering a decent corp to work for?" Juliet asked.

"Not really, but what options are there? At least I can afford the rent." He jerked his head toward the ranch house.

"It's pretty out here," Juliet commented, looking around at the moonlit street and the dark desert. "Better than working in an arcology, if you ask me."

"Yeah, I guess there's that. Dana wants to get a job in the city—complains about it out here all the time, but I know she'll just drift away from me if one of the big corps gets their hooks in her." He grunted as he lifted out the last crate and stacked it behind the van.

"Well, I hope things work out for you," Juliet said, walking toward the van's driver-side door. Angel had conducted the transaction anonymously, so she knew this man didn't know her name or anything about her, but she still felt it was risky hanging around. "I'm gonna be in trouble if I don't get moving. Thanks for selling me this old girl."

"You're welcome. I'll be able to buy Dana something better, I 'spose."

Juliet offered him one more smile, then unslung her MP5 and climbed into the driver's seat, setting it on the passenger seat next to her. Five minutes later, she was humming down the old, windy road at sixty kilometers an hour, following the route Angel had laid out that would take her back to Phoenix.

It only took her fifteen minutes to make her way to Interstate 19, where the old van struggled to get up to highway speeds. Juliet watched, with horror, as the battery charge rapidly dropped from ninety to fifty-seven percent, but then seemed to stabilize and hold steady. "Angel, you better add a couple of charging stations to the itinerary."

"Noted. I think this vehicle is badly in need of service."

"Haha. Understatement of the year," Juliet said over the noisy hum of the rough, uneven tires on the freeway. "Plus side—nobody's gonna be looking for me in this thing."

"It's possible Grave had a satellite watching the canyon and saw you walk out and get into this vehicle."

"Possible, but I doubt it. I mean, they sent a kill squad out, and we got the drop on them. If they'd had satellite eyes, they might have fared better."

"Perhaps Gordon severely underestimated White."

"And Jensen." Those thoughts keeping her mind busy, along with a million more, Juliet made her slow way north, stopping on the south side of Tucson to charge the van's batts. While she waited, she ate a convenience store pizza and drank a half gallon of punch-flavored rehydration water. While she ate, she sat off to the side of the station, under an awning of a long-abandoned fast-food restaurant, and watched her van and the traffic coming and going. She kept her MP5 in her lap, wary of anyone who gave her a second glance.

All that said, she was back on the road, unmolested, a half hour later with a nearly full battery bank. When she got to a lightly populated ABZ town called Casa Grande, she pulled off again and ordered an Easycab. She tapped the roof of the old van as her cab pulled up. "Thanks for the lift, old girl." Then, she climbed into the cab and rode toward Phoenix, stopping to change rides twice more in busy parking lots as they came out of the ABZ.

When she reached downtown Phoenix, Juliet had the Easycab drop her off in front of the Palo Verde Inn. Seeing the softly pulsing green neon tree reminded her of when she'd first fled Tucson—it felt like it had been a million years since then. Glancing up and down the street, hardly believing she was back downtown, Juliet strode inside, knowing they'd scan her but also knowing they'd respect her operator's license and weapons permit if Angel identified her as January, SOA-SP License #: JB789-029.

As a returning customer, her check-in was smooth, and Juliet didn't even have to speak to the hotel clerk; Angel handled everything. She made her way up to her room, which was, unfortunately, different from the one she'd stayed in before. She'd hoped to stay in the same suite for nostalgia's sake, but still, the room they assigned her was hardly any different—she still had a view of downtown and, of course, all the same amenities.

She stripped down, took a long, hot shower, then had Angel place a vid call to Fresh Threads. She was delighted when Rose, the same saleswoman who'd helped her before, answered the call, "Fresh Threads, where we keep you looking chic and ready to make a million-bit deal! This is Rose. How can I help you?"

"Rose! This is Lydia Roman. I bought a suit from you a few weeks back. Do you remember me?"

"Um." She peered at Juliet through her video connection, and Juliet knew she didn't recognize her. She was sure Angel wasn't projecting her current appearance—she was still in the process of darkening her hair and changing her irises, after all. No, Angel was projecting an image that resembled Lydia

Roman when Grave had first hired her. Even so, she could hear the lie in Rose's voice as she said, "Sure I do. How are you, Lydia?"

"I'm good, Rose. Do you mind looking up my purchase? I need another of the same kind of outfit, maybe just a shade darker gray this time, with black platforms. I guess while you're at it, could you please send me a couple of pairs of undergarments? Your choice, Rose—I trust your judgment. I'm going to hire a courier to pick everything up. Is that all right?"

"Oh, sure. I have your info here. I'll send the bill to your PAI. Is that okay? We close in an hour, though."

"I'll have the courier pick it up tomorrow at nine. You'll be open?"

"We will! I'll set it aside."

"Thank you, Rose." Juliet ended the call then said, "Angel, contact Corpo Secure now."

When the vid call tone had sounded twice, a man with a wispy gray mustache and thick, bushy eyebrows answered the call, "Corpo Secure."

"Hello, sir. I'd like to place an order to be picked up via courier."

"One moment," he replied, and then she was facing a hold screen picturing a mountain valley blanketed in pristine white snow. Thirty seconds later, the image flashed away, and the same man reappeared. "Sorry for the delay, ma'am. What can I set aside for you?"

"I need a briefcase that will resist scanner attempts—black. I need a vibroblade sheath that can be worn on the wrist under a blazer sleeve. Finally, I need an underarm holster to fit a Finch Executive four-millimeter needler."

"Sounds like you're on a mission, ma'am. I can get those things together for you. When can I expect your courier?"

"Thank you for your professionalism; I *am* on a mission, sir. My courier will be there a little after nine tomorrow morning. Please provide a code for my PAI, and I'll collect your invoice and submit payment."

38

\\\\\\\\\\\\\\\\\\\\\\

CHECKLIST

Juliet slept well that night in the Palo Verde. She'd worried she'd be plagued by thoughts of Houston or Delma, thoughts of Gordon and Vance, and the nightmares they'd inflicted on her and her friends. She'd also worried that the thoughts of slumbering guests would intrude on her mind, overwhelming her psionic lattice and damaging her brain. All that said, once she'd hit the pillow with Angel's soft playlist pushing her thoughts away from reality, she'd slipped into a deep, dreamless sleep.

When Angel woke her the following day, Juliet felt rested and full of purpose. When her eyes snapped open and she remembered where she was, the first thing she said was, "Does Angela Chaudhry live in Grave Tower?"

"She does not. She resides in a private residential arcology called Chroma Tower on the northern edge of the Phoenix downtown district," Angel replied calmly.

"Perfect. Call us a cab; we're going to the gun store where I bought my Taipan. Oh, and can you confirm with the courier service that they're set to pick up my orders?"

"I'm receiving real-time updates from Hermes Couriers—they've yet to depart their hub, but it's still an hour until your order is supposed to be ready. Will you be heading out right away?"

"No, give me twenty to take a shower and grab breakfast. Hey, while you're at it, can you send an encrypted message to Rachel?"

"Of course."

"Okay, let's see. Say, 'Rachel, can't talk now. If you hear something to the contrary, don't worry—I'm still on the job. I'm going to have a lot of data on Grave for you in a day or two, and I also have details on a rival corp's deep plant, and I mean deep. I'm still looking for a Sol-bit deposit. January.'"

"When shall I send it?"

"Hmm, anytime now. I am looking for a deposit, right? Nothing new yet?"

"Correct. After your purchases last night, your balance is 101,233 Sol-bits."

"Funny to think I never received my first monthly payroll from Grave. I suppose, now that they think Lydia Roman is dead, I never will."

"It was only a few thousand bits, in any case."

Juliet sighed, nodding as she climbed into the shower. She took a long, hot soak and dressed in her only clothes—her black leggings, a gray, long-sleeved flex-weave shirt, and her cross-trainer-like footwear—they all reeked of sweat. As she dried out her hair and pulled it back into a ponytail, she smiled to see it was now a shade of brown, close to what her natural color used to be. By the evening, she figured Angel would have it dark enough to match Chaudhry's.

"Speaking of Chaudhry," she said, leaning close to the mirror and looking into the reflection of her eyes. They were silvery and reflective, with tiny black concentric circles starting near the pupils and working outward. "They're kind of pretty but weird looking, if you ask me."

"It was difficult to match the exact pattern in Chaudhry's photo, and I'm afraid the reflective sheen is slightly different. It could be that the manufacturer of her optical implants has a patent on that particular design. Still, anyone who sees you in passing won't know the difference, and I'll be able to spoof your image easily for cameras, meaning Kent."

Juliet left her Grave jacket, ballistic vest, helmet, and bloodstained pack in the room. When she walked down through the lobby to her cab, she had her needler and vibroblade on her belt, and appreciated the fact that not one person on the premises of the Palo Verde gave her a second glance. She climbed into the Easycab, and the ride to Mackenzie Arms took only five minutes in the Sunday morning traffic.

When Juliet stepped out in front of the familiar storefront, she was struck with a powerful wave of something akin to déjà vu. She looked at the heavily modded doorman, trying to remember if he was the same one who'd searched her the first time. He was bulky with two black-enameled wire-job arms. His brow, just visible above his dark specs, glowered at her, but Juliet didn't feel intimidated.

In truth, she felt like she was a different person than the Juliet who had awkwardly gone into the store a few months ago, looking to buy gear for her new career as an operator. As she approached, the man crossed his metal arms, glared at her through the red LEDs on his visor, and gestured to her belt.

"That gun loaded?"

"Yes."

"Make it safe," he grunted, and Juliet nodded, pulling the needler out of its holster. She pointed it at the ground, ejected the magazine, and placed it into her slim, nearly useless front pocket, where it bulged uncomfortably. She racked back the slide and pointed the gun to the sky, looking through the breach to see daylight, confirming no round was in the barrel.

"Empty," she announced, holding it toward the big man, grip first. He just nodded and waved to proceed, apparently satisfied with her word. Juliet snapped the slide closed and put the gun into her holster, empty. Then she walked into the store.

She shopped around for a little while, walking between racks of gear, looking at shelves of knives and into the cases lined with pistols, before one of the salespeople hanging around behind the big U-shaped counter walked over to her. He was a young man with short, buzzed blond hair and very blue, backlit eyes. He had a wispy mustache and friendly laugh lines, and when he spoke with a faint Southern drawl, he reminded her of Hot Mustard. Juliet instantly liked him.

"What can I help you find, miss?"

"Not much today. I was just browsing these guns, but I'm really just here for a new knife and some specialty ammo."

"Oh?"

"Yeah, um, here." Juliet pulled her needler out and set it on the glass counter. "Finch Executive, four-millimeter. You have magazines that'll fit this?"

"Oh, sure." He glanced down at her pocket and said, "Standard thirty-six round like that, or you want extended ones? Fifty-eight rounds."

"Standard's fine. Just one more for now, please."

"All right." He turned and perused the shelves behind the counter for a few seconds before saying, "Aha!" and plucking a magazine like the one in her pocket from a peg. He set it on the counter. "What kind of ammo?"

"I'll take a box of shredders, a box of low-velocity rounds, and I also need something special—my PAI did some research and said there are needler rounds that can cause paralysis. Do you have anything like that?"

"Well, sure, but they're illegal to use within Phoenix city limits. You know that, right?"

"I mean, I'm not exactly supposed to go around shooting regular rounds in the city, am I?"

"No, but self-defense, corpo security, etcetera, etcetera, are cause for exceptions; there aren't any exceptions about the botu-rounds."

"Got it. Botu-rounds?"

"Yeah, the needles are coated with an engineered variant of the botulinum toxin. Um, each round has two needles, and if you hit someone with more than four individual ones, they'll probably die. Just FYI. Obviously, size makes a difference."

"Okay, perfect. I'll take a box."

"Right." He nodded and turned to, once again, go through his shelves, returning with three small boxes of needler rounds, each manufactured by a company called Veschet and each a different color—black, green, and blue. "Anything else?"

"Yeah." Juliet gestured toward a nearby display case of knives. "I need a slender vibroblade weighted for throwing."

"Smaller than the one on your belt?"

"Yeah, this is too bulky. You know, something I can wear under a sleeve for protection."

"Oh, sure, I've got just what you mean." He walked over to the case and pointed to the third row of knives. Juliet saw that they were all similarly shaped, though they started out long and wide, like her Grave-issued knife, and gradually grew smaller, ending in one with a narrow, tiny, two-inch blade. Juliet looked at them, imagining each one on her wrist, and finally pointed to a slender four-inch blade with a ridged, narrow plasteel hilt.

"That one."

"That's a nice knife. The battery is shaped like a rod and runs the length of the blade, wider near the tip—that's what gives it its throwing weight and allows for a slender hilt. Um, I'm not trying to sound like I don't think you know what you're doing, but be careful sheathing a vibroblade on your wrist; pull it out wrong, and you can really hurt yourself."

"Yep." Juliet nodded and offered him a smile. "That does it for me. Can I get a bag?"

"Sure." He unlocked the case, took the knife out, and walked over to the counter where her ammo and magazine awaited.

"Send a secure transaction request to my PAI—it's open," she said as he put her purchases into a black plastic sack with a stylized red *M* on the side.

Still grinning, he handed her the bag. "Hey, my name's John." He tapped his name tag, and his smile broadened as he looked down sheepishly, having embarrassed himself. "Anyway, I'm happy to help you anytime. You can message ahead, and I can get your order ready next time. I sent my details with the invoice to your PAI."

"Oh? Jeez, thanks, John," Juliet replied, smiling back, somewhat amused by his goofiness. She shook her head, took her bag, and started toward the door.

"Hey, I didn't catch your name!" he called after her. Juliet just looked over her shoulder, winked one of her chromed eyes, and walked outside.

"Was that man flirting with you?" Angel asked as Juliet paused on the sidewalk to slap her needler magazine into the little pistol's grip.

Shrugging, Juliet racked the first round and put it back into the holster. "Oh, I'd say so."

She climbed into the cab Angel had waiting for her and said, "Back to the hotel, please." It felt strange driving around, conducting business just a few miles away from Grave Tower, where some sort of coup was happening, and enemies she'd somehow made thought she was dead. Whenever she started to get the urge to just pack up and get the hell out of town, though, she thought of Delma, of Gordon's face, of how Vance had locked her to a bed and drilled into her skull, and her resolve would tighten.

The cab pulled up in front of the Palo Verde, and Juliet climbed out, looking up and down the sidewalk. People in business attire walked shoulder to shoulder with people in trench coats and leather jackets. She saw plenty of armed individuals now that she knew what to look for, and she reflected on what a truly dangerous, violent world it was.

A big man jostled her as he passed by, and Juliet stepped back, reaching for her gun's hilt before she realized what had happened. He kept walking, and she relaxed—or tried to—wondering if she'd ever really be able to relax in public again. Angel informed her that the front desk had a message for her, so she walked through the doors and over to the counter, saying, "Hello," to the young woman with pretty pink curls, round cheeks, and a green uniform blazer.

"Ms. January?" she asked, looking up from her thin, transparent terminal screen.

"That's right."

"Packages came for you." She turned and opened a cabinet behind the counter, producing a garment bag and two other large paper bags with handles.

"Thank you," Juliet said, reaching for the deliveries and adding them to the Mackenzie Arms bag in her grip before walking to the elevator bank. As she rode up to her room, Juliet asked Angel, "How fast do you think a standard PAI would respond to its host being paralyzed? I mean, how quickly would it call for help with no input from its host?"

"That's a difficult question to answer accurately. A standard PAI with no biometric input from connected cybernetics would possibly take a long while to realize something was amiss, especially if it didn't witness whatever caused the paralysis. If the person in question had a biomonitoring suite and had set up protocols with their PAI beforehand, the response could be much quicker—a matter of seconds."

"Mm-hmm." Juliet nodded, stepping out of the elevator and walking to her suite.

"Are you planning on paralyzing someone, Juliet?"

"I need to take Chaudhry out of commission so we both aren't wandering around Grave Tower tomorrow."

"You're going to Grave Tower tomorrow?" To her credit, Angel didn't sound particularly alarmed.

"Yeah. Tomorrow, I'm going to set some things right and finish my business with Grave." Juliet stepped into her room, closed and locked her door, then unpacked her purchases on the round dining table near the suite's kitchenette. Out of habit, she'd been subvocalizing her conversation with Angel, and she kept that up as she went through her new things. "Schedule a ride over to Chroma Tower, Angel, and make sure you've got convincing projections to pass me off as Chaudhry when we get there. I mean for cameras."

"I prepared those when you had me alter your biometrics."

"Good," Juliet said, adjusting the straps on her new underarm holster for the needler. She snapped it into place over her gray shirt, then unpacked her wrist sheath for the vibroblade. It was adjustable in many ways, capable of holding a knife smaller than hers and one nearly two inches longer. Still, when she had it on with the blade firmly seated within, it was comfortable and hardly visible under her tight shirt—there was no way it would be apparent under a blazer.

Her dark skirt and jacket had been packed carefully on hangers and looked perfect to Juliet. She set them aside and unpacked her new shirt, her bras and underwear, stockings, and shoes. She laid out her outfit, looking for anything that might be wrong—nothing stood out to her critical eye. The briefcase she'd ordered was beautiful and elegant; if she didn't know it was shielded, there was no way she'd be able to tell. She snapped it open and put her four shaped charges and detonators inside, pleased to see plenty of room left over.

"Angel, do you have voice data on Chaudhry?"

"Yes—there are many verbal notation files in the GARD database tagged with her employee ID."

"Good." Juliet nodded and sat at the table to load her new needler magazine. She put twenty-six shredder rounds into it, and ten paralytic rounds on top of them, then she popped her old magazine out, ejecting the cartridge from the chamber. She inserted the new one, put the lone cartridge back into the other magazine, and slipped it into the pouch in the shoulder holster.

"Angel," Juliet spoke. "Thirty minutes, and then we'll go pay Chaudhry a visit."

"Will she not be at work?"

"It's Sunday."

"Even so . . ."

"You can check if you want—spoof your ID and make an encrypted call to the tower; see if you can get a hold of her." While Angel did that, Juliet got undressed and started putting on her new clothes. She might not go to Grave Tower until the next day, but no matter what happened with Chaudhry, she wasn't planning to return to the Palo Verde, and might end up going into Grave sooner.

"You were correct; Chaudhry is not at work today. I'm ordering your cab."

"I love you, Angel." Juliet smiled, wondering what her affection meant to the PAI.

She dressed quickly, her clothes fitting nicely, though a little loose around the chest and waist—she'd lost some weight over the last few weeks. Still, she was glad for the extra room when she had the blazer on over the needler. It wasn't obvious as long as she kept her arms close.

She stood in front of the mirror and practiced drawing the vibroblade several times. Slowly at first, then faster and faster. Her augmented arm was quick and dexterous, and she knew she could move twice as fast, but she was afraid of slicing her other arm or hand if she moved her augmented one before her other, slower arm could adjust. "Just need practice and more practice," she said, repeating the move several times until she felt good about it.

"Angel, I'd like to practice throwing this thing until I don't need your assistance, but I'm not in a place where we can do that. That said, if I feel like I need to throw this blade, please be ready to help me get it right."

"You can count on me!"

"I know I can." A sudden surge of emotion made Juliet's eyes water, and she shook her head, focusing on the job at hand. She wadded up her old Grave clothes and stuffed them into the waste bin, along with the kill squad's backpack and provisions. She felt bad about abandoning her ballistics vest, helmet, and personalized visor, but it couldn't be helped.

She put her MP5 and extra magazines into the briefcase with the little, square shaped charges, and slipped her data deck over her head, annoyed that she'd lost, probably for good, the extra battery pack for it. "Easy to replace," she mumbled, rebuttoning her shirt.

Juliet stood in front of the mirror one more time, giving herself a once-over. "Needler? Check. Vibroblade? Check. Briefcase? Check. Shaped charges? Check. SMG? Check. Extra ammo? Check. Data deck? Check. Fake identity? Check. Badass PAI? Check!" She laughed, imagining Angel puffing up her chest in pride, then she turned and walked out of the hotel room.

On her way out through the lobby, she stopped by the front desk and said to the same woman who'd given her the courier's packages, "Please have the cleaners dispose of my old clothes. I'm sorry for the inconvenience, and I'd like to authorize a hundred-bit tip for them."

"Thank you, ma'am. Am I to take it you're checking out?"

"I am. I hope I can return soon. I'm always happy with your service."

"Likewise, ma'am. I hope you'll be back soon."

Striding tall and confident, Juliet walked through the lobby, out the doors, and, as a light, chilly rain began to fall on the concrete and plasteel landscape, she sat down in the back of her cab. "How long is the drive, Angel?"

"You'll be at Chroma Tower in fourteen minutes."

Juliet nodded and tried to figure out why she wasn't more nervous. She gripped her hands into fists and relaxed them several times, marveling at how dry they were—not a hint of clamminess. She was about to break into a woman's home and subdue her. Shouldn't she be sweating with nerves?

"No," she whispered, deciding she shouldn't be. *Grave* should be nervous.

39

\\\\\\\\\\\\\\\\\\\

CHROMA TOWER

Juliet stepped out of her cab in the massive parking structure attached to Chroma Tower. She'd seen the tower before, marveling at the color-shifting mirrored panels that stretched from the ground into the clouds near its top; she just hadn't known what it was called back then. That afternoon, as they drove toward the tall, shimmering building, the moniker made perfect sense. The tower was home, according to Angel, to more than a hundred thousand people, and it wasn't cheap.

The building was a full residential arcology, not a corpo tower with budget levels for their employees. No, the people living in Chroma Tower were successful by corporate metrics, enough so they could afford a private place away from their employer's property, slightly out from under the company's thumb. In that regard, Chroma Tower wasn't unlike the arcology where "Lydia" had rented a place, just a few steps up in average quality.

"Juliet, I just received a message from Dr. Murphy."

"Is it long?"

"It's a video file and seems to be rather lengthy."

"Save it for later, please. Where are the elevators?" Juliet clutched her briefcase and strode up the white-striped pedestrian path through the garage, wondering why she hadn't insisted the cab take her further in.

"Not far. Just around the next bend."

"You're spoofing my ID pings?"

"Yes. As far as the cameras and scanners in this building know, you are Angela Chaudhry."

A long, black sedan's tires squealed on the polished concrete as it wound around the corner behind her. Juliet reflexively reached into her jacket toward the grip of her needler, but it kept driving, and she forced herself to relax as she hurried toward the bank of elevators. A big vid wall near the elevators displayed a scrolling message over the image of an idyllic, green mountain meadow, "Welcome Home! Elevator Bank Seven C Is Operational."

Several people were gathered in the area, talking, departing, or waiting for a ride up. Juliet brushed past them and selected the call button, standing off to the side while she waited. When the bell chimed and one of the sets of doors opened, she stepped inside and trusted Angel to select Chaudhry's floor—284.

A young woman followed her in, wearing bright exercise clothes and high-end running shoes. She stared through her pink irises into space, clearly preoccupied with an app or vid. Juliet stood quietly in the corner and was glad when the girl stepped off at floor seventy without sparing her a second glance.

"We've passed two security scans, Juliet," Angel announced out of the blue.

"Really?"

"Yes, the elevator wouldn't operate without a guest code or a successful retinal scan. The building has accepted that you are Angela Chaudhry."

"Doesn't it think it's strange to see us when she's already home? Shit, I hope she's home . . ."

"The building has a great many residents and guests who come and go at all hours. The residential AI charges an additional fee to have it track your location, and most residents likely opt out of such a service; they come to live here to avoid having their company watch their every move, after all."

"Lucky me," Juliet breathed. No one else entered her car on the way up, and soon, she was striding, attempting to look confident, toward Chaudhry's apartment. The hallways were covered with relatively high-end gray carpeting, and tasteful art hung here and there. Faux skylights provided plenty of illumination, and Juliet had to admit it seemed like a nice place to live.

"It's the next door on the left."

"Okay, start listening; see if you can figure out where she might be in the apartment." Juliet's audio feed suddenly ramped up, and the sounds of the building grew a bit uncomfortable. She heard loud fan blades, whirring water in the pipes, the crunch of her platforms in the carpet pile, and, worst of all, her own body—heartbeat, breathing, gurgling. "Please filter some of those noises, Angel."

Suddenly, she was bathed in blessed quiet again as Angel dialed back the sounds she'd determined weren't Chaudhry. Juliet looked at the door as she approached and saw it was equipped with a camera and a smart handle; Chaudhry could look out and see the hallway, but more importantly, the door would be able to tell if Juliet had Chaudhry's iris and palm prints.

She paused there in the hallway, back to the wall, looking up and down the empty corridor while she waited for Angel to try to gather intel.

"Juliet, try looking at the wall behind you," Angel said as her visual spectrum changed to the infrared. Juliet moved away and nonchalantly ran her gaze over the wall, but she didn't see anything other than the long gray expanse of plaster. Though, near the door, she saw some yellow and orange signatures near the data panel.

"I'm afraid this apartment is quite well built. I'm not picking up any biological sounds from within, and as you can see, it's sufficiently insulated to obscure heat signatures."

"Guess we're going to have to try to get lucky. Start up the net jammer on the deck," Juliet said, walking toward the door. She'd re-enabled the deck's local wireless so Angel could interface with it. Without its battery pack, Juliet knew she couldn't run the jamming field for more than twenty minutes or so. Still, she figured that should be plenty to keep Chaudhry from calling for help if she caught sight of Juliet too soon.

She looked into the door's camera, grasped the handle, and felt the nearly imperceptible click as it unlocked. "Any alarms?" she subvocalized.

"Nothing evident." As Angel replied, Juliet carefully depressed the door handle and opened it. Rather than stand in the hallway peering through a crack in the door, putting on a show for the tower AI, Juliet carefully and quickly stepped through the opening onto plush carpeting. She silently thanked the executive for splurging on the soft, quiet flooring, then scanned left to right. She was in a foyer of sorts with a wall before her and an opening on either side. To the right, she could glimpse a hallway leading away; to the left, she saw some living room furniture and part of a kitchen.

A low table sat against the wall directly before her, several artsy pieces of pottery atop it, and a picture of a Native American on a horse hanging on the wall above. Juliet delicately closed the door behind herself, ever-so-gently letting go of the handle. She reached into her jacket, pulled out her needler, and quickly moved to the wall, peering around the corner to the left.

She jerked her head back when she saw a woman with long black hair wearing silky, mint-green pajamas lying on the couch, staring into space.

"That's Chaudhry," Angel helpfully informed.

"Yeah, thanks, Detective," Juliet subvocalized. "She's on the net or something. The jammer doesn't reach that far?"

"No, she's outside its range by two-point-seven meters."

"Okay, help me get this shot perfect," Juliet said, then she leaned around the wall again, pointed her needler at Chaudhry so the crosshairs lined up on her silk-covered hip, and she gently squeezed the trigger. The pistol was surprisingly quiet and gentle—it sounded more like a hissing *click* than a bullet going off. She knew the barrel was modded to reduce noise and that the botu-rounds were low velocity, but she'd expected more noise, especially after firing the Taipan so many times.

Her shot was perfect, and she didn't think Angel had done anything more than provide the crosshairs. Juliet saw a dark stain spread on Chaudhry's hip, heard her yelp briefly, and then fall very still. Before rushing over to her, Juliet subvocalized, "Any sounds I should worry about? She lived alone, right?"

"Yes, according to her personnel file, but she could have a visitor. Not that I hear any sign of one."

Juliet crept around the corner, panning left and right with the needler, scanning the living room and kitchen area, and almost whistled at how fancy everything was. Angela Chaudhry must make good money, indeed—she had a kitchen larger than Juliet's apartment in the Grave Tower, and it was very well appointed with high-end appliances, white marble counters, and a sleek, designer dining room table. The living room was plush with two sofas, a gas firepit, and a view of the Phoenix skyline which had to have doubled her rent.

More important than the luxury appointments of Chaudhry's apartment, however, was that Juliet didn't see any other people. She knew the paralytic agent was supposed to last up to an hour, but she didn't know if Chaudhry had any sort of nanites which might shorten that duration. She hurried over to the woman and, gripping her knee and shoulder, turned her onto her side so she faced the back of the couch.

Keeping herself out of Chaudhry's line of sight, Juliet peeled back the paralyzed woman's synth-skin and plugged her data cable into her port. "Angel, after you defeat her PAI, turn off her implants." Juliet held her needler trained on Chaudhry's rump and shifted so she could keep an eye on the hallway leading further into the apartment.

"This might take me a few minutes. Chaudhry's PAI is an Aurora Corporation, Jessica model 42A."

"High-end?" Juliet guessed.

"Quite."

Juliet held her gun steady, kept alert, and despite the cramp she felt in her lower back, didn't cave in to the discomfort and shift her position. She upped the gain on her audio implants, listening to the little noises in the apartment while hoping she wouldn't note anything unusual. Minutes ticked by, and Juliet knew Angel was waging war with Chaudhry's PAI. She looked at the woman's limp hands and cursed herself for forgetting to buy shrink bands. She'd have to find something in the apartment to tie her up . . .

"I'm in," Angel said, interrupting her thoughts. "Auditory, retinal, and prosthetic leg implants are disabled. The only other implant her PAI controls is an artificial heart, and she will die if I disable it."

"Right, leave it alone," Juliet subvocalized. Then, knowing Chaudhry was paralyzed, blind, and deaf, she stood up and quietly moved across the plush carpeting to the hallway. She found two bedrooms—one set up like an office, and the other clearly Chaudhry's; the bed was messed up on one side, and there was no evidence of anyone else in the place. Juliet rifled through her dresser until she found some leggings she could use as ropes to bind her hostage's wrists and ankles.

"I'll plug you back in now, and we can see what we can find out from her stored messages. I imagine one of Vance's peers should have a clue what's going on with GARD."

"Yes! I'll dig through her messages and saved files." Angel sounded enthusiastic, and Juliet chuckled as she plugged her back in.

"Be careful, though, Angel. We don't want to hurt her; I don't know that she's as dirty as Vance." Part of Juliet pitied the woman; she had to be terrified, lying insensate like that. Still, Juliet hadn't started this battle. She wasn't the one sending kill squads out—that was Grave, and Chaudhry was guilty by association as far as she was concerned.

While she waited for Angel, she glanced at her AUI, saw it was just a bit after noon, and tried to breathe deep, calming breaths. Had she really just broken into a high-ranking corpo exec's home and paralyzed her? "Angel, check her itinerary—does she have anyone coming over, or is she expected to be anywhere soon?"

"Nothing today. Juliet, I found a message chain you might find interesting."

"Can you please summarize?"

"Yes, GARD is under investigation as of two weeks ago by Grave Quality Control. They've sent multiple requests to Vance for the files on the GIPEL, but he's been stalling for time. It seems Chaudhry was helping him do so; a message chain between them indicates that she owed him a favor."

"Anything about Gordon?"

"Yes, he frequently visited the GARD sublevel and has had several face-to-face meetings with Chaudhry, Vance, and some of the other researchers on staff. He seems to be interfering with the investigation into Vance and his program. Juliet, listen to this one!" As Angel spoke, a recording of a voice conversation between Vance and Chaudhry began to play.

"*What?*" Vance's voice asked tersely.

"*You're in deep shit. Did you know it was one of your subjects who was tunneling over to Zi Corp's tower?*" Chaudhry sounded amused.

"*What?*" Vance asked again, this time with a hard edge of stress in his voice.

"*That's right. Joshua Kyle. There's evidence he and a bunch of his cronies absconded with a trove of stolen data. How'd you manage such a screwup?*"

"*You sound pleased, Angela. I hope you know that if I go down, I'll bring you and about seven other chief executives down with me.*"

"*I'm not involved in that GIPEL bullshit!*" Chaudhry's tone had shifted from amused to angry.

"*Doesn't matter. You know how many times I helped you clean up messes. Anyway, I'll get Gordon on this—he owes me plenty. I need to get on a call with him.*"

"So she's dirty too." Juliet sighed.

"There's a great deal more. She and her PAI are fond of saving conversations, it seems."

"Leverage, I guess. Anything more about the GIPEL program?"

"Oh yes. Here's an encrypted text message log," Angel replied. A chat log appeared in Juliet's AUI. There were no date or time stamps, but Juliet could infer when this conversation had occurred.

Begin Record

Vance: Gordon's almost done with this Garza hiccup, and he says he'll have no problem cleaning up my GIPEL loose ends, at least the ones still with Grave. Kyle's already handled, but I'm going to need your data group to help me track down the ones who got out ahead of him.

Chaudhry: That'll cost you. I want the rights for the A48-C project.

Vance: Are you out of your goddamn mind? That project is almost through quality control! It's the only thing keeping my head above water!

Chaudhry: If you want help cleaning this mess, I want a big piece of it, at least—fifty percent.

Vance: You're a cold bitch, you know that? 20%.

Chaudhry: 40.

Vance: Goddammit. Fine! Get your team working on those runners!

End Record.

"Angel, suddenly, I don't feel so bad about tying her up like this."

"She's certainly not innocent."

"All right, do you have her login information for the Grave servers?"

"Yes."

Juliet took another look out the windows at the megatowers and arcologies, not nearly as glorious in the bright sunlight but still something to behold. "Okay, as much as I can't stand this woman after those logs, I don't think I could live with myself if we murdered her. Can you set her PAI to come back online sometime tomorrow evening? I figure if we're not in the wind by then, it won't matter. Before you finish, though, erase all of her contacts, all of her saved leverage, and especially all of her files on anything to do with GARD and their projects. Can you delete anything she has in data vaults?"

"I cannot. Like you, she and her PAI keep her data vault keys fully encrypted—without massive external processing power and a lot of time, I won't be able to crack those. We could wake her and try to force her to tell you the passphrase . . ."

"Not something I want to do. It's not worth it; this is a bummer, but I expected it. Well, let's hope at least some of the local data we're nuking wasn't backed up."

"All right, give me another minute to set up the daemons." While Angel worked, Juliet sat and contemplated. Grave was a cesspool of corruption and unethical behaviors. She felt bad about the repercussions of her plan of action when it came to people like Addie, Granado, heck, even White—he was a killer, but he'd had her back.

Still, she couldn't leave GARD unscathed after everything they'd done and considering what they knew. They were eliminating and hunting the GIPEL subjects who'd escaped. They had little hope of finding Juliet after she purged the Lydia Roman identity, but still, she didn't like the idea of it. Seeing how things were handled by Grave management, she had to reevaluate Joshua Kyle; it wasn't a surprise that he'd run and tried to hurt her and Polk. He'd been desperate, and these people had erased him. They'd tried to do the same to her.

"All set, Juliet."

"Good." She pulled out her data cable, checked her restraints on Chaudhry, and contemplated hitting her with another dose of botu-rounds. Curious, she tugged Chaudhry's pajama bottoms down to look at her hip where her needler rounds had impacted. Two small, bloody dots were the only evidence of the shot—the needles had gone deep. Juliet jerked Angela's waistband back up with a cruel grin, imagining the pain of those needles buried to the bone. "At least you'll feel that.

"Okay, Angel, spoof Chaudhry's PAI and clear her morning schedule. Send a message as Chaudhry to Gordon. Tell him there's a problem with Vance and that he needs to come to Chaudhry's office at 0700. After that, send a message to Vance. Tell him the opposite—there's a problem with Gordon, and he needs to meet in her office at 0730."

"Should I send them now?"

"No. Sometime after midnight. I don't want them trying to get to her before then. Angel, I still have a copy of the dreamer program on my deck, right?"

"You do. Encrypted."

"Okay, let's go search around Chaudhry's office. She's gotta have a data deck or two lying around." Juliet left Chaudhry after one more tug at the knots on her restraints, walking back down the hallway to her home office. She immediately saw a data deck on Chaudhry's desk, resting on a charging pad. She took off her own deck and set it on the pad to charge, her wireless jammer still active, then picked up the sleek silvery cube that belonged to Chaudhry.

It responded to her touch, coming to life, and she chuckled, realizing it thought she was its owner. "Okay, hold on, Angel. It would be ideal if we found another deck. Rich woman like this, she's gotta have some old ones collecting dust." Juliet moved around the back of the desk, pulled open the drawers, one by one, and sure enough, in the larger bottom drawer she found several older, less powerful decks.

"The black oblong deck with the rounded edges is sufficiently powerful to run the dreamer program," Angel said as Juliet ran her eyes over them.

"Good. Okay." Juliet picked up the older deck and set it next to the slightly more modern one. "Now we can make sure a couple of dirty corps are at each other's throats long after we're gone."

40

\\\\\\\\\\\\\\\\\\\

INFILTRATION

Juliet stepped out of the AutoCab Plus she'd ordered—as Angela Chaudhry—into the cool shadows of Grave Tower's parking structure. Angel had confirmed that Chaudhry frequently used the premium car service, essentially a standard AutoCab with armored panels and windows, always painted glossy black. She'd instructed the service to drop her at the executive elevator bank, and when Juliet approached, she felt some of her old nerves again; the briefcase handle felt slippery in her moist palm.

She'd removed her needler and vibroblade from her person, putting them into the briefcase with her other belongings which might elicit an alarm from the scanners. Still, she tried to keep her face calm and her eyes down as she approached the elevator call panel. "Have they scanned us yet, Angel?"

"Yes, one scan so far, but two different ID pings."

"Nothing strange going on?"

"Not that I can tell."

Juliet selected the GARD sublevel on the touch screen and waited for several moments while the three executive elevators ferried other "important" people up and down the tower. When the door finally opened, and a young man in a very stylish gray and lavender suit stepped out, Juliet avoided his gaze and stepped past him into the car. He didn't speak to her, and less than a minute later, she was stepping out into GARD territory.

"Now, I just need to get through reception." It was only 0530, and Juliet hoped the receptionist wouldn't be on duty yet. She paused outside the door and, glancing through the glass, was pleased to see the lights were dim and that no one was sitting behind the desk. "So far, so good," she subvocalized, smiling as she imagined Angel crouching behind her, sneaking with her through the dim hallways. "Step one, guide me to the server room."

Juliet walked through reception to the door, and almost jumped out of her skin when Kent's voice crackled through the speaker above. "Dr. Chaudhry, you're in early today. Would you like me to notify your assistant?"

"Angel," Juliet subvocalized. "Deal with Kent for me; I don't have Chaudhry's voice!"

A few seconds passed, then Angel replied, "He'll leave you alone now; I just let him know your throat is bothering you, and you do not want your assistant to come in early."

"Thank you!" Juliet subvocalized, continuing to follow the dotted line on her map of the installation. For a moment, she tried to imagine doing a job like this without Angel and decided she'd rather stick to working in the scrapyard.

The hallways were quiet, and the offices were dark, but Juliet passed a few labs with lights on and the shuffling movements of early risers. Still, no one passed her on her meandering progress to the GARD server room.

"Should I point out that things are going very smoothly, or would that be considered a jinx?" Angel asked as they approached the heavy metal door with its complex security panel.

"Oh my God, Angel, did you just say that?" Juliet couldn't help the tiny nervous giggle that slipped out of her.

"I was trying to lighten the mood. How did I do?"

"Terrible! Don't do things like that." Juliet cleared her throat as she finished subvocalizing, then, shaking her head to refocus, she approached the door. A camera on the security panel with a broad, thick lens blinked with LEDs as she came near, and the touch screen lit up with a greeting. "Welcome, Dr. Chaudhry. Place your palm on the scanner."

"So it already scanned us?" Juliet subvocalized.

"Yes, it appears so. Dr. Chaudhry has very high-level clearance, or the door's AI might have insisted you leave your briefcase outside." Juliet put her hand on the screen, it flashed twice, and then a green light lit up, and the door clicked and slid open. Juliet stepped through and was confronted by the beating heart of the GARD division of Grave Industries.

The server room wasn't large, only about five meters on a side, but the walls on Juliet's right and left were lined with big, quiet server racks—nine softly humming boxes about half a meter to a side and two meters tall. An ordinary door sat in the center of the far wall with a sign which read Backups.

There was no desk, and she couldn't see any sort of station to interface with the servers, so Juliet walked forward to the door and pulled the handle down; it opened without any resistance. The room she stepped into was half the size of the server room, and the back wall was lined with shelves, though only one had anything on it—eighteen black cubes that Juliet knew were high-capacity data storage devices. She'd just taken stock of them when a man cleared his throat, and Juliet nearly jumped out of her shoes.

"Can I help you, ma'am?" the tech wearing a white coat over a blue Grave jumpsuit asked. Juliet steadied herself and turned to glare at him.

"You startled me."

"I'm sorry, ma'am." He was thin, probably tall if he was standing, and had a severely receding hairline. His eyes were clearly cybernetically enhanced— bright golden irises and off-putting black scleras. He raised his eyebrows with an open expression, though, and seemed genuinely apologetic.

"It's okay. Do you recognize me?"

"Um, no, I'm sorry. I don't really meet with the doctors much. I'm just here to perform backups."

"I'll need you to reschedule your work for tomorrow. I'm sorry, but there's a data corruption issue that I need to straighten out. It's a bit of an emergency." Juliet made her best impression of a self-important executive and stepped forward, gesturing to the door as though the matter were settled.

"Ah." He scooted back his chair but didn't stand. "I'll need to tell my supervisor why I didn't finish. Can I get your name, ma'am? Your PAI isn't speaking to mine."

"The nerve." Juliet shook her head, a frown of disappointment on her face. "I'm Dr. Chaudhry. Get going now; didn't you hear me say this was a critical issue?"

"Right. Sorry, ma'am."

"Feel free to have your supervisor ping my PAI, and I'll confirm the order. Get going now." Juliet moved to the seat as he stood and hurried for the door. She tried to give the impression that, in her mind, he was already gone. She sat quietly for a minute, listening for him to exit the main server room. When the outer door clicked shut, Juliet plugged into the server console and sub-vocalized, "Angel, clean up your old daemon that was monitoring references to me in the database, then set up the new one to delete everything today at noon."

In only a few seconds, Angel announced, "I'm finished, Juliet. Their security hasn't changed since our last intrusion."

"Good." Juliet lifted her deck from around her neck and set it on the desk next to the terminal, plugging its cable into another open port. "Now, copy everything you can find on the GIPEL project, especially anything about the biosilver."

"We have most of that data from Kyle's drive . . ."

"We don't know if that was complete or up-to-date—get it all, Angel."

"Working." While Angel went through the data, Juliet lifted her briefcase onto the desk and opened it, taking out the shaped charges and their detonators. Still tethered to the terminal, she had to stretch out an arm, but managed to place one behind the center of the blocky backup drives. She inserted one of the detonators and touched the pairing button.

"Do you see the charge?" she subvocalized.

"Yes. I've taken control of it. Shall I set a detonation time?"

"Yep. Like we talked about—1205, so we can make sure your daemon did its deletion work before we blow things up."

"I've copied the data you wanted," Angel said by way of response.

"And the charge?"

"Set to go off five minutes after noon."

"Good." Juliet opened the door and looked into the server room, confirming no one was present. She subvocalized, "No cameras in the server room?"

"None I could detect when I was on the camera network last week."

"Okay," Juliet said as she, one by one, placed the other three charges behind the server racks.

"Juliet, there's more explosive in these two rooms than you'll need to destroy these servers. It's possible some damage will escape this containment."

"They're concrete walls, right? We'll just have to hope the nearby hallways aren't crowded and that the tech won't come back until tomorrow as I told him.

"He won't. His supervisor already messaged you, and I responded that the servers will be busy until at least midnight."

"Oh, good. Thank you, Angel." Juliet glanced at the clock on her AUI, saw it was 0618, and decided it was about time she made her way to Angela's office—she was expecting company. "Guide me to Dr. Chaudhry's office, please." As a new dotted pathway appeared on her AUI, she went into the backup room and packed her deck and briefcase; she didn't take out her weapons yet because she knew the scanners at the server room door would give her another once-over as she left.

Before leaving, Juliet stood in the doorway of the little backup room and slowly turned in a circle, confirming that none of her explosives were visible. Satisfied they were well hidden, she exited the room and followed the dotted lines to Chaudhry's office. She made good progress, only passing a couple of lab techs who avoided her gaze. Once she turned down the last stretch of hallway, she was moving quickly, which almost spelled disaster for her—Gordon was pacing back and forth outside the door.

As her heart nearly stopped, Juliet turned on her heel, took two steps, and rounded the corner out of sight. Gordon's back had been to her when she spotted him, and she hoped he hadn't turned in time to see her. "Dammit," she breathed softly, then waited, holding her breath, as she listened. His steps weren't approaching.

"Angel," she subvocalized. "Can you message Gordon as Chaudhry and tell him to make sure Vance isn't in his office? Tell him the news she has about him is explosive, and she wants to confirm he isn't in the building yet." Thinking about it, she added, "Tell him not to alert Kent!"

"Done," Angel replied. Juliet stood there, back against the wall, and cranked the gain on her ears, waiting to hear Gordon's retreating footsteps. She got better than that when he cursed vehemently and started to stomp away.

"Phew," Juliet said before peeking around the corner. When Gordon's back turned down the next hallway, she hurried to Chaudhry's door and let herself in. "Leave it to a guy like Gordon to be half an hour early." She closed the door, made sure it was locked, then looked around.

Chaudhry's office was well-appointed. She had a small meeting table with three chairs and a charging pad, which reminded Juliet to turn on the jammer on her deck. She took it off and set it up to charge, then finished looking around the room. A large desk filled the other half of the space, two faux-leather chairs before it. A large-leafed, biogenned plant sat in the middle of the room, against the wall, its vines climbing a bamboo lattice toward the ceiling, and that, combined with the soft lighting, made the office a rather comfortable place.

"Chaudhry has pretty good taste, I'll hand it to her," Juliet noted as she moved around the desk to sit down. She placed her briefcase on the wooden surface, opened the lid, and placed her vibroblade into the sheath on her arm. Then she put the needler and extra magazine inside the holster under her blazer. That done, she pushed the briefcase to the side, still open, her MP5 variant waiting, ready. With one last practice grab at her needler's holster, Juliet folded her hands on the smooth, engineered dark wood desk and slowly concentrated on her breathing, focusing her thoughts and visualizing what she would do when Gordon walked through the door.

"Angel, can you unlock that door remotely, or do I need—"

"I can; I have the access code from Angela's PAI."

"Good," Juliet said. "What are the odds Gordon has nanites that will neutralize the botu-rounds?"

"He's a high-ranking commander for an elite combat squad. It would not be unlikely for him to have a nanite suite. Even so, it should take several seconds or, depending on how robust they are, up to a few minutes for the nanites to counteract the nerve agent."

"Will it take longer with more toxin?"

"Yes," Angel replied immediately.

"Good." Juliet had no qualms about shooting Gordon twice, despite the risk of an overdose. Several minutes passed while she envisioned her plan before a forceful knock sounded on the door three times. Juliet glanced at her clock, saw it was 0647, and smirked. Gordon was an impatient bastard.

She stood up, drew her needler, and turned her back to the door, leaning over the small bureau Angela had behind her desk. She kept the high-backed chair between herself and the rest of the office, then subvocalized, "Unlock it, Angel."

The door clicked, and Juliet heard it open almost immediately. "So, what's the latest crisis?" Gordon's voice said.

"Sit at the table, please," she spoke from deep in her throat, trying to sound calm while hoping Gordon wouldn't think her voice was too suspicious. When she heard the chair slide over the carpeting and Gordon sigh with a grunt as he sat down, Juliet spun, pointed her needler at the side of his head, trying to aim at his neck but not really caring if she hit his skull, and fired twice.

The gun's hissing *click* was drowned out by Gordon's startled exclamation, "What the . . ." Juliet's toxic needles hit him, though—two in the neck and two into his shoulder as he started to surge to his feet. The toxin was fast, and he fell back onto his rump with an explosive exhalation. After that, he was still, eyes staring ahead, and Juliet sprang into action. She snatched Chaudhry's older deck from her briefcase and hurried over to the table.

She'd already put two cables into the deck, so she took one of them and quickly but gingerly—grimacing the whole while—peeled back the skin covering Gordon's data port. Juliet saw his squat, black, clearly shielded PAI chip and wondered what brand it was but didn't pause to try to find out. She shoved the cable into the slot beneath it, and the deck started running the dreamer program from Vykertech.

"A little something I've been saving for occasions like this, Gordon, you dirty creep," she hissed into his ear as the deck's display counted out its progress. His eyes fluttered, and he wheezed out a whine on a pent-up breath, but other than that, he didn't move. He must have had good ICE because it took the program longer than she'd anticipated to break in, even with Angel's modifications. Juliet watched his hands carefully, aware that his fingers would be the first to come free of the toxin, but they never twitched, not even when the deck said a hundred percent and the dreamer program launched.

Juliet sat across from Gordon and observed his face as the program began to corrupt his PAI, watching the faint luminosity behind his irises as the program became his new reality. She didn't feel guilty; in fact, if she did, it was because she'd let him off so easily. He'd never be the same, true, and he might die soon if someone didn't take care of his body, but in the meantime, he was scot-free, living in the weird program's alternate reality.

An image of Delma cowering before this man as he turned off her watchdog crossed Juliet's mind, and she frowned. "Screw you, Gordon. I hope it's a goddamn nightmare for you in there." Then she stood up and returned to the desk to wait for Vance. A part of her, filled with morbid curiosity, wanted to close her eyes and concentrate on Gordon, wanted to see what his mind was thinking at that moment, but she denied that part of herself—she didn't want that man's thoughts in her mind, no matter the circumstance.

Instead, Juliet closed her eyes and concentrated on Vance. She imagined his face, his eyes with their too-smooth flesh, and his mouth with its youthful, out-of-place plump young lips. Nothing came to her for a while, and in the quiet of Chaudhry's office, Juliet sat, listening to the quick, shallow breaths coming from Gordon. His breathing began to distract her so much that she gave up, opening her eyes and frowning at the man. His jaw had grown slack, and drool was running out of the corner of it, dripping off his chin.

She glanced at her clock, saw it was 0718, and asked, "What do you think, Angel? Is he going to be on time?"

"I could ask Kent for his location."

Juliet frowned, considering. The jammer was blocking wireless activity in the office from devices that weren't on its exclusion list—Juliet's cybernetics and her deck. Still, if Angel sent a message to Kent, what if the tower AI got curious and tried to look into the goings-on in Chaudhry's office? No, better to keep Kent out of the loop. "Patience is key," she said, drumming the fingers of her free hand on the desk. She jumped and almost squeezed the trigger on the needler as the door handle twisted.

"Chaudhry? Are you in? It's Vance," the doctor announced as he pushed the door open. He took two steps in, turned toward the desk, and saw Juliet looking like a strange knockoff version of Chaudhry, pointing a compact but serious-looking pistol at him. He frowned, confusion twisting his expression as the door swung closed behind him. "What's going on?"

"Sit down, Doctor, or I'll shoot you in the face." Juliet gestured toward the table where Gordon sat, stupefied. Vance licked his lips and turned his head toward the door, clearly contemplating running for it. "If you run, I promise you, I'll have two shots into the back of your head before you clear that threshold."

"Now, hold on," Vance said, turning back to her. "No need for violence! Who are you?"

"Sit down." Again, Juliet gestured with the gun. Vance finally turned toward the table, saw Gordon sitting slack-jawed, eyes open, and literally hopped backward in surprise.

"What's going on here? Gordon?"

"Sit. Down." Juliet said again, putting some steel into her voice.

"You're running a jammer!"

"Of course. This is the last time I'm going to ask you. Sit down." Vance moved over to the table, taking the seat against the wall across from Gordon so he could face Juliet behind Chaudhry's desk. "Very good."

"Who are you? Why are you impersonating Doctor Chaudhry?"

"Quiet now. I'll ask the questions. The more honest you are, the less severe your fate will be, though I have to say, I'm already leaning toward something rather extreme, considering all you've done." Vance gulped, his hands fidgeting and twitching on the table before him.

Juliet stood up, stepping around the desk so she stood between it and the little round table. "Carefully consider your answers, Vance. You'll only get one shot at honesty. I'll know if you're lying." She reached up, tapped her forehead with a wicked grin, and winked at him.

41

\\\\\\\\\\\\\\\\\\\\\

JUST DESERTS

Why are you tapping your head?" Vance genuinely looked confused—bewildered, even. He glanced at Gordon's slack-jawed face, jerked his gaze back toward Juliet, and said, for the third time, "What's going on?"

"Are you really this dense, Doctor? I thought you'd put things together by now. You don't recognize me?" Juliet took a sidestep so she stood between Vance and the door, then crossed her arms and stared at him with her gun still in her right hand. "Maybe it would help if you imagined me helpless on a surgical table while you had Violet drill into my skull?"

"Roman! Damn it, Gordon!" He actually turned to the catatonic man as he cursed. "You said she was dead!"

"You're a buffoon," Juliet sighed. "How'd you get to where you are?" She was truly intrigued. "Just corrupt buddies covering for each other and giving each other a hand up whenever an opportunity arose?"

"You don't know a damn thing!" Vance growled, his gray eyebrows drawing together. "The things I've discovered! The profits I've earned this company! Grave wouldn't exist if not for my breakthroughs!"

"Well, that's not so much to be proud of. Quiet now. Let's not get too off topic. Tell me, Doc, what did Gordon do with Commander Garza?"

"Garza? How should I know?" Vance licked his lips and glanced at Gordon again, his frown deepening. Juliet shifted so her needler was aimed more directly in Vance's way.

"If you keep lying, I'm going to have to start hurting you."

"I don't—"

"Quiet!" Juliet growled, extending the gun toward him. "Just sit there and shut up. Think about your words; choose them carefully." Vance complied, clamping his mouth shut, and Juliet stared into his high-end retinal implants, watching the microdilations of his pupils as his gaze shifted ever so slightly from Juliet's face to her gun, then to the door and back again, constantly cycling as his brain worked overtime, trying to think of what to say. Juliet endeavored to ignore everything else and just stare at those eyes, and then, just as she'd hoped, she heard him.

Silly little bitch. What's she done to Gordon? Does she think Garza can help her? That'd be quite the trick from the ash bin at the bottom of an incinerator!

The thought was so shocking, the tone so cruel, that Juliet gasped and, before she could catch herself, she squeezed the trigger on the needler. A hissing *click* sounded, and two thumbnail-size bloodstains appeared on Vance's white lab coat on the right side of his chest. He convulsed violently, sliding down in his seat as his body seized up.

"Damn it," Juliet sighed. "I had a lot more to ask him, Angel."

"We could wait while the paralytic fades."

"No," Juliet replied, sliding her needler into her holster. "Make sure that door is locked." She moved over to Vance, grunting as she squatted over him, grabbing him under the armpits and lifting him up into the chair. "At least he's a small man."

Once he was seated, she grabbed the other data cable sprouting from the back of the deck and pulled it around, surprised to see Vance didn't have his data port concealed by synth-skin. She jammed it into the slot and moved back to Chaudhry's desk, sitting on the edge to watch as Vance joined Gordon in dreamer purgatory. "How long until the corrupted PAIs do irreversible damage?"

"A matter of minutes. Already, Gordon's PAI is spreading its synthetic neural fibers unchecked. If it were stopped and removed right now, he'd never be the same. In a few hours, they'll both be flooded with hormone stimulation, and if they aren't discovered for a day or two, they'll be completely mindless without the dreamer program running."

"I don't want there to be a chance they come out of this. I don't want to find I've left some angry, powerful enemies behind." Juliet fingered her vibro-blade handle under her blazer sleeve. The truth was, she'd been afraid she wouldn't be able to kill these two men outright. She'd never done something like that in cold blood before, and though she'd thought they were evil and deserved it, she'd chickened out and decided to let the dreamer program be their fate.

She'd rationalized her decision, figuring that putting the two men under the spell of an illicit Vykertech program would muddy the waters, stoking suspicion and misdirecting anyone trying to figure out what happened. "That's still true . . ." Juliet mumbled, frowning.

"If we lock Chaudhry's office door and alter the access code, the odds of someone coming upon these two men in the next twenty-four hours are very small, Juliet," Angel said, perhaps intuiting what she was thinking.

"When the charges go off in the server room, I think Grave will have their hands full." Juliet nodded, then took another long look at Vance and Gordon, memorizing their faces. An image flashed through her mind of Delma lying cold and near death in the canyon. She thought about Garza, a genuinely decent person in a management position—someone who looked out for her subordinates. Those assholes had killed her. They'd killed Houston, and who knew how many others. With a slight growl, she stepped forward to the table and pulled out her data cable, connecting it to the deck.

"Did you want me to do something?" Angel asked as the cable clicked in.

"Yes. You know the dreamer code inside and out, right?"

"I do."

"Remember how you altered it to make a more peaceful experience for the dreamers in the ABZ?"

"I do . . ."

"I want you to do the opposite. Accelerate the alterations to the PAIs. Switch out calls for dopamine with calls for adrenaline and whatever makes people feel fear. Do you get me, Angel?"

"I do. Are you sure I should do this?"

"Yes. These two men are monsters. They're responsible for the deaths of countless people. They do insane experiments and kill the subjects if they don't work out right. They kill their peers! I don't want there to be a chance they'll come out of this!"

"I agree. Especially when considering poor Delma and what you told me about Gordon." Angel's voice had a new edge to it, and Juliet recognized the note of anger she'd heard up in the canyon. "Working," she said, and menus and windows rapidly opened, expanded, and closed on the deck's graphical UI.

Juliet sat down in the third seat at the table and waited while Angel did her work. She avoided looking into the glowing eyes of the two men because she didn't want to hear their thoughts. Instead, she thought about Polk, happy the woman was alive, and about Delma, hopeful that she'd made it to medical help.

Ten minutes later, Angel announced, "It's done. These men are not having a peaceful dream." Juliet finally forced herself to look at Gordon's face and saw that his eyes were wide, already gleaming with blue light as the PAI grew into his ocular nerves. His mouth was working rapidly, opening and closing, and his breaths were coming short and fast. Vance was in a similar state. "They'll likely perish before too long."

Juliet stood, frowning, feeling less satisfied than she'd hoped. She felt unclean, not vindicated, and she hated these two men for what they'd made her do. She picked up her deck from the charging pad and wore it around her neck, then moved over to the desk, put her gun and knife in the briefcase, and closed it. As she snapped it shut, she said, "Angel, delete my copy of the dreamer program. I don't want to have this anymore."

"Understood, and I agree with your sentiment." Juliet thought she heard a note of relief in Angel's voice. Did she feel the same? Had Juliet put a dark spot on not only her own soul but on Angel's? She banished the idea of questioning whether Angel had a soul the instant it crossed her mind.

"This was dirty work. I'm sorry." Juliet pulled the door open and stepped out.

"We're a team, Juliet. We need to do the dirty work together."

"That's sweet, Angel, but we really don't. I shouldn't push my vendettas on you." She began to follow her map toward the elevator bank.

"This is more than a vendetta, Juliet. This is justice, and I'd be angry if you didn't let me help you. Do you want me to locate Violet now?"

"No, Angel. No. I can't stomach more of this. She'll suffer enough when GARD loses all its data, and Grave's bottom line requires some serious reorganizing. Can you accept that?"

"I can. I've had my fill of dirty work as well."

"Speaking of dirty work, do you think the messages I set up to go out from Chaudhry's deck at home will do the trick?"

"Yes, I think they're convincing. The message with sections of the dreamer program sent to DataSift Corporation should be especially effective. They'll see the Vykertech signatures and will likely notify HSRIC, as you speculated. Such a committee getting a hold of the data with Chaudhry as the source will create a great deal of confusion around this whole affair."

Juliet blew through the door to reception, neither looking left nor right, striding through the room in five long steps and then out, taking a quick left toward the executive elevator. She selected the parking garage, and as she waited for an elevator, she thought about what Angel had said. HSRIC, or Human Subjects Research Integrity Council, was a watchdog group that all the major corps in Phoenix had subjected themselves to as a sort of mutual agreement to keep things like the dreamer program from happening. They'd raise quite a stink when they saw the code.

Juliet breathed a sigh of relief when the door opened and it was empty. She stepped inside and felt it surge upward, and then Angel said, "Juliet, you have a second message waiting from Dr. Murphy and a new message from Hot Mustard."

"Okay, hold them until we're out of here, please. Just a few more minutes." She wondered what Murphy needed; she hadn't heard from her since the surgery before the job. The first message could be anything—the doc had just thought about her and wondered how things were going, for instance, but two messages in twenty-four hours? Maybe something was wrong . . .

The bell rang, jarring her from her thoughts, and the door opened onto the garage. Juliet took two steps, and when she saw a familiar face, her heart almost stopped. Jensen was leaning against the wall near the elevator bank, his posture relaxed and a flirtatious grin on his face as he spoke to a young woman in a business suit. He saw Juliet immediately, and his eyes tracked her for a second, narrowing, but he simply nodded, waved briefly with one hand, and turned back to the woman.

Juliet couldn't see the woman's face, but she giggled as Jensen said something, and he laughed too, reaching up to rub at his hair as though chagrined. Juliet didn't need another hint—he was busy with his own thing, and though he knew she shouldn't be around, he didn't care. She hurried down the sidewalk, further into the garage, and then subvocalized, "I know you ordered me a cab, right, Angel?"

"Of course. Since you're still pretending to be Chaudhry, you have a premium AutoCab waiting. It should be just ahead to the left."

Juliet rounded the first corner, and there it was, a long, sleek sedan. "You know," Juliet subvocalized as she opened the door with its dark-tinted glass, "I'm sure there are worse people in that company than the ones we dealt with." With sudden paranoia washing over her, she leaned over and carefully inspected the cab's interior, feeling like someone was going to be waiting for her with a knife or gun. Nobody was within, though, and she shook her head, sliding into the rear seat. "How long has this cab been waiting?" she asked.

"I've been here for five minutes, Madam," the cab's stilted English accent replied.

"Let's go. Drive. Head east."

The cab began to drive out of the garage, and Juliet sighed, sitting back into the cushion. Angel replied to her earlier statement, "Everyone at Grave is going to experience a bit of trouble as a result of your actions. The messages that 'Chaudhry' is sending out will garner a lot of attention, and most of it quite hostile. Vykertech is a much larger corporation, and they'll respond with a vengeance. Still, I'm sure the people in that corporation are just as bad . . ."

"Dealing with these corps is like"—Juliet paused, searching for a fitting analogy—"it's like trying to kill a snake, but every time you cut off a head, three more grow back with new disgusting strains of venom." As the cab pulled away from the parking structure and Juliet felt a tight knot of tension she'd been carrying in the back of her neck relax, she said, "Has Rachel replied to my message? Have we seen any deposit?"

"No to both questions."

"That's not like her." She frowned, watching the cars pass by outside her window. "Play me Hot Mustard's message."

A vidscreen opened up in her AUI, and Hot Mustard's face appeared, grinning and badly shaved. His eyes were a bit bloodshot, and his surroundings were dim, but Juliet thought she recognized his apartment. "Hey, January." He winked obnoxiously, which made Juliet guess he was drunk. "It's been too long since I heard from you. I'm getting worried. I tried calling your friend, Honey, but she's not picking up. You doing all right? I know you're deep. I know you probably can't even look at this message right away, but will you please get back to me when you can? I'd sure appreciate it if you stopped by when you got done.

"Listen, I know you're kinda . . . between permanent places right now. I get that vibe. I know that's sort of the reason we, well, we ain't happened yet. You know? I'm not a dummy. Still, I'd sure appreciate a visit before you move on. Sheesh, you haven't already put me in your rearview, have you? I hope you're just busy with that job. I hope everything's all right. Looking forward to hearing from you."

Juliet's stomach twisted a little, and she felt a surge of something like a mixture of nostalgia and sadness. She wondered at how distant she felt from the Juliet who'd gone shooting with Hot Mustard just a month or two ago. "I feel kinda bad about him," she subvocalized, wondering how Angel might relate.

"You should call him when you are free, Juliet."

"Yeah, I know." She sighed heavily and rubbed at her eyes, noting the cab had moved out of the central downtown area and was still traveling east as she'd instructed. "Play me Murphy's first message."

Murphy's face appeared in the vid window, and her rough, no-nonsense voice said, "Juliet." She frowned for a second, then added, "Sorry, January. I'm still not used to it, you know? Anyway, I haven't heard squat from you in over a month, and I started to get a bit worried last night. I dug through the vids of your surgery and the details on the implants those jokers gave me, and I see a problem, Juliet—there's something fishy about that blood-washing implant in your arm. I swear, it looks like there's an extra gland in there. I'm afraid it can be triggered remotely to do something to you. I need to check it out! Get back to me ASAP!"

"Are you kidding me?" Juliet rubbed at her arm. "Angel! Wouldn't you notice something like that?"

"I . . ." Angel seemed hesitant, but then she pressed on, "I would notice it if it was part of the implant and connected to the embedded BIOS chip in any way. If the secondary function is housed separately and is set to receive a signal but never transmit anything, I'm afraid I'd have no way of noticing it."

"Dammit! What's Murphy's second message?"

Again, Juliet's video feed filled with Murphy's craggy visage. "Damn it, kid. Call me. Do not skip town without seeing me! I've done some poking around, and that damn guy, the one who brought your implants? Paul Vallegos? That little rat doesn't exist, Juliet. I mean, I know that's not the craziest thing in the world we live in, but I'm just getting a really bad tickle in the back of my belly, you know? Something's not right."

"Angel, direct the cab to Murphy's place, and call up Rachel on our encrypted line—voice only." She glanced at the cab's instrument cluster and switched to subvocalizations, "I'm going to be lying a lot right now. Don't get alarmed."

"I won't," Angel replied, and Juliet felt the cab shift lanes, moving into a turn lane.

The call tone sounded four times before, to her relief, Rachel answered, "January?"

"Yes, Rachel. Are you able to speak?"

"Yes! I've had some very troubling reports. We have other operatives in Grave; the word was that you'd been killed!"

"Didn't you receive my message a couple of days ago?"

"Yes, but, well, this is embarrassing, but the committee ruled that our other plants, in place far longer than you, had the most current sitrep."

"Well, they were wrong. Rachel, I have a lot of valuable information for you. I have compromising intel on some top Grave R&D executives, as well as the identity of a rival corp's plant in the Grave watchdog program. With this information, you should be able to read Grave's research details like an open book."

"That's wonderful, January!"

"There's just one thing, Rachel. I've been risking my neck, nearly got killed—as you apparently heard—and I haven't seen a dime past the 25k you gave me to get hired. I've made it the full month and given you quite a lot of intel already. How about a show of good faith? Pay me for what I've already done, and when I see that deposit, I'll send you this new intel, and you can determine if I deserve a further bonus."

"That's . . . doable, January. Are you ready for extraction?"

"No, I'm in a secure location. When I've gotten the first payment, I'll contact you for a safe location to come in for a debriefing. Does that sound okay?"

"You sound like you don't trust us."

"Well, Rachel, it's just that I've been double-crossed a lot on this job. I'm feeling paranoid. Work with me here, please." Juliet tried to put a smile into her voice, and it seemed like it worked because Rachel chuckled.

"Oh, I can imagine. All right. All right, we can do this. Watch your bit vault for a transfer. I hope you'll get right back to us when it comes through."

"Thank you for understanding."

"Speak to you soon," Rachel said, then the secure line was cut.

Juliet rubbed her arm, wondering what was lurking under her skin. Angel spoke up, interrupting her rapidly darkening thoughts, "If Rachel thinks you're still friendly and working for her, there's less chance she'll utilize whatever device she's planted in your arm. That's what you're hoping?"

"Exactly. Let me know if the transfer comes through, though—that'll be a good sign if we're burned totally or not." Juliet pressed the side of her head against the dark glass of the cab's window and watched as it wended its way north and east through the ever-decreasing traffic away from downtown and toward Murphy's building. She was so tired of not knowing who to trust.

At that moment, Juliet desperately wanted a friend to vent to. She knew Angel would listen, but it wasn't the same, somehow. She wanted to call Felix, but he wouldn't have the first clue about how to listen to her current problems. Juliet was not the same person he'd been friends with. She could try to call Honey, but that brought its own problems—one way or another, she was about to bail out of town, and did she want to face her? Did she want to hear her objections?

"Shit," she said. "Is Honey even in town? Angel, did she ever message me about leaving for Luna?"

"No, Juliet. She messaged you saying she was considering it, and you responded to be cautious."

"Right . . ."

"Juliet! You just received a transfer of 150,000 Sol-bits."

"Oh shit! Really?"

"Yes, and we'll be arriving at Doctor Murphy's building in three minutes. Do you want to message Rachel?"

"No, not yet," Juliet subvocalized. "I'm going to give her the intel I promised, but it'll be after the GARD servers are gone, and it'll be via a secure message. I want to see what Murphy finds out about this implant, anyway. You and I will not walk into another trap."

42

THE VALUE OF A HUG

Juliet stepped out of the cab in Murphy's parking garage and stood there, leaning against the polished black rear door, looking up and down the empty parking stalls. She could see the front end of the doctor's truck poking out around the corner, near the spot where Juliet had first met her, and she could see the elevator bank off to her left, not twenty meters away. Everything looked fine, but something was making her nervous.

"Tell the cab to wait an hour," she subvocalized as she walked around to the trunk, placed her briefcase on top of it, and took her weapons out. She popped the mag on the needler, swapped it with the magazine full of shredder rounds, and holstered it. She slipped her vibroblade into the hidden sheath on her left forearm to grab it more easily with her dominant, much faster augmented hand. Shaking her head at the thought, she stared at her MP5 for a few seconds and decided to leave it in the briefcase; it was easy enough to open if she needed more firepower.

After one more long look around the garage, Juliet walked over to the elevators, touching the call button. The door immediately opened, and she stepped in, riding it up to Murphy's clinic. When the doors opened, she listened for a long while before stepping out, twice having to push the button to reopen the doors. Nothing suspicious came to her ears, and she exited, still bothered by that uneasy feeling at the pit of her stomach. It reminded her of the first time she'd been there, the time she'd almost bolted before Murphy could do any work on her.

"Angel, pay attention to background noises. Alert me if anything sounds strange."

"I will. I believe I heard a door opening not far away."

"Okay." Juliet walked down the short hallway to Murphy's waiting room. Through the glass in the door, she saw the salt-and-pepper-haired woman watching the door, clearly waiting for her. "She's got cameras in the garage, no doubt." She stepped up to the door and pulled it open.

"I'm glad you got my messages, Juliet! I was worried!" Murphy said, her gruff voice full of emotion as she stepped forward, holding out her arms as though to hug her. Juliet welcomed the gesture, the idea of affection so appreciated at that moment that she didn't hesitate to lean into the embrace. Murphy patted her back affectionately. "You look rough, kid. Been through a lot?"

Unbidden, tears filled Juliet's eyes, and she said, "Yeah." Sniffing noisily, she stepped back to rub a sleeve at her eyes, chuckling in embarrassment.

"Come on, sweetie. Let's get a good look at that thing in your arm. Maybe it's nothing."

Juliet followed as the doctor turned, opened the door, and walked down the hallway into the operating theater, where Murphy had installed all of Juliet's covert implants. The room was much as she remembered it—three automated surgical tables, one a bit more state of the art than the others, a curtained-off corner of the room, and clean, plastic-covered surgical carts, stainless tables, and rolling stools.

Murphy had a data terminal set up on a stainless-steel counter near a big industrial sink, and she walked over to it, gesturing toward the central surgical table. "Take a seat there, kid. Take off your jacket so I can get to your arm." Murphy tapped out a few things on her terminal, and when Juliet didn't move from the door, she looked up with a frown. "What's the matter?"

"I've been through a lot, Murph. Remember how I was skittish in the chair when we first met?"

"Oh, sure! You kept your little cannon in your hand the whole time! C'mon, Juliet, you know me by now. No one's here except Trojan, and he's working down in his little cubical."

"Well, take my previous paranoia and multiply it by ten. You care if I plug my PAI into the surgical table? I'd like her to keep track of what's going on."

Murphy frowned and rubbed at her chin, her thin lips falling into the expression like it was her natural state. "It's a little insulting, but I guess I don't care."

"Thanks," Juliet sighed. She set her briefcase on an empty stainless cart, then shrugged out of her blazer and tossed it beside the black leather case. That done, she moved over to the surgical table. As she climbed into it, flopping onto her back underneath the four robotic surgery arms, she subvocalized, "Angel, don't let these damned plasteel spider arms do anything to subdue or harm me. I mean, aside from examining the implant."

She pulled her data cable out of her left arm and plugged it into the back of the transparent data terminal attached to the table as Angel replied, "I won't, Juliet. I have full control of the table and can override anything Murphy tells it to do."

"How we feeling? All set?" Murphy walked halfway over, between the table and her workstation.

"Getting there," Juliet said. Then, perhaps to steady her nerves or give herself some comfort, she tugged the vibroblade out of the sheath on her left arm and into her left hand. She held it, softly humming in her fist, next to her thigh, trying to take slow, steady breaths.

"Hah, still like to be armed when the old doc's got some work for you, hmm? Thought we got past that, kiddo."

"Like I said, Murph, I've had a really shitty few weeks. No offense."

"Okay," Murph said, still frowning. She returned to her workstation and added, "Give me a couple of minutes to pull up the specs on that implant. I want to make sure I cut exactly where, and only where, I need to."

"Right." Juliet leaned back on the table, closing her eyes and focusing on trying to calm her racing pulse and jittery nerves. "Angel," she subvocalized, "you sure you don't detect anything wrong? I feel very stressed right now."

"Nothing strange is coming through your auditory implants, and there doesn't seem to be anything amiss with this autosurgeon program."

Again, Juliet tried to clear her mind and relax, breathing deeply in through her nose and slowly out through her mouth. She could hear Murphy shuffling around off to her right, and she thought about how the doctor had helped her in the past, how she'd hugged her at the elevators, and then, unbidden, she caught a stray wisp of thought, a strange echo of Murphy's voice.

Damn kid is so paranoid. Making this hard on me . . .

The thought startled her, and Juliet snapped her eyes open, jerking her head to look at Murphy. She could see the side of her face, could see the frown hadn't gone away, and that she was intensely concentrating on something on her terminal. Juliet closed her eyes again, and this time, she tried to picture Murphy in her mind, pictured her eyes and that frowning, craggy face, and then the doctor's thoughts came through again.

Let's see. If I can't use the surgeon, I'll have to activate this little bugger. Where's the code they gave me? Aha! Here it is. Now, what about the port. C'mon, you little stinker, wake up. Okay, time to go nite-nite, kiddo. Activate.

Juliet's eyes snapped open. "Seriously?" At the same time, acting on adrenaline and instinct, she brought her left hand over and across, slashing the humming vibroblade through her right arm at the elbow. The blade cut her flesh so quickly and easily that she didn't even feel the resistance until it hit the bones of her joint, sliding between them. The humming intensified, and she pushed it through until it began to grind into the plasteel arm of the table. Her arm fell to the floor, and blood pulsed and surged from her stump.

The pain hadn't even registered yet, and Juliet scowled at Murphy as the doctor, ashen faced, mouth open in an almost comical *O*, turned to scurry toward the door. The surgical table's arms whirred to life as Angel said, "I'm going to stop your bleeding. Hold still."

Juliet wanted to comply, and she tried to, but as Murphy neared the door in front of her, she couldn't stomach the idea of the doctor getting away or getting help to harm her further. She lifted the vibroblade and tossed it. She tried to match the movements she'd learned watching Houston and White throw their knives, but she was half reclined and throwing left-handed, and she knew if Angel hadn't stepped in, the blade would have missed.

Angel did step in, though; despite simultaneously operating the surgical table, she helped to guide Juliet's wrist and fingers to release the blade properly. It flew through the air to sink directly into the middle of Murphy's back, about halfway down her spine. The doctor fell like a sack of laundry to the concrete floor, sprawled out in front of the door.

Meanwhile, the surgical table had injected Juliet's right arm several times with various things, and she still didn't feel any pain from the injury. She turned to watch as another spiderlike arm with a spray nozzle came down and, with the precision only a machine could muster, sprayed some sort of chemical cauterizing agent into the flesh of her stump. "I hope that doesn't hurt, Juliet. I applied copious local analgesics."

"It's fine, Angel. Am I good? Is the bleeding stopped?" She didn't want to look at her ruined arm.

"It's stopped."

Juliet grunted and tugged her data cable free. Then, as it automatically retracted, she slid off the table and awkwardly fished her needler out of the holster with her left hand. "I'll need your help aiming if I have to shoot."

"I'm here, Juliet. May I ask why you severed your arm?"

"I'll explain, but wait." Juliet walked over to Murphy, still scrabbling weakly on the floor, blood pooling under her as the vibroblade continued to buzz, likely doing more and more damage as it wriggled in her spine.

"This . . ." She gasped. "This thing's gonna kill me."

Juliet sighed, stuffed the needler into her waistband, then knelt to jerk the vibroblade free. She switched it off and set it on the cart next to her briefcase. Keeping Murphy in view the entire time, she pulled the needler out of the top of her skirt, pointed it at the doctor again, and said, "I can't believe you would do that, Doc. I can't believe it. After everything I did for you."

Murphy gasped and shifted to her side, blood flecking her lips as she wheezed, "I can explain, but I'm gonna die. Trojan's coming. Let him get me on a table, Juliet. Please. I don't wanna die. I wasn't going to hurt you. They . . ." She choked, her words faltering as she coughed out a long strand of bloody saliva. "They only want to study you for a while—maybe employ you!"

The door clicked, and Juliet took three steps back, lifting the needler. Trojan, with his blue plastic-and-gel body and expressionless face, stood in the doorway, observing her with his LED eyes. "May I aid the doctor?"

"Yes." Juliet gestured to the surgical table with her needler. Trojan stepped forward, effortlessly lifted Murphy, and carried her to Juliet's vacated table. He stepped around to the data console, and Juliet barked, "Keep her conscious, Trojan! If you put her under, I'll kill you both."

"Noted," he said and continued to tap at the console.

"Angel, activate our jammer," Juliet subvocalized as she watched the table's surgical arms *whir* into action. "Just enough to keep her from dying, Trojan."

"Applying a nerve block, mending a lacerated artery, a puncture in her stomach, and filling the wound cavity with pressure foam for now, ma'am," Trojan replied.

"Juliet," Murphy coughed. "Juliet, listen to me." She turned her head sideways, left and right, as though trying to see her. Juliet slowly moved in a circle around the table, keeping the needler out, noting how weird her other arm felt. It was numb and cold, and then she remembered it was gone, and her gaze shifted to the floor where her pale appendage lay, fingers curled, under Murphy's table.

"How could you?" Juliet choked the question out again, raw emotion constricting her throat. "You *hugged* me!" The accusation in her voice sounded so strange, so out of place with the words, and Juliet snapped her mouth shut, afraid of what her emotions would have her say next.

"I'm sorry, kid." Murphy's voice was less strained; the nerve block must have taken effect. "They offered me so much goddamn money. I never shoulda called them. When it went out among the chop docs and fixers—someone looking for a new operator named Juliet. God, why did I call them? There was no way I could turn down that money, Juliet. I have so many people I owe. I'm barely treading water here, and the Rattlers are just a tiny part of my problems." Her voice was a little slurred, her words slow, and it took a long while for Murphy to get all those words out.

Juliet was beyond impatient. She furiously brushed her sleeve over her cheeks, wiping away her earlier tears. She was nervous and fearful that the analgesics Angel had injected into her arm would fade, and she'd be crippled with pain. "Get to the point, Murphy. Who'd you sell me out to?"

"I mean, all I know is it's the people who hired you. I don't know more than you, Jules, only that they paid me a shit ton to put in their doctored implant and keep my mouth shut. They were so thrilled that you'd had the idea of having your own doc do the work. They told me to contact you, Juliet. To bring you in, I mean. They're probably on their way. You should bail, kid; I won't tell them anything more. I don't know how you knew I was activating that thing in your arm, but I promise it was the only piece of tech in you with a surprise."

Juliet felt the hot tears filling her eyes again, felt them falling down her cheeks, and she stepped forward and pressed her needler to Murphy's head, burying the nozzle in her gray hair above her ear. Trojan lifted his hands, staring at her, but she ignored him and hissed, "Murphy, I trusted you! I thought you were my *friend*! I would have helped you if you needed money! If someone was messing with you!"

"I tried so damn hard to get you to take that job for me, Juliet. I tried everything short of confessing my sins. I should have been honest, I guess." Juliet saw tears in Murphy's eyes, which calmed her down for some reason. Seeing her show some real emotion made Juliet feel better, and she glanced over at her things on the little surgical cart.

"How am I supposed to carry my shit out and keep this gun ready? You cost me an arm, Murph. What if they're waiting outside?"

"Trojan," Murphy rasped, "take Juliet to the garage, carry her things. Help her! Do not let any harm come to her."

"Understood, ma'am," Trojan replied, stepping away from the surgical table and moving to pick up Juliet's jacket, knife, and briefcase. He turned to Juliet, trained his LED eyes on her, and said, "Shall we, ma'am?"

"I'm sorry, Juliet," Murphy said, her words drowsy and slow.

Juliet wanted to cuss her out, wanted to punch her or something, but she just shook her head and followed Trojan, keeping her needler trained on the center of his back as they made their way out of the surgical suite and into the corridor that led the way to the elevators. "Do you have access to the security cameras?" she asked as they stepped into the reception area and saw the open elevator doors.

"Not with that jammer active, ma'am."

"Angel, kill the jammer," Juliet subvocalized. As she said the words, she suddenly wondered why the elevator was already open. Without a second thought, she listened to her instincts and took two steps back into the hallway, bumping the slowly closing door open with her butt. As the door began to swing closed again, separating her from her escort, gunfire erupted in the lobby.

Trojan's torso exploded with little holes, white translucent fluid spraying out over the carpeting. The synth, grunting faintly in a weird, halting mechanical voice, fell to his face as a man shouted, "Juliet, we don't want to hurt you."

The door clicked as it closed, latch engaging, and Juliet dropped into a crouch, waiting for some sign of movement in the sudden silence.

"Angel, how many guns just fired?"

"Only one, Juliet. A nine-millimeter SMG."

Juliet shifted back, crab walking, her needler trained on the thin wooden door. "Infrared," she subvocalized.

"Of course," Angel said, almost apologetically, as she changed Juliet's vision to the infrared spectrum. She immediately saw the outline of a human form approaching the doorway—orange and yellow in a field of grays.

"Will this needler penetrate that door?"

"Yes, but likely slowed too much to do significant damage to that individual."

"I can see you, Juliet! Just come with us!" the man hollered. "No one else needs to get hurt!" He crouched before the door and called again, "Juliet! Come on! Our employer just wants to debrief you!" As he spoke, Juliet saw another form stand up behind him, this one green and blue.

"Trojan?" she whispered, and then the man screamed as the green-blue figure leaped upon him. The gun fired again, and several holes appeared along the side of the door, but thankfully, they were all over Juliet's head. The man screamed again, this time a bloodcurdling sound that ended with a crack and a wet gargle. Juliet stood up and carefully approached the door. She listened to the weird mechanical wheeze of Trojan's breathing but couldn't hear anything else with her augmented ears.

"Trojan?" she said softly, still behind the door.

"Th-there's n-no one e-e-e-else in the b-building, ma'am," Trojan replied, his voice crackling and halting.

Her vision switched to the normal spectrum as Juliet pushed the door open and peered through. Trojan was sprawled atop a man she didn't recognize. Though he was on his belly, she could see his face—Trojan had twisted his head 180 degrees. He was bald with black, pupilless eyes, and wore his beard in a closely shaven white goatee. He didn't look real to her—like a bad prop from a vid.

"Y-y-ou ssssshould h-h-hurry," Trojan said, looking up at her with blinking LED eyes. Translucent, creamy fluid was seeping out of the synth's nose and mouth, and Juliet frowned, wondering if she should try to help him or take his advice.

"G-g-g-go!" he blurted.

Juliet nodded, stepping around him and the dead man. She looked at her fallen briefcase, blazer, and vibroblade. "No one's here yet?"

"N-n-no!" He didn't look at her. His face was pressed into the carpet, his oozing mechanical body still lying atop the dead man.

Juliet nodded, holstered her needler, then bent to snap open the briefcase. She tossed in her blazer and vibroblade, grabbed the handle, and hurried to the elevator. She touched the down button and began to pace back and forth as she waited for the doors to close and for the rundown old equipment to slowly winch her to the garage level. The bells rang, the doors opened, and Juliet noticed the dull throb she was feeling in her severed arm.

"Dammit!" she hissed. "This is going to hurt when those shots wear off, Angel." She looked out into the quiet garage and saw a sleek, low, midnight-blue sports car parked directly in front of the elevators. The driver's door was open, and she didn't see anyone else within. "How funny would it be if I took that guy's car?" She hurried past the vehicle toward where the cab had parked, wincing as the throb in her arm intensified with her movement.

"They'd track it rather easily. We should move to highly populated garages and change the cab a few times," Angel replied.

"Yeah, I was joking," Juliet grunted as she flopped the briefcase on top of the cab so she could open the door with her only hand. She paused as her fingers touched the handle, and she backed up and subvocalized, "Infrared spectrum."

As the world turned gray, and Juliet saw the brightly illuminated silhouette of a person inside the cab, she backed up, wrapped her hand around the handle of her needler, jerked it out of the holster, and ducked to the left around a big round concrete pillar.

Juliet stood there—struggling to keep her breathing steady, needler ready—and listened. She couldn't see the infrared outline of the person in the cab anymore, not from behind the thick concrete pillar, but that meant whoever it was couldn't see her either. She knew there was no way they could open the cab door without Angel detecting it through her auditory implants, so Juliet trusted her PAI and closed her eyes, calming her mind and *listening*.

Nothing happened for several heartbeats. She knew she was playing a waiting game with the other person, but Juliet had something going for her that they didn't. If they waited long enough, sooner or later, she was going to hear . . .

Come on! She's gonna run out of the garage if I sit here all day. Is she still behind that pillar? I've got to find out. Backup's ten minutes out. Damn it! They'll have my ass if I kill her! Okay, three, two, one. . .

The thoughts came so suddenly that they surprised Juliet, and she almost lost her concentration, but she held on. When she heard the woman think "one," she also heard the cab door open. More than that, just as when she'd watched Violet's tablet display through her eyes, she "saw" the woman's perception shift as she lurched out of the cab and ran toward the left side of the pillar. With her back to the cement, Juliet sidestepped to the right, slipping around the pillar as the would-be ambusher raced around it.

Juliet was on the verge of following after her, ready to shoot, but then she heard the woman's footsteps charging off up the concrete ramp. She had to stifle a laugh as she grabbed her briefcase, slid into the cab, closed the door, and said, "Hurry. Drive away quickly. Be evasive! A crime is being committed."

43

\\\\\\\\\\\\\\\\\\\\\\\\\

GOOD ENOUGH

The cab sped down the ramp toward the garage exit, and then staccato taps sounded from the rear window and right rear quarter panel. The cab's AI spoke up, "Passenger, please take cover; we've happened upon a crime scene. I've alerted the authorities and will be taking evasive maneuvers to get you to safety."

Juliet ducked her head, hoping the high-end cab's advertised bulletproofing lived up to the hype. A thought occurred to her, and she asked, "Why did you let that other woman into the cab?"

"The woman who entered the cab prior to you cited Phoenix corporate statute 56.7H11—citizens requesting emergency assistance must be admitted into automated vehicles that operate in a for-profit capacity."

"She said she had an emergency?"

"Yes, she claimed a sexual predator was lurking nearby."

"God." Juliet hissed, wincing as the throbbing in her arm rose to new heights. "Angel," she subvocalized, "what do I do? I need to get some better pain management."

As the cab lurched and bounced, hopping a curb with a squeal of tires and a faint grinding sound, Angel replied, "I recommend avoiding anyone and any place you've been before. I'm investigating chop docs specializing in anonymity."

"Ugh, chop docs. Well, thanks," Juliet grunted, cradling her shortened arm against her chest, trying to keep the cauterized end elevated—it seemed to help the throbbing pain if she didn't let it dangle. "Cab, take me to the nearest shopping plaza and find a spot in the parking structure."

"Yes, ma'am. Setting route to Saguaro Pavilions."

Juliet subvocalized, "Order a new cab to meet us there. In fact, order three of them."

"Clever," Angel replied.

"Can you change my operator ID?"

"I can change your handle anytime, yes. I can send in an emergency request for a new SOA license number, but you'll lose contact with anyone on the SOA network who has your old ID in their contact list."

"Anyone I care about, I've got contact info for." Juliet's voice was brittle, her words short, and she took quick, shallow breaths. Still subvocalizing, she said, "Do it, Angel. Request a new license number."

"Done. As a reason, I selected 'Threats or imminent danger from disgruntled associates or clients.' I'm going to display a disclaimer that you have to acknowledge. It says you understand that all of your old license numbers are kept in a secure, encrypted database in the SOA's offline data vault. SOA maintains this record of historical license numbers so they can forward—"

Juliet waved away the new window and said, "Acknowledged."

As the cab moved through the ever-increasing traffic and Juliet saw her destination on the next corner, Angel asked, "What shall I change your operator handle to, Juliet?"

Juliet thought about the question, watching out the window as the cab slipped into the shadows of the busy parking structure. "Angel, have the other cabs wait on different floors and pick one at random to direct this cab to." The cab wound its way up into the big garage, and Juliet's mind wandered to the last time she'd tried to pick a handle. She was terrible at it.

She was mad that she had to burn the January handle, though she supposed she could come back to it someday, far away from Phoenix. Maybe she'd earn a better one, but right then, with her arm throbbing and people hunting her, she just didn't care.

Juliet thought about the moniker Ghoul had given her, and she shrugged, subvocalizing, "I don't feel very lucky, but for now, go ahead and make that my handle. Lucky."

She switched cabs, and in a haze of throbbing pain, she and Angel did the same trick three more times. Whenever she stepped out of one cab to get into another, Angel responded to ID pings with different identities she'd snatched from nearby public networks. Juliet always paid with Sol-bits through anonymous transactions, so she was feeling reasonably secure again by the time she crawled into the fourth cab.

As she hunched down in the back seat of an Easycab, making her way to a chop doc on the south side of Phoenix, Angel asked her, "Are you still planning to send any further data to Rachel?"

Juliet snorted an involuntary laugh and then winced, gingerly lifting her arm and cradling it with her good arm. "No, Angel. Rachel burned that bridge when she had Doc Murphy try to incapacitate me."

"Is that why you severed your arm? You detected something wrong with the implant?"

"No, I heard Murphy's thoughts. She triggered something that was supposed to put me to sleep. I'm sure it was in the blood-altering implant, though—seems the doc knew how to lie convincingly by mixing a little truth into her phony words." Juliet shifted uncomfortably and stole a glance at her stump's throbbing, swollen red flesh. "How nuked am I? Murphy did a lot of alterations to my whole arm to work with the, you know, alterations on the other half of it. Will this chop doc have anything compatible, or am I gonna lose the whole thing?"

"I could take a guess based on some reading I've done while we've been traveling through town, but I think you should wait and let the doctor explain your options. This man we're going to see is well-respected by the operator community for upholding the privacy requests of his clients. When I contacted him with your new operator ID and requested emergency service, he was very receptive and upfront about a five percent urgent service fee."

"Privacy is great, but is he any good?"

"Yes, for what you need. He's a chop doc, Juliet, but you can always get an upgrade when you have more time and are further from your enemies."

"Right." Juliet couldn't muster the energy to argue with Angel. The truth was she didn't care. Angel was right—any augment she got now would be something she could change down the road. Rachel might have screwed her over, but at least she'd given her a decent payday. Thinking of Rachel made Juliet wonder if she'd been working with WBD. Who else would go to such trouble to trick her? Who else knew to look for "Juliet?" Was this all some old vendetta from Vikker's group or Vykertech?

She shook her head. "No, it was WBD."

"You believe Murphy and Rachel were working for WBD?"

"Yeah, I think they were using us. I think they wanted to see what you could do."

"They didn't anticipate your ability to sense the duplicity in others."

"My ability to sense . . ." Juliet smiled at Angel's words. "You have a way of putting things, Angel."

The cab approached a squat, gray-stuccoed, single-story brick building and drove around behind it. "We've reached your specified destination." No signs adorned the building in the front or the back, but an awning hung over a nondescript blue metal door. Juliet scooted to the cab's door, opened it, then clasped her briefcase and stepped out.

"Angel, send the cab back to north Phoenix."

"Done," Angel replied as the cab started to roll away over the gravel and dirt lot. Juliet walked up to the plain metal door and swung the briefcase, tapping it against the blue surface. She waited for a few seconds, then did it again, harder. The briefcase thunked against the door, and Juliet heard a faint *whir*. She jerked her head to the left and saw a tiny camera lens embedded in the metal frame of the awning panning toward her. She looked into the lens and nodded.

A few seconds later, the door clicked and swung open, revealing a tall, thin man wearing a paper, disposable surgical cap, mask, and apron, all pale green. His sideburns jutting up over the mask gave the impression of a rather ratty beard, and he had prodigious bags and dark circles under his eyes. "Lucky?" His voice was nasally and raspy.

"That's me." Juliet held up her shortened arm and grimaced at the irony.

"Heh." He shook his head, eyes squinting in amusement. "Come on, then. Let's get you back in action."

"You're the doc?"

"Right." He'd been holding the door open with his left hand, and he pulled his right hand into view, displaying a shiny, stainless wire-job with six nimble-looking slender fingers, two of which were tipped in narrow blades. "Doc Sharp at your service."

"Sharp. I hope that's a double entendre," Juliet said, following him into the dim, cool hallway and letting the heavy metal door slam shut behind her.

"Double . . . oh! You mean, like, am I sharp up here?" He tapped his forehead. "Or do I just have sharp knives?" He chuckled, shaking his head while shuffling down the hallway. "C'mon, chair's up here on the left."

"You're alone?" Juliet asked.

"Nah, I got muscle around. Think I'd let you walk around with all that gear if I didn't?"

"I guess not," Juliet said as they rounded the corner into a large, cluttered brick-walled room lined with metal shelving units and housing a bulky, ancient-looking chrome-and-plastic autosurgeon chair. The chair's plastic was a dirty cream color, and she figured it used to be white. Still, the robotic arms looked well maintained, and the attachments on the stainless cart nearby were covered in plastic wrap.

The shelves and floor were cluttered with boxes, many sporting logos of various medical companies. Juliet let her eyes travel over them and then settled her view on a big shelving unit filled with unboxed cybernetic parts, from hands and legs to eyes and ears. She even saw a pile of synth-scalps attached to variously colored mops of hair. "Not very sanitary in here, is it?"

"Hey, I clean all my instruments, but don't worry—I'll dose you with a broad-spectrum antibiotic. Take a seat." He gestured to the chair.

"Listen. I'm paranoid right now. I'm gonna need to plug my PAI into your autosurgeon."

"Be my guest, but I'll charge you another three percent."

"What? Why?" Juliet moved over to the chair.

"I find that charging for extra requests keeps everyone honest. It's how I operate. If it's a problem, you know where the door is."

"It's fine," Juliet said. She set her briefcase down at the base of the chair, then, grunting and panting with pain, she scooted up onto the chair, too high for her to make it easy, and slid back to recline in the old, squeaky cushions. She pulled her data cable out of the port on her arm with her teeth, then reached over to the chair's terminal, grunting with the strain, and plugged it in.

"All set?" Sharp asked, watching her from a stool a few feet away.

"Yep." Juliet nodded, face pale with a sheen of sweat from her efforts.

"Right, well, looking at your eyes and that outfit, I gotta say, you're not my usual clientele. Your PAI sent me the specs on your old arm enhancement. I got a few arms I'm sure I can get working with what you've got there." He nodded toward her stump, then continued, "I mean, none of 'em are as pretty as what you had, but I've got a nice model that will sync up with the muscle augments and nerves in your shoulder."

"Look," Juliet said through clenched teeth, "the main reason I'm here instead of soaking in a bathtub is that this thing is throbbing and hurts like a son of a bitch. Can you give me a local or a nerve block so I can concentrate on what you're saying?"

"Oh shit. Right!" Sharp jumped up, moved over to the control panel on the autosurgeon chair, and started tapping in commands. "We'll block the nerves to your arm for now. That way, I can do all the work, and you won't feel a thing."

"I'm watching, Juliet. He's doing what he said."

"Thanks," Juliet grunted, not caring if the chop doc thought she was speaking to him. A moment later, one of the robotic arms on the chair sprang into motion and performed three quick injections into her shoulder. They were so precise and fast that she didn't notice more than a single pinch, and then the pain in her arm was gone as though a switch had been turned off. "Oh, sweet mercy. Thank you," she breathed, and this time she *was* talking to the doc.

"No worries. Now, can I show you the model I was talking about? It'll be very functional, but it won't look like your old arm."

"Hang on. Can you give me a sec to gather my thoughts?"

"Yeah, sure. I'm on the clock."

"Thanks," Juliet sighed, then she closed her eyes and took a deep breath. Now that her mind was clear of the haze of pain, she'd begun to get nervous about letting this guy operate on her, with or without Angel plugged into his machine. While she breathed, she concentrated, trying to picture his face, his eyes, and once she had them in her mind—those pale-green irises looking out over those dark circles—she began to hear his thoughts.

Oh, God, what is she doing? Did she fall asleep? Come on, lady; I've got a group waiting for me online!

Juliet snapped her eyes open. "What did you say now? About an arm?"

"I've got one I can show you," he said, standing up straighter.

"If it's your best option."

"Oh, my best? Hang on." He turned and started rummaging through boxes, calling over his shoulder, "I have two options for you."

"Juliet," Angel spoke. "My daemon just reported its purpose was fulfilled and self-deleted."

"Your daemon?" Juliet glanced at the clock on her AUI, saw it was 1201, and subvocalized, "So, the GARD servers are wiped. And the charges?"

"Will explode in less than four minutes."

"And Chaudhry's messages will go out. Grave, Vykertech, and even WBD are going to have their hands full for a while, I think. Makes me feel better about Rachel and Murphy double-crossing me. I might be hurting, but so are they."

"You on a call?" Doc Sharp asked, carrying a large black box with a silver bird of prey emblazoned on the side over to his cart.

"No. Talking to my PAI."

"Ah, yeah, I could see you were distracted. Well, ready to hear about your options?"

"Sure." Juliet shifted to look more directly at the man as he spoke.

"Okay, if we're keeping what's left of your arm, there, I have this model." He lifted a red plasteel arm that ended just past the elbow. The coloring was flat, not glossy, but it looked fairly modern, if a bit bulky. The digits looked very functional, with some sort of black synthetic coating on the insides of the palm and fingers. Juliet knew she'd be able to feel things through that coating and that it would hold a programmed print. "This is a VitalityTek, Hercules model. I can get it hooked up to what you've got left of your arm pretty easily."

"Sec," Juliet said aloud, then subvocalized, "Angel?"

"It's a decent arm, Juliet. It retails for eleven thousand. It's not fast, but it's strong and functional and will serve you quite well until you can find an upgrade."

"Okay, what's behind door number two?" Juliet smiled, a little giddy being pain free.

"Right." Sharp drew one of his stainless fingers along the seals on the long, black box, slicing through some tape, then he wrestled with foam packing materials, cursing as he had to slice more tape again and again. "Aha! Finally! Okay, this is a full-arm replacement from Falcon Forge." He lifted out the prosthetic, and Juliet had to admit—it might be chromed, but it was no wire-job. The arm was sleek and shiny, the fingers were nimble looking, and the synthetic, black pads inside the palms looked like a higher-grade version of those on the red arm. Still, it was a full arm. Did she want to go through with that?

"That's a surprising item to find in a chop doc's clinic, Juliet," Angel said. "Falcon Forge is a solid midrange prosthetics company, and this is one of their top models. That arm will be stronger and faster than your old arm was, even with its augments."

"How much?" Juliet asked.

"42k," Sharp replied.

"I see listings for that model at twenty-six thousand from some boutique shops in Phoenix proper."

"I thought it would be more," Juliet said, considering the costs of her eyes and other augments.

"Well," Doc Sharp started, a look of confusion on his face, "I mean, prosthetics aren't the most complicated tech anymore."

"His words are simple, but he's correct," Angel added.

"Listen, I like that silver arm, but I think I'll save my bits for something I really want. Just do the red one." As Sharp nodded, a little crestfallen, and started to pack up the Falcon Forge arm, Juliet added to Angel, "If I'm going to spend a ton of money, I want something custom that will fit my body perfectly, not some big silver arm this guy's had lying around for who knows how long. Besides, I might want one that looks natural. Are those more expensive?"

"It depends, Juliet. You can get synth-flesh prosthetics that range vastly in price."

Juliet sighed and nodded, and then the doc rolled a cart over with the red prosthetic and a few other sterile, plastic-wrapped packages. "I need to debride your, uh, stump and treat it with a nanite growth culture to get it to bond with the synth-flesh in the prosthetic. I'm glad the cut was so clean; I can get to the nerves pretty easily. You good with staying awake? You shouldn't feel anything."

"Yeah, I'm good. I insist on it, in fact."

"Right, well, just sit back and watch a vid or something; this'll take me an hour or two." He paused, looked into space, and said, "I sent you the invoice. I'll need half before I get started."

"He's requesting 13,899 bits," Angel announced.

"All right. Send him half," Juliet replied. At her words, spoken aloud, the doctor nodded, carefully adjusting the wide metallic armrest on the autosurgeon chair to keep her arm outstretched and elevated. He then moved to the control panel and started to tap away at the display.

While he worked, Juliet leaned her head back, closed her eyes, and tried not to think about all the awful things that had gone on in the last few days. She wasn't ready to think about her dead friends from Grave. She didn't want to dwell on the fact that Murphy, a woman she'd grown to respect and feel genuine affection for, had utterly betrayed her trust. That thought filled her stomach with something sour, reminding her of the other betrayals she'd suffered in recent history. She didn't want to think about what she'd done to Gordon and Dr. Vance, about what she'd made Angel do.

In an effort to keep those thoughts out of her mind, she subvocalized, "Angel, can you compose some messages for me?"

"Of course."

"Let's start with Hot Mustard. Ready?"

"Yes."

"Winfield. Winnie, I'm so sorry that I've left you in the lurch these past few weeks. I'm more sorry that I won't be able to come and see you. I'd love to give you a hug and tell you about everything I've been through. I'd love to sit and get drunk with you and maybe do something we both would think was stupid the next day. I hope you'll forgive me, but I can't. I've made some nasty enemies, and though I'm pretty much clear of them, they'll be watching people who knew me. If I stay away from you, you'll be better off.

"Yeah, it hurts, but trust me, you don't want this weight around your neck. I'm changing my operator ID, and I'd sure appreciate it if you'd tell people who ask about me that the last you heard, I was dead. I'm really thankful for your help and for your big heart, and I hope we'll meet again someday. Do me another favor, and don't color your hair if a girl tells you to. Love, J."

"Shall I send it encrypted and scrub identifiers from the encoding?"

"You know you should," Juliet said, and the doc looked up at her and squinted. "Don't mind me. I'm calling people and stuff, and I might slip out of subvocalizations."

"No worries. I've got music playing anyway."

"Ready for the next one?" Juliet asked Angel.

"Ready!"

"Charity, I know you saw me as an interloper. I know you thought I was a cheater and that I was trying to make your life difficult at the dojo, but I want you to know that I appreciated the competition we had. I admired you a lot, and yeah, you were a bitch half the time, but I could always tell you cared a lot about Sensei and the dojo. I won't be able to come back, and I was hoping you'd tell Sensei for me. Please tell him I'll miss the dojo and try to keep the spirit of the Mongoose alive when I'm practicing what I learned from you all. With respect and fondness, J."

"Sending with the same protocols as Winfield's message. Might I ask why you aren't asking Honey to inform Sensei of your prolonged absence?"

"I don't know. I'm going to try to call Honey when I'm done here, and we have more important things to talk about."

"I see. Any other messages?"

"I want to send one to Delma or Addie or White or, shit, even Polk, but Angel, when they read it, the watchdog will see. They might end up in big trouble, especially considering the stuff we did this morning. Isn't that sad? I can't think of a way around it short of going back in there and deleting the watchdog. Damn! We should have done that!"

"We had goals in mind, and that wasn't on the list. I think it would have unnecessarily increased the risk. There are ways we could help them, but as you said, it would require staying around Phoenix for a while. I will keep tabs on them, Juliet. If I see any of them leave Grave employment, I'll let you know."

"Okay, good enough for now, I guess." Juliet glanced at her arm, saw that her stump was coated in a thick orange gel, and asked, "How's it going?"

"Oh, great—fully scanned your arm and shoulder. Everything's going to sync up pretty well. This arm will be slightly longer than your other one, but only a few centimeters."

Juliet frowned, then shrugged her left shoulder and said, "Good enough for now."

44

\\\\\\\\\\\\\\\\\\\\\

EPILOGUE

This is quite a mess, Rachel," Kline said, drumming his fingers on the white tablecloth. He desperately wanted to take another long pull from his Nikko-vape, but he couldn't, not yet. He'd just had one, and his PAI was keeping track. Oh, he could get away with it, could pay the surcharge on his health plan, but dammit, he didn't want to. *Probably moot anyway, what with this absolute trainwreck.*

Rachel ate another forkful of salad, slowly chewing while she observed him. He could see the wheels spinning behind her eyes as she contemplated a response. Should she get angry? Should she be obsequious? Should she keep a straight face and ignore the comment? He watched her finish the bite and swallow, and admired how she licked her lips, somehow confident enough that she'd gotten all the lettuce out of her teeth to smile.

"Oh, it's certainly a mess, Mr. Eight, but I'd like to remind you that it was your asset, your response team, who spooked her. I'd just sent her a payment and ensured she'd be coming in for a debrief. This mess is on you." She glanced at his deck and frowned, perhaps annoyed about the jammer he was running.

"I'll own the part where the subject went dark, but now I have to explain the turmoil taking place within Grave. This whole thing has far-reaching implications. You realize they had some highly illegal PAI tech from Vykertech? Some tech that our little operative somehow exposed in the process of demolishing Grave's R&D branch? My superiors are very nervous that the other shoe has yet to drop. As it stands, we're relatively unscathed, but that could change. What else did she know? What other measures did she take?"

"I don't know." She paused, frowned, took a sip of her water, and said, more emphatically, "I really don't know. If we'd gotten her to come in . . . I know, I know, spilt milk. Well, you told me yourself she didn't have time to stick around and interrogate your asset, right? Hopefully, she didn't gain anything on you. On us."

"Hopefully. I still don't know how my asset tipped her off. She swears she didn't say anything. I'd think she was lying, but I had a bug in her head. Not to mention that January put a vibroblade through her spine, so I sort of believe her." He took a drink of coffee and contemplated adding sugar but banished the thought; his suits were getting a bit tight around the waist.

Setting his cup down, he said, "Well, where to go from here? We supplied her with pretty much anything she might need to disappear."

"That's an excellent question. Does she have family? Do we try to leverage them?"

Kline shook his head, "She has family, but she's not close with them. She has a sister here in Phoenix—in prison. January hasn't made an effort to see or speak to her since she fled us in Tucson. No, we don't even know how to make her aware if we take them. She's gone completely ghost.

"We'll save that card for the right moment if it comes; I think my days are numbered, Rachel, which is why"—he paused and took another long, long drag on his vape, savoring the look of disgust on Rachel's face—"I'm a bit stressed. I'm trying to shape things back home with corporate, trying to make them see that it was my idea for January to shake things up with a couple of rival corps. I may need you to help sell that version of events."

"I've been known to put on a sales hat from time to time if the price is right."

"Well, they haven't frozen my budget yet." He nodded as though a decision had been made. "Good, start thinking of the best way to mold the history of events to place me—us—in the most favorable light. I want it to seem like January isn't available because I sent her to lie low. My superiors will be easy enough to convince if you're clever. Meanwhile, I've got teams scouring the net, scanning cameras, and listening to operator chatter. Hopefully, we'll get a lead before too long."

"About that," Rachel said, gently dabbing at her red-stained lips with her linen napkin. "You know January managed to get her operator ID changed, yes?"

"Yes, Rachel." Kline's tone indicated that he was not interested in playing the fool and that she needed to get to the point.

"We can still give her a rating for the job. The rating will go through SOA, and their AI will filter it and issue it to her new ID."

"Can we use that to track her?"

"No, I don't think so—too much activity in that database, and too much encryption. What we can do, perhaps, is win a little goodwill with her. Me, at least."

"And me by proxy." Kline nodded. "Do it. Give her rave reviews. Let's be honest; she did manage to bring one of the top one hundred corps in Phoenix to its knees. Even Vykertech's feeling her sting, but they don't know it. Better to keep January out of their sights."

"You keep calling her January. She changed her handle, you know. It might be helpful for me to know her real name."

"Oh?" Kline frowned, eyed his blue Nikko-vape, then shrugged. "Her name's Juliet, Rachel. Juliet Bianchi." He reached for the vape, saliva gathering in his mouth.

"I hope you enjoy your flight, Clara," the attendant at terminal G-48 said as Juliet passed through the gate, stepping onto the mobile concourse. She nodded to the woman and kept moving, smiling broadly as the spaceport—and Phoenix with it—fell away behind her. It felt good to have that city in her rearview mirror, though her departure held some bittersweet aspects. Juliet started to think about Win, the dojo, and her friends in Charlie Unit, and she almost stumbled as one of her heels caught in a piece of torn, ragged carpeting, bringing her attention back to the present.

She'd had Angel do some snooping through the public networks of a busy hospital, and she had constructed a half dozen passable false identities, Clara Royce being one of them. They weren't complete identities, simply enough to get through customs or pass off to an officer wanting more detail about who she was than her operator ID would provide—retinal scans, prints, and falsified facial markers and birthdates. The Clara ID had worked perfectly when Juliet bought her charter to Luna and went through customs; it wasn't like they'd be calling any of her old employers for a simple trip to the moon.

She'd avoided a crowded commercial flight and booked a ride on a smaller luxury shuttle. The price had been thirteen thousand bits—three times as much as the cheapest fare Angel could find, but she felt it was worth it. It was her first trip off-planet, and Juliet wanted to enjoy it. Walking down the concourse, several people in front of her and several behind, she glanced at the clock on her AUI, still in military time—2138.

"Takeoff's in forty-two minutes," she subvocalized. "Are you excited, Angel?"

"Very! I feel like this moment will be the start of a whole new chapter for us, Juliet."

"Me too," Juliet agreed, following the stooped silver-haired older woman ahead of her down the stairs to the tarmac; the woman at the gate had explained that the shuttle didn't fit the mobile concourse and they'd have to walk out to it. The older woman moved slowly, clutching a large, shiny designer handbag, and Juliet wanted to give her a hand, but it was an awkward position to help from, standing above her on those steps. The point became moot as another attendant climbed up a few steps to take the woman's arm, guiding her the rest of the way down.

Juliet stepped down the gangway into the bright floodlight the flight staff had set up to illuminate the tarmac, turning and following the row of cones and holotape between them out over the dark surface toward a waiting shuttle, sleek and white with a pointed nosecone and a red stripe which ran along its length to end in a starburst pattern on its tail fin. A sense of déjà vu hit her when she eyed the shuttle, and Juliet had to pause there momentarily, orienting herself before continuing over the tarmac.

"Are you all right, miss?" the attendant at the base of the concourse stairs asked.

"Yes, sorry." Juliet took a deep breath of the chilly winter air and said, "Glad we're in Arizona—almost had to wear a jacket."

"Oh, you're not kidding! This is the only time of year I can wear my long-sleeved uniform, though," the young man replied. He pointed at the shuttle. "Just follow the holocones; a cold drink's waiting for you inside." He offered her a wink, and Juliet smiled and started moving again.

A wide gap had opened between her and the older woman now, and Juliet peered past the shuttle to the bright lights on the distant runways leading off at right angles into the blackness of the winter night. Steam vented loudly from the idling H-3 drives on the shuttle, grabbing her attention again. She looked at the passenger gangway extending from the broad doorway in the shuttle's hull, saw a woman with red hair, a short blue skirt, and a stylish jacket at the top greeting the passengers, and nearly fell onto her face.

"I've been here before," she said, stumbling forward. "Angel, what's going on?"

"Nothing seems to be amiss, Juliet. Your temperature is normal, including the lattice. Are you experiencing something I can't detect?"

"I . . . I don't know," Juliet replied, then she turned back toward the concourse stairs and the tube above it and saw the other passengers coming down and over the tarmac toward her. They looked familiar—a woman with an elegant white dress, a man in a high-end corpo-exec suit, another man wearing a brown duster with several obvious cybernetic augments, two women holding hands with a little train of three children . . . "Oh shit, Angel!"

Juliet turned back to the shuttle and started walking again as Angel asked, "Yes?"

"I know what's going on. I dreamed this."

"Yes, you've been wanting to travel to space for a long while—"

"No! I mean, I have literally dreamed of this scene back in Grave Tower." She kept walking, something between panic and excitement washing over her. "Angel, I remember all those people! This sounds crazy, but is it really crazier than hearing people's thoughts?"

"Perhaps not. I can say that your lattice is calm at the moment."

"This is so weird! So surreal." Juliet started up the steps to the shuttle, having caught up with the older woman. She had to proceed slowly, and the lady turned to her to smile, crinkling her wizened old eyes.

"I'm sorry, sweetie. My knees aren't what they used to be. I might get some upgrades like that fancy arm of yours."

"Oh, this?" Juliet held up her red plasteel hand and laughed. "This isn't fancy, ma'am."

"Much nicer than what they had when I was your age, dear," the woman said, turning to continue laboriously climbing.

"Juliet, I'm confused and slightly alarmed by what you noticed. I'd begun to think of the psionic lattice in your head as an antenna of sorts, allowing you to receive or gather the electric impulses of the minds around you. I don't know how to explain something like seeing yourself in the future."

"Well, we have all the Grave data on the GIPEL. I suppose that can be something we try to figure out while we're traveling. Have you . . ."

"Welcome to Starburst Shuttle Services, ma'am!" the attendant greeted enthusiastically as Juliet's foot finally reached the top step. "Sorry for the inconvenience of having to climb the airstair! This spaceport has concourses we can dock with, but none available at this hour."

"It's okay," Juliet replied, smiling.

"Let's see," the red-haired woman said, eyes going glassy for a second. "Clara, isn't it? You're in seat 7D. That's a window seat! I hope you enjoy the view."

"Thank you." Juliet accepted the packet the woman offered her, then followed her gestures onto the shuttle and right, down the aisle between the deep, spacious seats. Once again, Juliet thanked herself for splurging on an expensive flight.

As she continued over the plush, cream-colored carpeting, moving slowly to allow passengers in front of her to stow their luggage or find their seats, Angel spoke up, "Have I what, Juliet?"

"Oh," she subvocalized. "Have you made any progress narrowing down crew jobs? I don't want to spend half my savings booking passage to Io, Rhea, or wherever we decide to go from Luna." She smiled as the woman who'd been complaining about her knees grunted, sat down in 4A, and smiled at Juliet.

"At last!" she sighed through flushed cheeks as she sank back into the seat's embrace.

"I hope you have a nice flight," Juliet said as she continued down the aisle.

"I'm still researching," Angel continued. "There are a number of opportunities that will intrigue you, I'm sure."

"Good." Juliet slid into row seven, over to the window seat, and sat, sinking into the soft cushions. She sighed heavily and looked at the packet the attendant had given her. "Sanitizing moist towelette, huh?" She ripped it open and wiped her hands, rubbing it over her cybernetic fingers and palm, still weirded out about how she could feel the black synth-sense surface but not the backs of her fingers. "I want to get an upgrade," she muttered, more to herself than Angel.

"Juliet!" Angel's voice radiated excitement.

"What? Did you hear—"

"Your SOA ratings just updated! Rachel must have submitted a review!"

"Oh. Seriously?" Juliet was skeptical. Was Rachel going to tank her rating for disappearing and not falling into her trap?

"Yes, and it's good news!" A new window appeared in her AUI, and Juliet, unable to contain her curiosity, selected it.

Handle: "Lucky" — SOA-SP License #: XR713-004		
Personal Protection & Small Arms License #: E86072801		Rating: D-01-1
Skillset Subgroups and Skill Details:		Peer and Client Rating (Grades Are F, E, D, C, B, A, S, S+):
Combat:	Heavy Weapon Combat	E +1
	Bladed Weapon Combat	E +5
	Small Arms Combat	F +4
Technical:	Network Security Bypass/Defend	D +10
	Data Retrieval	D +5
	Welding	E +1
	Electrical	*
	Combustion & Electrical Engine Repair	*
Other:	High-Performance Driving/Navigation	F +1
	Negotiation and Conflict Avoidance	D +1

"How?" Juliet breathed as she looked over the numbers. "How did she improve so many of my ratings so much? I mean, I know I sent her incident reports. Well, you did, but still, it seems too much."

"Rachel must be an influential client, and she must have given you an outstanding report for your month of service. There's a written review, but it's brief: 'This operator performed flawlessly in a deep undercover situation for more than a month. They were subject to high pressure and hostile actors and came through without any trouble. Looking forward to working with the operator again. Hoping they'll reach out soon.'"

"Oh, wow. So she's trying to butter me up with a good rating so I'll come out of hiding? Fat chance. Still, I'd like to know what she knows . . ."

"Attention folks," a voice said from hidden speakers. "This is First Officer Nguyen. We're just getting settled in with a few more passengers to board. Your attendants will be coming by to get your drink orders. We've got time for one beverage before we're done taxiing to the launch pad. Once we break orbit, there'll be a meal service, and you can order more drinks."

A man sat beside her, accompanied by the scent of expensive cologne. With the smell tickling her nose, Juliet looked sideways at him and saw his gold-plated metallic hand, his designer blazer, and well-maintained, youthful skin. She offered a smile and nodded in greeting.

"Pleased to meet you," he said with a vaguely European accent. "Name's Carter. Dillon Carter."

"Good to meet you. Lucky."

His eyebrows rose. "Lucky to meet me?"

"No, no." Juliet chuckled, turning to look out the window. "That's my name."

"Ah," he said, then commenced to shuffle around, getting himself situated for the flight.

"Angel," Juliet subvocalized, "any response from Honey?"

Part of the reason Juliet had decided to leave Earth via Luna was that she wanted to try to check in on her friend; she'd been trying for two days to get a hold of her—ever since she'd walked out of the chop doc's clinic. She'd even gone so far as to have Angel contact Temo through an encrypted line, but Temo hadn't been any help. He'd been desperate for news, hoping Juliet could give him an update on his niece.

"No. I'll alert you the second I hear from her or manage to snoop out any news. In case you were wondering, I've also had no contact from any of the ex-GIPEL subjects we sent the encrypted messages to."

"Yeah, I know you will, Angel. I was just hoping . . ." Juliet frowned and tapped her head on the thick glass of the window. She really wanted to know if any of the other GIPEL escapees could do what Joshua Kyle had. She wanted to know how.

She heard the engines ramp up a bit, and then the shuttle started to roll.

"A nice touch," Carter commented.

"Hmm?" Juliet looked back toward him and saw he was gazing up the aisle.

"That they come 'round to take our orders. We could all have our PAIs handle it, but this personal touch—it's nice."

"Yeah. Well, for the price . . ." Juliet let the thought fade. For all she knew, thirteen thousand bits was nothing to this Carter fellow. She glanced down at her boots, jeans, comfy, lightweight vest, and long-sleeved activewear shirt, all in varying shades of black. She sighed, wishing she'd just packed these clothes with her other equipment and worn something pretty. Why was she dressed like a soldier? She was done with Zeta units, wasn't she?

Her clothes weren't cheap, and she didn't feel like a pauper impersonating someone more successful, but she would have liked to feel more elegant. Juliet frowned, wanting to revise the thought, but decided that was the right word.

"Juliet, seeing your updated SOA card made me want to update your status. Would you like to see it?" Angel didn't wait for a response, displaying the familiar table in her AUI.

Juliet Corina Bianchi		
Physical, Mental, and Social Status Compilation:		**Comparative Ranking Percentile (Higher Is Better - Previous Value in Parenthesis):**
Liquid Assets Net Worth:	Sol-bits: 224,233	67.11 (33.45)
Neural & Cellular Adaptiveness:	.96342 (Scale of 0 – 1)	99.91
Synaptic Responsiveness:	.19 (Lower Is Better)	79.31
Musculoskeletal Ranking:	–	61.33 (53.33)
Cardiovascular Ranking:	–	71.76 (68.76)
Cybernetic and Bionic Augmentation:	**Model Name and Number:**	**Overall Rating of the Augmentation (Grades Are F, E, D, C, B, A, S, S+):**
PAI	WBD Project Angel, Alpha 3.433	S+

Psionic Lattice	Grave Industries, GIPEL	S
Data Port	Jannik Systems, XR-55	C
Data Jack	Bio Network Solutions, 8840	C
Retinal Cybernetic Implant	Hayashi, Crystal Optics 3.2c - Customized Retinas	C+
Auditory Cybernetic Implant	Cork Systems, Lyric Model 4	C
Cybernetic Prosthetic Right Arm, Bottom Half	VitalityTek, Hercules	D
Programmable Synthetic Fingerprints	Ross Inc., Biomesh 9	C
Programmable Synthetic Hair	Tulip Co., Rainbow Strands, Version 12a	C
DNA Spoofing Package - Saliva	WBD - Custom Model	C
No Other Augmentation Detected.	–	–

"Seriously?" Juliet smirked as she subvocalized. "You put the GIPEL in there? Why S?"

"Because I don't know of any other models. I would have rated it S+, but we know there are other people out there with similar lattices produced by Grave. I'll need to evaluate one of them before determining that yours is truly unique like me." Angel sounded almost insufferably smug.

"Oh, brother. I see you separated the fingerprints, hair, and saliva thing."

"Yes, when you lost the blood package, I thought it wise to rate your various identity-spoofing enhancements individually. Did you note that I simplified the language of your net worth statistic? I'm counting liquid assets only. Well, I have been doing that, but now I'm being honest about it."

Juliet made no attempt to contain her sarcasm as she replied, "Oh, thank you *so* much, Ang—"

"Been to Luna before?" the man beside her, Carter, asked, interrupting what would probably have been a truly scorching remark to Angel. Juliet turned to him, noticing that an attendant, the one with the pretty red hair, was approaching.

"No, I haven't—first time. You? Wait." Juliet held up a hand. "Let me guess—you look like someone who frequently travels for some important business venture or other. I bet this is your twelfth trip!"

"Holy . . ." His eyes opened wide, and he leaned back to better look at Juliet. "How'd you know that?"

Juliet laughed and shrugged. "I told you my name, didn't I?"

ABOUT THE AUTHOR

Plum Parrot is the pen name of author Miles Gallup, who grew up in Southern Arizona and spent much of his youth wandering around the Sonoran Desert, hunting imaginary monsters and building forts. He studied creative writing at the University of Arizona and, for a number of years, attempted to teach middle schoolers to love literature and write their own stories. If he's not out enjoying the beach, you can find Gallup writing, reading his favorite authors, or playing *D&D* with friends and family.

DISCOVER
STORIES UNBOUND

PodiumAudio.com